INTO THE FIRE

HAYLEY REESE CHOW

INTO THE FIRE

HAYLEY REESE CHOW

Whimsical
Publishing & Illustration

For information address Whimsical Publishing, whimsicalpublishing.ca

ISBN: 978-1-998195-12-1

Edited by Micheline Ryckman and Deborah O'Carroll
Cover art by Gabriella Bujdoso
Cover design by Micheline Ryckman
Map by Micheline Ryckman

For Brighton, and all my other big dreamers.

CASOLLA SYSTEM.

OBRONE

CASOLLA

EXA-STATION

BELETHEA

WORM GATE
BETA3

OTHO

NORTHERN
OUTPOST

WESTERN
OUTPOST

EASTERN
OUTPOST

ALPHA
BASE

SOUTHERN
OUTPOST

MT. AGUYA

DRIETIS

CHAPTER 1

8.10.43B: T-minus 8 days until Mt. Aguya's Eruption

AFTER SPENDING MOST of the last year vying for the attention of the race royale fans, Ezren Hart now wanted nothing more than to escape from them. She ducked beneath the raised stage in the center of Petraskis, a holopro of a pink-tinged sunrise crawling over the dome above as she hid from the thousands of spectators jostling in the central garden. She tugged at the dozen belts that wrapped around the torso of her ruffled dress and tried not to focus on the weather readout on her goggs.

Outside, on Belethea's capricious surface, the wind was blowing at a reasonable twenty knots, with only a three percent chance of precipitation in the next six hours. It was so clear out there, she could probably even catch a glimpse of Casolla's other twenty-one moons and still have time to watch a *real* sunrise.

Except, she couldn't—because she had to be *here*.

"There you are!" Sylvia's commanding voice cut through the milling security and event managers. Silver ink swirled around her eyes in a mask-like design, and the vibrant colors of her rainbow brows stood bright against her light brown complexion. "What're you doing back here?" She pushed her waterfall of black curls behind her shoulders as she cut through the crowd. "We still need to style your hair and face."

"Have you seen Foster yet?" Ezren peered around the tents for his broad-shouldered form. He'd been touring the stations on a PR round with his mother for the last three weeks, but he was supposed to be back for this. And it was the only reason she wasn't making a break for the surface right now. Well, that, and with the ambassadors here from the three major planets and the Delegation of Stations... Sylvia would probably kill her.

A holopro of a schedule, detailed to the quarter hour, flashed out from the electric-purple goggs perched atop Sylvia's head. "He's with the stylist." She cut Ezren a glare. "Just like you should be. And then he has an interview with *Belethea Talks* before we go on stage."

Ezren winced. She didn't envy him the interview, but at this rate, she'd be seeing him for the first time in nearly a month in front of half of Petraskis. If it were any other social manager, Ezren would've thought Sylvia had arranged it on purpose for the VSoc clout, but she trusted Sylvia with every fiber of her being. Unfortunately, after Ezren and Foster's BRR win, it was just an acknowledged truth that their schedules had grown into uncontrollable twin monsters.

But, suns, did she miss Foster.

"I promise I set aside two hours for you to relax together this afternoon, but right now we've got to move." Sylvia herded her toward one of the many small tents housing the athletes, politicians, hologgers, and race royale officials from across the system, all prepping for what Virtual Society promised to be the broadcast of the century. The news was so tightly under wraps that even Ezren didn't know what they were announcing, yet the rumors on VSoc ran rampant.

. . .

After eight grueling minutes, Sylvia guided her back out, Ezren's mahogany hair now braided in an intricate crown atop her head. Streaks of orange and magenta crisscrossed elegantly beneath the teal goggs nestled in her hair and swirling gold ink curled around her eyes. Ezren would've much preferred her leggings and oversized sweater, but now that she was a Belethea athlete ambassador, she was expected to put on a show at every appearance.

What Sylvia had once deemed her "fan face" now seemed to be her everyday face. Ezren, surface rat and terraforming intern of backwater Tuzuno outpost was no more to be found. In her place, the BRR Champion, Belethean Athlete Ambassador, and de facto voice of the terraforming movement had taken over her every waking moment.

And there was no end in sight.

They'd barely stepped out of the tent when a blue-haired hololodger accosted them with no less than three hovercams circling her head, red recording eyes gleaming.

"Ezren Hart! We're here reporting for *The Royaler Review*. Any hint what the big announcement is? With the BRR board in chaos, and Calderon's ongoing trial, rumors are they're canceling the BRR this year? Is that true?"

Ezren's gaze darted to Sylvia, who stepped in front. "Not a chance."

Skin prickling, Ezren swallowed hard as she thought of how her suit had constricted around her body at the finish line of last year's BRR. The searing heat against every inch of her— how she'd fought to breathe as it closed around her neck, her lungs—

Sylvia's hand found hers and squeezed. A message popped up in front of Ezren's eyes, a tiny personal holo projected from the goggs nestled in her hair.

SYLVIA: BREATHE.

Ezren sucked in a deep breath, filling her lungs slowly before letting the air hiss out through her lips.

"Well, that's a relief." The hololologger beamed, oblivious to the turmoil raging through Ezren. "Inter-system tensions have been so high lately with the cheating scandal and terranium debates." She peeked around Sylvia at Ezren. "Speaking of scandals, this is your first appearance with Sterling in over a month. Has your relationship suffered without the royale—"

"Always the chaffing *Royaler Review*." Sylvia practically pushed Ezren toward the stage, not quite stemming Ezren's urge to punch the hololologger straight in her fan-face. She and Foster were *fine*, no thanks to the gross VSoc gossip hololologs betting on how much longer their relationship would last.

Out of earshot of the milling crowd, Ezren reluctantly let her hands unclench. "Why do we have to do these things, again? We're not even technically royalers anymore."

"Because you're an athlete ambassador, Ezren." Sylvia's gaze flicked to something flashing in her goggs, the practiced words rolling smoothly off her tongue. "And we're trying to unite the system under the shared love of the royale. Like it or not, your influence and voice matter."

Ezren suppressed a groan. She'd thought she was done with all the VSoc shenanigans after they'd won the BRR, but it had only swung back stronger than ever. While the win had given her a platform to raise money for Belethea's terraforming effort, it had also seemed to trap her in place. According to her contract, she was on the hook to be a VSoc monkey until her BRR eligibility was up in two years.

"Right." She glanced up at the holopro technicians scurrying across the stage, her heart skipping at the possibility of an unexpected speech. She really did need to start reading Sylvia's messages. "So, what am I supposed to do here again?"

"Just smile and be present for the cause." Sylvia reached

out and tucked a rogue strand of hair behind Ezren's ear, the crowd's clamor rising and falling just on the other side of the tent. Her gaze toggled to one side as a message chimed in her goggs. "They're ready for you backstage. Let's go." With that, they stepped out from behind the tent, and the crowd erupted at the sight of them.

Though the noise was nearly deafening, they weren't all cheers. In fact, jeering protesters took up the whole front row, their holopros projected above them.

"We don't want Ezren's sky, we want Belethea's."

"Terraforming is planet murder!"

"We stand with Calderon, a true Belethea hero."

"Terra-fod-off!"

Ezren flashed her Sylvia-approved smile at the throng, even as anger bubbled in her belly. The man was a murderer for suns' sake. "I don't think my presence is helping the cause," she gritted out under her stiff grin. "Calderon's supporters are everywhere."

"Exactly." Sylvia's jaw flexed through her own frozen smile. "That's why you need to be here to head them off. If we sit around while they shape the message, they'll win the hearts and minds, and then Calderon will be as good as free." Sylvia ushered her up the stairs into a backstage area holding a crowd of other well-dressed VIPs.

Ezren tried to squeeze a breath into her buckle-constricted chest. The more Calderon twisted the details, the more public opinion seemed to shift against her. Some increasingly vocal Belethea nationalists were now preaching he was doing what was really in their planet's best interest—to preserve both Belethea's character and place in the galactic order. Ezren was even starting to receive threats over it.

And the only thing she could do to retaliate was stand on stage in a dress? The thought made her want to sprint for the closest exit and run for days. She peeked out again at the raucous crowd.

"Free Calderon. Free Belethea. Free Calderon. Free Belethea!"

Another group of Obronians jostled beside the Never-Terras with their own anti-Belethea messages.

"Belethea cheaters!"

"Ban Belethea!"

"Ugh." Sylvia grabbed the jacket of a passing event worker. "Can we please get some security out there? This is getting out of hand."

Ezren tugged at the buckles on her dress, her chest tight. It was still hard to believe only a few months ago they had been shouting *her* name. She glanced at the Obronian delegation in their barely-there shorts and translucent shirts—the same people who claimed Calderon was just the scapegoat for a wider Belethean conspiracy. An allegation which now brought the protesters screaming to her door.

"Stop glaring at the Obronians," Sylvia whispered.

"They're glaring at *me*," Ezren grumbled, obediently looking away to where the Dreitians, in their full robes, were also scowling at her. Finally, her gaze settled on the safe skyline of Petraskis's spindly towers against the holopro of a blue sky. "Couldn't we have done this whole song and dance at the thing next week?" Surely one excruciating Casolla family reunion was torture enough for everyone.

"Do you ever read my messages?" Sylvia planted her fists on her round hips. "The Casolla Ambassador Summit is bigger than the race roy—"

"Ezren Hart." A sharp voice sliced through the din.

A hard-eyed woman with sleek gold goggs atop her gray-streaked bob glided across the stage toward them in thigh-high boots and a collared jacket with at least a dozen bronze buttons.

Ezren would've recognized Catalina Villegas, the prime ambassador of Belethea, anywhere. At one point, Ezren had even looked up to her after she'd fought to get Belethea an equal voice on Casolla's diplomatic stage.

But that was before she'd accused Ezren of stirring the political pot for her own aims and made her out to be an attention-seeking Obronian masquerading as a Belethean. Belethea's prime ambassador kept her displeasure no secret after the BRR scandal, and her VSoc onslaughts against Ezren appeared on a weekly basis. Ezren had a strong suspicion she would've been happier having Calderon continue his schemes if it meant she didn't have to clean up the ensuing political shaft storm.

Which all meant that keeping her face blank was a bit of a struggle.

EZREN: DON'T TELL ME THIS WHOLE EVENT IS JUST ANOTHER OPPORTUNITY FOR VILLEGAS TO TORMENT ME IN PERSON.

SYLVIA: I SWEAR IF I'D KNOWN SHE WAS COMING, I WOULD'VE WARNED YOU. THAT'S AMBASSADOR OLIVER YORK FROM THE DELEGATION OF STATIONS NEXT TO HER. DON'T FORGET TO BOW.

The spacer beside Ambassador Villegas grinned from behind his one-eyed half visor, his sleek jumpsuit rolling with a stormy holopro. The smile even reached his eyes. Huh. Strange for a politician.

Ezren obediently bobbed her head. "Ambassadors. It's a pleasure."

"York was just sharing his concerns about your ambassador duties interfering with your training." Villegas's steely gaze slewed to Sylvia. "But I assured him that you have it all under control."

"Give them a break, Cat." York elbowed the stiff-necked Villegas with a grin and ran a hand through his swath of thick auburn hair. "Isn't one win enough? Has a champion royale pair ever gone back for more?"

"Honorable York"—Villegas raised a disapproving black eyebrow at him—"don't tell me your spacers are scared of losing again. After all, why would we waste a perfectly valid contract?"

Ezren's stomach dropped, and she glanced at Sylvia. "But we won't be—"

"Definitely under control." Sylvia cut her off with a subtle widening of her eyes. "Just working out a few details."

Before Ezren had a chance to hyperventilate, a silent message slid into her goggs.

Sylvia: Go with it. I'll figure it out later.

"Excellent." Villegas's frown cut into the well-worn lines on her face. "And I presume your address is already prepared for the Casolla summit? I have full confidence you'll uphold Belethea's reputation—it could go a long way to repairing last year's"—her cold smile pierced Ezren with barely repressed resentment—"damage."

"Oh, c'mon." York's warm eyes favored Ezren with a wink. "Hart's speeches always go viral. There's a reason she's one of the biggest names in the system." He put his hands up as if he could picture the words. "*Forget everything else, we just want to race.*"

He remembered her speech at the BRR banquet? Ezren's chest warmed at the compliment, but Villegas's frigid stare smothered the spark in an instant.

"It had better be," Villegas said. "It'll take more than a pair of fast legs to keep the other planets from disemboweling Belethea's political autonomy."

Cheeks burning, Ezren lifted her chin, forcing the words through gritted teeth. "If my legs are no good, maybe I should just focus on my ambassador duties. We have other competitive royalers ready to carry the team, and I was planning to attend Petraskis Univers—"

"Now, now, don't misunderstand. While not enough on their own, your legs are the ones I want in the race." Villegas's thin lips crooked up. "You'll have plenty of time for school after your contract expires."

Ezren's ears buzzed as if refusing to process the words. Would this woman really make them race again? They'd barely survived the first time. Her pulse quickened as her skin remembered catching fire in the final stretch.

York frowned, sympathy lining his brow. "Well, of course, I think one thing we can all agree on is getting the BRR back on track." His gaze flicked to someone behind them. "You'll have to excuse me, but it was a pleasure to meet you, Ezren."

A message lit up Ezren's goggs.

YORK: HANG IN THERE, THIS WILL ALL BLOW OVER BEFORE YOU KNOW IT.

Ezren bobbed her head again with a grateful smile before he disappeared toward the edge of the stage.

"Indeed." Villegas's attention swiveled to something in her goggs. "Kicking off the season next week with a sparring exhibition against the Belethean MMA champion will be a great way to show everyone you're back in the ring."

"What? But I haven't been training," Ezren spluttered, side-eyeing a confused Sylvia. That definitely hadn't been in the schedule—not to mention the fists had never been her strong suit anyway. Indignation needled her skin. "Do you want me to get beaten bloody on VSoc?"

"Don't be so dramatic." Villegas waved her off with knobby fingers. "You've always been the underdog. Honestly, it's where you thrive."

"Fod off, she said she's not doing it."

Tension unspooled from Ezren's shoulders, relief cascading

through her as she turned to see Foster Yunin-Sterling, resplendent in his three-piece and messenger hat, holding two cups of coffee. "It's not consistent with the BRR message. We always have a team."

But Villegas's shark-like smile only widened. "Ah, yes. The second half of the contract has arrived. I think—"

"Please, everyone, if you could quiet down, we'll begin," an announcer blared from the speakers.

Villegas gave them all one last piercing look, lingering on Ezren. "Just remember, you both belong to Belethea. So act like it." With a condescending whirl of her skirts, she strode toward a beckoning organizer.

Foster pushed the coffee cups into Sylvia's hands, his scowl softening as he turned to Ezren, the stormy greens and grays of his irises swirling. "You okay?"

Everything else left Ezren's mind in that moment, and she could've melted right there backstage. Three weeks was way too chaffing long. A wave of emotions too big to name swelled through her chest, but in the end, all that escaped her was a breathless whisper. "Foster."

Then his lips were on hers, his hand cupping her cheek as his arm curled around her back, pressing their bodies together. He tasted of coffee and cinnamon and just so completely Foster, his mouth warm as it moved against hers, skirting the edge of restraint. The cams whirled around them with a clamor of hoots and hollers that Ezren tried to block out. Because Foster was here. And that's all that mattered.

Pulling back, he slid his warm cheek against her cool one, his breath hot against her ear. "Suns, I missed you."

Ezren pressed herself to him, unable to get close enough as she nuzzled her face into his neck. "Let's just run away," she whispered, only half-teasing as buoyant joy threatened to lift her into the air. "No one would catch us."

Sylvia cleared her throat, and they both turned to where she leveled them with hooded eyes above a barely concealed smile. "As cute as this is, they're about to call you on stage."

Ezren shared one last rueful look with Foster before stepping away. "There's always something."

"It's okay." Foster's hand found hers. "We'll have time later."

"That's what I've been trying to tell her." Sylvia jerked away from a hovercam that veered too close. "Besides"—she proffered the two cups of coffee with a wry smirk—"as your official coffee holder, it's getting cold."

Ezren smiled as she took the cup and glanced back at Foster, every inch of her tingling with heat. "Thank you."

His hand snaked around her waist, and he pressed a kiss to the crown of her head. "Anything for you."

Their gazes met again, and Ezren swore she wouldn't make it until later. But then Villegas's voice echoed through the speakers, rudely bringing her back to the event at hand.

Foster's scowl returned too, and he raised his cup toward Sylvia. "So what's Villegas's problem today? Tell me they didn't pick her as the Belethean team steward. She acts like we're enemy number one."

"All the ambassadors are on edge lately with the terranium rights discussions." Sylvia's jaw flexed as she brought up her holo. "But don't worry, we'll figure this out."

Ezren offered Foster a weak smile. "It's been a rough morning."

"Sorry I was late; trying to find coffee in this place was nearly impossible." He blew on the steam rising from his drink. "Did you call Sam for his first day?"

"Asdef," Ezren swore, nearly spilling her coffee. "I completely forgot."

"Don't worry." Sylvia held out a placating hand, the

schedule flashing before her. "They're just doing an intro right now so you have a couple minutes if you can make it quick."

With Foster as her shadow, Ezren scampered to the side of the stage and fished the hovercam from the many folds of her dress. With a mental command, it hummed into the air, and Foster leaned in close to her as it scanned their faces. A moment later, her brother's holo lit up the air before them, and he flashed a bright smile. His own round hummingbot, Giles, projected their images in front of the impressively verdant school campus sprawling behind him.

"Hey Sam!" Ezren raised her voice to be heard over the clamor. "Happy first day!"

"Yeah, hope you like the new place," Foster said from beside her.

"Hey, thanks." In the holopro, Sam had all the sharp angles of a thirteen-year-old just hitting his growth spurt. Though Ezren had seen him less than a month ago, it already seemed like an eon, and she couldn't help but notice with each gained inch, she saw more of their father in his aquiline nose and broadening shoulders. "But aren't you supposed to be at a big announcement or something?"

"Yeah, but I didn't want to miss your first day. Belethea STEM academy is a big deal, and it looks gorgeous." Her smile slipped with an ache deep in her chest. "Wish I could've been there."

"It's cool." Sam reached down so that Waffle, his dog-capybara hybrid with a resting bored face, could investigate the cam. "The support team's all here." The cam shifted to show her mom's, Micah's, and Davis's matching grins.

His words punched Ezren in the gut. *The support team's all here.* Apparently she was no longer part of it. And her dad... well, Sammy barely remembered him, but she didn't think she'd ever unsee the hole where he was supposed to be.

The silence his booming laugh should have filled. *Stop it, Ezren.*

"Oh good, I'm glad," she managed, hoping he couldn't hear the tremor in her voice.

SYLVIA: WRAP IT UP, THEY WANT YOU OUT HERE IN TWO MINUTES.

"Okay, well we've gotta go, but we'll visit soon," Ezren rushed out.

"Sure thing." Sam waved. "See ya." And before Ezren could get another word out, her brother ended the call.

She turned to Foster, the smile melting from her face. Sam was starting his first day at Belethea's premiere boarding school without his dad or sister beside him, and she hadn't even remembered to call on time.

"It's all right." Foster's hand found hers and squeezed, as if he could read her mind. "He understands, and he seems happy."

Ezren's mouth tightened. "Yeah, it's just, days like this make me really miss my dad, you know?"

Ten years ago, her dad had accepted a remote job to help pay for Sam's regen surgery, but after a few years, the messages slowed to a trickle. Then, shortly after she turned fourteen, they'd disappeared entirely—and so, it seemed, had her father. After a thorough search, the investigators had concluded that her father had traveled through the system's wormgate to start anew with the settlers of a different system. Due to the incredible stress of remote jobs, it was a common occurrence, but that didn't make his abandonment any easier to swallow.

"There's a part of me that knows I should just stop thinking about him, but I still wish I knew where he was right now," Ezren said.

"I get it." Foster's stormy irises swirled with an expression Ezren couldn't quite decipher, and he tucked a strand of magenta hair behind her ear. "And I definitely think it's some-thing we should talk about when we get out of here."

"You mean *if* we ever get out of here." The throb in her chest only deepened as she took in the sea of well-dressed holologgers and VIPs chattering around them. She was so tired of not being where she wanted to be. Ezren grabbed a handful of her skirts and lifted them helplessly. "I can't keep doing this, Foster."

His eyes softened, and he leaned in closer, his forehead nearly pressed to hers. "I know, Ezren, but—"

Sylvia's head of wild curls popped through the crowd. "You two, on stage, now."

Foster frowned, but he guided Ezren toward the beckoning stage manager. "We'll make it through. One step at a time."

Ezren nodded. Though his words didn't diminish the throat-closing sense of being trapped, they were the only answer they had. Together, they pasted on their fan-ready smiles and walked onto the stage, the crowd erupting into a feverish cheer. Above the roar, the Obronians and Never-Terra protesters blasted their hateful slogans at max volume as if trying to drown each other out.

Ambassador Villegas stood at the podium, saying some-thing about returning to the great tradition of the Belethea Race Royale, but Ezren could barely hear her over the cacophony of the throng. Two figures collided in the front row, and the opposing factions clashed with renewed vigor—a pair of protesters now smashing together with swinging fists.

The violence of it even gave the ambassador pause as secu-rity infiltrated the crowd, only to be rebuffed. Villegas's voice rose above the clamor, her stony countenance unruffled. "Everyone calm down, Warner Calderon himself is—"

The mention of his name only whipped the crowd into a frenzy.

Even Ezren spun toward the ambassador, a suspicion crawling through her. "Calderon's here."

"Cheat!" The mob surged forward, security just barely holding them back in their bid to climb the stage. "Calderon is Belethea's true heart!"

"There's no way." Foster's gaze whipped around. "They wouldn't do that to us."

"To move forward, we need to make peace with the past," Villegas said. "So, I present—"

A silver-haired man strode toward the podium, and Ezren locked gazes with Calderon's ice-pick glare at the same time one of the protesters broke free and rushed the stage.

"He has a weapon!" someone shouted.

Ezren whirled just in time to see a man charging toward them in a heavy coat, pulling apart his lapels to reveal a bulky vest bristling with wires, his face a hard, desperate mask.

Bomb.

"Ezren, get back!" Foster seized her elbow, yanking her away from the stage's edge. She barely had time to process before Foster tugged her into his chest and turned his back to the crowd.

Just before everything exploded around them.

CHAPTER 2

8.10.43B: T-minus 8 days until Mt. Aguya's Eruption

FOSTER STOOD in the steel interior of the police station's waiting room, the nanite bandages itching at his skin where they wrapped around his arms. Like the topsuits that protected them on Belethea's harsh surface, the textured lattice injected nanites directly into the bloodstream to harvest energy from the user's cells. But while topsuits used their energy toll to increase athletic performance and enable suit repair, the medical nanolattice stimulated accelerated healing of the body itself.

Still, the nanites did nothing for the rage coiled in Foster's chest, scratching at his bones from the inside. This was not at all how today was supposed to go. He and Ezren were supposed to make a brief public appearance, and then he was going to spring the surprise he'd been cooking for the last four months.

Instead, someone had tried to chaffing kill them. Because of course.

Now, he was still waiting for Ezren to finish giving her statement, and the murderer who'd tried to off them during the BRR was also here somewhere. His fingers spasmed at his side, a lasting, and irritating, reminder of the royale accident that had taken his hand, and the ensuing regeneration treatment that had grown it back. He massaged it into submission as he paced back and forth among the metal chairs where a scattering of other uninjured VIPs waited.

Since the terrorist who caused the explosion died from his injuries, it was unclear who the intended target was. Had it been one of the Obronians targeting Calderon? (Honestly, he couldn't blame them.) Or had it been one of the Never-Terras gunning for Ezren? After all, according to the organizers, only Ambassador Villegas and a few others had even known Calderon was going to be there.

His shoulders tightened at the horrifying possibility.

Though the activists had been threatening violence for weeks now, no one thought they would escalate this quickly. He sucked in a deep breath, trying to calm his spinning thoughts. Maybe this would finally convince Belethea's governing stiffs to let them lie low for a while. After weeks on the political campaign, he and Ezren certainly deserved a break. Especially with the news he had for her. His pulse stuttered at the thought.

The hiss of the doors to the interview room drew Foster's gaze, the tension in his shoulders easing at the thought of finally grabbing Ezren and getting out of there.

Instead, Warner Calderon stepped into the foyer, flanked by none other than Ambassadors Villegas and York as well as a third muscle-bound man Foster could only assume was Calderon's bodyguard.

Shaft.

Foster froze, his fists clenching at his sides. It was as if he'd been transported back to that day almost a year ago when Calderon had first announced Harland and Sylvia as the new team handlers. Now Harland was behind bars in a prison station somewhere—he and Lucian Talmadge taking the brunt of the litany of charges levied against Calderon. So were these his new lackeys? Did his reach really go so far?

The burly one stepped forward, a wolfish smile on his meaty face, as if tempting Foster to attack. Foster drew in a steadying breath, hyper aware of the array of cams peering at them from every corner of the room and the bandages encasing his arms. Straightening, Foster stepped to one side, mutely extending a hand to usher them to the exit—anywhere away from him.

But Villegas hardly acknowledged his presence as she addressed Calderon with her usual cold clip. "I apologize for the fuss, Executive Calderon." She adjusted her black goggs with two manicured fingers. "We already have a security team diagnosing how they slipped through our protocols."

Calderon shifted his top hat and cane to the same hand. "Indeed. But this shows exactly why we need the BRR. It not only unites Belethea, but the entire system." He looked up as if to peer at Obrone and Dreitis somewhere far above. "Without it, we truly are at risk for war."

Every muscle in Foster's body constricted. Was it possible Calderon had planned the attack to paint himself as a victim? To try to shove his anti-terraforming message down people's throats? After all, what was another body on the pile? The thought made him want to kill him right there in the lobby. Consequences be shafted.

Burly raised a brow at Foster, as if sensing his thoughts. His grin widened, and the image of a red horse galloped around his throat, so fast Foster almost missed it. Foster forced himself to smother any outward expression of surprise, but inwardly he balked. A nanite tattoo? Though he'd never seen one in person before, he knew they were used almost exclusively in the underworld for a variety of purposes.

And this one had obviously been a warning.

Calderon had connections with the dark syndicates. Foster didn't even know why he hadn't guessed it before. After all,

Calderon never killed anyone with his own hands—he always got someone else to do it for him. No wonder he'd excused himself from the trial with a snap of his fingers.

This day. What in the actual fod?

York flashed an easy smile, his loose posture at ease. "Relax, Warner, it won't come to that. With Belethea and the stations in lockstep, we won't let the Obronian radicals shout us down." York's gaze alighted on Foster, his grin broadening as if they were old friends. "And of course, you'll have your BRR champions to lead the charge."

Villegas's granite stare turned to Foster, like she was trying to send him a message he couldn't begin to comprehend. "Yes, they'll be advocating for peace and unity at the ambassador summit for just that reason. Isn't that right, Sterling?"

Foster's skin went cold as he took in the four sets of expectant stares: two politicians, a murderer, and his pet mobster. Calderon had already attempted to kill him, and only one of them looked like he hadn't recently considered Foster's assassination himself. He could already see them justifying his martyrdom as a call for *unity*.

"I—" A chill ran down Foster's spine, and his jaw clenched, the moment stretching in the brittle air. He felt the trap ready to snap shut around him, but he had no idea how to escape. "We'll do what we have to."

"I wouldn't expect anything less." Villegas dipped her sharp chin toward Calderon. "Now if you'll excuse me."

She'd scarcely walked out the front door before Calderon turned to his other two companions. "If you could give us a moment as well, I need a word with Sterling."

"Of course." York's gaze darted to Burly before he tossed one last grin at Foster. "I'm sure you two have a lot to catch up on, but I hope we'll get the chance to chat next time, Foster." With that, the ambassador followed in Villegas's footsteps in long strides. Burly trailed after him, offering one last feral smile before the door hissed shut.

Foster looked around for the other VIPs, only to find they'd disappeared as well. *Not a coincidence.* "What makes you think I'm going to stay in this room alone with you?" Foster scoffed.

"Don't tell me you're scared of an old man?" Flashing his too-sharp teeth, Calderon splayed his empty hand in front of him in a poor show of innocence.

A bead of cold sweat ran down Foster's temple as he realized he almost certainly had control of the cams. But surely if Calderon meant him harm, he wouldn't do so in a police station of all places. Calderon scraped a metal chair across the floor and lowered his bent body into it. "Come, do sit." He gestured to the chair across the table from him with his cane.

"I know you're behind this." Foster hesitated on the other side of the table, curiosity and rage warring within him. "I guess you're not going to stop until we're all dead."

Calderon shifted his old-fashioned brass goggs in his silver hair with a sigh. "I can assure you this attack wasn't caused by me. I know you believe I'm the villain in the story, but you need to start thinking in grays instead of black-and-white. If you accept that, then you'll be able to think ahead instead of just reacting."

Foster leaned against the far wall, putting as much space between them as possible, and crossed his arms. "Murder seems very black-and-white."

Calderon waved him off impatiently. "Your hatred for me is clouding your judgment, so let's cut to the chase, shall we?" He stood and paced slowly toward Foster. "The case against Calderon Industries is over. Lucian and Harland have taken full responsibility for acting independently, there's no proof of any rigging, and the terranium distribution is fully in our purview."

Foster's gaze narrowed, his nerves calcifying with bitter-
ness. As much as he hated Calderon's words, he couldn't
dispute them. "Are you here to gloat then?"

"No, gloating is a young man's game, Foster." He folded his
hands on his cane, his shoulders falling. "I need your help."

Foster blinked, once... twice. But the words still didn't make
sense. "Help?" This was one of the most powerful men in the
system. What could he possibly need from Foster? His gaze
narrowed in suspicion. "I'm not going to go back on my statement for this unity chaff. Every word I said was true."

Calderon pressed on as if he hadn't spoken. "You have the
influence, the resources, the experience, and the history to
shoulder Belethea's Race Royale legacy. You were born to be a
royaler, and you carried your doubles partner across the finish
line, just as I once did." He lifted his chin. "Now, if you really
love Belethea, we need to work together to keep the rest of the
system from scrapping her for parts."

Foster's mind raced. Just what was Calderon's game here?
"I'm done with the BRR, and I don't even want to be on the
same planet as you, much less work for you."

"*With* me, Foster, not for me." Calderon's eyes gleamed
with fervor. "And if you don't, the BRR will fall into a power
vacuum that will end the race and tear Belethea apart. It *will*
lead to war. Perhaps one Casolla may never escape."

"You're bluffing." Even as he denied it, he couldn't block
out the dozens upon dozens of VSoc articles that had postu-
lated the very same thing. But that wasn't his problem. He was
just a royaler, and he'd already crossed the finish line. "Is this
why Villegas is trying to force us to race again?"

Calderon inclined his head. "Which we all know is ridiculous, of course. You're so much more than a royaler now.
Catalina is thinking small." Calderon leaned forward, his face
now only inches from Foster's. "With Hart's rabid terraforming

fanbase, Catalina wishes to remove you from the real playing field. If you accept my offer—if you let me guide you—you'll be able to do so much more."

"Not interested," Foster ground out, his skin crawling at the man's closeness. "Find someone else."

"I cannot. Unfortunately, your position is unique." Calderon straightened. "I'll need your answer at the summit on Obrone."

"Or what?"

"You and I will either lead together or we will all be forced down a darker path. One that will undoubtedly take you into the Churn Belt once again." Calderon drew himself up, assessing Foster. "The choice is yours."

Foster's hand spasmed, and he grimaced, massaging it with the other. "Did you forget you tried to kill me only a couple months ago?"

"I never forget anything. Especially a race royale finish for the history books." Calderon replaced his top hat on his head, exposing his sharpened canines in an almost wistful smile. "But one must learn to adapt to survive on a harsh planet such as ours. It's a lesson I learned decades ago, and one I imagine you will soon be well acquainted with. So, as a token of my good-will, I'll offer you another piece of free advice you'd do well to keep close." He paused in front of the door and looked over his shoulder, piercing Foster with his icy gaze. "You can be afraid of the arena, but if you want to stay alive, you'll enter anyway, always keeping your enemies where you can see them."

Then the door hissed open and Calderon walked out, his muscular bodyguard waiting for him with a savage grin.

Foster could only stare as the door closed behind Calderon, leaving him alone in the silence.

What the fod had just happened?

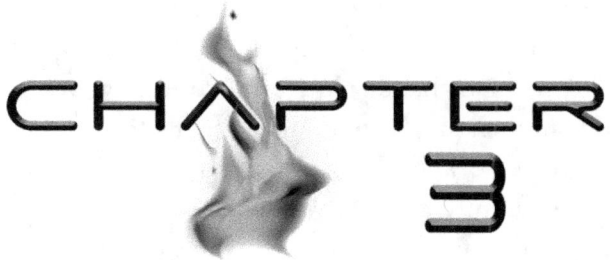

CHAPTER 3

8.10.43B: T-minus 8 days until Mt. Aguya's Eruption

AFTER A DAY that felt like a week, Foster, Sylvia, and Ezren walked into Carmella's lobby as afternoon gave way to evening. With their other teammates, Simon Grady and Bex Gunderson, no doubt training on one of the upper floors, the common area was blessedly quiet. Plush cushions, sprawling couches, and holo-games took up half of the large space that had clearly been designed for a fully equipped roster of sixteen. The other half held an open kitchen area complete with two well-stocked refrigerators and an oversized kitchen island with a half dozen stools lining one side. The familiarity of it soothed Foster with a bittersweet comfort. Carmella Hall had been home base for two years—a place where they'd grieved and celebrated—but now all he wanted to do was break free of it.

Though the Belethea team encompassed only the five of them, with the official start of the race royale season, new racers would be pouring in soon—filling the space with their laughter, chatter, and dreams. Meanwhile, he and Ezren were supposed to be turning a new page and moving to the university across town, a hope that was drifting farther away with every second.

He knew it was well within their contract for Villegas to force them to race, he'd just never expected it to happen. With the fatality risk so high, most BRR champions rode off into the sunset, fame and fortune tucked under their wings—no one had ever won twice. He frowned, thinking of Villegas standing at Calderon's right hand. He'd been sure they were working together, but then they'd contradicted each other.

And now he and Ezren had two threats to deal with. Because, apparently, one wasn't enough.

Still in his rumpled three-piece, Foster collapsed onto a couch with a sigh. In another beat, Ezren flopped beside him, and he automatically folded her into his chest. He inhaled her familiar scent of lemon and sage as her head nestled perfectly into the hollow of his neck, and his muscles finally relaxed. Once they got a moment alone, he could lay it all out for her, and they would figure it out together. Just like they always did.

"Tell me we get a break now, Syl," Ezren mumbled, her breath warm on his neck as one of their ever-circling hovercams captured a holo for VSoc.

The rage of it all surged in him again, and he just managed to restrain himself from slapping it out of the air.

Sylvia leaned against the back of the couch and projected the schedule in front of her. "Well, the good news is—"

"Are you all okay?" Black curls askew in a way that still managed to look fashionable, Grady strode into the room in his teal-and-black warm-ups, sweat shining on his brown skin.

Bex followed him like a pale ghost, her spiky white hair damp and her muscles rippling beneath her porcelain complexion. "The explosion was all over VSoc."

Foster met Grady's gaze. "Calderon was there."

Grady's nostrils flared with rage, and satisfaction heated Foster at the sight of someone finally reflecting his own ire. It had hit them all hard when their doubles partner, Genevieve Navarro, died in the royale qualifier two years ago, but even after they discovered Calderon had been behind it and then tried to murder the rest of them as well—no one seemed to be filled with righteous fury like Grady and him.

Grady's hands fisted at his sides. "Did you at least get a punch in?"

Ignoring Grady, Bex's stare sharpened on Foster. "Do you think he was behind the attack?"

Foster exchanged a glance with Ezren, wishing they'd had a chance to talk it over first before everyone else weighed in. "I don't know."

Ezren's coffee-colored irises shimmered with a mixture of confusion and, strangely, sorrow. "I think it was sloppy for someone like Calderon. He's too smart for something chaotic like that. It could have easily gone wrong, and he could've gotten hurt as well. Maybe even died." Her teeth worried at her lower lip. "It was probably one of the Never-Terra groups. They've been threatening violence for weeks now."

Foster's brows knitted as he stroked Ezren's magenta-streaked hair. She was speaking sense, but if the Never-Terras were really out to get them now, why would they stop at just one attack? The thought of the Beletheans they represented turning against them made his shoulders tense. And the worst part was, since Ezren had become the voice of the terraforming movement, she took the brunt of it. His arm tightened around her.

"Just fodding blime," Grady muttered, twirling one of his dangling gold earrings around a finger.

"But Sylvia, weren't you saying something about good news?" Ezren asked.

Sylvia straightened and offered her a grin. "Yes, the meet-and-greet has been canceled for safety reasons, so your night is free."

A cheer went up from Ezren that Foster couldn't help but smile along with.

"But..." Sylvia swiped through what looked like a million and three unread messages on her holopro. "I think I can still salvage dinner with your dad, Foster."

"What?" Ezren's jaw dropped, and she turned to Foster. "I didn't know he was in the city. Do I get to come too?"

Foster frowned. "Wait, what dinner?" He checked his goggs for any message from his dad, but the last one had been his usual bland check-in weeks ago. Though Foster hadn't seen his dad since the new year, his latest update said he was still touring on Dreitis with his band. Then again, it would be just like him to show up at the worst time—on their only night off in months.

Sylvia pushed an errant curl away from her face with a huff. "I swear, I don't know why I send you the daily schedule if you don't bother to read it. His PA sent an invitation this morning." She projected a holo of a formal dinner invitation.

Gerard Y would like to treat the Belethean Champion Royalers to a congratulatory dinner.

Grady lurched toward the holo, his hazel eyes wide. "What? Please tell me Bex and I were invited too. I'm such a huge fan."

"I made a reservation for the four of you, but it's Foster's dad, so..." Sylvia shrugged at him.

Grady turned in Foster's direction, his expression morphing into that dumb pouting thing he did on VSoc. Foster waved him off before he could make a plea. "It's fine. He's just using us for publicity anyway." The more people to act as a buffer between him and his father, the better.

"As if Gerard Y needs publicity." Grady barked out a scoffing laugh. "He's an original Casolla music legend. He can use me all he wants."

"And now it's weird," Foster said.

Ezren giggled beside him, her face glowing. "This will be so fun."

"Does this mean I have to go too?" Bex crossed her arms, tone flat.

"Nobody get too excited." Foster rubbed a circle with his thumb on the top of Ezren's hand. "The odds that he'll flake are at least ninety percent."

"Oh, cut him some slack." Sylvia swiped away her holo before giving him a reproachful frown. "He *is* one of the busiest celebs in the system." Her gaze softened as it slid across the team. "But this could be the last event with just the four of you before the recruits get here next week."

"Does that mean the lovebirds are moving out then?" Grady smirked. "I mean I can handle anybody if I don't have to put up with Sterling anymore."

"Well, I hope you're not too sick of us." Ezren plucked at the ruffles of her dress, her gaze darting to Foster and then Sylvia. "Because if Ambassador Villegas's contract dispute holds up, it looks like we'll be staying."

Bex straightened. "Wait, what?"

"Villegas is trying to force Ezren and Foster to race again." Though annoyance edged Sylvia's tone, she couldn't hide the worried furrow of her brow.

Foster's jaw tightened, and he could practically hear his teeth grinding. "Because risking our lives for Belethea once wasn't enough." He thought of Ezren's screams beneath the twisters of the Churn Belt, the stony flatness of Villegas's stare. And he couldn't shake the feeling that another race would be a death sentence. *She wishes to remove you from the real playing field...*

Beside him, Ezren shuddered, as if reading his thoughts. "I don't know if I could do it again."

"Don't worry, we won't let it happen." Sylvia put a protective hand on her shoulder, her older-sister mode fully engaged. "I'm working on it."

Grady vaulted over the back of the couch to sit on Ezren's other side. "Yeah, besides, you're Sterling chaffing Hart." He flashed one of his winning smiles, the kind that had charmed half of VSoc even when they were a nobody underdog team. "I'm pretty sure you call the shots now."

"I don't know, kin, I think Villegas thinks her name is on the back of your topsuit, not Belethea," Foster said.

"Well, forget her, then." Bex crossed the room, a fire in her ice-blue eyes. "And forget Calderon. Because royalers look out for each other." Her thin lips curved up, but the expression held more warning than mirth. "And they already know we're hard to kill."

The five of them regarded each other, heads close, tied together by too many brushes with death to breathe easy.

Finally, Ezren cracked a smile. "Eh, well, Sylvia's VSoc schedule may still kill me."

A chuckle rippled through them, and Sylvia raised a fist in feigned outrage. "You all never—"

The hiss of the front door cut through Sylvia's mock tirade, and a man in a long trench coat with a thick crop of tangled black hair walked into the room.

Foster leapt from the couch, his muscles coiling as Sylvia stepped forward. "Um, excuse me, you can't just—"

"I'm Inspector Ian Shiro." A holo of a badge glowed from the black, military-grade goggs hidden in his untamed hair.

Sylvia crossed her arms. "Okay, Inspector, but our gates were locked."

His holopro winked out and he shrugged, slipping his hands into his coat pockets. "I have an urgent appointment with Foster Yunin-Sterling, so I let myself in."

Oh shaft. All eyes turned to where Foster rocked on his

heels in the middle of the room. This was totally not how he'd planned this. "Look, I meant to shoot you a message, but this really isn't a good—"

"It's time sensitive, Sterling." He rubbed an agitated hand across the five-o'clock shadow darkening his angular face. "He's alive. I found him."

And even though Foster had been thinking about this moment for months, he suddenly realized he didn't know if this was a good thing or a bad one. He stiffened, ears buzzing, as every face in the room turned to him, varying levels of confusion flickering over the Belethea Race Royale team.

It certainly didn't feel like a good moment.

"I've located Hart, but he's in a precarious situation," Shiro continued from where he stood in the lobby, looking out of place amid the teal décor in his dark trench coat. "And if it were my dad, I'd want to know."

He found him? Joy and fear coursed through Foster in equal measures. His gaze shot to Ezren, time stretching as he watched comprehension sink in, her body shooting upright as she jolted up from the couch. Her wide eyes toggled from Foster to Shiro and back, her hands twisting in the interminable ruffles of her skirt. "Wait, what's going on? Hart? Does this have to do with me?"

Fod. Fod. Fod. Fod.

Foster glanced at Grady, Sylvia, and Bex, but the three of them had shrunk back into an uncertain knot. Though their faces all mirrored a perplexed blankness, from their silence, they obviously sensed the gravity of the situation. Still, all Foster could think was, *This wasn't how this was supposed to go.*

He was supposed to get the facts and then figure out how to break it to Ezren. And now here this rando was, in the lobby full of an audience, with some hot news on her missing father who'd walked out four years ago and not looked back. He shoved the frustration down. Considering it was already going, there was nothing he could do but roll with it.

"Ezren." He took her hands, holding her gaze. "A few months ago, I hired a private investigator to find out what happened to your dad."

The color drained from her face, a hand flying to cover her open mouth.

"Oh. So this is his daughter?" Shiro's dark eyes slid to the gawking trio, and he finally seemed to twig that this was, in fact, the wrong place for this conversation. "Do we want to move somewhere more private?"

Foster puffed out a breath of relief. "Ye—"

"No." Ezren's gaze sharpened, closing in on the man as if she were on the attack. "It's fine. You said you found him. Is he alive?"

"Yes." Shiro took a hesitant step backward from her charge, his mag-boots clicking on the gray tile floor. "But he may not be for long."

A gasp slipped from Sylvia and maybe Grady too, and Ezren swayed on her feet. Foster stepped to her side, anchoring her with a hand on her elbow. "Ezren, maybe you should sit down." Was this good news? Bad news? He really couldn't tell yet. Honestly, when he'd hired the investigator, he thought it might give Ezren some closure on when and how her dad left the system—not whatever this was.

"But how?" Ezren murmured, her eyes shining like wet opals. "Where is he?"

Shiro's inscrutable gaze flicked to the gawkers again before settling on her. "He was transferred to a top-secret terraforming project on Otho."

"So he's still in the system after all." Ezren shook her head, this concrete information seeming to steady her somehow. "But that planet was deemed unsuitable for terraforming."

"Eh." Shiro lifted one shoulder in a half-shrug, and in that movement, Foster realized he probably wasn't much older than mid-twenties—Sylvia's age. "I'm no scientist, but he's definitely there, along with a bunch of other smart types who allegedly disappeared."

"How did you find out?" Foster asked. While Shiro's services had cost him a pretty penny, he never could've expected one person to uncover this level of conspiracy. Especially not when the Harts' own attempts to find their missing member had failed.

"If you ask the right people the right questions, you find things." Shiro paced the room now, almost casually. "I located a guy who'd escaped the place, and though he couldn't tell me what they were working on, he confirmed the identities of quite a few missing folks." He glanced at Ezren. "Hart included."

"Sounds like a chaffing mess," Grady piped up from the other side of the room, Bex looking on with narrowed eyes beside him.

"We're still missing a lot of details." Shiro idly turned on one of the holo games set up in a corner, and a translucent steering wheel appeared in the space before him. With another command from his chip, he turned it off. "But not for long, I'd bet."

Foster's gaze followed him around the room, unease roiling in his chest. Something about this guy didn't feel quite right—a forced ease to his movements and words that set Foster's teeth on edge. "Why's that?"

Shiro rolled his shoulders, continuing his circular stroll. "Baxter Research, a renowned terraforming group, was forcibly bought out by Calderon Industries a few months ago with the intent to shut it down. Apparently, Baxter fought back. With the ongoing court case, I heard Calderon was getting rid of them entirely, but now that they're in the clear, I'm sure it'll all come out. The bad, ugly, and hideous."

"Getting rid of them how?" Sylvia shifted from one high heel to the other.

"In a way I think you're familiar with. Last week, Gobrion Station authorities found three purged labs that used to belong to Baxter. Absolutely nothing and no one left. Since it's still under investigation, they're trying to keep it hush-hush, but I'd say they've only got a few days before it hits VSoc." His tone was offhand, almost cheerful, and Ezren swayed again.

Foster curled an arm around her waist, letting her lean into him as he turned to Shiro. "I think we need some time to process."

Shiro's professional, close-mouthed grin glided around the room as if he were memorizing the place. "Sure thing." His goggs flashed, and Foster's and Ezren's goggs chirped in kind. "I've sent the brief to your inbox with my contact info. If I can be of further service, drop me a line." He paused at the threshold, his dark gaze falling to Ezren with a wince. "Sorry the news was mixed, but for what it's worth, I've had to deliver worse."

In another breath, Shiro swept out the door as quickly as he'd come, taking all the air out of the room with him. Foster glanced at Ezren, her face a mask of shock. She'd mentioned more than once that not knowing what had happened to her dad ate away at her, but perhaps intervening hadn't been his place. She certainly looked anything but pleased. Suns, this was the worst day he'd had... well... since the BRR.

Finally, Bex pointed to the stairs, dragging Sylvia and Grady by the elbow. "We're going."

Grady resisted her pull. "C'mon, Bex, Ezren said it was fine. Don't you want to—"

"Shut up, Grady." Bex yanked on his elbow like he was a stubborn puppy. "Sylvia, help."

But Sylvia was looking at Ezren, worry wrinkling her brow. "Well..."

They'd barely made it two steps before Ezren's eyes cleared. "I'm going to Otho."

Everyone froze, and Foster's stomach turned to lead.

But Grady found his words first. "Um, what?"

Ezren lifted her chin and shifted away from Foster, standing taller, as if her mettle had seeped back into her. "If my dad's in trouble, I need to go get him." Her gaze darted to the mass of skirts still swathing her legs. "Or at least talk to him."

"Whoa." Foster held up his hands. "Let's tell the interplanetary authorities first. If he's in danger on Otho, it's their job to protect him and everyone else out there."

Ezren turned to him, her stare hard in a way he hadn't seen before. "The authorities that haven't found him in four years? Or the ones that bungled Calderon's prosecution? The police that Calderon probably has in his pocket?" She shook her head, and he could almost hear the gears whirring in her mind. "The closer the authorities get, the faster Calderon will move to destroy Baxter and the people working there."

"And what do you think Calderon Industries would do if they find *you* out there, Ezren?" Foster's voice rose with an edge of desperation. "You know they'd jump at the chance to make you disappear right along with them."

"But this is my dad's life we're talking about." Now Ezren was pacing too, her brow furrowed in thought. "It's only a week-long journey, if I could get ahead of—"

"But how would you get in?" Grady interrupted, and for once Foster was thankful for his input. "That guy said it was top secret, right? They might even kill you for knocking on the door."

"Especially if you're already on Calderon's hit list," Bex said.

"Your dad wouldn't want you to take that risk," Sylvia added, her gaze soft.

But the stubborn set of Ezren's jaw didn't ease.

"Look, we're athlete ambassadors, right?" Foster said. "Maybe Sylvia can ask around and see if there's someone more discreet we can report this to."

"Absolutely." Sylvia projected a list of names and faces from her goggs. "Anonymous reporting is a thing for a reason, and I can definitely get you a contact."

Still, Ezren's face betrayed no emotion—no sign of giving way. Instead, she turned her steely stare to Sylvia. "Can you give us a minute?"

"Of course." Sylvia dipped her chin as she ushered the other two out, her goggs chiming with another message. "Oh, Foster, your dad just canceled dinner tonight."

"C'mon," Grady groaned, throwing his head back dramatically while Bex practically shoved him up the stairs. "I can't believe I missed my chance again."

Foster's lips twisted, grateful for once that his dad was completely unreliable. He really didn't need that drama on top of the shaft day he was already having. Turning to Ezren in the almost perfect quiet of Carmella's empty common room, he studied the worry etched into every curve of her small frame, and a frown dug into the corner of his mouth.

"Thank you for finding my dad, Foster." Though Ezren's voice was soft, there was no uncertainty in it. "But you have to realize that now I know he's alive, I can't just stay here while Calderon murders him."

Foster's gut swirled with guilt and a strange foreboding that seemed to deaden the air. "Ezren, that's madness. You're talking about running into a lethal situation with zero preparation." He tunneled an agitated hand through his hair. "We haven't even verified this guy's story yet; he could be totally off base."

"But it's a lead," Ezren insisted, a fire lighting her from the inside. "And if he's telling the truth then we don't have time to verify the details and report it to the authorities. That could take weeks that my dad doesn't have."

"Ezren, you're not going to help anyone if you go off half-cocked." Foster's neck heated with the need to convince her. "You could quite possibly make a delicate situation worse."

"How does it get worse than my dad being in Calderon's line of fire?" she shouted.

Foster pressed his lips together, his spine rigid with the obvious impasse before them. Where had this conversation gone wrong? The odds of this being a suicide mission were a coin flip, and yet she was staring at him as if he were the one that didn't understand. He let out a sigh and propped his hands on his hips.

"Look, I really can't imagine how you must be feeling right now. I know it's a lot, and it's been a crazy day." He swallowed, trying to find the way out of this. "But at least give me twenty-four hours to verify this guy's story and see if we can get some help before we go racing off across the system." Maybe then, she would listen to reason. He just had to stall her. "Please, Ezren."

"I..." Ezren let out a long breath, her shoulders caving as she squeezed her temples—her coffee-brown eyes overbright. "I need to go for a run."

The *by myself* was unspoken, and he couldn't help the disappointment curdling through him. Still, if she could take some time to work through this—absorb it—maybe that was for the best. "Yeah, okay."

After all, this wasn't about him. After years of wondering,

Ezren finally knew where her dad was, yet somehow they were left with more questions than answers. And if it was bothering him, it must've been killing her.

He looked down at her skirt and boots. "Are you going to change before you go?"

"It's okay. I have my stuff stashed in the Marble Street airlock." Ezren strode out of Carmella's sliding doors, and Foster trailed behind her, the argument still too huge between them.

As they stepped into the faux evening twilight of Petraskis's holo-dome, disquiet rippled through Foster at the thought of Ezren going out alone after the morning's explosion. The anxiety only snowballed as his mind jumped to Calderon's news... which he obviously couldn't drop on Ezren now when she was already dealing with *this*. A breath puffed out through his cheeks. It was only a few hours—it could wait.

He turned to her with a wistful smile that felt too heavy to lift. After weeks away, he'd wanted nothing more than to hold her all night and into the next day, and here he was letting her go. "Be careful out there, okay?" He opened his arms, and to his relief, she slid into them without hesitation, burying her face in his chest. "They still don't know who was behind the attack this morning. There could be more of them."

"I will." Ezren pulled back to look up at him, her expression tender with a love that seemed to break him and put him back together every time he saw her.

Suns, he'd missed this—her scent, her touch, how the edges of her face softened when she looked at him. He'd never get enough.

He held her gaze, something urgent and fierce bubbling up in his chest. "I love you, Ezren."

She returned his weighted smile, something about it too

bittersweet as she pressed a warm kiss to his lips. "I love you too."

She started to drift away, but he pulled her close one more time. "Tell me again," he breathed.

Her hands circled his back as he deepened the kiss, the warmth smoldering into a blazing heat that filled him from toes to fingertips. The two of them melding into one as they moved together. Sterling/Hart. Hart/Sterling. Like two halves to a whole. Completely right.

When they finally parted, she had a real grin on her lips as she rose on tiptoes to whisper in his ear. "I love you, Foster Sterling."

With that, she retreated into the gathering shadows, and all at once, he couldn't shake the feeling that the darkness was falling much too fast.

But before he could call her back, Ezren had disappeared into its tenebrous embrace.

CHAPTER 4

8.11.43B: T-minus 7 days until Mt. Aguya's Eruption

EZREN HURTLED across the mauve landscape, the navy clouds racing her across the teal sky. The giant form of Casolla stared through the atmosphere with Dreitis, Obrone, and her other moons gathered around her orange-streaked face. Under their celestial watch, Ezren climbed one of Belethea's serrated spires, pulling her body up hand over hand until she stood atop the peak, thunder rumbling in the distance. Chest heaving and muscles rubbery under her form-fitting topsuit, Ezren's gaze drifted upward again, trying to spy Otho among Casolla's attendants, but the whipping clouds had already obscured the heavens.

Was her father up there on Otho right now? Otho was half the size of Belethea, but from what she'd read, its surface was like one giant lunar volcano, rendering its burning atmosphere toxic. So much so, that it had been deemed unterraformable decades ago. So what was her father, an atmospheric scientist, doing there now?

Her legs trembled as familiar, painful questions spun through her with a fresh vengeance. Had he chosen to leave them for his work, or had he been deceived somehow? After the budget P.I. her mother hired years ago had failed to find him, they'd presumed he'd left through the wormgate for a new life.

Many such travelers changed their names in an attempt to escape their pasts, making the theory impossible to confirm, and the lingering question had kept her up more times than she could count.

But if the secrecy of his work had kept him from contacting them, perhaps... Hot tears filled her eyes under her goggs, her mind unable to finish the thought—the hope was too much. But what did she do with it now?

She couldn't tease the possibility to her brother and mom—not when they could still lose him all over again. For better or for worse, she had to see him with her own eyes and get the truth from his mouth.

The certainty centered her again, filling her legs with steel on her twenty-mile run back to Petraskis's armored dome. The storm above thickened into menacing funnel clouds as she entered the airlock with one last wistful glance at her beloved Belethea. The rain pattered down, and lightning branched through the teal sky, illuminating its jagged mauve landscape. No matter what anyone said on VSoc, she loved her planet, in all its raw glory.

The door clanged shut on the visage, and Ezren quickly stripped off her topsuit, shoving it into the duffel bag from her locker. She threw on a frayed oversized sweater of Foster's and a pair of leggings before slinging her bag over a shoulder and stalking onto the nearly empty streets of Petraskis. She'd been out for hours, and the dome above reflected a clear starry sky, the streetlights illuminating pools of gold in the dark of the predawn.

A part of her wanted to return to Carmella, melt in a hot shower, and then lose herself in Foster's solid arms. But as soon as she leaned in that direction, Shiro's warning blared through her thoughts:

It's time sensitive. Your dad may not be alive for long.

There was no way she could rest with the seconds ticking away on her dad's life. If he died while she lay curled safe in bed, while she *knew* he was in danger, she'd never be able to look her mother in the eye again.

But what could she do about it?

Lost in a cloud of anxious indecision, she let her feet take her to her favorite café and slid into a booth. With a thought from her chip, she ordered a large hazelnut cream, her mind still running at a million miles a minute as she shifted her attention to her goggs.

First, she tapped into her newsfeed where theories on yesterday's bombing flooded every hololog from Belethea to Obrone. From there, she veered into the latest on Calderon's activities—a topic she'd been avoiding as much as humanly possible throughout the trial—and found that Shiro had been telling the truth. Apparently, Calderon bought out Baxter Research sometime before the BRR and had been systematically shutting down their research sites one by one. One of the sites had allegedly fallen victim to a catastrophic fire with dozens dead, some of whom hadn't been heard from in years.

Her stomach dropped. She knew Calderon was a murderer, but now it seemed like he wasn't even bothering to hide it. Still, why Otho? Had Baxter unlocked a leap forward in terraforming technology? Was that what Calderon and his Never-Terras had been so desperate to snuff out?

She swiped away the updates to find her mom's holos from Sam's first day of school. But despite the smiling faces of her mom and Sam, the only thing she could see was the glaring hole where her dad could've been. Should've been.

There was no question; this was something she had to do. With a deep breath, she pulled up Foster's name in her goggs, her gaze running over their last messages.

Foster: Hey, I'm going to pass out. Stay safe and wake me up when you get in.

Ezren: Okay, I think I'm going to make it a long one. My mind is all over the place, and I'm struggling with this.

Foster must've fallen asleep before he read her message, and it would probably be another hour before he woke up. She thought of Foster's request to delay her decision. While she understood the reasoning, the urgency of the situation threatened to choke her. Like every childhood nightmare of her father's death was coming true. But if she was going to convince Foster, she needed more information first. And she needed it now.

Swallowing the knot of guilt in her throat, she pulled up Shiro's contact information and sent him a chip message.

Ezren: Hey, I want to know more.

His response was immediate.

Shiro: I figured you would.

Ezren bit the inside of her cheek. Ian Shiro's VSoc footprint was minimal, giving her few clues about his background, but if Foster had hired him, and he'd managed to actually find her dad, that must be worth something. She sent him her location.

Ezren: I know it's early, but I'm here if you can meet me.

Shiro: Give me thirty.

Shiro made it in twenty, looking exactly as he had when he'd waltzed into Carmella Hall over twelve hours before. Almost as if he'd been waiting for her this whole time. His black goggs glowed as he ordered himself a drink, and then he spread his long arms across the back of the booth, scanning the empty café.

"So, what information can I interest you with, Ezren Hart of Belethea? Or should I say Obrone? Do you prefer to claim Tuzuno, specifically?"

Well, someone had done their homework. "Your VSoc says you offer investigative services, and you pilot your own lunar hopper." Her hands tightened around her oversized mug. "Could you take Foster and me to Otho?"

"Depends." His angular face held no surprise as he kept her gaze. "How much can you pay?" A service port hissed open in the table, and a small platform rose to deliver his mug. Which seemed to be more syn-whip cream and choc drizzle than actual caffeine.

For once in her life, the question held no fear for Ezren. After winning the BRR, creds were no longer an issue. "How much are you asking?"

"Forty thousand."

Ezren raised a brow, surprised that the offer was, in fact, reasonable. Was that suspicious in and of itself? Then again, she didn't know how much inspectors made. "Okay. A third now, a third when we find my dad, and a third when we get home."

He stirred the cream into the dark liquid of his beverage. "Done."

For a moment, Ezren could only blink at him. She hadn't really known what to expect, but she'd thought it would be more difficult than this. "How do I know you'll get us there and this isn't some bizarre kidnapping scheme?"

"While I'm sure you're used to everything on this rock revolving around you, I have my own business on Otho." He tapped his finger on his mug, looking for all the world like he didn't care if she believed him or not. "But as it is a venture that requires some funding, I'm more than happy to take you along."

Ezren nodded, something about his matter-of-fact air

quelling her doubts. That, and it was hard to be suspicious of a man with sugary white foam coating his upper lip. "Can you be ready to leave by tomorrow morning?" That would give Foster the twenty-four hours he'd asked for, although she highly suspected he'd continue to stall as long as he could.

"Well..." Shiro took a noisy slurp from his drink. "The thing is, Baxter's region of Otho is on the cusp of a once-in-a-millennia volcanic event." He pulled up a holo of a giant volcano belching a sparking column of black ash into an orange sky. "Mt. Aguya is scheduled to erupt in seven days, and I'm concerned Calderon is going to take the opportunity to trap Baxter's researchers on the surface and wipe them out. Even if he doesn't though, no one will be flying in or out of there for months after it blows."

A shadow passed across his face as he met her gaze. "And as much as I want your money, I can't afford to miss my window."

Ezren's brows knitted, her fingers tightening on her mug. "So what are you saying?"

He downed the rest of his drink and stood with an air of finality that sent Ezren's heart racing. "I'm saying I'm leaving in an hour whether you're on board or not."

"An hour?" Ezren nearly choked on her coffee. "That's barely enough time for me to get to the spaceport."

"Then you'd better stop fritzing around." He started toward the door and paused, his thin lips pressed into a firm line. "Look, I can't guarantee your dad will be alive when we get there, but I can say, with complete confidence, this is the only chance you're going to get."

Ezren swallowed. "We'll be there."

With a nod, he was gone.

Her hands trembling, Ezren slid both of their mugs onto the service platform, and it dipped down into the depths of the table with the dishes. With the first rays of simulated sunlight peeking through the windows, she glanced around the café once to confirm she was alone before she pulled a hovercam from her pocket and called Foster.

Scarcely had she sent the command than his face appeared before her, his dark brown hair brushed away from his forehead and his expression dark with some mixture of fatigue and annoyance. "Hey, where are you? Is everything okay?"

"I'm at Small Hour Café." Ezren frowned at the chatter of people in the background. "Wait, where are you?"

"Sylvia had me scheduled for an interview this morning." He gestured to someone behind the cam and walked into what she could only assume was a closet, closing the door behind him. "Did you not get her message? I think you have one too in another hour."

"Oh, right, it's probably in my inbox somewhere." Ezren ran a hand over her face, her heart still pumping wildly in her chest. They didn't have time for this. "Foster..." She bit her lip, tapping her fingers on the table. "Don't hate me, but I just met with Shiro. He's leaving for Otho in an hour with or without us... and if I miss this chance, I don't think I'll ever be able to forgive myself if something happens to my dad. I know it's dangerous, and a long-shot, and maybe kind of crazy, but I *have* to go." She met his gaze, his brows low over his stormy eyes. "Please say you'll go with me."

For a moment, they only stared at each other, their past and future stretching between them like a taut wire. They'd faced impossible odds before. Storms. Murder. Death. She knew if anyone could do it, they could. But what if he said no? After all, he'd made his objections perfectly clear yesterday. And when they were fighting so hard to escape the death sentence of another BRR, how could she drag him into a fiery unknown that promised to be so much worse? Especially after he'd already gotten hurt protecting her from the explosion yesterday. Ezren's breath caught in her closing throat as guilt and desperation warred within her. She couldn't ask this of him. It wasn't—

"Fine." Foster let out a long breath and pinched the bridge of his nose. "Look, I'm not far from Carmella. So let me get out of this, grab our stuff, and I'll meet you at the port."

"Wait, what?" Ezren dared not breathe, sure she misheard him as someone knocked on the door beside his head. "But yesterday, you were so against it."

Another knock rapped on the door, and Foster pounded on it with a hoarse bark. "I said just a second." He turned back to the cam. "Yeah, Ezren, I'd rather you not run off to the most dangerous planet in the system in direct line of sight of a murderer, but I'd rather cut off my hand again than let you do it alone. Besides..." He massaged his right palm, his face softening. "It's your dad. I get it."

An unexpected sob caught in Ezren's chest, relief and love cascading through her. "Thank you, Foster."

"Don't get me wrong though. I'm still not thrilled about it. And I definitely don't trust this Shiro guy. But I guess we can figure that out on the way." He raised a brow. "Just don't leave without me."

A grin stretched across Ezren's face as she swiped a tear from her cheek. "Right. My travel bag's by the door in my room." Ezren said a silent thanks that Sylvia made them keep one packed for last-minute commitments. "Just don't be late, Foster Sterling."

"Well, it is hard to keep up with Ezren Hart." The corner of his mouth twitched up in a wry grin. "See you in an hour."

The call ended, and Ezren nearly melted into a pool of jelly right there in the booth. They were really doing this. A glance at the clock forced her to her feet, and she nearly ran out of the café, hopeful anticipation buzzing through her. Despite everything else going on with Calderon's trial, the Never-Terras, and the threat of another race royale, this was a problem she could do something about. Right now.

After all, she needed her dad. And it was quite possible he needed her too.

CHAPTER 5

8.11.43B: T-minus 7 days until Mt. Aguya's Eruption

FOSTER BURST from the closet into the open room cram-packed with an expectant production crew encircling an impatient holol">logger perched on a stool under a legion of overbright lights. And despite the shaft storm he was surely running towards, he couldn't help but feel a grim satisfaction that he was at least escaping this debacle.

He held up his hands in a placating gesture as he edged toward the exit. "Sorry, there's been an emergency. You can contact my manager, Sylvia Long, to reschedule."

The holol"logger popped up from her stool with renewed interest, her slick black hair cascading around her shoulders beneath the fluffy pink goggs cocked to one side on her head. "What kind of emergency?" A trio of hovercams whizzed around her as she practically chased after him.

"The personal kind," he muttered as he shouldered his way to the exit.

"Relationship drama, then," the holol"logger said with an air of confidence. "Is that why you and Ezren Hart have been spending so much time apart?" She looked into one of the cams, its red eye staring directly at her. "Statistically speaking, only 0.9% of royale doubles stay together long-term." She turned back to him as he pushed out the door into a bright hallway lined with a weird carnival holopro. "Was it the distance that got you? Or the lack of common ground without the pressure of the royale holding you together?"

Foster's lips flattened into a thin line, and he had to force his tone to remain civil. "As we've said many times, Ezren and I prefer to keep the details of our relationship private."

His reaction only seemed to goad the holollogger, as if she could scent drama like a shark to blood. "There have also been rumors that Ezren is refusing to race." She lowered her voice. "Would you consider racing with another double? I've heard you've been seen a lot with the royale recruit Iris Holloway. Could there be a team Sterling/Holloway in our future?"

Foster bared his smile again, even as his teeth gritted together. "Thank you so much for this opportunity, but I really have to run." With that, he charged through the front door and literally ran down the street, the holol!ogger's protests fading in the crowd behind him.

The throng on the walk parted with a wave of *oohs* and *ahs* as recognition rippled through them. Pulling up an algorithm Ezren had made him to avoid crowds, he turned sharply down a side street and stuffed his newsboy cap on his head. He yanked his scarf over his face as he ran toward Carmella, relishing the feel of the ground beneath his feet.

Though he'd never particularly loved one leg of the BRR over the others, after Ezren had entered his life, her love for the run had spilled over to him, and he'd missed the stretch of his legs on those weeks aboard the stations. But now, they were going back out into orbit. Though not his first choice, at least he'd be with Ezren. That made all the difference. Maybe they could even use the time to plan what to do about Calderon.

He turned onto Carmella Hall's broad street and slipped into the small side gate. Jogging across the trim lawn, he unlocked the back door and took the stairs two at time. He briefly considered letting Sylvia, Grady, and Bex in on what was happening, but another glance at his goggs confirmed that he didn't have time for explanations. They'd have to settle for a message once they were off the ground, and even then, he'd probably hear Sylvia blow a gasket from orbit.

Still, his lips curved up at the thought of missing out on two full weeks of VSoc antics. He jogged to his room first and grabbed the travel bag that he'd dropped in his closet only yesterday. His door hissed shut again as he started toward Ezren's room, only to pause halfway at the sound of a muffled crash and harsh voices echoing down the hall.

"She's not here."

"Tell them to blow location two."

Adrenaline prickled across his skin as he noticed Ezren's door was slightly ajar. In three steps, he strode to the entryway and shoved the sliding door open—to reveal chaos.

Words in dripping red graffiti covered the walls.

Fod off Terraformer.

Cheating parasite.

You should be dead already.

Obronian traitor.

The mattress had been stripped from her bed and ripped apart, her drawers torn from the walls, her clothes shredded and strewn about the room, her window busted.

And in the center of it stood four hulking men, their faces obscured by static holos projected from their goggs, brandishing jolt bars—retractable rods crackling with electricity—and what looked like restraining cords. *Mother. Suns. What would they have done to her if she'd been here?*

Foster's hand curled tightly around his bag, fury pulsing through him in hot waves. "You have three seconds to get the fod out."

"It's not her," said one. "It's her doubles partner."

Foster's muscles tightened, but inwardly, his mind whirled. Outnumbered and without his topsuit to narrow the size advantage, these men could easily overpower him. He thought out a quick message in his goggs.

FOSTER: EZREN'S ROOM. SCRAP. NEED—

Another one lifted his jolt bar. "He'll do."

Foster barely had time to react before the man charged him. Taking a step forward, Foster kicked him directly in the diaphragm, and he crumpled to the floor. Foster turned and raised his bag in time to block the second man's jolt bar whipping toward him. He swung with the other fist, catching the man in the jaw.

Another jolt bar arced toward him, and he just managed to twist to catch the blow on his shoulder instead of his head. Electricity crackled through him with a bolt of white-hot pain just as another blow caught him in the thigh, and his knees buckled. Someone punched him in the jaw, and his vision whirled as he staggered backward into the hall, desperately trying to give himself time to recover.

His thoughts stuttered over the thunder of his pulse pounding in his ears. *Need to get to Ezren. No time for this.* Another jolt bar came for him, and Foster raised his bag—much too late.

"Foster!"

The figure paused at the shout, turning to face the newcomer just as Simon Grady tackled him from behind. The jolt bar flew from the intruder's hands, and Foster seized it from the ground. With a huge swing, he cracked it against the head of the next man running out of the room to his friend's aid. The man fell to the ground in a fit of convulsions, and Foster seized his jolt bar as well. *One down.*

"Grady!" He tossed the weapon to where Grady wrestled the larger man in the hall, trading blows.

"Thanks, kin." Grady snatched the bar from mid-air and brought it down on the man's chest with another surge of electricity. *Two down.*

Foster turned to face the last two when a muted boom rumbled through the air, like distant thunder, shaking the ground beneath their feet.

The men paused, turning their holo-obscured faces toward one another. "New direction. Time to move." The larger one unhooked a small sphere from his belt and dropped it to the floor. It had scarcely impacted on the ground before it erupted in a burst of smoke with an ear-splitting whine.

Foster leapt backward, instinctively dropping his bag and clapping his hands to his ears. "Grady!" The smoke stung his eyes as it enveloped the corridor in a thick cloud, clogging in his throat as he choked on his words. "Grady, are you okay?"

Grady's voice just barely pitched over the horrid screeching of the device. "I'm fine. Where are they?"

"I don't know." With a wary eye ready for attack, Foster moved toward the squealing device still spewing smoke before stomping on it with his mag-boot. It took three solid slams before the squealing finally stopped and the spray of smoke lessened to a fizzle. Foster waved an arm to dissipate the gray mass, only to reveal an empty corridor, Grady with his back to the wall, and Ezren's ruined room beyond.

"Shaft," Grady hissed, holding a hand to his side. "What was that about?"

Foster's gaze scoured the disaster of the room one more time, adrenaline and questions clotting his brain. Had they been there to hurt Ezren? Take her? Kill her? He shook his head, tearing his gaze away. "Where are Sylvia and Bex? We need to—" Foster's goggs chimed with a message, and his gaze flicked to the holopro.s**EZREN:** FOSTER, YOU HAVE TO HURRY!

Something's happened, and Shiro's accelerated the schedule. You have to get here NOW!

Foster: What's happened? I'm on my way.

"Sylvia and Bex both aren't responding." Grady's gaze sharpened on Foster. "Do you think this has to do with that weird inspector guy? Or that terrorist yesterday? I mean it sounded like there was another explosion."

Foster gritted his teeth, impatient misgivings scrabbling at his gut. "Look, all I know is I have to get to the spaceport right now." He picked up his bag and strode down the hall, not waiting to see if Grady followed.

"Hey, wait up, Sterling." Grady jogged after him as he pushed into the stairwell. "I don't know what's going on, or where the suns everyone is, but those guys are still out there."

Foster shoved open Carmella's back door, trying to ignore the pain now forcing its way to the forefront of his mind. "Grady, I can't stay here when Ezren's—"

"I know. That's why I'm coming with." Foster paused at the back gate and looked at Grady only to find his expression serious. "Royalers don't go alone, Sterling." His lips curved into a smile. "I mean, I did just save your ass after all."

For a breath, Foster held Grady's stare, the last two years churning between them. They'd competed fiercely that first year, then grieved separately after Genevieve's death, their guilt festering into bad blood and then jealousy once Ezren came along. It was really her bright smile and unending resolve that had finally brought the four of them together as a team.

But she wasn't here.

And balancing on the edge of running into the dark after her, he was strangely grateful that Grady was beside him. Still, he couldn't ignore the uncertainty scraping at his ribs. If he let Grady come along, his life would be in danger, no doubt about it. But with two attacks in two days, leaving him behind could be just as bad.

And in the end, he was right. They were stronger together.

He let out a long breath and held out his forearm. "Thanks, kin."

"All right." Grady knocked his arm against Foster's. "Let's go see just what's going on out there."

As they ducked through the gate and took off running through the crowd, Foster checked his messages, but there was no reply from Ezren.

Foster: Are you okay? What's going on there?

Foster: Are you still at the port?

Foster: Ezren??

As Foster and Grady barreled through the crowd and smoke rose somewhere in the distance, Foster's goggs remained silent.

More than the explosions, the shouts, or the crowd, it was that silence that cemented his uncertainty into dread.

CHAPTER 6

8.11.43B: T-minus 7 days until Mt. Aguya's Eruption

(TEN MINUTES earlier)

After a zigzagging sprint across Petraskis, Ezren stepped onto the metal floor of the cramped private dock that looked more like a metal cube than anything else. She raised a brow, vicious doubt cycling for the hundredth time in the last hour. "Are we sure this is a ship?" Patches of yellow hinted at a paintjob that had to be decades old, and its chunky, bulbous frame showcased a design from the previous century. The two distinctly unimpressive main engines hanging from a cylindrical fuselage didn't help, and neither did the tiny spherical gravity chamber tagging along in the rear. "Because it kind of looks like a piece of chaff."

With his usual air of unruffled amusement, Inspector Ian Shiro patted the belly of the small ship with a hollow clang. "I think the phrase you're looking for is 'under the radar.' When you're trying to break into a top-secret facility, you don't really want to attract a lot of attention."

The boarding ramp lowered with a sputtering hiss, and Ezren stifled a snort as she checked her goggs for an update from Foster. Nothing yet, but he still had thirty minutes. "Is it even going to make it to Otho?"

"In fact, it is not." Though his dark trench coat still

enfolded him, Shiro had traded out his Belethea-style button-down for a spacer's one piece, and his goggs for a translucent half-visor.

Ezren frowned at the shift, realizing none of his VSoc profiles had mentioned where he was from.

"This one's just getting us to Exa Station," he continued, "and from there, we'll be picking up a new ride."

Ezren cocked her head as the bay's metal shield slid open above them, revealing a savage maelstrom roiling through the dark beyond a blast-proof glass ceiling. Shiro started up the boarding ramp, but Ezren paused, her fingers curling in the overlong sleeves of Foster's hooded sweater. Once she got on that ship, there would be no going back.

Sensing her hesitation, Shiro smirked at her over his shoulder. "Oh, so now you're getting second thoughts? Are they on a delay or something?"

"You have to admit"—Ezren gestured to the ship as she walked up the ramp toward him—"this screams dodgy."

"Well, of course, I'm a private investigator. Dodgy is literally my business." He leaned against the dented archway to his ship to give her enough room to pass. "But I'm glad you're having reservations. It means you're not stupid, and"—he chuckled under his breath—"that you might not be too angry."

"Angry about wh—"

And that's when Ezren saw Sylvia and Bex waiting in the ship's common area. For a moment, Ezren froze, eyes wide as her mind sputtered to process what was in front of her.

Bex turned to Sylvia, arms crossed as she leaned against the wall segmented into a hundred different drawers. "See. I told you she was going."

Sylvia wiped a hand over her face before standing, outrage and exasperation making her seem a lot taller than her completely average height. "Ezren, what were you thinking?

We've got the ambassador summit coming up in *eight* days, Ambassador Villegas is on our ass, there was a terrorist attack on one of your public events yesterday, and you were just planning on disappearing?"

Ezren flapped her hands, still trying to comprehend Sylvia and Bex's presence. Had Foster sent them? If so, then where was he? "How are you even here?"

Bex jerked a thumb at Shiro. "We paid him to tell us if you did anything stupid."

Ezren turned to the boarding ramp entrance where Shiro watched the proceedings as if it were the day's entertainment. "You sold me out."

He hooked his hands onto the lapels of his trench coat with a placating grin. "I had a previous arrangement that was in your best interest."

Ezren crossed her arms, her annoyance turning her mouth sour. "You're a mercenary."

Sylvia rolled her eyes. "Now she gets it."

Ezren continued on as if Sylvia hadn't spoken. "How am I supposed to trust you to get me to Otho if you don't have my back on Belethea?"

"You *don't* trust him," Bex supplied.

"No." Sylvia pointed a finger at Ezren, her silver nails flashing. "You don't *go*. Period."

Ezren's voice pitched, her confusion and desperation bubbling into a shout. "But this is my *dad*!"

Memories of her father welled up in a visceral wave—her dad teaching her Casolla's stories in his deep bass, letting her ride on his shoulders to the first day of school, cheering her on despite his haggard, sunken face in a holopro from the other side of the system.

"I have to go." Ezren looked from Sylvia to Bex and back, both of them shocked into silence. "I'm not going to miss my chance." She swallowed, her voice lowering to a whisper. "Not when he's caught in Calderon's murder web."

For a moment, only Ezren's ragged breaths filled her ears as Bex and Sylvia exchanged a glance she couldn't read. Even Shiro seemed to be weighing the moment.

"Well, yeah." Bex pushed off from the wall. "That's why we're not here to stop you."

Ezren blinked. "You're not?"

Sylvia shot Bex a hostile side-eye. "Well, that was plan A."

"We're royalers, aren't we?" Bex crossed the cramped ship, her ice-chip eyes boring into Ezren's. "*We're* the ones who've got your back." She lifted her chin at Shiro as he slipped past them into the cockpit. "Not some rando."

"Well, I did tell Foster." Ezren ran her fingers across the smooth wall of the ship, trying to school her emotions before they spilled out in an anxious mess of gratitude and embarrassment. "He's on his way now."

Sylvia tossed a triumphant grin toward Bex. "See, I told you they would work it out."

"But it wasn't a guarantee," Bex replied, her flat countenance unchanged. "And I'd much rather go to some murder-moon than get in the middle of their lovers' quarrel."

Murder-moon. Ezren's shoulders fell, the fire in her doused with fear. This was exactly why she hadn't told them. It was one thing to put her own life at risk on this deadly fool's errand —but her friends? "Bex, you don't have to—"

"I know," she said.

"Look, this is sweet and all." Shiro's half-visor connected with the ship's holo heads-up display in a myriad of numbers and panels. "But you all brought your bags, right? We can wait twenty more minutes and then we're—"

A distant explosion rumbled through the air and the metal ship shuddered under its vibrating bellow.

Ezren looked from Sylvia to Bex to Shiro, their faces matching expressions of confusion. "What was that? Another explosion?"

Bex strode to the boarding ramp, her pale brows drawn low over her hard blue eyes. "It sounded close."

Sylvia's holopro flashed from her purple goggs, VSoc glowing brightly within the small ship as she scrolled with blinding speed. "Updating ... updating ... Okay, here. Got it. Explosion of unidentified cause at—" She stopped, her eyes rounding.

Shiro looked up from his control panel. "What's with the dramatic pause? Where was it?"

Paralyzing fear spiked through Ezren. "Please don't say Carmella."

Finally, Sylvia seemed to find her voice, but it came out distant—almost detached. "No, it was the news holo station."

Bex visibly relaxed and a small puff of air escaped Ezren's lips. "How weird they would target a news station after yesterday. It's so random."

"No, Ezren." Sylvia took a small step toward her, lines creasing her brow. "That's the thing. It was the news station you were supposed to have an interview at this morning."

For a moment, Ezren could only stare at Sylvia as her ears buzzed, and all she could think was, *Well, that makes more sense.*

"Right." Shiro turned back to his holo control panel, and the ship rumbled to life. "Change of schedule. We're leaving."

"No, we can't." Ezren glanced toward the door of the bay, hoping against hope that Foster would appear on command. "You said twenty minutes. Foster's not here yet. He can't be far." Pulling up her goggs, she sent him a frantic message urging him to hurry.

Shiro turned to her with an incredulous expression. "Okay,

but you realize that was before we knew that someone is targeting you specifically. One explosion I can accept as a possible coincidence. But two?" He shook his head. "We need to get off this plan—"

The bang of a door bursting open yanked Ezren's attention toward the hangar's entrance. Her heart lifted as she jogged down the boarding plank, relief already washing through her at the prospect of finding Foster running toward them. Of pulling him aboard and finally leaving the ground.

Instead, she found a man in a static holo-mask striding toward the ship. And he was pointing a gun at her.

She barely had time to register the danger before a gunshot echoed through the hangar. Ezren's arms flew to her chest, only to find that it was fully intact, and the man in front of her fell to the floor in a fit of convulsions. She turned to see Shiro lowering a black pistol, and for the first time, Ezren noticed the shoulder holster beneath his jacket. At least he'd only used bolt-ammo—it incapacitated, but didn't kill.

Shiro jerked his head toward the cockpit. "Like I was saying. We're—"

The door banged open again, but this time, not one, but a dozen men in masks flowed into the room with a chatter of gunfire. Swearing under his breath, Shiro returned a volley of shots, and then stabbed a finger at Bex. "Get her inside. We're taking off." Then he turned and raced back to the HUD, the boarding plank already rising beneath Ezren's feet.

"No!" She started for the door, only for two strong arms to grab her from behind and haul her bodily up the ship. "Bex, Foster will be running straight into them!"

Sylvia slid into one of the worn seats and yanked the netting-style restraints over her chest. "It'll be okay, Ezren, the port's security team just busted into the hangar too."

Above them the glass ceiling rolled back to unleash the

storm raging above. Through the viewports, Ezren could make out the strong winds buffeting the armed men. Were they really going to leave without Foster?

Bex pushed Ezren into a seat before finding her own. The netting ensnared her broad shoulders as the ship lifted from the ground. "We really should've known Calderon would go after her as soon as his trial was over."

"Yeah, a little warning would've been great," Shiro called from the front. "They're trying to close the entire port. I'm going dark so they don't follow us."

"Wait, what?" Ezren's stomach sank, and she paused on Foster's last messages he'd sent only a minute before:

Foster: Are you still at the port?

Foster: Ezren??

And she wouldn't even be able to answer them. While she understood the need to hide their position, going dark meant she wouldn't be able to send or receive any messages from Foster. She had to know he was okay.

Sylvia scowled at Shiro where he guided them out of the hangar. "This was all your idea. If you'd had better timing, none of this would've happ—" A deep pink, six-tailed cat jumped up on the seat beside Bex with a soft mew, interrupting Sylvia's latest lecture. "Why is there a tiny cat?"

Shiro flicked something across his holo as the ship accelerated into Belethea's stormy atmosphere, the storm winds buffeting them from side to side. "It came with the ship. Could someone hold on to it, please?"

Showing no sign of surprise, Bex picked up the cat and tucked it into her own harness as if she'd done it a million times before.

Shiro punched another control, and the pressure doubled on Ezren's shoulders as the lunar hopper cut through Belethea's layer of storms, clouds already obscuring Petraskis's dome below them. "We have to go back for Foster."

A dry laugh escaped Shiro. "Um, no. Calderon will have a welcome party waiting for you the second we re-enter the atmosphere. Not to mention if we go back, we can kiss our window to get to Otho goodbye." He turned in his seat, his dark eyes grave. "Are you in or not?"

Ezren's hands knotted in her long sleeves. She thought of Foster winning the brawl in the BRR for them. Of him carrying her across the finish line. There was nothing Foster Sterling, race royale prodigy, couldn't do... but her? "I... I don't know if I can do this alone."

Sylvia reached out and squeezed her arm. "Well, it's a good thing you're not alone."

Ezren looked from Sylvia's soft expression of understanding to Bex's set jaw, and her voice dropped to a choked whisper. "Thank you."

Sylvia gave her a reassuring pat, her full lips curving into a wry grin. "Yes, well, I think I can say with confidence that there are exactly zero other VSoc managers that will go to the ends of Casolla to make sure their athletes live to see another day." Her gaze hardened beneath her rainbow brows. "But I want to make it clear that the only reason I agreed to this was because *Shiro*, here, said that after this little adventure, he'd be able to get us to the ambassador summit in time. Right, Shiro?"

"I'm not going to lie"—Shiro pushed his tangled hair away from his forehead with a chuckle—"I'm a little impressed that someone just tried to blow you up, and then shot at you, and you're still thinking eight days ahead."

"We have to. At this rate, Calderon will never stop coming after us." Ezren squeezed Sylvia's hand again, this time in complete agreement. "It'll be our chance to expose Calderon for his latest series of crimes. With evidence from Petraskis and Otho, we might be able to make the charges stick this time."

At last, the vessel broke through Belethea's atmosphere, and the pressure lifted from Ezren. The ship's inner liner hummed to life, spinning to give them at least 0.25 Egrav of normalcy. Unbuckling, Bex freed the cat and drifted to her knees, gazing out the circular viewport at the cloudy, teal mass of Belethea already far below them.

"Fill our wings with fair winds, Mother Belethea, till your solid ground is beneath our feet once more." The cat trilled beside her, and Bex bowed her head, her voice barely a whisper. "Keep us safe."

The words sent an icy trickle down Ezren's spine, a cold disquiet soaking into her skin. She sent up her own silent prayer that Foster was safe down there and that he would forgive her for leaving without him.

"It's okay, Hart," Bex said, running a hand along the cat's back. "He'll understand."

With a nod, Ezren took a deep breath of the air that would have to be recycled for however many days until they got to Exa Station and stared out the viewport into the blackness. At least, no matter the dangers they faced on Otho, Foster would be safe on Belethea. After all, Calderon was trying to silence her voice —the voice of terraforming—not Foster's. He would be fine, and she would see him in eight days at the ambassador summit, just like Sylvia had planned. From here, there was nowhere to go but forward.

She pressed her fingers to the viewport over Belethea's teal face one last time. *I'll meet you on Obrone.*

Ezren had to believe that or she couldn't do this. And she *had* to do this. Her dad was worth it.

Or at least, he had been once.

CHAPTER 7

8.11.43B: T-minus 7 days until Mt. Aguya's Eruption

FOSTER STARED at the empty hangar where gun shots scorched the metal of the floor, and beyond the clear ceiling, the Belethean storms swirled with no less than three funnel clouds. Two police officers stood in the center questioning what looked like a spaceport employee while other officials peppered the chaotic spaceport. After the explosion at the news station and the subsequent attack here, Petraskis had completely shut down all atmospheric traffic.

Right after a class six lunar hopper registered under Ian Shiro had left from this hangar.

Grady walked up behind Foster. "I talked to the authorities, and they're claiming the violence was caused by the Never-Terras still in the city after the exposition yesterday. They arrested someone, but I've never seen him before."

Foster nodded, unsurprised. If Calderon hadn't been in the middle of the explosion yesterday and given him his weird little talk afterward, Foster would've been sure he was the puppet master here. But while his cult of Never-Terras made sense, they'd never been this organized before. So who else could be behind it?

"I checked the security footage, and Bex and Sylvia were

on board too," Foster said. "They must've also talked to Shiro sometime last night."

"I can't believe they left me out." Grady adjusted his octagonal goggs in his dark curls, which, even after a scrap and a sprint from Carmella, looked immaculate. "I mean, what is this, some kind of girls' trip?"

A kindred annoyance crawled through Foster. He should've thought to call Shiro last night too. Should've known there'd be no holding Ezren back. Should've run after her and insisted they work through it together rather than wait until the last minute. Chaff, if it weren't for him, they could've all been on Shiro's ship last night and avoided all this.

But he'd hesitated, and now Ezren was in more danger than ever. He thought of how they'd clashed, how desperate she'd been, and the uncertainty as she'd looked at him in the dark last night. Now, with attacks coming from no one knew where, he wasn't there for her. His shoulder blades tightened with an internal rage that had nowhere to go. "Looks like they made it out okay, but they've gone dark since they left."

"Probably to keep the Never-Terra psychos from coming after them." Grady's holopro flashed out from his goggs. "At this point, it's pretty obvious they're targeting Ezren, but the good news is it's definitely given Ezren an edge over Calderon in VSoc favor for the moment."

Foster gritted his teeth—of course Grady would be thinking of VSoc, of all things.

"And at least Bex and Syl are with her," Grady continued, his tone light, as if half of their team wasn't speeding away toward a death planet without them at that very moment. "I guess it could be worse."

"I'm not waiting for it to get worse." Seething, Foster spun on his heel and stalked toward the exit. "I'm going after them."

"You mean *we're* going after them." Grady grinned, matching him stride for stride.

Foster side-eyed him, but inwardly, a knot loosened in his chest. While they both knew the team should've stayed together from the start, it was still a big ask. "Are you sure? I don't know this Shiro guy, and with the asschaffs targeting Ezren, this is already way messier than our average royale."

Grady flashed his VSoc-gold smile. "Which is why I know you'll need help." They walked out of the port into the milling street, pulling their scarves up over their faces in tandem. "But we're already behind, and they're not letting any ships take off from here for another twenty-four hours, so how're we getting out of here?"

Foster flicked to the messages in his goggs, a bitter tang coating his tongue at the favor he was about to call in. "I know of a ship and a private hangar just outside Petraskis we can use."

"Really?" Grady's face brightened with interest as he followed him, the thrill of their endeavor glinting beneath his long lashes. "I'm impressed, Sterling. Those are some hidden depths. But can you pilot it?"

"I thought that was your job. You're the wheels after all." Grady had been a street jetracer until he'd broken his spine in a crash, and his parents had revectored him into BRR training. He had yet to lose his penchant for near-death experiences or wild schemes, but he was, without a doubt, Belethea's best driver of any vehicle on sea or land.

"Across interplanetary space?" Grady scoffed. "Nah, kin, I *am* amazing, but the BRR doesn't leave orbit, or re-enter it for that matter. And landing... yeah, that's a no."

"Well, shaft." Foster paused, ducking into an alley to give them space to think. "We need someone we can trust, and we need them today." He squinted at the overcast sky projected on

Petraskis's dome as if he could somehow see Ezren flying through the dark space above. "If they get too far ahead, we'll never catch up."

They were silent for a breath before Grady slapped his hands together. "You know what, don't worry about it. I know a guy."

And honestly, Foster didn't know if that was a good thing or a bad thing.

Foster stood in the small hangar and checked his goggs for the tenth time. There was still no answer from his dad, but he hadn't exactly been expecting one. Not that his message had been a question anyway.

Foster: Heads-up, I'm taking the ship for a couple weeks.

He looked up at the first-class lunar hopper before him—sleek and gold and three times bigger than a hopper had any right to be. Since his dad mostly traveled with his entourage in their band's much larger cruiser, it hadn't even left Belethea in over a year.

The familiar low-grade annoyance prickled through him, as it did any time he thought of his not-quite absentee father. His dad rarely messaged him outside his twice-a-month check-in. And they were usually just quick one-liners that Foster half-expected his manager wrote for him ahead of time.

But at least in this case, it had worked out for Foster. He'd never taken out one of his dad's ships before, but like the mansion outside of Petraskis, he was supposed to be welcome to use it. Per, once again, his dad's manager, who he actually kind of liked now that he thought about it.

He looked around the empty hangar again, his gear already stowed aboard. It was 1230 station time, which meant Ezren and the others had over a five-hour lead on them, but the maintainers had needed time to prep the ship, and Grady was supposed to be pulling a pilot out of thin air. Still, he said he'd be ready by—

The door hissed open, and Grady rolled in with three hover-dollies of luggage.

Foster barked out an unsurprised laugh. "You know we'll be only gone for like a week, right?"

"You said there was plenty of room," Grady replied, directing his luggage up the boarding ramp with a command from his goggs.

"Yes, but it's also fully stocked."

"Then don't be asking to borrow my stuff when you run out of shampoo." Grady smirked.

"Right." Foster's lips quirked up. He was still surprised at the ease that had grown up between them in the last few months. Something he never would've thought possible after Vieve's death. "Did you pack our pilot in there too?"

"No, I'm right here."

Foster frowned at the vague familiarity of the voice but couldn't quite pinpoint its owner until he glanced at the doorway. There, a guy his own age stood with dark hair styled into a sweep, an olive glow to his complexion, and a spacer's half-visor over one eye.

Davis Banda. No fodding way.

Foster's head whipped back to Grady with a barely suppressed growl. "That's our pilot?"

"Oh, chill your chip." Grady's grin only widened, his eyes glinting with amusement. "We needed someone we can trust, with an interplanetary pilot license, on a minute's notice. Who better than a friend of Ezren's?"

Foster took in a controlled breath and folded his arms. The problem with Davis was that he'd once been more than Ezren's friend, and even after all this time, he *knew* Davis would've welcomed more. Paradoxically, there was a part of Foster that personally hated Davis for breaking Ezren's heart, but he had to admit, he'd always been there for her in a pinch. And at least this way, he didn't have to worry about this episode getting leaked on VSoc.

But he still didn't like it.

Adjusting the bag on his shoulder, Davis admired the ship with a low whistle. "Well, isn't she blime?" He turned to Foster with a friendly smile. "Are we all ready to ship out then?"

For a moment, Foster studied Davis, but there was only open curiosity in his countenance. Which was exactly what infuriated him most about Davis—he was impossible to hate. Still, that didn't mean he was off the hook. "Did Ezren tell you she was leaving?"

"I had no idea." Davis's smile flattened into a frown, and he dropped his bag onto one of Grady's dollies. "But after Simon told me about the update on her dad, it doesn't surprise me." His lips pursed with a shrug. "That's what I would've done too."

"Have you met him?" Foster kicked at the metal floor of the hangar, hating the advantage of history Davis still had on him. "Her dad, I mean?"

"No." Davis gave the dolly a push toward the lowered boarding ramp, and it hummed away. "But they were in Tuzuno when they hired that first P.I. who couldn't find him. Sammy didn't remember him much, but it hit Ezren and her mom hard."

"Shaft." Foster's shoulders dropped, his arms falling to his sides. Ezren had thought her dad abandoned her. He hated even thinking about how much pain that must've put her through, and yet they'd been wrong all along. "The ship's prepped for take-off, but we're already behind. So we'd better get going."

He turned and walked up the boarding ramp, Grady and Davis trailing behind him. The ship opened into a spacious cockpit with seats for six and separate rooms branching off for the cargo, private bunks, exercise room, kitchen, and common area. Though the layout was still small by most planet-sider standards, by a spacer's measuring stick, it was lavish. And he'd certainly need the room if he was going to survive Grady and Davis for a week.

"You should've seen Ezren when she got the news." Grady chuckled, nudging Davis. "It totally looked like a bomb went off when she found out." He opened the door to the storage room and sent his dollies in. "I have to admit, that girl's reaction time is fast, but she really has a bad habit of running off in a fritz. Remember that time she ran out into a blizzard to find you, Sterling?"

Guilt wriggled through Foster's already tense muscles. He should have seen this coming—should've told her he'd go right away. But then again, he still didn't have a good read on Shiro and couldn't she at least have called him *before* the shady P.I.?

"If I'd known this would happen, I wouldn't have hired the inspector in the first place." Foster closed the boarding ramp with a chip command and dropped into a plush passenger seat in the cockpit, yanking at the restraints.

Davis slid into the faux-leather captain's seat, the spherical holo heads-up display coming to life around him. He glanced sideways at Foster. "Yeah, but hiring a P.I. to find her dad was a pretty blime thing to do, Foster. At least she has a chance to find him now."

Foster let out a long sigh. He really didn't want to like

Davis, so why'd he have to be so nice? "Yeah, well, it went down kind of rough."

"It definitely did." Grady fell into the seat beside Foster with a laugh. "But now we have the chance to help her find her dad." His gaze darkened as he looked at Foster. "And take down Calderon Industries while we're at it."

Davis paused, his expression unreadable as he looked over his shoulder at the two of them.

"I just want her safe." Foster gestured toward the hangar ceiling as it opened above them to an oddly calm teal sky, dawn sunlight peeking through thanks to Belethea's short sols. "Do you think we can catch up to them?"

Davis turned back to his holo, a thousand different readouts flashing that only looked half familiar. "Maybe—this ship's actually incredibly fast. If you know what lunar hopper model Ezren and the others are on, I should be able to locate it and calculate our intercept."

"They went dark after launch, and I haven't seen their signature pop up yet." Grady flicked the image of a squat, round ship onto the cockpit's holo sphere encasing them.

A cold chill ran across Foster's neck as the ship's engine began to rumble. Even though he understood the reasoning, he still didn't like the feeling that Ezren could be anywhere right now. Or nowhere at all. "Can you still track it?

"Maybe. What do you know about the Shiro guy? We could try to see what routes he's taken in the past." Davis jostled against his restraints as the ship lifted into the air.

"I tried to look the guy up, but his VSoc accounts are almost blank." Grady leaned forward in his seat, projecting a picture of Shiro's angular face. "They really don't say anything more than we already know."

No one spoke over the roar of the engine while the ship executed its take-off protocols, the Gs pressing down on them as it cut through the atmosphere. Looking out the forward view holo, Foster tried to focus on his breathing. Within minutes, Belethea's clouds blurred by and the great volcanic face of Casolla greeted them—indigo and tangerine against the deep black of space.

And in that great nothingness, Ezren was out there somewhere.

Finally, Davis broke the silence with the question that'd been floating unspoken between the three of them.

"What if this guy works for Calderon?"

It was the question Foster had been studiously avoiding, but there it was, out in the open, and there was no ignoring it now. What if Shiro was manipulating Ezren to coerce Foster into cooperating with Calderon? Or what if he were trying to remove Ezren entirely? After all, though Calderon had tried to convince Foster to work for him, he hadn't said anything about Ezren.

Foster's mouth went dry, his stomach quailing in a way that had nothing to do with the Gs.

"Nah, it's probably just standard P.I. ops. Especially with the attacks." Grady reached over and squeezed Foster's shoulder. "He seemed legit."

"Yeah," Davis said. "Even if this is a plot to lure Ezren off Belethea, it seems overly complicated." The ship now safely coasting on course, and the generated gravity humming, Davis unbuckled his restraints and swiveled around to face them. "How do you know this guy anyway?"

"I..." A cold sweat broke out on Foster's brow, and he swallowed the boulder in his throat. "I didn't know him. I put out a call for an experienced P.I., and he contacted me." Foster ran a shaky hand across his face as the full realization of it hit him. "It was right before the BRR, so I wasn't even thinking of Calderon or threats or anything." *Mother suns.* He put his spinning head between his knees. Everything had happened so fast, he hadn't thought to look into it harder. The guy had found *him*, and now he basically didn't exist.

Ezren's life was in danger because of him.

Davis and Grady traded a grim look, but Davis was the first to speak, his voice low. "It's okay, Foster, you couldn't have known this would happen."

"Yeah, kin, and he still might be fine," Grady added. "We'll figure it out either way. Ezren's got Bex and Syl with her too, and you know Bex can take anybody."

Davis turned to the holo of the ship floating in the HUD and enlarged it. "I'll look over what we've got on the ship, and we'll put out a tracker to see if it pops up again. It's nearly impossible to go completely dark out here, and I'm betting they'll need to refuel before they get to Otho. Since we already have a good idea of their direction, there's a solid chance we'll find them."

Foster sucked in deep breaths as Grady moved into the copilot chair next to Davis, the two of them conferring over the ship's specs. He leaned back in his seat and looked out at the stars again, strangely grateful to have these two guys who usually irritated the chaff out of him.

They weren't Ezren. Not his double. But they were on his team. And right now, he needed that. He took another glance around the streamlined cockpit, the vibration of the engines purring through metal under his feet. Though he didn't know much about lunar hoppers, he'd already confirmed that this ship was much faster than a standard vessel. The thought struck a cautious spark in his chest. They were only five hours behind, but it would be days before Ezren landed on Otho. Grady knew more about vehicles than anyone, and Davis obviously knew what he was doing too. They were a better crew than he could've hoped for, and they both knew the stakes.

If anyone could outpace this Shiro guy, it was them.

One of the doors hissed open, and Foster's head jerked up as a tall figure stumbled into the cargo area.

"Hey, kin. What the fod. I'm trying to nurse a hangover back here."

Grady and Davis leapt from their seats, Grady's hands automatically raising for a fight, while Davis pulled a jolt bar from his belt.

"Who are you and what're you doing here?" Davis barked.

The figure slumped into a spare chair, his head lolling back and his long hair tied in a high knot. "Mother suns, don't shout. My head..."

Realizing he wasn't a threat, Davis's shoulders relaxed, but not before Grady belted out a rich laugh and slapped a hand on Davis's back. "Hold up, kin. It's Gerard Y."

Davis raised a brow with a cautious smile. "Tell me that's not a famous assassin."

"Worse." Foster scowled, his hands curling into fists as his jaw worked. "It's my dad."

CHAPTER 8

8.12.43B: T-minus 6 days until Mt. Aguya's Eruption

THE LAST TIME Ezren had been on a ship it had been with her mom and brother, and they'd been leaving their crowded home planet of Obrone for a new life on Belethea. She'd been fourteen then, and her father's messages had completely stopped. At that point, her mother had already stopped talking about him, and they would only receive one more cred transfer before they never heard from him again. Sam, at nine, was still so little, and while his regen procedures had been a cautious success, they'd yet to find the appropriate medication to manage his pain. So even though it cost a fortune for their capy-bog, Waffle, to travel with him—they'd paid it.

They couldn't afford to leave behind more family.

Those were dark years with few smiles, and Ezren had apparently managed to repress the memories with some success. So it was only natural that she'd forgotten how much she hated interlunar travel.

Hated.

The *Tumble Bucket*, as the ship was so aptly named, had only three connected rooms. The cockpit, a living space with fold-away bunks and a heating cube for the morale meals that supplemented their tasteless nutrition sludge, and a tiny 0.7-G exercise sphere with a weight bench and a treadmill—where

Ezren was currently pounding out the virtual miles. Not a foot away from her, Bex and Sylvia ran through hand-to-hand drills, the irregular slaps of their feet and hands punctuating the air.

The astounding part was that allegedly the *Bucket* could hold eight "comfortably." They were only at half capacity and already felt packed in like sardines. Which was exactly everything that was wrong with the space arks that had come through the wormgates and the stations they'd been converted into. But even in the cramped space, Foster's absence haunted her. She'd left him behind in a spray of bullets, and now she couldn't even contact him. What must he—

No, don't think about that. They were after you. Foster will be fine.

Ezren pushed herself harder, her goggs projecting a simulated Belethean track she'd used many times in Carmella. But the recycled air tasted stale, the hum of the exercise sphere's spinning gravity liner grated on her ears, and the cold pulse of the vastness of space stretched out all around her.

Involuntarily, her mind drifted to the day her father had left Obrone—a memory she'd forced herself not to think about for the last four years. How he'd tapped her on the nose, tears budding in his eyes. *"No matter how far I go, my heart is always right here with yours. I love you all so much, you'll feel it, even from here. Whenever you look up at the sky, know that I'm looking right back down at you."*

The pronouncement of his abandonment had turned those words into a lie, but now... she gazed out into the darkness again. Was it possible he'd been looking this whole time? Had she been the first one to turn away? She couldn't even remember how long it'd been since she'd dared to hope.

A voice punched through her thoughts. "So, this is what you royalers do, huh?"

Blinking damp eyes, Ezren turned to the entryway to find Shiro leaning against the threshold with a bemused smile.

"Right. Who would've thought royalers actually run and spar?" Sylvia put her hands on her hips, a challenge glinting beneath her lashes. "Do they even teach hand-to-hand under whatever rock you P.I.s crawl out of? Or do you just hide behind a gun?"

"Not to brag, but the P.I. rock is pretty cozy." Shiro toed out of his boots and slipped out of his coat. "Maybe you can teach me a thing or two?"

"It's the least I can do, I'm sure," Sylvia drawled. Though she didn't have Bex's rippling muscles or Ezren's lean build, Sylvia's skills were nothing to sneeze at.

Ezren's stare caught on the gun holster still strapped to his chest with a black pistol slotted into it, and a distant anxiety fluttered through her as she thought of him laying down fire at the port. Despite Sylvia's light tone, this man was dangerous. But he unbuckled the weapon too, leaving him in a sleeveless spacer's jumpsuit that showed off his well-defined shoulders and biceps. Apparently, he was no slouch either.

Ezren stepped off the treadmill, and Bex edged out of the way as Shiro approached the mat with an easy grin. But Sylvia had no patience for that. She feinted a jab at his nose, and Shiro circled away in the cramped space, his hands loose at his sides.

"So I know about the others, but you ran royales too, right?" His tone was teasing as he easily blocked another punch. "What was your specialty?" Sylvia edged too close, and Shiro darted in with whip-like speed. In a breath, he had her trapped against him with full control of her arms. His movements were so smooth, it almost seemed like a dance.

"Well, it certainly wasn't the fists." Sylvia strained against him, frustration twisting her face though not hurt in the slightest—another testament to his skill. "But they recruited me for my wheels."

"Ah." Shiro released her, and she stepped away with a scowl. "Well, I suppose we'll have to see what you can do in the cockpit."

"Why don't you try a real fighter instead?" Bex stepped forward, her cold gaze running from Shiro's stocking feet to his wild thatch of dark hair.

"It'd be my honor." He spread his hands in a wide invitation.

Leaning against the wall, Ezren and Sylvia exchanged a smirk. Without a topsuit to narrow the strength gap, his height and weight had given him an advantage on Sylvia. But Bex was as tall as he was, and while he had the wiry build of someone who spent a lot of time in low G, Bex never went a day without honing her body.

Once again, Shiro waited for her to attack. This time, it only took one move. Shiro may have been fast, but Bex was lightning. Closing the gap, she seized his jumpsuit and, with a sharp twist of her body, slammed him to the ground. In another second, she had her knee resting lightly on his neck, a fist an inch from his nose.

Ezren chuckled in sympathy at Shiro's shell-shocked expression. "We call that hard mode."

"Are you saying I'm easy mode?" Sylvia glared at her with mock outrage. "Extra cultural etiquette quizzes for you."

Ezren groaned, trying not to think about the two she'd already failed that day. "There's nothing easy about you, Syl."

"Okay, I gotcha." Shiro accepted Bex's outstretched hand and got to his feet with a chuckle. "But can you handle a gun?"

Ezren shook her head, the uneasiness once again quaking through her. "Guns aren't allowed in the BRR."

With a flick of his hand, his pistol flew from his holster and into his practiced grip. Only then did Ezren notice the thin metal bracelet around his wrist. A magnetic caller. Similar to their mag-boots, it had a very specific attraction that could be turned on and off. With a command from his half-visor, the walls disappeared around them, replaced with a sim of a shooting range with a variety of figures standing in a field of tall grass. He raised the gun with bent elbows and pulled the trigger, nailing five targets in quick succession.

The word "bullseye" appeared above each target before fading into the blue sky holopro.

Strangely though, there was no pride in his expression—only a sort of grim satisfaction. "The weapon's on sim mode. Most tactical topsuits will assist your aim, but no software can beat practice." He offered the handle of the gun to Bex. "Care to give it a try?"

"Royalers don't use guns." Bex stepped away from him, her lips curling in distaste. "It's an ignoble weapon."

"If people are murdering your teammates, maybe you should." He shrugged, the gun falling to his side. "Training would at least pass the time."

Sylvia raised a skeptical brow, and the cat chirped as it entered the room, tails raised curiously. "Have you ever killed anyone?"

The recycled air grew decidedly heavier, and though he smiled, Ezren thought his gaze softened with something like sorrow. "That's classified." He opened his arms, and the cat leapt into them with a satisfied purr.

"That's a yes," Sylvia said.

Ezren chuckled nervously, trying to lighten the mood. "He's a cat person, how bad could he be?"

"Are you joking?" Bex strode across the room and leaned against the wall with them—a united front. "Calderon has three cats."

"No way." Ezren frowned. "How do you even know that?"

Sylvia reached out to scratch the cat's head in Shiro's arms, and it preened under her attention. "The more I find out about you, Ian Shiro, the more suspicious you seem."

His grin widened, and this time, it creased the laugh lines edging his face. "And you know what, Sylvia Long, I think you like it."

Ezren stifled a snort and peeked at Bex. But if Bex was picking up on the flirtatious tension between these two, she wasn't showing it.

Sylvia pressed her lips together, flicking a curl away from her face. "I think I'm considering the escape pod."

The cat jumped away, and Shiro rubbed a hand over his perpetual five-o'clock shadow. "Eh, well, in three days we'll be at Exa to get the latest Otho entry codes and one of Baxter's supply ships. If you have cold feet, you can exit the ride there if you want." He brushed past her to pick up his holster and rebuckled it around his chest.

Ezren shifted from one foot to the other. "So it's a stolen ship then?"

"Nonsense. It went off course, and we're simply returning it." Shiro smirked as he slid into his coat.

Sylvia drummed her fingers on the drawers of supplies lining the wall. "Just how illegal is all this?"

"What? Breaking into a murderer's secret facility? I'd say it's all grays at this point. Unfortunately, I'd call it a bullet-shade of gray." He opened one of the wall-drawers at waist-height. "So, if you get tired of throwing each other around, there are a few sim-guns in here you can practice with." His gaze hardened for just a moment, and the drawer snapped shut. "I highly recommend you do." With that, he turned and walked back to the cockpit, the cat on his heels.

Ezren, Bex, and Sylvia exchanged a glance. Sylvia's skeptical. Bex's indifferent. And Ezren's worried. The unknowns of what she'd gotten them into seemed ready to swallow them. Running away from danger, running toward danger—and despite what Shiro said about Exa, she couldn't see any escaping it at this point.

Ezren eyed the drawer of sim guns. "You all should bail at Exa. This is way too dangerous."

"Don't let him shake you," Bex said. "It's dangerous, but if there's one thing royalers know, it's how to get in and out of danger. There's no one better to run in there and figure out what's going on." Her gaze drifted toward the cockpit, her lips twisting thoughtfully. "And I think he knows that."

"Fod it." Sylvia sighed and yanked open the weapon drawer. "As much as he annoys the chaff out of me, he's also right about the guns. If we're going up against Calderon, he's not going to hold back. We need to be prepared." She took a pistol out for herself and handed one to Ezren.

For a moment, Ezren hesitated, then she reached out and took it.

Bex was right. It was an ignoble weapon. But if Calderon came for them, he wouldn't be restrained by the appearance of any rules this time. He was killing people.

Her grip tightened on the cold metal, the weapon heavy in her hand. She would learn to use it, but she prayed to the suns she wouldn't need it.

CHAPTER 9

8.15.43B: T-minus 3 days until Mt. Aguya's Eruption

FOSTER LAY on the wide couch in the ship's recreation room, scrolling through the latest VSoc rumors. Speculation was running rampant on the mysterious training camp the Belethean Race Royale team had disappeared to on the tail of another terrorist attack. While the hologgers laid out their weirdest conspiracy theories, Grady and his dad played some kind of drinking game he didn't understand. Twin hovercams spun around them as his dad knocked a card out of Grady's hand with a whoop.

"Can you at least keep it down?" Foster scowled at them from the couch. "Haven't you run out of booze yet?"

His father glanced at him with a slapdash smile. "But what else's there to do up here?"

"Yeah." Grady swayed slightly. "And besides, we'll need VSoc holos to post of this thing when we get back."

Foster's glare homed in on his dad. His straight black hair was tied high on his head and a thick beard edged his face. They were so different in looks and personality, there'd been times when Foster wondered if Gerard was even his father. This was one of them. "You could just take the escape pod and leave if you're so bored."

Gerard closed his eyes and tilted his head back with a

smile, completely relaxed, with no regard for his assistant, agent, and bandmates who were probably fritzing out about his absence down on Belethea. "I could," he said, his voice a melodious bass even when speaking. "But the break couldn't have had better timing. I'm supposed to be working on my next album, but they had me on a big publicity rush for no reason. Now I finally have time to think." His grin widened, his gray eyes twinkling in the low light. "I ought to be thanking you for kidnapping me."

Grady cocked his head thoughtfully, toying with one of his earrings. "Your publicity team was probably trying to capitalize on Foster's recent VSoc skyrocket."

Gerard let out a low chortle. "Am I really such an old washed-up rock star that I need to rely on my son to boost my music?"

"Yes," Foster said flatly, overlapping with Grady's, "Of course not."

"Always so harsh to your old man." Gerard laughed again, and Foster couldn't help but notice that despite his father's fifty-odd years, they probably looked closer to brothers than father and son. He must've paid a fortune in fodding youth-enhancing cell regen treatments. There were even rumors on VSoc of some black-market varieties that were near magic these days.

"You could come play with us," his father continued, lifting his glass to Foster. "Get some bonding time in."

"Big pass." Foster sat up, ready to flee if need be. By definition, lunar hoppers weren't huge, but he'd rather be in the cargo hold than drink with his father. "I've got stuff to do."

Before he could make his escape though, Davis strolled into the room and sat purposely next to him. Foster scowled, but Davis's lips only quirked into a polite smile. "Do you mind?"

"Go right ahead," Foster said. Though he still didn't like

Davis, he had to admit that his company had been better than Grady and Gerard's on this bizarre expedition.

"I've got good news." Davis folded his hands together, elbows resting on his knees. "I just got a tag on Shiro's ship when he docked at Exa Station."

"How far are we?" Foster snapped to attention, his muscles tightening as if he could run the rest of the way.

Davis's grin curved in a relaxed tilt. "Only a couple hours."

Foster nodded, his thoughts tripping over each other. "If they're there for fuel and supplies, we might be able to catch them."

"Did you say Exa Station?" Gerard swirled the golden liquid in his cup, the wave bobbing above the rim in the reduced gravity and a furrow cutting between his dark brows. "That place is a hotbed of organized crime. Are you sure you want to go there?"

Prickles of disquiet stabbed Foster in a thousand places, sharpening his tone. "If Ezren is there, that's even more reason to go."

"There are other, safer stations they could've refueled out of." Davis's expression darkened as he met Foster's gaze. "If he took them there, it doesn't bode well."

"We still don't know anything." Grady waved them off, picking up his hand of cards with another flick of his wrist. "No use worrying until you have to."

Foster ignored him, pulling up his VSoc holo again.

"Ezren's family and Micah are doing well," Davis said quietly. "It sounds like whatever Ezren decided to do, she didn't tell them. So I let them know she was going to be out of comms for a while but not to worry."

"Oh." Foster's lips tightened. With everything going on, he'd completely forgotten to check in with them. "That was... thoughtful. Thanks."

Davis nodded to the headlines in Foster's holopro. "I guess a lot of people have noticed you two are missing already?"

"Yeah, but Sylvia covered for us with some away messages before she left. She's delayed the recruits' starting dates but it looks like Villegas has done a decent job of shifting the focus to them in the meantime He grimaced. "Though Sylvia will have a conniption if we don't make that stupid ambassador summit in four days."

"The one where they're debating the diplomatic impacts of the investigation on the BRR and reviewing terranium right distribution?" Davis asked in a tone that sounded like he fodding well knew, so why was he asking?

"Yeah, it's all a load of shaft." Foster's hand spasmed, and he covered it with the other. Beside him, Grady fell back onto the plush rug with a victory howl as Gerard took another obligatory swig from his tumbler. "Ezren and I did our part, so we should be done with this chaff."

"But you can't be done. It's not that easy." Though Davis's gaze followed the game, his tone was earnest, nearly vibrating with intent.

Frustration welled up in Foster like blood from a fresh wound. "Right, because winning the BRR was easy."

"I didn't say that," Davis replied with all the infuriating patience of a centenarian monk. "But if you want real change, you have to be in it for the long game. And honestly, with your influence, you could be a huge help in getting Belethea back to a new normal. Or a huge hindrance." Davis rubbed his palms together, sincerity emanating from his every pore. "With that power, you have greater opportunities. Opportunities others would die for. How many people get to have a voice at the Casolla summit?"

Foster rolled out his shoulders, tired of this conversation before it'd even begun. How had Ezren put up with all his preaching? "Opportunity makes it sound crisp and all, but it's really just more work."

"Yes." Davis leaned closer, refusing to let up. "But your work has a chance to make a real difference. Obrone's orbit will take it close to Otho next week, so there's still a chance you could get there in time."

Before Foster could respond, Gerard called over to them, "What are you two looking all serious about?"

Davis smiled, but a tightness tugged at the corners of his eyes. "Your son doesn't want to be famous."

"But..." Gerard frowned, squinting in confusion. "We've always been famous."

Chaff, how did Foster end up on a ship with *three* insufferable people? "Ah yes, and it was always such a treat having my every move documented on VSoc growing up."

"Yeah, yeah, you can boohoo about it all you want." Gerard waved at him with his glass, the sphere of liquid lifting out of the cup before he caught it again. "But whatever troubles your fame and fortune get you into, they can get you out of too." He took another sip. "That's the whole point."

Foster shot to his feet, turning his back on his father as he faced Davis. "What's our ETA on Exa?"

Davis didn't even hesitate. "Two hours and fifteen minutes."

Thank the suns. "I'll be in the gym." Unable to stand it any longer, Foster stalked off, leaving Grady and Gerard guffawing over their asinine game. Still, adrenaline coiled through him at their destination's proximity. What if something had already happened to Ezren? He had to know she was okay, and more than that, he needed to get off this ship before he strangled his dad and started to like Davis Banda.

CHAPTER 10

8.15.43B: T-minus 3 days until Mt. Aguya's Eruption

BY THE TIME they reached Exa Station on the fourth day, Ezren was ready to crawl out of her skin. As soon as the boarding ramp lowered, she burst into the bustling hangar and spun around in the somewhat larger enclosed space. Anything was better than Shiro's scratched tin can.

"Finally." She smiled back at Bex and Sylvia as they followed behind with the baggage hover-dolly.

The ill-fitting spacer jumpsuits Shiro had procured for Bex and Ezren hung loose from their limbs, and the half-visors looked out of place over their left eyes. Ezren imagined she looked even more unrecognizable with her hair dyed back to her natural mousy brown and a gray scarf covering the lower half of her face. Or at least, she hoped she would be unrecognizable, because there was nowhere to run if she was mobbed in here.

Sylvia stepped to her side, already sniping at Shiro, her new favorite hobby over the past few days. "Are you sure our bags are going to make it to the new ship?" She stuffed her goggs down her well-fitted, purple one-piece and straightened her matching half-visor—which she'd apparently brought along for the possibility of a station appearance. "I have important stuff in there."

Shiro took her jibes with an easy grin as the boarding plank raised behind him, the pink cat—who Ezren had finally dubbed Turnip—darting out at the last second. "Yes, yes, don't worry, all your hair products are going to make it." With a chip message, the dolly closed into a hovering cube. Turnip only just managed to jump onto the top before it trundled off to their presumed destination with the pink cat as its strange captain.

"Are you sure we can't carry anything, just in case?" Ezren frowned, already missing her tattered sweater and goggs.

"We want to avoid anything that's going to mark you as an outsider," Shiro said, adjusting his coat over an olive green one piece that made him look like a shabby mechanic more than a spacer.

A bandana covered Bex's white hair as her gaze took in the crowded hangar around them. "Not exactly a high-end station, is it?"

Ezren cocked her head, re-examining it. People milled to and fro as ships filled with passengers, supplies, and cargo lined up to go in and out of the airlocks. Exa was one of the bigger stations, population-wise, but the hangar still felt overstuffed, the walls plastered with holo-ads for budget nutrition and shuttle services. Not only that, but there was a palpable roughness to the spacers here. Many glanced at them with hard eyes, some with torn jumpsuits and cracked half-visors. A few even openly sported nano-tattoos crawling across their skin that Ezren knew blared their syndicate affiliations, while one—a shabby fellow curled in the corner—had a scar carved into the right side of his face.

"Don't stare," Shiro said in a low voice. "The scar is for those who have gone against the Kalashnik. Exa is their territory, and a good reason to step lightly here. The black-market drug game has spiked off the charts in the past few years, and the Kalashnik have the influence to prove it."

Wordlessly, the three of them followed Shiro as he strode to one of the nearby corridors. While the scowls drifted over and past them, Ezren's gaze flicked to the pistol she knew lay holstered somewhere under Shiro's jacket. At least the claustrophobic boredom of the last few days had made her a decent shot, although not nearly as good as Bex. That girl had a laser eye that made Ezren wonder if she was genetically engineered for combat. But the thought of a gun fight breaking out in a crowded station made her stomach roll.

The mag train was packed to its limit as they shuffled in, bodies pressed together from every side, and Ezren found herself wishing for the tin can again. In the silent mass of bodies, a group message illuminated Ezren's half-visor.

SYLVIA: WHERE ARE WE GOING, SHIRO? SHOULDN'T THE NEW SHIP BE AT THE HANGAR DOCK WITH THE OTHERS?

SHIRO: I HAVE SOMEONE TO MEET FIRST, AND WHILE WE'RE ON STATION, TREAT ALL CHIP MESSAGES AS PUBLIC. THE NUMBER OF HACKERS MINING DATA HERE WOULD FRITZ YOUR MIND.

Ezren shared an uneasy glance with Sylvia and Bex. Bex's posture was rigid, but Sylvia's lips pursed briefly with doubt before she glared at Shiro once more.

SYLVIA: IF THIS ALL GOES SOUTH, I'M HOLDING YOU PERSONALLY RESPONSIBLE.

Shiro smiled at her, leaning close. "I think you'll find we all went south together as soon as we started this little adventure," he whispered.

Sylvia didn't back down, the two of them only inches apart as she punched a finger in his chest, her voice equally low. "You got us here, so you'd better get us out."

"Whatever you say." His eyes flicked to her lips so quickly that for a second Ezren thought she imagined it. Sylvia's eyes flashed before she turned away, giving him a face full of her curls.

Ezren stifled a snort. She couldn't help but wonder if either of them had acted on their obvious attraction. Not that it was any of her business, and she wasn't sure if she trusted Shiro, but it was the first time she'd seen someone fluster Sylvia. It was good for her, and Ezren couldn't help but root for them. Even if it only made her miss Foster more. Suns, she hoped he was safe.

But as they delved deeper into the belly of Exa, a small part of her was relieved he wasn't there. After all, she had no doubt that if someone tried to shoot her—*again*—Foster would be the first to jump in front of the bullet. Dents peppered the walls and floor, dust coated the air vents and swirled in the sour air, and they passed a trio of scorches on the wall she swore were from gunfire. Yes, Foster was safer on Belethea.

The hubbub of the hangar evaporated as they walked, now replaced by strangely silent passersby with their heads down under the flickering holos and dim lighting. Wordlessly, Bex moved to Ezren's other side, sandwiching her in between the three of them.

Ezren's emotions roiled, caught with the fear of what would happen to them if she was recognized alongside the indignation that she had to be protected when this was her idea. The conflict only made her want to move faster.

At last, Shiro stepped into what looked like a relatively respectable café. He nodded to the man at the entrance before leading them to one of the circular booths in the back, cased in by curved glass walls. Ezren couldn't see anyone else in the café, but a few of the other opaque barriers could've hidden customers inside.

"Well, this doesn't seem so bad." Ezren offered a tentative smile as she slid in beside him, praying they had coffee. Would it be weird to order cake?

The door hissed shut behind them, and Bex's shrewd gaze slewed across the spartan establishment with holos of authentic burgers and alcohol adorning the walls. "Money in an unmoneyed place. Sound barriers around the booths." She sat back and crossed her arms. "We're not paying for food here; we're paying for discretion."

"But the food's good too." Shiro projected a menu from his visor. "And we'll still need to use a distorter, of course."

Ezren cocked her head at Bex. "How'd you know that?"

"Petraskis has places like this too." Bex touched the glass barrier, and a thick frost spread from her fingers, turning the window white to hide them from wandering eyes. "My father's MMA gym didn't take off until I was ten or eleven, and even now, my family doesn't exactly run with the most reputable of crowds."

"Look at you with your hidden depths." Shiro's lips curved in a stretched smile that didn't reach his eyes. "I'm glad at least one of you knows what we're dealing with." He turned his dark gaze on Ezren. "Information is money here, and money is power. So when my contact arrives, none of you says a word." He looked at each of them in turn. "Even if he asks you a question, don't answer. From here on out, we don't trust anybody."

Sylvia let out a long-suffering sigh as she projected the menu from her half-visor. "Just when I thought you couldn't get any sketchier."

Ezren folded her arms around herself, a chill crawling up her spine without the protection of her thick sweater. The stations never seemed to completely keep out the cold of space. "But who are you—"

The door to their booth sliced open, and Ezren closed her mouth with a click.

An older man with a receding hairline and a paunchy middle straining against his patched jumpsuit shuffled in. His features sagged with a tired weight as he eased into the booth across from Shiro. Beside him, Bex scooted closer to Ezren and Sylvia, the three of them packed tight on the bench between Shiro and the newcomer. The door rolled shut, closing them in, and suddenly Ezren had the distinct feeling of being trapped inside a box inside yet another, even smaller box.

"We have seven minutes." The man folded his hands on the table. "But your order is ready and waiting."

A hole slid open in the middle of the faux-wood table, and five plated burgers, each surrounded in a halo of fries, rose on a circular platter. "My man, of course it is." Shiro took one of the plates and slid it to his contact with a smile. "Try some for yourself."

Something flashed in Shiro's visor, and a low buzzing filled the enclosed space.

The man didn't look at them as he grabbed a burger with wrinkled hands, taking a bite as Shiro passed the other plates around. "Are you still planning on your trip?" the man said around a bite.

"We are." Shiro delicately crunched into a golden fry. "And I was wondering if you had some more tourism advice for us. My friends are new to the area."

"My advice is don't go." The man's gaze skewed to Ezren, his expression softening, almost sympathetic.

From Shiro's description, Ezren had been expecting someone dangerous, but it was obvious this guy was anything but. The horrors of a victim were etched into every line of his face, every measured movement, and even the hunch of his shoulders.

"It was dangerous before, but now it's suicide." He took another decisive bite of the burger.

Ezren's chest iced over, and any regard for Shiro's rules went out the airlock. "What's changed?" she whispered.

Shiro, Bex, and Sylvia all shot her matching glares, but if the man recognized her, he didn't show it. Instead, he leaned forward, all pretense evaporating as he lowered his voice.

"The scientists on Otho are resisting Calderon's attempts to shut them down, and it's devolved into a full-scale conflict." He shook his head. "Not only is their communication with the outside limited, but now, comms are jammed all over Otho. It's basically guerrilla warfare down there between Calderon and Baxter." His doughy lips tightened, and his deep-set eyes locked on Ezren's. "I don't know what secret they're hiding, but the bottom line is, people are dying over it. And with it so hush-hush, there's gotta be someone higher covering it up."

Bex's brows knitted as she studied him. "You were there."

Shiro audibly slapped a hand to his forehead, but they were beyond his suspicions now.

"I was just the supply runner." He straightened again, shifting on the cheap vinyl seat. "And even I barely got out."

Ezren's breath caught in her chest. "So, how did the scientists get there?" The curiosity clawed at her from the inside out —the need to know impossible to stifle. "Did they choose to go?"

He barked out a dry laugh. "If they did, they quickly realized their mistake."

Ezren's mind raced, trying to piece together this new information. "It was a terraforming breakthrough," she whispered. "It had to be."

There was no way Calderon would risk that getting out with the resurgence of the terraforming movement. If Baxter had figured out a way to terraform a toxic planet like Otho, the implications were boundless. There would be no stopping terraforming then, with eighteen other moons waiting for just such a breakthrough.

"Indeed." Shiro wiped his mouth with a napkin and tossed it onto the table. "Perhaps we could discuss this lat—"

"Why not just kill them like he did the others on Gobrion?" Bex interrupted.

"I don't know about Gobrion, but with the firefight on Otho now, I'd hazard a guess the scientists foresaw that eventuality." The man shrugged, his face drooping even lower. "Then again, maybe they're already dead. I had an inside guy who was supposed to send me an SOS message with proof for the Calderon trial, but he's two weeks late."

Ezren's body went rigid, the blood draining from her face. "But surely there's some way to tell—"

The blast of four successive shots rang through the air, followed by the crash of breaking glass. Simultaneously, the four of them ducked as a calm voice echoed through the café. "We are now closed, please make your way to the exits."

"Shaft." The man's face hardened, and he slid a folded piece of paper to Shiro before locking eyes with Ezren one last time. "Tell your dad I tried to warn you." With that, he manually shoved the door to one side and ran out.

He didn't make it two steps before shots burst out again. He fell to the ground, blood seeping across the floor, eyes staring.

Dead.

Then all Ezren could hear were screams.

CHAPTER 11

8.15.43B: T-minus 3 days until Mt. Aguya's Eruption

EZREN'S MOUTH fell open as Sylvia's shrieks echoed in her ears and dark blood burgeoned across the metal floor. Like Shiro, most law enforcement officers used bolt-ammo, but these were laser-lead—meant to kill while not ricocheting off the metal walls of the space station.

Mother suns.

Shiro reached out and slid the door closed as a fresh volley of bullets rattled the glass.

"Is there another way out?" Sylvia screamed as Bex simultaneously yelled, "Are they here for us?"

Neither got an answer before the glass shattered around them, raining down in razor shards. Shiro grabbed Sylvia's arm and yanked her low in the booth. "Stop talking and run for the back door! I'll cover you." Shifting in his seat, he raised his gun over the lip of the booth and fired off five quick shots. Together, Ezren, Bex, and Sylvia sprinted for the back of the café where an old-fashioned hinged door stood like a portal to safety. Bex had just rounded the corner when Sylvia let out a blood-freezing scream, and Ezren turned to find her on the ground, blood gushing from her leg.

Before Ezren could react, Shiro scooped her from the floor and threw her over his shoulder, still firing at their attackers. In two steps he made the door and slammed it shut behind them, a manual bolt sliding home. "This way," he grunted, striding off down a narrow maintenance corridor.

"But there were still people back there," Ezren said with half a mind to unlock the door and throw it open.

"And I feel for them, I do." Shiro's mag-boots echoed in the metal hallway with battered doors peppering the walls. "But our time is up, and we have a ride waiting."

"Am I dying?" Sylvia moaned from his shoulder, a trail of crimson dripping from her leg.

"If you are, I'm seriously impressed with your lucidity." Shiro took a sharp corner, adjusting her on his shoulder.

"Who were they?" Bex's eyes darted behind them as she brought up the rear. "Do you think they'll follow us?"

"The Kalashniks, Calderon, the actual authorities—who knows? You people are *so* popular." He put Sylvia down and looked at Bex, sweat slicking his forehead. "We'll need to carry her between us so she doesn't draw so much attention." Bex nodded, pulling one of Sylvia's arms around her shoulders as Shiro shoved open a side door into a wider hall with a stream of people flowing through it. "See the door third on the left, private dock seven-two? That's us."

They'd almost made it to the metal dock when a deep voice shouted from behind them. "Out of the way! Stop those four!"

Shiro turned as a man barreled toward them, pulling a gun from his hip. With Sylvia in his arms, he wasn't going to have time to disarm him. In a blink, his gaze jumped to Ezren and she nodded, hundreds of hours of Bex's hand-to-hand training surging through her in a rush of adrenaline.

With a lunge, Ezren grabbed the man's arm and used his momentum to flip him over her hip. He slammed into the floor, and twisting his hand, she wrested the gun from his fist, just as she'd practiced on Bex a hundred plus times in the past few days.

"C'mon!" Shiro shouted from the open door, guiding Sylvia inside while Bex shoved off an aggressive bystander. "Stop fritzin' around."

Ezren ran for the door, but before she got there, someone grabbed her arm and threw her to the ground. She tensed as the mag-boot swung toward her, but Bex's fist found his face first. Ezren scrambled from the floor only to stop dead, looking straight down the barrel of a gun.

Ezren didn't get a breath before a blast nearly deafened her, and the crowd ducked in a swell of screams.

But it had been Shiro's gun, and the man before her crumpled to the ground in a convulsive fit.

"I said come *on*," Shiro yelled, the words serrated with agitation.

Finally, Bex and Ezren ducked into the doorway, and Shiro banged it closed behind him. With another chip command, the dead bolt clanked into place. Apparently this place did not fritz around with security. That done, Shiro turned on his heel and picked up Sylvia from where she leaned against the wall. Though his hands were gentle as he lifted her into a bridal-carry, her eyes screwed shut in pain.

"Say hello to our new home." He jerked his chin at the ship before them, but there was nothing easy about his expression now—the lines in his face taut with strain.

Ezren turned and stopped mid-step, her mouth falling open. This ship was nothing like the *Tumble Bucket*. In fact, this was about as far away from a bucket as it got. Its enormous frame was built like a torpedo, and she had no doubt it flew as well through air as it did through space. Beefy engines hung from its sleek wings, and she even spied a landing craft and escape pods snug against its broad belly. The only blot marring its militant precision was the pink six-tailed cat waiting for them on the boarding ramp with a soft meow. Well, at least they knew their stuff made it.

"Are those *cannons*?" she asked.

Bex grabbed her arm and yanked her along. "It's a military-grade stealth ship."

"Now you're getting it," Shiro said, stalking up the boarding ramp.

The cockpit to this new ship was spacious but efficient, with a floor-to-ceiling holodash in front of the pilot's seat and doors branching out to other bays. Everything here was sleek and new, the heads-up holo chock-full of controls and a full 360-view of the hangar. Four seats lined the nose for the crew along with jump-seats edging the side and what looked like endless storage tucked in its walls.

Now *this* was a ship.

Sylvia looked up at Shiro beneath knitted rainbow brows. "Who the chaff *are* you?"

"A private investigator, a pilot, your current savior." He smiled down at her as he lowered her into the copilot chair and strapped her in. "I wear lots of hats."

"I'm checking the other rooms for unwanted visitors," Bex said, taking off through the ship at a run.

"Is there a bandage for Sylvia's leg?" Ezren asked, eyeing the blood trail spattering the pristine deck. The boarding ramp snapped shut behind them on well-oiled gears, making Turnip jump.

"There will be time to play nurse later." Shiro's fingers flew through the holos as the ship powered up, and Ezren frowned at his familiarity with the controls. Could one of his hats be military pilot as well? "Right now, we need to get out of here, so strap in."

No sooner had the words left his mouth than the door to the hangar burst open with a controlled explosion.

"Pulse shields up," he barked. "Open airlock doors, initiate take-off protocol, and override host communication." The ship responded with alacrity, the laser-fueled shields absorbing the energy of the bullets as Shiro smiled. "Finally. Nothing says warm and cozy like superior firepower."

"Stop crowing already and get us out of here," Sylvia snapped.

"If a bullet won't get her down, I'm beginning to think nothing will," Shiro said, the ship easing off the ground and into the airlock.

Bex ran back into the cockpit with Turnip in her arms and slid into a seat. "The other rooms are clear."

The robotic male drone of the ship leaked into their visors. "Take-off permission denied. Airlock door closed."

Another volley of gunfire echoed through the hangar as a group of heavily armed men rushed the ship. *Mother suns.* What would they do if they couldn't take off? If those men had explosives, it would only be a matter of time before they boarded. Ezren's heart pounded in her chest as she scrambled for a plan and came up with nothing.

Shiro squinted at the scrap of paper in his hand. "Override 034-November-9-Echo-22."

A beat, and then the ship's voice answered. "Take-off permission granted. Safe travels."

The airlock doors opened one after the other to reveal a blanket of stars lost in perpetual night, welcoming the ship into open space. Ezren let out a tense breath—only to be interrupted by a percussive boom that shook the vessel, punctuated by Sylvia's yelp.

Ezren white-knuckled her restraints, sure her heart would burst at any second. "What the chaff was that?"

But Shiro's focus remained on the ship. "Return fire, perform evasive maneuver ninety-three, and initiate stealth cloak."

The ship vibrated again as its own shots rattled off, and Ezren reached out to grip Bex's hand. "I really don't want to die in space." Ezren's breaths pumped too fast. "I want to die on an actual planet." She wanted to be on Belethea with the wind around her when she bit it, not here in the void.

With Turnip zipped into her spacer jumpsuit, Bex squeezed Ezren's hand, her own gaze steady. "You're not dying today, Hart. Just breathe."

The ship jerked in a series of nauseating, unpredictable maneuvers, and the accompanying Gs slammed into Ezren's chest like a ten-ton brick. Her stomach was threatening to give up its contents when they finally leveled out. As Ezren re-inflated her poor squished lungs, an eerie quiet fell over the ship.

Shiro stretched his arms out above him, tilting his head from one side to another, as if waking from a nap. "Well, that went better than I thought."

Ezren looked up, sweat trickling down her brow and still clutching Bex's hand. "You mean, it's over? Just like that?"

"Just like that. All thanks to a little stealth technology and a man who knows how to use it." Shiro grinned. "It's okay, you can hold your applause."

"There's something seriously wrong with you," Sylvia wheezed, her pant leg dark with blood.

"Oh, right." Shiro lurched into action. "Don't worry, there's a med bay through here." Unbuckling her restraints, he swept her into his arms and carried her through one of the side doors. Sylvia's long eyelashes fluttered, her light brown skin three shades too pale.

Ezren and Bex followed behind them, watching as Shiro

laid Sylvia on a metal cot. He projected a holopro, and with a few commands, the black, crawling nanites swarmed from the table over her injured leg.

Bex removed the bandana from her white hair, and Turnip squirmed free of her jumpsuit. "So, if this was better than you thought, how did you think it was going to go?"

Satisfied with the nanites' progress, Shiro chuckled as he turned toward them. "Look, we just chartered a stolen military vessel, received the intel codes of a secret base, survived a firefight with the local syndicate, and got away with a completely treatable injury." He shook his head as he brushed a lock of dark hair out of his eyes. "If that scares you, then you're definitely not going to like what's on Otho."

Sylvia rubbed a hand across her damp forehead, her breathing ragged. "I can't decide if I'm impressed or disgusted with you right now."

The corner of Shiro's mouth twitched up. "Did I mention your entire wardrobe made it safely aboard?" Turnip curled around his ankle with a chirpy mew as if to corroborate this story.

The ghost of a grin tugged at Sylvia's lips. "Okay, maybe not completely disgusted."

"I do have that effect on people." Shiro straightened, puffing out his chest dramatically.

Ezren's muscles relaxed with their banter, and she turned away, their dead informant still frozen in her mind. She hadn't even known his name. Breathing deep, she tried to siphon the tension from her bones. Someone had just *shot Sylvia.* Thank the suns Foster hadn't been there, and she desperately hoped he didn't find out somehow before they got back. Surely the syndicate would keep their attacks hushed up, especially if they were linked to Calderon's own murderous activities. In fact, now that she thought about it, they probably were.

Yet even with the blasts of gunfire still ricocheting through her ears, she couldn't regret coming. *Tell your father...* She knew in her blood that her father was alive on Otho somewhere, but one question still dominated her every moment. Because the man had been right, people were dying to keep Calderon's secret, and there were forces at play here that she didn't understand.

But what was on Otho that was worth all this?

CHAPTER 12

8.15.43B: T-minus 3 days until Mt. Aguya's Eruption

FOSTER DIDN'T KNOW what he'd been expecting from Exa Station, but it wasn't the absolute shaft storm they walked into. People were running through the row of ships in the docking bay, and he could've sworn the faraway crack of gunshots echoed through the crowded hangar.

He turned to Davis standing beside him on the boarding ramp. "What in the chaff is going on?"

Davis's holopro blinked out from his half-visor. "From VSoc, it looks like there's some kind of syndicate altercation going on, but I can't find anything more than that."

"Ugh, why is it so loud?" Grady stepped beside them, squeezing his temples. "Let's find E and the others and get out of here."

"Ah, Exa." Gerard swaggered out from the ship, stifling a yawn as the steam from his mug of syn-coffee wafted into the air. "Always a pleasure to visit the armpit of the Casolla system." He slurped his drink, and his expression sobered. "In all seriousness, this place is more off-balance than usual. Simon's right. We need to leave as soon as we can."

"Shiro's ship is actually only two docks from us." Davis nodded down the line of lunar hoppers, and Foster craned his neck to get a look. The ship he'd indicated was barely more than a scrap of metal with an engine.

"The one that's half-rusted?" Foster's balance shifted with unease. "You're sure?"

Davis had barely nodded before Grady strode toward it. "Well, let's go get them already."

Foster jogged after him, stabbing a finger at Gerard over his shoulder. "Guard the ship, we'll be right back."

Gerard smirked and gave him a little salute with a lift of his mug. "Sure thing, Foster Sterling. It's not like I own it or anything."

A reedy man in a frayed jumpsuit was muttering to himself over a shallow gash in the hull of Shiro's ship when Foster, Davis, and Grady approached, but he wasn't the shady inspector from Belethea.

"Hey," Foster called to him. "Do you know where the owner of this ship is?"

The haggard man turned to him with small, suspicious eyes. "That'd be me."

Foster raised a brow at Davis, who was already rechecking his holopro. "But that can't be right. Ian Shiro took off in this ship from Belethea four days ago."

"I don't give a rat's ass what happened four days ago." The man bristled. "I bought it fair and clear two hours ago."

Grady narrowed his gaze at the man before turning to them and lowering his voice. "Doesn't look like he's lying. But why would they sell their ship if they're still going to Otho?"

Foster frowned, the ripple of misgiving turning into a wave. "Do you know where the previous owner went? Did you see some girls with him?"

"Look here, dust mite." The man folded his arms, a tattoo of throwing knives slicing along his grease-stained muscles.

"Around here, nobody sees nothin' without some creds. And sometimes not even then."

"Fine." With a thought, Foster transferred him a hundred creds, his voice lowering. "Did you see them?"

"Nope." The man relaxed into the sneer of a successful swindler. "But I did hear there were some girls in that hush bar that got busted down."

Foster couldn't breathe, and by his side, Davis went rigid. "Was anyone hurt?"

"You mean besides the three goons that died?" The man let out a humorless laugh. "Good riddance to 'em, leaves a little more air for the rest of us."

The blood drained from Foster's face, but Grady's stare was focused as he scrolled through VSoc, flicking a message to Foster.

GRADY: Relax. They've already released the names. It wasn't them.

Drawing in a ragged, furious breath, Foster took three steps forward until he towered over the man, his fists clenching as he forced the words out in a low growl. "Where'd. They. Go."

The man met his gaze with cool indifference, but then his eyes sparked with recognition. "You... you're Foster Sterling."

Shaft. The last thing they needed was to be recognized when this place was already on the edge of a riot. Foster drove a frustrated fist into the hull an inch from the man's head. "*Where?*"

The man flinched, raising his hands in surrender. "That's all I know, I swear."

Foster turned away with a huff, already pulling up his holo. "Can we crack into the surveillance cams?"

"Don't have to," Grady said. "It's already on VSoc—happened less than an hour ago."

The holo blinked into Foster's goggs, and stepping between the ships out of the crowd, he projected it in front of him. The glowing image showed a packed, narrow Exa hallway from a wide-angle view. Though the cam was to their backs, he could recognize Ezren from any angle, her hair any color, wearing any clothing. The way she moved and carried herself was as familiar as his own shadow. With her gaze on a swivel, she trailed behind Shiro and Bex as they practically dragged Sylvia through the crowd.

Foster's spine whipped straight as a trio of muscular men shouldered through the throng in Ezren's direction. The one on the left drew a gun, and the crowd obscured the clip before it ended in shots.

He whirled on Grady. "Where's the rest? What happened?"

Davis shook his head as he swiped through his holo. "There's no more. Someone posted the clip trying to get an ID on them, but it's already been taken down. It looked like they were heading into another bay though. Give me a second, maybe I can find the ship."

"They must've made it." Grady curled a strand of hair in his fingers as he played the footage again. Around them it seemed like every ship in the station was vying to take off. "Otherwise these thugs wouldn't be looking—"

Foster's goggs chimed with a message, and his pulse leapt. Ezren. Maybe she was still here. He pulled it up, and the faint hope shattered.

DAD: SYNDICATE TRYING TO HIJACK THE SHIP. GET HELP.

Foster swore. "Someone's trying to steal our ride."

"Looks like everyone's itching to get out of here." Davis's eyes widened at the roaring crescendo of chaos around them—

people running up boarding ramps, voices raised, engines heating the air as ships vied for the airlock. "If they leave with it, we could get stranded here."

"Fod that. Your dad says there's only two of them." Grady slapped Foster on the back and jogged toward the ship. "C'mon."

Foster ran after him, strangely glad for something—for *someone*—to bear his fury. He relished the stretch of each long stride taking him toward a good scrap, barely registering Davis's protests as he lagged behind.

The boarding ramp was already closing when they arrived, but Foster clamped a hand on Grady's shoulder just as he was about to charge in. He looked at Davis. "Is there another way aboard? These guys will be armed." Were they the same ones that had shot at Ezren? Acting on Calderon's direction?

"We should be able to manually open one of the escape pods." Davis pointed to one of the cylinders recessed in the underbelly of the ship.

"I'm on it." Slipping from Foster's grasp, Grady darted away beneath the hull, his goggs lighting up in the shadow.

Foster followed him, glancing over his shoulder at Davis once more. "When I signal, I need you to open it again."

Davis's olive skin blanched. "There's got to be a safer way."

"Sure, you sit out here and think about it," Foster said. The escape pod's hatch swung open with a hiss, and Grady pulled himself into the tight, dark space within. "And if they *do* off us, use your perfect plan and go rescue Ezren for me."

"Wow, you're going to let Davis rescue Ezren?" Grady smirked, offering him a hand up.

"Literally over my dead body." Foster's adrenaline shot through him in an electrifying buzz as he climbed into the escape pod.

FOSTER: NO MORE TALKING. THEY MIGHT HEAR US.

GRADY: I'M NOT AN IDIOT, STERLING.

FOSTER: MAYBE. BUT SOMETIMES YOU STILL DO IDIOT THINGS.

GRADY: YOU GOT THAT FROM SYL, DIDN'T YOU?

FOSTER: GUILTY.

Foster paused and pressed his ear to the escape pod's door, but all was quiet. He slowly slid it open and stepped into the private bedroom where raised voices echoed from the cockpit. Foster peeked through the door's circular window to find two nearly identical men with shaved heads and large rifles standing over his father, who flashed them a bloody smile from where he lay on the floor.

"You'd make this easier if you'd just give us the access code," a deep voice said.

"I'm sure if you hit me again, it'd help me remember," Foster's dad replied with his usual irritating joviality.

"We're going to hack into it before long, and we'll remember you were less than cooperative," said a second, nasally voice.

FOSTER: DAVIS, OPEN THE BOARDING RAMP. GRADY, AS SOON AS THEY'RE DISTRACTED, WE'RE JUMPING IN.

Grady shifted from foot to foot with an excited grin.

GRADY: I CALL THE NEAR ONE.

FOSTER: JUST DON'T GET SHOT. AND DON'T LET HIM SHOOT ME EITHER.

The ship shifted as the boarding door opened, and both men pointed their rifles aft, but if they were going to attack from behind, Foster needed them to take at least three steps forward. Beside him, Grady frowned, apparently noticing the same thing.

GRADY: DAVIS, WE NEED MORE OF A DISTRACTION. CAN YOU LURE THEM OUT?

FOSTER: WHAT THE FOD, GRADY, THEY COULD SHOOT HIM.

GRADY: THEY COULD SHOOT YOUR DAD, TOO.

Foster didn't have time for a plan B before Davis's voice echoed through the ship. "Hey, Gerard, are you still in here?" He walked up the ramp with an oblivious smile on his face.

"What're you doing, Davis?" Gerard's face contorted with pain as he twisted toward him. "Get out of here."

"He's right, asschaff, you've got the wrong ship," said one of the men, his face a cold mask as a red horse ran across his thick neck.

Davis stopped in his tracks, his jaw dropping in feigned shock. "Who are you?" Foster had to give it to him, he was a decent actor, but it didn't quite belie the sweat trickling down his temple. "Gerard, are you okay?"

The men edged forward just a little. "You have to the count of three to get out of here."

"We're wasting time," the other said, raising his gun. "We'll use this one as leverage."

FOSTER: Now.

He charged through the door, grabbing for the far one's weapon. A shot went off with a deafening crack and someone yelled while Foster and the brute went tumbling to the ground. Though the man was perhaps bigger in bulk, he had neither the training nor the solid body of muscle Foster had been honing his whole life.

Controlling the muzzle with one hand, Foster slammed the thug's head into the ground with the other, stunning him. With another yank, he freed the rifle and knocked the man's head with the butt one more time. His eyes rolled back in his head, and his hand fell limp to the floor.

Foster whipped around to find Davis holding the other gun, while Grady, with blood flowing from a cut in his forehead, restrained the second man.

"Others will have heard the shots." Gerard struggled to his feet, holding his side where Foster highly suspected the thugs had cracked a few ribs. "Hurry up and throw them off before more get here."

"Wait, first I want to know." Foster pointed the rifle at the intruder as Grady pinned the man's arms behind him. "Why did you try for this ship? Are you targeting us?"

The man let out a rough laugh, the red horse racing across his throat again. "It was a ritzy ship without Kalashnik protection, of course I was targeting it, even before the Otho news."

Foster's grip tightened on the gun. "What Otho news?"

"Fod of—"

Before the man could get the word out, Foster whipped the barrel across his face, eliciting a screech of pain. "Try again." When the man didn't respond, Foster raised the gun.

"Fine." The man spat blood onto the metal floor. "It's no secret. Fifteen minutes ago, an anonymous source leaked that Calderon found terranium on Otho and was trying to keep it quiet for himself. Now every syndicate in Casolla and their spacer grandmother is trying to get a ship out there to stake a claim."

Another volley of shots echoed from the spaceport, and Davis flinched as Gerard stumbled to the cockpit. "We're leaving now."

"Fine, get rid of him." Foster dismissed Grady with a jerk of his chin and grabbed the other unconscious body, keeping one hand on the gun as he dragged him off the boarding ramp. Grady shoved the second thug off with a kick to the back, and the man disappeared into the seething crowd without a backward glance. Another man charged the ramp, but Foster raised his rifle, stopping him in his tracks. Blood still boiling, Foster and Grady backed into the ship, away from the swarming anthill of Exa Station.

"Shutting the doors and readying for takeoff." Davis threw the other rifle into a wall compartment as he ran for the pilot's seat, their ramp already closing. "Strap in."

Gerard pulled himself into the copilot chair before looking over at Foster. "You need to get a med kit."

"Speak for yourself," Foster snapped, even as his vision spun.

"Whoa, kin, at least sit down." Grady caught his arm and lowered him into a seat. "Shaft, were you shot? I'll get the bandages."

Foster's head was whirling so fast now, he could barely focus. Ezren wasn't here. People had been shooting at her—at them. Was she even alive? What if she hadn't made it off Exa, and he was leaving her there? Amidst it all, he held on to his anger like a spar in a rough sea.

"Foster—" his dad started as they lifted in the air.

"I told you to guard the ship," Foster cut him off, swaying in his seat as the ship took flight.

"And you were supposed to get help." A deep furrow slashed through his father's eyebrows, and in that expression, Foster distantly thought that perhaps there might be a resemblance between them after all.

"Is everyone strapped in?" Davis yelled, guiding the ship around the anarchy that was now the airspace of Exa Station.

"In." With med kit in hand, Grady lurched into the seat next to Foster, the auto-harness buckling him in place. "Get us outta here, D."

"Did you look up the terranium news that guy was talking about?" Foster asked, his words ragged.

"Yeah, he wasn't lying. The leaks have basically sparked off a terranium rush between the station syndicates." Grady pulled off Foster's jacket, exposing the channel the laser-lead had carved into his bicep, blood dripping from the uneven graze onto the floor.

Foster's eyes drooped. "You weren't supposed to let me get shot."

Grady sized the bandage and adhered it to the wound. "*Let* is a strong word here."

"But terranium mines are a Casolla-owned resource," Davis said, finally jostling them out of the airlock into open space. "Private citizens and companies can't claim them."

"Yeah, well, the syndicates answer to the black market, not the law," Gerard said, his face oddly tight as he looked at Foster. "And if the looters are in and out before the authorities get there, who would know?"

Grady regarded the holo projecting dots of light all around them—dozens of ships all headed in the same direction they were. "So basically, what you're telling me is that every spacer pod-tick with a ship is on their way to Otho right now?"

Gerard scrubbed a hand through his beard, wiping the blood from his cut lip. "Yep."

Davis stared at the holo with him. "In better news, I looked up the Exa dock logs and think I've ID'd Ezren's new ship. It left forty-three minutes ago, but it's been completely dark since."

"Which means, if they're not accepting comms, they may not even know about all the fritzing terranium pirates on their tail," Grady said, rubbing his jaw where a bruise already darkened his brown skin.

"And Otho's going to turn into a shoot-out in a hot minute, if it isn't already," Gerard said, his voice sure and even.

Huh. If Foster's father was pretending to be an adult, it must be serious. Foster took a deep breath, the drain of the nanites threatening to take him under. "Forty-three minutes isn't a lot though. We should be able to catch them."

"Foster, the ship they're in now..." Davis turned to meet his gaze. "It's military-grade, with stealth and weapons and everything." He shared a brief glance with Grady, his voice almost gentle. "I don't think Ian Shiro is just any private investigator."

For a moment, a thick silence stretched over them for the first time since they'd discovered his father on board.

Foster's hand cramped, but when he reached for it with the injured one, a fork of pain bolted up his arm. He winced. "Well, this just got a whole lot more dangerous." He met each of their gazes in turn. "If anyone wants to take an escape pod and bail, now's the time."

Grady snorted, his gaze sweeping around the four of them. "Look, Sterling, nobody here is leaving."

Davis nodded, his smooth jaw flexing. "Otho may be the most dangerous planet in the system right now, and if Ezren and the others are really going down there, they're going to need our help."

Foster let his eyes close for just a second, absorbing his words before turning to Gerard. "Dad, you—" His hand cramped again, and he scowled down at it, swearing under his breath.

"Don't say another word." Gerard leaned forward to check his bandage. "I'm not going to stop you from going in there. If anyone can get in and out of Otho before they shoot it to space-dust, it's Belethea's champion royale team." He flashed a grim smile that didn't reach his eyes. "But I'm not going to be the dad that lets his son go it alone either. And... I do have one recommendation."

Lacking the energy to argue, Foster let himself sag into the seat, his chest roiling with rage and fear, but also with a warm gratitude that he wasn't in this alone. The storm of emotions threatened to pull him under. "What's that?"

His dad picked up one of the rifles. "I think we're going to want to learn to use these."

CHAPTER 13

8.17.43B: T-minus 1 day until Mt. Aguya's Eruption

EZREN GROANED as she missed the twenty-eighth assailant crashing down from the ceiling and virtual blood splashed across her goggs. "C'mon! I was so close!"

"I win again," Bex said from where she dodged a hand-to-hand combat bot. "That means I get tomorrow's morale meal."

Ezren flopped onto the mat of the fully-padded exercise room big enough for at least six. "What happened to guns being a cowardly weapon or whatever?" After two days of practically living in this room, her muscles felt sore but stronger, the grip of a pistol disturbingly familiar in her hands.

The combat bot landed a punch square in Bex's hard stomach, and she grunted before kicking it across the room. Flashing red with a low battery, it rolled off to its charging station.

"It still is, and one I refuse to die by." Bex stretched across the floor beside Ezren, staring up at the holo of the teal Belethean sky. "I'm going to make sure we get home, even if that means fighting fire with fire."

The click of mag-boots stopped at the doorway. "I thought you were supposed to be training?" Ezren didn't have to look at Shiro to know he was giving them his stupid haughty grin. "Did you beat my high score yet?"

"Are you going to tell us how a private investigator got his hands on a first-class military vessel yet?" Ezren pushed a magenta strand of hair from her forehead, her usual look restored for Sylvia's proverbial "just in case."

"I thought you would've liked the upgrade," Shiro said, Turnip curling around his legs with all six tails flicking. "But all I get are complaints."

"It'd be better if you hadn't come with it," Bex deadpanned.

"After all I've done for you." He let out an overloud sigh.

Sylvia's voice came over the ship's speaker system. "Hey, stop messing around in there, we're going to be at Otho in three hours."

"Three?" Ezren bolted upright as Bex kick-jumped to her feet.

Shiro's demeanor changed in an instant, so much so that he almost looked like a different person. All levity dropped from his face, replaced instead by a dark tension. "So it's finally time."

Ezren side-eyed Shiro, pursing her lips. Despite their direct questions about his true identity, Shiro was still playing the P.I. card. But even though he had yet to come clean, she couldn't help but trust him, and she knew she wasn't the only one. Ezren called up the room's parameters in her goggs, commanding the holo to display their view of Otho. Swaths of bright orange lava burned across its garnet-red face—the angriest jewel in the system.

Beside her, Bex fell to her knees, her eyes fixed on the planet, and her words barely audible. "Sister Otho, Mother Belethea brings her greetings and asks you watch over her children while they're in your care."

Stomach churning with nerves, Ezren pulled up the planet's specs in her goggs, projecting them in bright teal letters in front of her:

Gravity: 0.6 Egrav

Sol: 26 hours
Air quality: Toxic
Temperature: 128° F
Recommended exposure time: 0 hours
Survivable exposure time: 27 minutes
Warnings: Extreme volcanic and tectonic activity. Unsuited to human habitation and current terraforming technology.

Shiro took a step forward, narrowing his eyes at the moon as if he had a personal vendetta against it. "Not a lot to recommend the rock."

"I went ahead and put us on a course to orbit." Sylvia poked her head in the door, her curls double their usual volume. Though the ship's med bay wasn't quite as well-equipped as their recovery room on Belethea, two days in the nanite paramedic chair at least had her back on her feet. "So, what's the plan?" Shifting on her still bandaged leg, she looked from one to the other before raising a doubtful brow at Shiro. "You do have a plan, right? That's why we put up with you this whole time."

The corner of Shiro's mouth twitched upward as he faced Sylvia. "We're going to try to be as fast as possible. With their extra armor, the tactical topsuits will keep us alive down there, but since I'm a half decade past my royaler window, they'll also do a number on my body, so I want to minimize time in it. Bex and Ezren will be fine though, and I've updated the aim-steadying routines in their suits." He stuffed his hands in the pockets of his long coat, leaning against the wall next to Sylvia as his gaze found Otho again. "We're taking one of the shuttle pods in, finding Ezren's dad, and getting out of there with or without him. I'm hoping to be down and up before the sun next sets in"—he checked his half-visor—"eight hours and thirty-one minutes. Which gives us about seven hours before volcanic disaster."

"Well, that's specific," Bex snorted, rising to her feet. "Absolutely no way that's going wrong."

"So we'll have seven hours of cushion if it does." Ezren ran a trembling hand along Turnip's back as she pushed her nose into Ezren's leg. "Do you know where my dad is down there?"

"According to our unfortunate contact, he was working at the south research outpost as of four weeks ago." Shiro scratched the back of his head with a sigh, his dark hair flopping onto his forehead. "Baxter has three other posts on this planet, but since most of the surface is unlivable, they're grouped roughly together. So we could plausibly travel to all of them if we have to."

"Before sundown?" Ezren frowned, Turnip's tails tickling her arms. "But your contact said it was like civil war down there. Somehow, I don't think that's going to make travel easier."

"And that'll be the tricky part." Shiro chuckled humorlessly. "We're unfamiliar with the terrain, and we don't know the particulars of the violence between Calderon and Baxter."

Sylvia's fingernails tapped against the wall. "Did you ever figure out what these people are researching?"

"Nope." Shiro flashed her a bright smile.

"So, that plan's shaft." Bex bent her neck to one side with a pop of her bones, her white hair freshly cropped short. "What's the real plan?"

"The good news is," Shiro continued, pointedly ignoring Bex, "that we're well-equipped for the mission."

Ezren ran her fingers along the textured mat as she tried to visualize the plan. "But if we're taking one of the pods, who's staying on the ship?"

"No worries there." Shiro beamed at Sylvia, holding out his hands as if presenting her like a prize. "Our lovely Sylvia Long here will be our getaway driver."

Sylvia dug her fists into her hips. "I'm going to be the what?"

"Oh, c'mon, you've been lurking over my shoulder in the cockpit for the last week."

"That's because I didn't trust you to get us where we're going." Sylvia gave him her patented unimpressed face, but Ezren couldn't help but notice she had a hard time not smiling when she looked at Shiro.

"Exactly, and I expertly used the time to teach you the controls and how to navigate, did I not?" He moved to put his arm around her, and she kept him at bay by pushing her finger directly into his forehead. "Besides, it's only eight hours, and it's not like you would trust me up here by myself either."

Ezren had to bite back a laugh as she stood and stretched her legs. Turnip skipped away with a meow of protest. Wow, Shiro certainly seemed to have a direct line into Sylvia's brain. What exactly had they been getting up to in all those hours in the cockpit? Maybe it was better she didn't know. She glanced at Bex to get her reaction, but her eyes were cold as ice.

"So it's only going to be the three of us? An odd number? That's bad luck." Bex's lips thinned into a hard, pale line. "The planets will take one to even it out."

Ezren's whole body buzzed with the notion—the certainty of Bex's words disturbingly premonitory. "No, you don't have to go, Bex. No one does. This is *my* dad, so the only one taking the risk should be me."

"Don't sweat it," Shiro said, capturing Sylvia's finger in his hand. "This is what we came for. We'll bring back your dad and be an even number. Happy planets. Happy Ezren. Happy Shiro gets paid."

Ezren shot him a wry look, seeing right through the lie this time, but she couldn't help being curious about what he really wanted here. Had he lost someone on Otho too?

Sylvia slipped her hand from Shiro's and squeezed between Ezren and Bex, hugging them both tight. "I'd say not to listen to him, but he's right. We've come this far, and you're the best royalers we've got. I know in my bones you can do this. And you..." She released them, stepping up to Shiro with narrowed eyes, her finger poking into his chest now. "You bring my team back safe."

"And you take care of my ship." He looked down into her brown eyes, his voice low as his hands rested on her hips. "And my cat."

Ezren turned away with a flush, the moment sending an anxious pang through her heart. Though she was more than happy for Sylvia, she couldn't help thinking of the hands she missed on her own skin. They hadn't been linked to comms at all since they left Exa, and she'd had exactly zero news of Foster. Ezren swiveled the holo view until the cloudy teal orb of Belethea appeared on the wall. What was he doing down there? Was he safe? She took a steadying breath. Eight hours.

After that, they'd be done with this. No matter what happened, she'd meet him on Obrone. She'd bury her face in his neck, and he'd wrap her in his arms—they'd be whole again.

She looked back at the fiery moon in front of them, pre-race nerves jittering through her. They could do this.

Three hours later, Sylvia's anxiety had escalated to tugging on her curly hair as they dressed in camouflaging tactical topsuits and packed supplies—food, water, nano-bandages, and an inordinate number of weapons.

Shiro's hands moved with sharp efficiency, and whoever he was, he knew what he was doing. Ezren and Bex stepped into the oblong expedition pod, and Shiro threw in one last monstrous bag while Sylvia practically bounced in place.

"I'm not fritzing around, Shiro. I'll be turning on the receiver to get an update every two hours, and I expect you back here irritating the chaff out of me before the sun sets down there."

"Every *three* hours." He turned to her, Turnip pawing at his shin. "Don't worry, we'll be back before curfew."

"Right." She wrapped her arms tightly around herself, an uncharacteristic waver in her voice. "But what do I do if you're *not* back, and I can't reach you?"

"Give it another twenty-four before going to the ambassador summit with everything. In case something happens, I've set up a delayed message for you to give to Commander Liassidi of Dreitis. He'll help you."

"What?" Sylvia's forehead wrinkled as she looked to Ezren and Bex. But they could only mirror her confusion. "That doesn't make me feel better. It was meant to be a rhetorical question."

"Well..." His roguish grin returned. "I wouldn't say no to a kiss if you're still worried. Odd numbers and all that."

Bex gave the curious Turnip one last scratch before strapping herself into the cushioned entry seats. "Hurry up, Shiro. We're already running out of time."

"All right, all right." Shiro chuckled, bending to step into the pod.

"Wait." Sylvia grabbed Shiro by the straps of his pack and tugged him into her. Their lips came together, and Ezren knew instantly that this wasn't their first kiss. Shiro cupped her face in his hands, and a hot blush scorched Ezren's cheeks as she averted her gaze with a knowing smile. Asdef, what *had* they been doing in that cockpit? Beside her, Bex let out a beleaguered sigh, no doubt counting the seconds.

Finally, Shiro pulled away, his dark eyes meeting Sylvia's. "We'll be back."

"You'd better be." Sylvia sniffed, gathering Turnip in her

arms as her gaze darted to the others. "And you'd better come back with four."

Then they were gone.

CHAPTER 14

8.17.43B: T-minus 12.5 hours until Mt. Aguya's Eruption

IF BELETHEA WAS a planet of storms, Otho was one of fire. As soon as Ezren stepped off the pod, the nanites in her suit whipped into overdrive, trying to protect her from the 115-degree heat. She sucked in a breath, and a shrill alarm went off in her goggs as it registered the dangerous levels of sulfur dioxide and hydrogen sulfide in the air. Even with her form-fitting suit covering every inch of her body, the air around her felt combustible, and the ground shuddered beneath her feet.

A steady, hot wind swept the gray clouds along overhead, and springs of boiling water, mud, and lava bubbled around them with a soft popping. On the horizon, a volcano belched black ash into the already crowded sky. It was as if they had stepped off the ship into the smithy of a fire god of old.

Bex dropped to one knee, her tactical topsuit turning burnt orange to match the landscape. Bowing her head, she murmured something inaudible as she dragged her fingers through the black grit underfoot. In another breath, she rose again and surveyed the scene. "I thought this was supposed to be the most survivable sector of Otho."

"It is." Shiro stepped beside her as their pod went into stealth mode behind him, perfectly camouflaging with its surroundings. "But even here, the probability of our pod taking on damage while out in the open is too great."

The ground beneath them trembled with a mild earthquake as if to emphasize his words, and Ezren adjusted the nutrition pack on her shoulders. Her father had been living here? The thought of it both sickened and thrilled her. While this place was obviously dangerous, it also emanated power. Its harsh, barren horizon held the allure of a land completely foreign—a place few others had laid eyes on. Like Belethea, she could not deny its savage beauty, and there was a part of her that wanted to take off running across the surface. The tactical topsuit was heavier than her racing model, but her body still felt light in the low-G, the adrenaline singing through her only tempered by the unfamiliar press of the pistol strapped to her thigh.

She sent a small prayer to Belethea that she wouldn't have to use it as she gazed at the ridges and valleys beneath the oddly calm skies. What was here that was worth killing for? There had been a long-standing theory that the energy concentration in terranium was what gave Belethea its volatile climate. But while Otho was obviously toxic, its atmosphere seemed relatively mild, at least for the moment. Did that mean there was no terranium here? If that was the case, then what could her father possibly be studying?

"Okay, listen up." Shiro lifted his rifle from where it hung around his chest. "Stay close to me. Don't shoot me. Don't shoot each other."

"Great pep talk." Bex stepped past him and put her hands on Ezren's shoulders, her blue eyes glinting beneath her steel goggs. "Listen, Hart, no matter what happens, we stay together." Her fingers squeezed. "We all know why you need to be here, but our number one priority is getting home alive. If we can save your dad, we will, but your mother and brother need you too. *Belethea* needs you."

Ezren swallowed, emotion tightening her throat. She sucked in a deep breath of filtered air, the wind whistling around them as she let Bex's steady strength ground her. "I'm glad you're here, Bex."

"Well, I couldn't let you get yourself killed." Bex released her, turning again to the smoky horizon. "There'd be no living with Sterling."

"Touching and all, but we need to head out." Shiro pointed to the east. "The south outpost's only a mile from here, but follow my steps exactly. If the tar melts through your boots, you get a one-way ticket straight back to the ship."

As Shiro bounded off, Bex and Ezren trailed behind him, carefully treading in his footprints to avoid the boiling pools. Ezren's nerves threatened to choke her at the thought of her father only a mile away, her constricting chest stealing her already thin air and sapping the strength from her legs. She had to think of something else if she wanted to stay focused.

Shaking her head, Ezren concentrated on mimicking Shiro's movements across the uneven terrain, her mind flying through various chip commands. She'd adapted her weather prediction algorithm based on the limited Otho data she had, but now she could feed it into a consistent update loop. Simultaneously, she started a data collection routine based on the ground beneath her. The soft ash compressed beneath her boots, but she could feel its heat through the soles. If she stepped in the wrong spot, she nurtured a sickening certainty her foot would find an underground channel of nanite-melting magma.

Even as she moved and fiddled with her goggs' data collection, her mind wandered to Shiro. Although he'd said he was unfamiliar with the landscape, he seemed to navigate its variability with confidence—was that hubris? Preparation? Or had he been here before? While she certainly didn't consider him a threat, her curiosity itched with the unsolved puzzle.

His military experience was obvious, but not unexpected from a P.I. And with Calderon and the syndicates mixed up in this, the situation grew seedier by the second. Was he tangled up with them somehow? Maybe his past wasn't something he was proud of.

Despite the mystery he posed, she couldn't deny that she had complete faith in him. Which probably marked her a desperate fool. But then again, at this point, what choice did she have? And if Sylvia liked him, that had to count for something.

Ten minutes later, Shiro held up a rigid fist on a low ridge. He peered down on a low metal building in the shallow crater, and Ezren's chest swelled with hope. After seven days traveling across the system, they'd finally made it.

"Remember, if we take fire, find cover first. Your topsuit will steady your hand and help you aim, so don't be afraid to squeeze the trigger." With a hop, Shiro slid on the loose ash down the gritty incline. Ezren followed after him with Bex bringing up the rear.

"So are you going to break into this place or what?" Bex called, her boots skating down the soft terrain in the low grav.

"I don't have to." Shiro arrived at the bottom first, holding his rifle tight to his body as he peered at the entrance. Skidding to a stop, Ezren carefully stepped behind Shiro to peek at the building, and her stomach dropped.

Though the door had to be six inches of blast-proof steel, it hung from its hinges, scorch marks blackening its face.

"So there really is a war," Bex muttered.

Shiro edged the door open and took a step into the dark,

boxy airlock, the interior entryway ajar in a similar battered condition. "Does that make you feel better or worse?"

The light from their goggs illuminated the hallway with scorches matching the door and a holo of open grass fields flickering on the walls. The click of their footsteps punctured the unmoving, deadened air as they stole through the silent building. Ezren stopped as her goggs lit up five rust streaks running along the wall before they connected to a deep maroon stain on the floor.

"It's dry." Bex gently nudged her forward as Shiro disappeared around the corner.

Cold sweat drenched Ezren's skin beneath her topsuit as the corridor led into an open laboratory space. And Ezren had to stifle a gag. Chairs had been knocked over, tables overturned, and shattered glass and melted metal littered the blood-stained floor.

So much chaffing blood.

Bex turned to Shiro. "Can we access any of their systems? Maybe there's a security holo."

"I've already checked. All virtual evidence has been destroyed in the site's mainframe." Shiro shook his head as he nudged a lump of molten metal with the barrel of his rifle. "From what I can tell, this was a Baxter base. They must've resisted when Calderon tried to shut them down."

"But where is everyone?" Ezren breathed, bracing herself for the answer.

The light from Shiro's goggs scanned the wreckage. "It's possible they evacuated to one of the other bases and are still alive, or Calderon might be holding prisoners somewhere."

"We can look outside for remains," Bex said, the words quiet even in the silence.

"Check inside first." The air of command in Shiro's words

cut through the buzz in Ezren's ears. "Spread out and see if you can find logs or anything else useful."

Ezren's feet moved to do as she was told, hyper-aware of the pistol strapped to her thigh. And despite the questions still whirling about Shiro's past, Ezren took comfort from his steely competence. She moved to the hall on the other side of the lab, desperate to get out of the destruction, and ducked into the first open door on her right.

A dark bunk room lay before her, three beds on each side. The light from her goggs played across the walls, illuminating plastic images of people and places tacked above the beds. Pictures. There were old-fashioned stills of children and families on stations and in sunny backgrounds she didn't recognize. She checked the lockers beside the bunks to find an assortment of hygienic supplies and jumpsuits in various arrays of casual organization, and her heart squeezed. Wherever these people went, it looked like they didn't have time to pack, but at least there wasn't any blood in here.

She was about to turn back into the hall when her light caught on a plastic square peeking from underneath one of the bunks. Crouching, she picked up the cracked picture and nearly dropped it again.

A pale eight-year-old girl with mousy hair and dark eyes stared out of the flat, glossy image—a younger version of herself. And not just her. Beside her, a pudgy little Sam, and her mom, ten years younger, smiled up from a small, worn couch. It was a photo from their apartment in Obrone—a single cramped room —with a round-cheeked Sammy wearing his prosthetics as they waited for regen to take hold.

She pressed the picture to her chest with a ragged gasp. Her father had been here, and he'd kept a picture of them close. *Whenever you look up at the sky, know that I'm looking right back down at you.* Tears sprang to her eyes, and any reservations about coming evaporated. She had to find him. Had to—

BEX: HART, BACK TO THE MAIN ROOM *NOW*.

Ezren tucked the picture in her pack and returned to the lab space. It was still several minutes before Bex and Shiro joined her. Shiro avoided her eyes, but Bex walked straight up to her, her gaze steady beneath her goggs.

Ezren shifted her weight from one foot to the other. "What's wrong?"

"Hart..." Bex glanced at Shiro, and Ezren's heart dropped into her stomach with an unsettled knowing.

"You found graves."

Bex's steady blue gaze held hers. "No graves. They were in body bags."

"How many?" Ezren asked, thinking of the beds lining the bunk room.

Bex blinked—once, twice. "Six."

All of them. Ezren swayed, but Shiro steadied her by the elbow.

"They were pretty roughed up." Apology laced his words. "I captured holos of the victims, but my facial recognition software isn't working properly. Do you think you could—"

"Send them to me." Ezren yanked her elbow away from him, his compassion too raw for the grief she didn't have time to feel—the hope she'd only just tasted obliterated in an instant. How late had they been? An hour? A day? They couldn't have missed them by much. "The faster I identify him, the faster we can get out of here."

Apparently, they'd be going home even sooner than she thought. How stupid she'd been to come all the way out here. To pin their lives on a chance slimmer than a blade of grass. Another of her naïve intentions ending in nothing but grief.

Ezren's goggs chimed with the file, but before she could

open it, her chip trilled again with an incoming call. She froze, frowning at Shiro and Bex while the ring echoed off the metal walls. "My goggs are supposed to be dark. Someone must've hacked into them somehow."

Shiro leaned closer, his gaze hardening. "Answer it."

Her heart pounding for reasons she didn't quite understand, Ezren accepted the call, projecting it for all of them to hear. Before she could get a word out, a familiar voice barked through the line.

"Get down!"

Time seemed to slow as Ezren fell to the floor, bringing Bex and Shiro with her, just before the flash of an explosion lit the room.

CHAPTER 15

8.17.43B: T-minus 12.5 hours until Mt. Aguya's Eruption

ALREADY IN HIS TOPSUIT, Foster leaned into the cockpit's holopro they'd streamed from an Otho satellite, squinting at the low metal buildings of Baxter's outposts projected on the HUD. "Have you found them?" From what he could see, nothing stirred on Otho's surface. Did that mean Baxter and Calderon had already evacuated?

Beside him, Grady, Davis, and Gerard stared over his shoulder at the scene. After another two days straight with the three of them, he was ready to jump in the shuttle for Otho's surface just for a little peace and quiet. If he had to hear his father crow about his shooting sim stats one more time, violence was a real possibility.

Davis zoomed out from the holos of the four outposts clustered on the volcanic moon. "Not yet. Their goggs are all dark."

"But you're sure they're here?" Grady asked, wearing his own teal topsuit. "Maybe we outpaced them."

"Did you see that military-grade ship they were in?" Davis snorted. "There's no way. And if they've been dark this whole time, they don't even know there's going to be terranium thugs raining down on this place in three hours."

"And you were sure they were headed to Otho?" Gerard centered the holo on one of the outposts with a cluster of tactical vehicles surrounding it. "If that Shiro character is dead set on obfuscating their movements, maybe he lied about their destination." As one, Grady, Foster, and Davis all turned to stare at him. He returned their gaze with an easy shrug. "What? You didn't think about it?"

Foster ground his teeth together. If he didn't get off this ship soon, he really was going to kill his dad. "If Shiro lied, they could be anywhere right now." The thought was enough to send a jolt of anxiety through him.

"Nah." Grady twisted one of his stud earrings, lines carved into his normally smooth brow. "I still think—"

"Wait," Davis cut in, zooming in on one of the holos. "I've got something."

Foster swiveled in the tight space, squinting at the black-and-red expanse with a spark of hope. "Is it them?"

"No." Davis pointed to a tac-V veering around a channel of black tar. "But this is the only movement I'm seeing on the surface right now."

"Look, there's another one." Grady pointed a well-mani-cured finger at another dark dot charging across the orange landscape. "Can you see where they're going?"

Davis extrapolated their course, tying it from one outpost to another on the screen. "It's this one." He pointed to a low building that nearly blended into the center of a deep crater.

"Okay." Disappointment quenched Foster's flicker of hope. "But that place looks abandoned, and I don't know where Shiro would get access to tactical vehicles."

"Unless he lured them there." Gerard stroked his beard as he squinted at the tac-V. "And that outpost door looks like it was blown off its hinges."

Foster glared at Gerard's casual tone, annoyance tightening his muscles. "So what? We don't know how long ago that happened. Davis, can we get a thermal scan on the trucks and outposts?"

Davis's brow furrowed beneath his half-visor as his gaze slewed across the sphere of holos around them. "Looks like I can get the trucks, but the outposts are obfuscated."

With another mental command, the feed zoomed in on the tac-Vs, and the holopro changed to a scale of high-contrast colors. The terrain morphed into a sea of red with two bright purple figures, bulky rifles strapped to their chests, riding in each vehicle. "Suns," Grady breathed. "Those look pretty soldiery for scientists, kin."

"And from their sizes, I don't think any of them are our girls," Davis said.

Foster tried not to bristle at the word "*our*" and failed. "So what do we do with this? Sounds like we still don't have anything."

"Hold on now." Gerard's brow furrowed. "Maybe this means your friends are there after all."

Foster's impatience flared, clipping his words. "Someone please make him make sense."

"Think about it for a second. If they're in the middle of a conflict, they'll definitely be surveilling their outposts." Gerard met his gaze, his gray eyes clear and grave, and Foster had to wonder the last time he'd been serious about anything. Had the run-in with the syndicate really affected him so much? "And if Ezren and the others recently arrived at one of their outposts— how do you think the residents would react?"

"They'd probably see any newcomers as a threat." Davis paced the cockpit, his hands clenching and unclenching at his sides. "But who's 'they'? Calderon or Baxter?"

"If they're both shooting, it doesn't matter." Grady bounced from foot to foot like he was getting ready for a brawl. "They're not riding hot to say hello."

Foster stared at the outpost again, but if there was any sign of Ezren, he couldn't find it. "That's all just a theory though. We don't know Ezren's there."

"And at this point, we're not going to know." Gerard's lips pressed together. "We'll have to make a decision with the information we have."

Davis's gaze moved to Foster, his olive complexion pale. "If they're surveilling the outpost, not only would they see an intruder, but it's possible Calderon could have recognized Ezren."

"It could be a great opportunity to make her disappear without any questions." Foster's pulse rattled as the trucks closed the distance to the outpost at an alarming rate. "But if we're wrong, we could be putting ourselves in the middle of a firefight we know almost nothing about."

"How long till they get there?" Grady picked up a nutri-pack and threw it over his shoulder. "Can we beat them?"

Davis's mouth twisted as his visor flashed with numbers. "We'll be directly overhead in three minutes. Your fastest egress will be the escape pod, but my numbers are predicting you're still going to be a few minutes behind."

They were working with a string of ifs, but if there was even a chance Ezren's life was on the line, there was only one choice. Foster grabbed his helmet, already striding to the shuttle. "I don't care. We're going."

"Now we're talking," Grady crowed, taking his own helmet.

"Foster, don't be an idiot." Gerard followed them as they crossed the deck. "Even if our theory is right, they outnumber you two to one."

"Not if you count Ezren, Bex, and Shiro," Foster replied.

"You're counting on the fact that they're actually in there." His dad's jaw flexed, and yeah, in that moment, they definitely looked alike. "*And* that Shiro didn't orchestrate the ambush."

"Yeah, well, we'll have the element of surprise either way." Foster slung the rifle they'd taken from the syndicate over his shoulder. The same one he'd been practicing with for the past two days. He wasn't a great shot, but he had to hope it would be enough. "Besides, it was *your* theory, wasn't it?"

"And I stand by it, but I'm just saying..." Reluctantly, his father stooped and picked up his pack, handing it to him. "Don't count on anything."

Grady was already slipping into the shuttle. "We'll be fine, Y. Royalers are fast, and we look out for each other. It's our whole thing."

"Grady's right," Foster said, surprised the words didn't burn his tongue. "It's just like another royale. We fly down, run in, scrap, and run some more."

"This isn't *just* anything, Foster. You're my son." Gerard ran an agitated hand through his long black hair. "I need you to come back."

Foster almost snorted at the ridiculousness of the statement. After all, his father hadn't seemed to be concerned when he was competing in the deadliest race in the system. But he supposed the bullets did lend it a different feel. "Oh, don't be dramatic, Dad." He stepped into the ship. "Sit back, have a drink, and we'll be back before you know it."

"Don't crash the ship while we're gone, D." Grady tucked a hovercam into his pack as a red recording dot appearing in his goggs, because apparently, he never stopped thinking about VSoc content.

"When you need an out, I'll be here." Davis's heavy gaze met Foster's, a shared urgency tying them together—a connection of complete understanding. "Just bring her back safe."

Foster slid his hand through Davis's to grip his arm, some part of him knowing that even if he hadn't come, Davis would still be here. "I will."

With that, the door hissed shut and they hurtled toward Otho.

Unfortunately, Davis's calculations turned out to be more accurate than Foster had wanted to believe. Foster and Grady just made the ridge, chests heaving, when the four armed figures slipped inside the open door.

"Fod it," Foster huffed, the air hot and stinking around them on the hostile terrain. "We've got to follow them."

"Sterling, did you see those guys? They were in tactical topsuits and packing some serious artillery." Grady shifted the rifle in his hands, and Foster could just make out the slight shake of his fingers. At least he was taking the situation seriously for once. "I mean, are we ready for this? We're talking life or death, and we don't know if they're in there."

"But we'd never forgive ourselves if they were." Foster's grip tightened on his own weapon. His only consolation was that the laser-lead wasn't usually fatal through a topsuit unless the shot hit the head or heart. Still, he knew where these guys would be aiming. "There's no one else to call for help." He turned to Grady, the seconds slipping away. He didn't want to go in without him, but he wouldn't force him either. "We either go in now, or we could be leaving Ezren and the others to die."

They were just words until the thunder of an explosion rent the air, punctuated by the rattle of automatic weapons. As one, Grady and Foster practically flew across the slope. With bullets flying, there was no more time for thinking. They sprinted through the door and down the hall, the gnashing of gunfire covering their footsteps as they rounded the corner, rifles at the ready.

Chaos and debris reigned across a dark lab, but it wasn't hard to pick out the four men laying fire from a hallway across the room. Someone returned shots from the shadows, but Foster couldn't pinpoint where in the mayhem. Adrenaline pounding in his ears, Foster aimed and squeezed the trigger. A figure fell in the darkness, but he didn't have time to linger on it before another gun muzzle swung toward him, spitting bullets. He dove behind a metal desk, just as the other man folded, presumably thanks to Grady's shots from the edge of the corridor.

But were Ezren and Bex here under fire too?

The men shouted at each other, their aim turning from the center of the room to Foster and Grady.

Foster swore under his breath.

FOSTER: GRADY, MAKE A RUN—

A small object sang through the air toward the aggressors, smacking one in the chest. A blinding explosion flared across the room. With a thunderous crack, Foster fell flat onto his back, pain tearing through his ribs. He staggered to his feet only to find the last man practically on top of him, his gun barrel canting toward Foster's chest.

He barely had time to register the regret that he still hadn't found Ezren when the shot rang through the air. For a second, Foster felt nothing, his body too electrified to process.

Then the man collapsed onto the floor, smoke pouring from his armored topsuit as he convulsed.

Foster fell to his knees, his legs jelly, and his chest heaving. Nausea rolled through his stomach, and he fought the urge to hurl right there in the middle of the chaos.

"Sterling!" Grady shouted. "Are you okay? Are there more?"

"I'm fine." Ears still ringing, Foster turned to where Ian Shiro lowered his rifle in his steel-colored tac gear, pieces of the smoking ceiling falling down on them. But was he friend or foe? "What'd you do with Ezren and Bex?" he coughed out.

Bex rose from a concealed corner behind a chair, a handgun as familiar in her hands as if she'd been born with it. "I'm here."

"Thank the suns," Grady said, his voice weak with relief from his spot in the hall.

Foster's stomach plummeted. If Bex was here and Ezren wasn't, that meant... "Bex, what—"

"Foster?"

Foster's heart nearly stopped as he looked to where Ezren shifted an overturned table from her body and rose to her feet. Immeasurable, all-encompassing relief surged through him. The fear that had been gnawing at him with sharp teeth for days finally eased. She was *here*. In seconds, he crossed the room, resisting the urge to throw his arms around her as his goggs assessed her topsuit for injuries. Though it looked okay, he could see a streak of blood behind her helmet, and her eyes looked unfocused.

"Ezren," he breathed, running his hands along her arms, noting that she also had a pistol in her grip. "You're bleeding. Are you okay?"

"I thought it was you, but I must be seeing things." She holstered the gun at her thigh, and her trembling hands gingerly closed around his elbows, as if to make sure he was real. "I thought you were on Belethea. Safe. How did you—"

"Ezren, I don't want to be safe when you're not." Foster gently knocked his helmet to hers, searching her coffee-dark eyes, trying to make her understand. He was always supposed to be here. Even if she was walking through hell, he would be there for her to lean on. "No matter what, if you'll have me, I'll be right here. With you."

For a moment, uncertainty flashed through her gaze, but

then her arms were wrapping around his waist, and he was pulling her close.

"I'm so glad you're here," she whispered, her body trembling. "I shouldn't be. But I am."

"Hey Sterling," Grady called from where he still stood in the hallway, his rifle half-raised. "What the fod do you want to do about this Ian Shiro guy?"

Bex cocked her head from where she leaned against the wall. "What's your problem with Shiro?"

Foster turned, his hand lacing with Ezren's as he edged between her and Shiro, unreadable behind his tac gear and goggs. "This guy isn't who he says he is."

"Well, yeah." Bex's blue eyes rolled beneath her goggs. "Give us some cred. We knew that before we left Belethea."

Ignoring her, Foster lifted his chin. Maybe the others could trust this guy, but there was no way he was turning his back on him without the truth. "Why are you really here? And don't give me that P.I. line."

"I suppose that's fair, at this point." Shiro moved to the bodies of their attackers on the floor, deftly incapacitating those that were still conscious with a small electric device and relieving them of their weapons. "My name is actually Shiro Tanaka, and I'm a dishonorably relieved agent of the interplanetary federation. I was investigating Baxter's illegal operations here when Calderon bought out Baxter, and he pulled strings to get the investigation shut down. I pressed harder and was put on an indefinite leave of absence." He pulled what looked like restraints from his pack and tied the soldiers' hands behind them. "So I decided to come back to complete the investigation on my own and clear my name. And I have... *had*"—he grimaced—"a contact here I'd left behind. Someone I'd promised to get out." Opening a door to a supply closet, he dragged the nearest of the unconscious men into it. "But I was short on funds to get the information and supplies I needed, so I started approaching family members tied to Otho, and you can figure out the rest."

Foster exchanged a glance with Grady, and his fingers tightened on Ezren's. "Quite the story, but where's the proof? What happened to your contact?"

Shiro stilled. "He's in a body bag in the hall with the rest of the scientists who worked here." He straightened again, his glare spearing Foster. "But if you need receipts, this might work."

With a chime, Shiro's credentials slid into Foster's goggs. The official ID holo showed Shiro's same lean face but with buzzed hair and in a crisp gray uniform decorated with various medals. There was some other information Foster didn't understand, but across the holo in bright red letters were the words *Inactive Duty*.

Grady whistled. "Checks out for me."

Foster's teeth ground together as he tried to gauge the risk. Ezren leaned into his arm, her voice low. "It's okay, Foster. He's saved our lives more than once. You can trust him."

Foster wished it was that easy, but after finally finding Ezren, he didn't want to leave anything to chance if he could help it.

"Look, I wish we had time for pleasantries." Shiro turned back to Foster, his gaze glinting with the dare of a challenge. "But it won't be long before these fellows are tagged as missing. So we need to hurry up and get out of here before their backup arrives."

Grady stepped forward from the hall. "Uh, it's worse than that." His gaze darted to Ezren and Bex. "Someone put the word out that they found terranium here, and now every gold-digging syndicate in Casolla is coming this way."

Shiro swore, hefting a chunky bag from the floor. "How long do we have?"

Foster checked the running count on his goggs. "By our last estimate, we have two hours before the first ships arrive."

Shiro let out a breath in a long hiss. "We can work with that." He bent and picked up a hefty rifle from his bag before tossing it to Grady. "Here. Trade up your goods."

Grady barked out a dry laugh. "Look, kin, we're not soldiers. We just came to grab Ezren and Bex and 'ject outta here."

Bex crossed her arms. "I thought you would've wanted evidence to put Calderon out an airlock."

Grady rolled out his right shoulder before favoring her with the artfully lopsided grin of a true adrenaline junkie. "Eh, I'm not saying I couldn't be convinced."

Foster resisted the urge to roll his eyes. So much for taking this seriously.

"No, I can't leave yet." Ezren slipped out of Foster's grasp. "My dad's here. He warned us just before the attack. We came all this way, and he's alive."

Bex exchanged a glance with Shiro. "Are you sure, Hart? With the message static, it would've been hard to recognize anyone. And the bodies... have you looked at the file?"

"I'll check the files, but I'm telling you I heard him." Ezren looked from Foster to Shiro and lifted her chin. "We still have time. I'm not going back now."

Shiro chuckled, his eyes crinkling beneath the goggs before he tossed another rifle to Bex. "Yeah, kind of looks like you're soldiers now."

Foster opened his mouth, but a wave of dizziness rocked him instead, and the world tilted.

"Foster!" Ezren moved to his side, putting an arm around his waist to support him, and a bolt of pain shot through his ribs. His jaw clenched as spots darkened his vision, and Ezren pulled her hand away, red reflecting from her gloves in the light of her goggs.

"Foster's hurt," Ezren said, her voice calm and even.

"I saw a first aid kit in the supply closet." Bex leapt into action from the corner. "And the air filters are decentralized here, so we should be able to close off one of these rooms so we can see the damage."

"Right." Shiro grabbed another man and pulled him into his makeshift holding cell. "Ezren, you help Foster. Simon and Bex, help me strip these guys for supplies and secure them." He pointed at Ezren. "Hurry it up though. We're leaving in fifteen minutes."

Foster let Ezren lead him into what looked like a kitchen area and leaned him against a table before closing the door behind her. Ezren's goggs lit up, and in another second, the lights flickered on with the hum of the air filter.

"They must get a lot of damage to the buildings to keep the air handlers separated like this. Either that or they're worried about contagion," Ezren said conversationally, as if they hadn't almost died. As if they weren't on the most dangerous planet in Casolla right now.

"Ezren—"

A gust of cool wind whipped through the space as the air filter cycled the room, and his goggs turned green in the breathable air. Ezren took off her helmet with a smile that didn't reach her eyes, her hair falling loose around her shoulders. "C'mon, Foster, we've got to fix you up and get out of here. I know you don't trust Shiro, but he's a good guy, and he knows what he's doing."

Foster lifted his arms to pull off his helmet, but winced as his side protested, the pain now lighting a fire through his muscles.

"Here, let me." Ezren gently pulled his helmet from his head.

"Ezren," Foster began again, his teeth gritting through the pain. "We have to get out of here."

"Foster, I didn't come all this way to leave." Ezren's gloved fingers fumbled with his topsuit before she unzipped her own, pulling her arms from the sleeves and letting it hang around her waist. Her pale skin practically glowed beneath her tank top. "I thought you understood."

"Ezren, how many times has someone tried to kill you now?" Foster said, breathing deep through the pain. "By my count, we're up to at least four."

"And you think it'll just stop if we leave this place?" The muscles in her shoulders flexed as she began on his topsuit again, gingerly peeling it down his body. "Calderon's trying to cover up something here, and I think it might be connected to the violence on Belethea as well. There's something he doesn't want us to know. If we dig deeper, maybe we can figure out how to stop it."

He flinched as she exposed the wound, and she winced with him. "So let Shiro do the digging," he rasped out. "That's what we paid him for."

"C'mon, Foster, you know he can't do it alone." She leaned closer to examine the jagged channel a piece of shrapnel had carved in his side. "I know it hurts, but it looks like a flesh wound. The nanite bandages will hold it together, but you'll still have to be careful with it until we can get it laserstitched."

But Foster could've cared less about the injury. "Ezren, *please*. In these last seven days, I think I've been more scared than I have in my whole life. Wondering if something had happened to you—if you were alive. I thought I was going to go insane with worry."

"I know." Ezren zipped open the first aid kit and extracted

a black bandage roll. Taking a small pair of scissors from the case, she cut through the nanitelattice in a long strip. "Because that's how I've been feeling about my dad since the moment Shiro said he was alive." Her voice softened as she applied the bandage to his side. "And I'm sorry. I wouldn't wish that on anyone, but... I thought when you agreed to come, you knew how I felt."

His skin prickled as the nanites entered his bloodstream, holding the wound together like thousands of tiny, wriggling stitches. But that small relief was replaced almost instantly by the characteristic itching caused by the bots' tiny movements. Ezren's hands drew away, but he caught one in his own. They were together again, but he couldn't stand the unsettled wrinkles between them.

"I... I do." Foster squeezed her hand, every muscle tight as he tried to find the right words for an emotion too huge to wrap his brain around. "It just feels like the BRR all over again, and we barely made it out once already. I don't know if we're lucky enough to survive twice."

"I know. Murderers, bullets, explosions... sometimes it feels like everyone has it out for us." Ezren's gaze darted away, her eyes shining. "But this isn't the BRR, Foster. I mean, I'm carrying a gun for suns' sake." She gestured to the pistol holstered at her thigh. "And look at you. Five minutes and you've already been shot. You shouldn't have to do this."

"None of that matters, Ezren. I'm not here because I have to be. The royale brought us together, but you and I—what we have—is so much bigger than that." Foster laced his fingers with hers. "I want to be the one that always has your back, no matter what. For as long as you want me."

"Of course I want you, Foster. I *always* want you with every piece of me, every fiber, since that first day I showed up at the starting line and you were there. And I know you're scared and worried; I am too. If I lose my dad and the person I love more than anything else in the 'verse today, I don't know that I'll survive it." She squeezed his hand, her gaze shining with intensity. "But there are bigger things going on, and now that we're here, I have to finish what I've started."

Foster regarded the stubborn set of her jaw, and understanding finally sank into his bones. Ezren never did anything halfway—it was why she made a difference when others couldn't. And he loved her for it.

"Okay, Ezren Hart." He cupped her jaw with one hand, stroking his thumb along her cheek. "I'm with you to the end." She relaxed against his palm, her lips quirking up, and he pressed on, "Because I trust you with everything that I am. But I need you to trust me too. I want to be the first person you call when you need to talk something through. When you have a problem big or small. Anything. Please, trust that you and I can work it out."

She nodded, her voice quiet over the hum of the air handler. "I believe in us, Foster Sterling. More than I ever thought it was possible to believe in anything." Placing her hand over his, she pressed her lips to his palm. "And I don't think I've ever been so glad to see anyone in my whole life."

"I've told you before, haven't I?" He shifted to sit on the table and tugged her closer, a fierce protectiveness burning through him. "I *always* come to get you."

"And not just you. This time it looks like I've dragged our whole team into this mess too." Ezren's fingers traced the bandage wrapping his side, regret lining her face in a way he hated. "I didn't mean for it to go this way."

"You came all this way for family, and your family came all this way for you." Foster shrugged, the corner of his lips tugging upward. "Are you really so surprised?"

"Family, huh?" Ezren's shoulders fell, a tender smile

creasing her face as she leaned into him, her hips between his knees. "I think our family is a magnet for danger."

Foster leaned his cheek against her hair, the warmth in his chest threatening to burst as he breathed her in. "Ezren, I don't care about the danger. I don't care what it took to get here, or what it takes to get out, all I care is that we're together. In storms or fire, I just want to be with you."

And then his lips were on hers, and he was whole. They were heat and electricity and some primal need lit within. Perhaps it was because they'd just escaped death, or the foreign planet under their feet, or the days apart, but they kissed as if there was nothing but this moment. He pulled her into his lap, his hands skating along her skin, and her hands in his hair, sure he'd never get enough. Trailing his lips down her neck, he savored the taste of her, the hitches in her breath, her fingers curling into his bare back. Because now that he'd found her again, he sure as chaff wasn't letting go.

And then Ezren's goggs lit up with a call.

CHAPTER 16

8.17.43B: T-minus 12 hours until Mt. Aguya's Eruption

EZREN'S EYES shot wide as her goggs chimed, and she jerked away from Foster to grab her helmet, answering the call through her chip as she did.

"D-Dad?"

Gaze darting to Foster, she reached out for his hand. He clutched it and squeezed. Then, with a rough wheeze, a voice came over the line, echoing through the room.

"...Ezren..."

Ezren would've wilted with relief if she had the time. Instead, she stuffed her arms into the sleeves of her topsuit, directing it to meld back together. "Dad, where are you?" She started for the med bag, but Foster already had it, his topsuit and helmet back in place as he strode for the door.

"Suns, that really is you." Her dad's ragged breath rasped across the line, his voice tight with emotion or pain, it was hard to tell. "Look, you've got to get out of here, Ezren. Run. Now. While you can."

Ezren stepped through the door and into the lab space where the others stuffed more scavenged supplies into one of Shiro's bags, and Foster said something to them in a low voice she didn't quite catch.

"Dad, what's going on? They say you've found terranium,

and now there's all kinds of syndicate ships on the way here to ransack this place. *Everyone's* got to get out of here."

"Oh, Ezzy." This time there was no mistaking the love in his voice. The heartbreak. "This is much bigger than terranium."

Shiro stepped closer to her, his eyes wide as he listened in, and Ezren bit hard into her lower lip while Foster and Simon gestured to each other in whispers, holos projecting from their goggs in the darkness. Bex only seemed to move faster as she loaded the bag.

"Look, Dad, it doesn't matter what it is. We're not leaving without you." She straightened, her doubts erased under her dad's voice—here, alive, and in danger. "Where are you?"

"Ezren, sweetheart, I—"

Silence dropped like a guillotine across the call, and Ezren leaned forward as if she could listen harder for the words that weren't there.

"Dad?" She checked her goggs and swore. "It cut out." A wash of irritation swept over her. Why couldn't he have just told them?

"Don't worry about it," Foster said. "Grady and I managed to get Davis to trace the call."

"Davis?" Ezren practically broke her neck to look at them. "You brought Davis Banda too?"

Foster rubbed the back of his neck. "Grady asked him to fly us."

"We needed a ride," Simon fired back.

Ezren's face heated with annoyance. "Please tell me you don't have Sam and Micah squirreled away up there too." At this point it seemed like everyone she ever cared about was here.

Ignoring the tense exchange, Shiro stalked toward Simon's holos. "Which outpost is it?"

"The one farthest away, of course." Simon smirked.

"That map can't be right." Shiro crossed his arms as he studied the building in the projection. "There are only four outposts."

"That you know of." Bex slung the bag over her shoulder as she stood. "The real question is, how're we getting there?"

Ezren tapped her fingers against her helmet while she thought. "If we take the shuttles, we'll need to go back to the ship to refuel and reposition. It'll take time." Her goggs glowed as she connected to the mainframe, looking for any information they could use. "Looks like it's a fingerprint and iris scan to get into the other outposts, but I think I can get into the repository here." Their physical security was ridiculously light, but then again, when you're the only show on the planet, they probably hadn't thought they had much to worry about.

"It's only seventy miles, and those guys drove here"—Simon jerked a thumb toward where their prisoners were trapped in the closet—"so let's just take their ride."

"I like it. Let's go." Shiro strode for the door. "Time's ticking."

Ezren barely had time to think before Foster's hand was on the small of her back, guiding her out of the room. She just managed to get the access codes as they jogged out to the two tactical rovers, guilt niggling in her gut. She was, without a doubt, putting everyone in danger. And while Shiro had his own reason to be here, the others didn't.

But Foster's words echoed in her head. *You came for family, and your family came for you.*

Now it would be up to her to make sure her family made it out.

They stepped out onto the ashy, fire-laced landscape of the crater surrounding the outpost. Like Simon had said, two tactical vehicles sat just outside the busted airlock door, as if waiting for them. The tac-V's looked like armored storm trucks from back home, riding on high wheels with thick heavy shells—perfect for rough terrain in low grav, especially if someone was shooting at you. She just hoped they were fast too.

"I'm driving," Simon called as he stepped up into one of the vehicles. "Bex, you're with me, and we'll take the special ops guy too."

Bex yanked the door open to the passenger seat. "Odd numbers are always bad luck."

"And we've got this one." Foster lifted his chin toward the farther vehicle, his gaze meeting Ezren's as he squeezed her arm.

Shiro opened the back seat to Simon's tac-V. "I understand that you're crack-shot drivers and everything, but keep in mind, you don't know this planet." Shiro gestured to the volcano spewing ember-sparking ash in the distance. "The auto-drive should be able to find the safest route, so don't mess with it unless you have to. Also, keep a safe distance from one another in case something does happen."

Wouldn't want both vehicles to be taken out at once. Ezren slid into a seat, her stomach flipping at the sickening thoughts of all the somethings that could happen. But the interior of the vehicle wasn't reassuring with a turret wedged immediately behind the driver's seat. No two bones about it—Calderon had come to this moon prepared for violence.

As Foster fired up the vehicle, he turned to her with crinkled eyes. "Just like another race royale, huh?"

"Kind of." Ezren tried for a weak chuckle. "How much longer did you say until the first ships get here?"

"Eighty-two minutes now."

Ezren nodded, her goggs linking to the tac-V's autodrive with an ETA of seventy minutes. "And what do you think the odds are that the syndicates will target the people on the surface first to try to get a location on the terranium?"

Foster glanced at her sideways as the tac-V began to move, its thermal regulator working overtime to compensate for the burning air threatening to bake them. "High."

Foster entwined his fingers with hers, and Ezren held on to him for dear life. Then the tac-V lurched out of the crater and onto Otho's surface.

The land spilled out before them in a wash of orange and black and Ezren couldn't contain an involuntary gasp as the wheels leapt off the ground in the low grav. The vehicle hummed, its magnetic coils adjusting, and they crashed back into the soft ground, grit spewing beneath the tires. The engine growled, HUD flashing latitude and longitude as the tac-V rumbled in a jagged path around the bubbling pools and deep beds of ash.

With Simon's vehicle swerving some ways ahead, Ezren dissected the data filtering through the auto-drive algorithm, assessing the variables and visual cues it used to calculate the temperature and solidity of the ground. Beside her, Foster's gaze raked across the mountains and valleys of ash, the smoky clouds swirling above them.

"You're itching to run through this mess, aren't you?" he said, his voice teasing.

Ezren smiled. "Just like you're dying to take the wheel, I'm sure."

His eyes curved into half-moons as they met hers. "I like to think my self-preservation instincts are stronger than that." But even as he said it, she could see his free hand tapping at the wheel.

"Well, I've already downloaded the driving algorithm and adapted it to my royale course guidance."

He cocked a brow beneath his goggs. "You planning a royale out here?"

Ezren shrugged with a laugh. "Don't give anyone any ideas."

But Foster's face darkened, his fingers drumming the steering wheel faster. "Ezren, something happened after the expo that day that I've been meaning to talk to you—"

An audio message cut Foster short as it blared through their control holo on a shared line.

"Heads-up, got a visual on two bogeys on our six," Shiro said.

"That's sooner than we thought." Ezren turned in her seat to peer behind them through the window. "Coming by land or sky? Are they armed?"

Foster scanned through the 360 holos on their dash, swearing under his breath. "Come on, Davis. Where's the chaffing warning?"

Ezren shook her head. "If he didn't spot them heading this way, they probably have some kind of stealth tech."

"That does not make me feel better," Foster said, just as another message flashed on the HUD.

"They look like off-world ships." Shiro's confident baritone filtered through the cabin.

Ezren opened her mouth to ask a question, when Simon beat her to it. "So why are they firing on us?"

"Because we're the competition for the terranium they're here to steal," Bex replied.

"Or maybe because they think we know where it is," Ezren said.

"Well, don't we?" Simon's high tone walked the fine line between humor and stress. "Why don't we just tell them your dad said there isn't any."

Even as Simon said it, Ezren's mind spun again with her

father's words. *Worse than terranium.* What could be worse than the high-density energy resource that practically ran the whole system? Did he mean more powerful? Obviously, whatever it was, Calderon had deemed it worth dying for. But why?

"Right," Bex said with cold sarcasm, "because the syndicate's looters would totally believe us."

"Enough." Foster cut through their banter. "Focus. What's the plan, Shiro?"

"I really hate to say this, but you're going to have to take it off auto," Shiro said, their truck weaving ahead over a dune of ash. "The tac-V's AI should lay out the track for you, but you're going to have to bust the safety constraints if we want to evade. The AI is too predictable."

"Oh yeah," Simon whooped. "Now we're talking. Sterling, see if you can keep up."

Simon's truck took off in a spew of gravel, and the blood drained from Ezren's face. Following suit, Foster slammed the manual release button, and the holodash lit up with their projected route. Ezren leaned against the window, spotting the two glinting black dots in the smoky sky.

"They're coming in fast." Ezren's pulse thrummed through every cell in her body. "There's no way we're going to outrun them."

"These are combat vehicles," Shiro replied, eerily calm. "Turn on the turret tracker, and it should have some basic anti-targeting defenses."

Ezren's chip connected to the vehicle's protection interface, and she found the routine he was referencing.

A spike of panic shot through her. "It's not automatic."

"You'll have to give verbal commands," Shiro said, as if he was telling her how to operate a dishwasher and not an anti-air gun.

"*Why?*" Ezren practically shouted, scanning through the

list of defenses. He couldn't expect her to shoot down a plane—she wasn't trained for this.

"Because AI can't use deadly force without your supervision," Shiro replied. "It's a *good* thing, Ezren."

"Forget about shooting," Bex cut in over the whine of an alarm filling their cabin. "What about the staying alive part? How are we supposed to stay in the solid areas if we're dodging bullets?"

"Do you have a better idea?" Shiro asked.

Another twin alarm blared through Ezren's goggs as one of the ships behind them locked on, and her pulse ratcheted into overdrive. "Foster, you're going to have to pull some evasive maneuvers."

"Right." Foster yanked the wheel hard to the left, trying to stay on the green-highlighted safe zones even as the safety sirens screeched at him. "You know, I really thought the BRR was hard enough without someone shooting at us."

"*Incoming missile,*" the tac-V chimed with an irritatingly cheery tone.

"Deploy anti-missile projectiles," Ezren snapped, holding on to the bracing bar as the truck leapt over a rock shelf. The tac-V jerked as artillery launched from the top of the vehicle, and the explosion propelled them forward. They bounced to the ground, somehow managing to land on solid rock, and the harness tightened around Ezren's pumping chest.

She scanned the terrain, but the other tac-V had disappeared. "Bex, Simon, are you still there?"

A volley of bullets lit into the stone beside them, the shots ricocheting off their exterior, and Foster jerked the tac-V into a serpentine. The two ships converged on them, trying to get another lock on the uneven landscape.

"And more importantly," Foster gritted out, gaze pinned on

the highlighted route of his HUD, "do we have any offensive weapons to shoot these fodders down?"

They hit a rise, and Ezren just caught a glimpse of Shiro popping his head out of the top of their tac-V with what looked like a giant cannon on his shoulder. A bright hot light shot out from the gun before detonating between the two ships in a percussive blast.

The bullets stopped abruptly as the ships veered away.

"Ezren," Shiro said, his words fast but clear, "there's a thermal cannon in the roof of the truck. It has auto-aim, so all you need to do is point and shoot."

"You want her to expose herself when they're gunning for us?" Foster asked, his voice pitching.

"Tell me when you're ready," Shiro said, ignoring Foster. "I've got one more shot. They'll dodge it again, but if we time it right, we should be able to get one."

"On it." Desperate and out of options, Ezren unbuckled her harness and moved to the turret behind their seats, bracing herself against it as they jolted along. Sure enough, the cannon waited for her there. Though it was almost as big as she was, the lower gravity and strength boost from her topsuit allowed her to lift it without much strain.

Hefting it onto her shoulder, she positioned herself beneath the turret roof's opening. "I've got the cannon."

Foster glanced back at her with desperation burning in his eyes. "Don't open the hatch until the shooting stops."

"I don't know if the shooting will ever stop." Ezren tried to mimic Shiro's calm, even as a storm of adrenaline spun in her chest. "We'll have to trust the pulse shields."

The bullets rained down on them in a hellish clatter, and Foster zagged around a rocky outcropping. As soon as the clang of the gunfire faded away, Ezren commanded the hatch to slide open, and a rush of hot air sang overhead. "Ready, Shiro."

His response was immediate. "Firing now."

Ezren straightened, the cannon rising with her, and though she couldn't see Shiro's truck, a bright flash lit the sky closer to their pursuers. Aiming in their general direction, Ezren didn't wait to squeeze the trigger, but she was in no way prepared for the backlash of the monstrous weapon.

Her goggs blackened to protect her eyes from the flash, but the force of it, combined with an unfortunate jolt of the truck, sent her spinning back and out of the hatch. She slid across the roof of the truck before her body collided with the ground, the cannon jolting from her grip. Ezren's helmet smashed against the rocks, and her ears rang with the impact as belated pain screamed through every part of her. She could barely process the messages lighting her goggs.

Foster: Ezren! Are you all right? Ezren's fallen out of the truck!

Shiro: Don't stop, Foster. They're—

Another explosion rent the air, and Ezren's goggs lightened enough for her to see Shiro's truck flip wheels over hood. It crunched into a solid wall of rock before sliding down into a boiling pool of tar. Ezren barely had time to scream before the plane turned on Foster's tac-V next, which was, of course, swerving toward her. Bullets rained down on the vehicle, overwhelming the translucent shields and bursting the tires.

"No!" Ezren yelled, a rush of adrenaline giving her body life as she grabbed the cannon and heaved it onto her shoulder. The weapon hummed as it poised to deliver the killing blow, and Ezren pulled the trigger. In a deafening crash, Ezren skidded backwards across the rock, stopping just short of a rivulet of bright lava cutting across the ground.

But her efforts were rewarded with a second explosion taking out a wing of the plane, and it fell in a wash of billowing fire.

Ezren sucked in a burning breath, all kinds of alerts zinging through her goggs, but none as powerful as the fear threatening to choke her.

Ezren: Foster!

She stumbled toward the battered and smoking vehicles, but she only took two steps before the ground threatened to give way beneath her feet, steam rising from below.

She swore, taking in another breath of superheated air. Her mind spun for a horrified moment before she remembered the mimic algorithm she'd attached to the vehicle's AI. "Suns, please tell me it's ready."

Through her goggs, the ground lit up beneath her feet, along with the words *Confidence: 85%.*

Ezren swore again. At least it was better than nothing. As she took her first step on the highlighted path, she skimmed the code for any obvious logic errors. The inputs mostly relied on visual cues, air quality, and temperature. She manually added the figures to her goggs display. After all, she could learn and adapt just like the code. With her added check, perhaps she could raise her odds.

Ezren: Foster, don't move, I'm coming toward you.

She swallowed, sweat stinging her eyes with every careful step, and suddenly she missed Belethea's cool temperatures. The ground trembled beneath her feet with a low rumble, and she tensed to keep her footing.

Ezren: Simon, Bex. Are you there?

No one answered, nothing but the quiet bubbling of the ground around her and the whistle of the air. Her heart thrummed with her rising panic. What if they were dead? The thought punched the breath from her lungs as her mind involuntarily leapt to the visceral nightmare of losing all three of them.

Stop.

She forcibly shook the image away. It was no good now, and if there was even a chance they were unconscious and needed her help, that was the straw she would grasp for. The hope she needed to keep going.

EZREN: HOLD ON, FOSTER, I'M COMING TO YOU FIRST.

There seemed to be something wrong with Ezren's shoulder as she tried to pump her arms, so she held it still as she shambled along. Dismissing the warnings that shrieked of suit damage, she approved the topsuit to absorb more of her energy for repair and kept a sharp eye on the environmental numbers as she moved.

"One step in front of the other," she whispered to herself.

When she reached the first tac-V, her heart only hammered harder in her chest. The embers on the hot wind sizzled against her suit's nanites as she took in the crunched front end, the shredded tires, and the bullet-ridden exterior. There would be no driving this thing again.

"Foster!" Ezren shouted.

A groan from the cockpit answered her, and she nearly collapsed with relief. The bent metal of the door squealed as she opened it and found Foster slumped over the steering wheel. "Are you okay?"

He looked up at her with bleary, unfocused eyes. "Ezren, thank the suns."

She gave him a once-over but could see no mortal wounds and allowed herself a flash of relief. "I think you hit your head pretty bad. Sit here while I check on the others." Taking a deep breath, she shuffled in the direction of the other car, her optimism buoyed. If Foster was okay, there was a good chance the others would be just fine as well. They would make it through this, odd numbers be scabbed.

Except the truck was almost completely submerged in a boiling pool of tar-like liquid.

Ezren's body went cold. No... they couldn't—

EZREN: BEX! SIMON!

For a beat, there was nothing. No movement from the truck except the superheated gasses rising into the already hot air. What did she do now? She glanced frantically around the pool, searching for where they could've gone. What if she couldn't find them? They had to be somewhere. She couldn't move on without them.

"Bex!" she shouted. "Simon!"

Only the wind answered her with a plaintive howl.

They couldn't just be gone.

Ezren was about to turn around when her goggs chimed.

SIMON: E, WE'RE ALIVE. BUT BEX AND SHIRO ARE HURT. I NEED SOME HELP.

Ezren's legs went weak with relief, and behind her, Foster stumbled from the car, his knees hitting the ground.

EZREN: WHERE ARE YOU?

SIMON: SENDING OUR LOCATION. WE'VE FALLEN THROUGH THE SURFACE INTO SOME KIND OF TUNNEL.

"A collapsed tunnel. Great." Foster stumbled to Ezren's side, a rifle strapped to his chest, and she reached out to steady him with her good hand.

They really *were* all busted up. She instinctively wanted him to stay by the tac-V, but she couldn't guarantee it would be safer. And she had to admit, with her non-functioning shoulder, she wasn't much better off than he was.

She squeezed his arm. "Try to walk in my footsteps. I've copied the tac-V's algorithm to show us a path." The solid ground here was narrow, the green dots surrounded by swaths of red as they made their way farther from the tar pool.

Foster kept looking over his shoulder, his eyes regaining focus as they strafed the sky. "Did you shoot both of the ships?"

Ezren nodded, her gaze catching on the others' footprints. "Yes, they definitely went down." Yet another mystery entity that had tried to kill them. A non-exclusive club whose membership grew by the day.

A faint shout drifted on the wind, and Ezren turned to see one of the wreckages smoking from a hillside, dark figures unloading smaller vehicles from its cargo hold. Ezren froze, her wide eyes meeting Foster's.

"They went down, but that doesn't mean they're dead," he muttered, throwing another glance behind him. "And look." He pointed to a black dot in the sky cutting low through the ashy clouds. "There are more on their way."

Ezren opened her mouth to respond when her goggs chirped a warning, drawing her attention to the ground. The algorithm painted the soil before them a danger red around a giant, gaping hole. She edged around the chasm, testing the surface with her mag-boots as she tried to peer down into the dark pit.

"Simon, are you down—" The chatter of gunfire shattered the silence, cutting her off. Foster crouched low, pulling her down with him. The crew of the wrecked ship was spitting bullets way too close for comfort, but she couldn't see what they were firing at. "Why are they shooting?"

"Another ship just cut in from the clouds, but they must be from different syndicates." Foster's tense gaze met hers. "Which means now they'll all be shooting anyone they don't recognize."

Ezren turned toward the hole with renewed desperation.

Ezren: Simon, can you see us up here? Stick to chip messages. The looters are still out there, and they're close.

SIMON: YEAH, I'M TOSSING UP THE ROPE NOW.

In the low G, the knot of rope sailed up through the hole with a low whoosh, but the deafening bursts of gunshots were nearing much too fast.

Ezren grabbed the rope out of the air, ready to anchor it to a boulder, when Foster put a hand on her shoulder.

FOSTER: IT'S NOT SAFE UP HERE. IS IT A MAN-MADE TUNNEL?

SHIRO: YES. I'M NOT SURE WHERE IT GOES, BUT I'D BE WILLING TO BET THAT IT WAS INTENDED FOR TRAVEL BETWEEN THE RESEARCH OUTPOSTS BEFORE THE QUAKES AND MAGMA GOT TO IT.

BEX: BUT WE DON'T KNOW IF IT HAS AN EXIT. WE COULD BE TRAPPED.

The shouts carried closer, and the telltale squeal of a vehicle door opening raked through the quiet. Ezren looked to Foster, noting how he favored one leg. "They'll be here in minutes. We have to make a choice."

Foster's gaze followed the small indents of their boots not quite whisked away by the wind. "If they're sharp, they'll know we came this way, but if we're lucky, they may chalk us up as dead from an incidental fall."

"Regardless, if we stay up here, it's a firefight." Ezren's hand moved to the gun holstered at her thigh.

Foster craned his neck over the edge. "It could still turn into a firefight down below."

"But at least then we'd have control over the entrance, besides"—Ezren held up the rope as proof—"we can't leave them down there." Another shout, closer.

Foster nodded once, sharp and decisive.

FOSTER: IT'S TOO DANGEROUS UP HERE, WE'RE COMING DOWN.

With that, he took a step and disappeared in a puff of ash. Ezren flinched as another volley of bullets sprayed somewhere behind her. *Infighting?* She chanced one last glance over her shoulder to see a dunecart's tires throwing up a cloud of ash before she disappeared into the cavern.

And as Ezren slipped into the belly of this beautiful and deadly planet, so different and yet so similar to her own, she could really only think one thing.

She absolutely fodding hated this place.

CHAPTER 17

8.17.43B: T-minus 11 hours until Mt. Aguya's Eruption

FOSTER'S HEAD pounded as he surveyed the tunnel, his entire body pulsing with pain as the stuffy heat threatened to suffocate him. It looked like an old magma tube had been reinforced with metal plating to create a man-made tunnel—big enough for a quad maybe, but not for any vehicle larger than that. The corroded escape hatch they'd fallen through didn't inspire much confidence in the integrity of the structure, but this section didn't look in danger of imminent collapse.

Thank the suns for small favors.

Ezren landed beside him, her mag-boots clanking on the metal floor as another volley of gunfire answered from above. She glanced up before grabbing his wrist and tugging him out of view of the surface.

"Are you okay?" she whispered, her gaze scraping him from head to foot yet again—as if he were the one who'd been forcibly ejected from the tac-V.

"I'm fine." Sharp pain stabbed the back of his eyes. "We need to reset your shoulder."

She nodded, her face white in some mixture of pain and shock behind her goggs. "Right. I'm ready."

He knew this wasn't her first time getting her shoulder reset, nor was this his first time resetting one. A year of royaler training did that to people. It had to be done, but he still hated to cause her pain.

Putting one hand on her shoulder, he gripped her wrist with the other. "Brace." Foster didn't hesitate—didn't even give her a moment to dread—before he yanked her arm back into place.

Muffling a cry, she crumpled into him, and he folded his arms around her. "It's okay, it's okay. It's done." He pressed his helmet to hers, sweat peppering her brow beneath her goggs. "Better?"

"Yes, thank you." She drew away. "But where ar—"

"Over here," Grady's low voice called from the darkness.

Together, Ezren and Foster turned, their gogg lights illuminating Grady where he crouched over their supply bag. He was digging for something as Bex leaned against the wall and Shiro lay across the floor.

Foster's shoulders tightened. He hadn't known what to expect, but this didn't look good. Foster walked toward them, noting Bex's taut fingers clutching at her bicep. "How bad is it?"

Bex shook her head, eyes screwed tight behind her goggs. "I'm fine. Just got cut through the arm." She jerked her chin at Shiro on the floor. "Check him."

"No need." Shiro's ragged breaths echoed in the enclosed space, his face twisted in pain. "I've got one shot in the shoulder... and my leg's broken below the knee."

Ezren took a step toward Grady. "I think we've got a splint in—"

Voices from above cut her off, and Foster's spine shot rigid.

Foster: No time now. We need to move. It won't be long before they come down here, and we need to be out of sight. Grady, help me with Shiro.

Ezren darted to the bag, snatching something from within

and zipping it shut as Grady moved to hoist Shiro from the ground. Running to his side, Ezren pressed the nanite patch to the hole in his shoulder. A stifled cry escaped him, and her dark brown eyes looked up at him apologetically.

Ezren: IT WON'T HEAL THE WOUND ITSELF, BUT AT LEAST IT'LL PROTECT YOU FROM EXPOSURE UNTIL THE NANITES PULL YOUR SUIT BACK TOGETHER.

Shiro: THE OUTPOST IS A FAIRLY STRAIGHT SHOT FROM HERE. IF WE FOLLOW THE TUNNEL NORTH, IT MAY TAKE US ALL THE WAY.

That sounded like a huge if, but Foster didn't have time or alternatives to argue.

Ezren: I DOWNLOADED THE TAC-V'S MAP FOR MY ALGORITHM. I'LL SEE IF I CAN CHECK OUR COURSE.

Foster positioned himself on Shiro's other side as he and Grady both pulled one of Shiro's arms around their shoulders. Shiro bit down on another cry, and Foster muffled a grunt as the wound in his own ribs stretched. But there was little they could do but start down the tunnel, the clacks of their mag-boots too loud in the silence. Ezren and Bex followed along behind them, Ezren with the huge supply bag slung across her back, and Bex with her rifle across her chest, still gripping her bleeding arm.

They were only a few steps though before a voice echoed through the tunnel behind them.

"Hey, what's this?"

Foster's wide eyes met Ezren's, but it was Shiro's message that spurred them into action.

Shiro: RUN.

They sprinted down the darkness, Grady and Foster practically bounding step for step in the low gravity as the voices continued on behind them.

"Looks like an air duct."

"Do you think something's down there?

"Better check it out."

EZREN: WE'RE NOT GOING TO MAKE IT.

GRADY: IF WE'RE GOING TO SHOOT, WE NEED TO LAY SHIRO DOWN.

Grady looked at Foster for confirmation, but he ran on, gritting his teeth. They may have done some virtual target practice on the ship, but they weren't hardened killers like these guys. Without Shiro, they'd be at a huge disadvantage. Especially since they didn't even know how many were up there. If there was a shoot-out down here, they'd be trapped like shiroach... to say nothing of a potential cave-in. He checked his goggs for the location Shiro had indicated, but it was a straight shot with no curves to hide behind. Could they hope for another access chute they could climb out of?

EZREN: WAIT, I CAN SEE THE TUNNEL ON THE MAP AND—

The world rocked beneath their feet, and they all stopped dead, the walls undulating around them.

Bex's unfocused eyes widened, her white hair plastered to her forehead beneath her goggs.

BEX: CAVE-IN.

SHIRO: NO, IT'S JUST AN EARTHQUAKE. SMALL ONE. THEY'RE COMMON HERE.

EZREN: WHICH IS WHY—

"Okay, I'm going to go check it out," one of the men called from the tunnel.

Though there was distance between them now, the words cut through the silence with perfect clarity. There was no more time for running.

GRADY: WE ARE TOTALLY CHAFFED.

Ezren waved frantically from the wall of the tunnel where she'd opened some sort of small access panel.

EZREN: HURRY! THERE'S A DISASTER SHELTER HERE.

Bex ducked in after her, and Foster pushed Grady and Shiro through with a rough shove. Climbing in the circular entry, he quickly closed the door behind him, thanking the suns for quiet hinges just as the clank of feet on metal echoed through the tunnel.

They froze as the voices rang out all too close.

"Do you see anything?"

"No, but the footsteps led to this tunnel."

"Well then let's sort it out."

A volley of bullets rattled through the small enclosure, a few sizzling as they hit close to the door. Ezren moved to Foster's side, lacing her fingers with his. Foster looked at her, his body coiled like a spring. He'd be chaffed if he let them touch her.

Another clank of footsteps and a shout. "You two walk in that direction, and we'll take this way."

FOSTER: IS THE ACCESS DOOR MARKED? WILL THEY SEE IT?

EZREN: THE MARKINGS ARE WORN AWAY. I ONLY NOTICED IT BECAUSE THERE WAS AN INDICATOR ON THE MAP. IT'S POSSIBLE THEY COULD MISS IT.

Grady shifted from foot to foot in front of the hatchway, still propping up a pale Shiro, while Bex leaned against the opposite wall.

GRADY: THE DOORWAY IS SMALL. WE CAN DEFEND IT.

BEX: UNLESS THEY THROW A GRENADE IN HERE, THEN WE'RE DEAD.

A deluge of swears ran through Foster's mind as he took in

the space. There were crates of emergency supplies tucked in the corners, but they were too small to hide anyone.

He took a deep, trembling breath, the footsteps only growing closer.

FOSTER: IF THEY OPEN THIS DOOR, WE'RE GOING TO HAVE TO SHOOT THEM AND MAKE A RUN FOR IT.

The problem was, at this point, two of them couldn't run.

BEX: I'M NOT GOING TO SLOW YOU DOWN.

EZREN: WE STAY TOGETHER.

Foster ignored them, straining to listen to the men outside.

"If they went this way, wouldn't we see them?" one said. "There's nowhere else to go."

Foster's hand stayed on the shallow indent that served as a door handle. If they so much as looked at it, he would rip the door off its hinges and start firing.

"But we saw—"

Another earthquake, this one bigger, shook the tunnel, the very walls rattling around them. Foster braced himself against the door, catching Ezren as she stumbled, and a spider-line crack ran through the worn metal reinforcements. Suns, if they stayed in here too long, Otho was likely to bring the tunnel down around them—which was probably why the researchers had abandoned it in the first place. Bile rose in his throat as he pictured the five of them buried alive down here.

"Fod this," said one of the men. "If they went this way, we know what outpost they're headed to. No use trying to catch them on foot in this death trap."

"Fine by me," said the other. "It's too chaffing hot down here anyway. Let's get topside."

Ezren drooped in Foster's arms, and Grady carefully laid Shiro on the floor, dropping to the ground beside him. But Foster didn't relax until the footsteps had long since fallen silent.

"Okay," Foster said. "I think we're clear."

Grady let out a long sigh. "That was *way* too close."

"I'm turning on the air filter and the thermal regulator," Ezren said, solar strips coming to life on the ceiling and cool air cycling with a low hum. She crossed to the supply bag with decisive steps. "First, we need to take care of Bex and Shiro's injuries, and then maybe we can check in with Sylvia on what's going on out there."

"Sylvia already... made contact," Shiro rasped, his eyes closed and sweat gleaming behind his goggs. "It's bad news."

Foster's overheated body went cold. "What do you mean bad news?"

With a wince, Shiro projected a holo from his black goggs into the air above him. "See for yourself."

SYLVIA: SHIRO, WHERE ARE YOU?! IS EVERYONE ALL RIGHT? THE SYNDICATES ARE TAKING OVER THE AIRSPACE ABOVE THE OUTPOSTS OUT HERE, AND NOW THE CASOLLA INTERPLANETARY FEDERATION HAS ANNOUNCED THAT THE LOOTERS WILL BE SHOT ON SIGHT. THEY'RE DECLARING EMERGENCY MARTIAL OWNERSHIP OF ALL OTHO RESEARCH OUTPOSTS, AND THREATENING WAR IF ANY INDIVIDUAL NATION TRIES TO MAKE A CLAIM. CALDERON AND BAXTER ARE BOTH LIVID, BUT SO FAR, THEY HAVEN'T BEEN ABLE TO OVERRULE IT. THE CIF'S TROOPS WILL BE HERE IN NINE HOURS TO OCCUPY THE RESEARCH OUTPOSTS POST-ERUPTION. SO WHATEVER YOU'RE DOING, STOP AND GET YOUR CHAFFING ASSES BACK ON THIS SHIP.

"So, she's basically saying if we're here when the military arrives, they'll kill us," Grady said with a wry smile as Ezren threw him a brace from the bag.

Bex shook her head from where she leaned against the wall. "This is all we need with inter-system tensions already high."

Foster swore, his goggs glowing green as the room achieved

breathable air quality. He pulled off his helmet and ruffled a hand through his damp hair. "I'll contact Davis to make sure he knows."

FOSTER: DAVIS, ARE YOU STILL ALIVE UP THERE? I'M SENDING YOU AN UPDATE ON THE SITUATION FROM SYLVIA.

DAVIS: YEAH, WE'RE WELL AWARE, KIN, BUT WE'RE LYING LOW. YOU JUST WORRY ABOUT YOU. I'LL SYNC WITH SYLVIA TO MAKE SURE WE'RE ON THE SAME PAGE.

DAD: WHERE ARE YOU? WE'VE LOST A LOCK ON YOUR LOCATION. ARE YOU OKAY?!

FOSTER: YEAH, WE FOUND EZREN AND THE OTHERS, BUT WE'RE IN TRANSIT. I'LL CONTACT AGAIN WHEN I HAVE AN UPDATE.

"How much farther do we have to get to the research outpost?" Grady asked, pulling Foster back to the cramped room.

"Fifty miles." Ezren projected the map from her goggs while she peeled back Shiro's topsuit with a nanite bandage in hand.

Beside her, Grady attached the brace to Shiro's right shin, lifting off his own helmet and then Shiro's. "No sweat. That's like an afternoon jog, especially in this gravity."

Ezren tugged off her helmet, and her worried gaze flicked to Foster's. Without words, he knew exactly what was going through her mind. Sure, they'd done it before, but not with gunshot wounds and a broken leg. Not to mention the toll Shiro's suit would exact on his body.

"In a straight-shot tunnel like this, we could make it in under five hours," Grady continued.

Ezren moved to Bex's side with another bandage. "Even so, we'll never make it there before those fritzers on wheels."

"Don't be so sure." Bex's hands shook as she moved to fold

down her topsuit, her normally pale skin practically translucent, and her words breathy. "On this terrain, there's no way they'll be able to travel in a direct route."

Ezren's hands paused, her eyes going round. "Bex," she whispered, something dripping on the floor.

The stench of iron flooded the air, and Foster moved to her side, a dark presage rippling through him. "What? What is it?"

"I'm fine," Bex said, but her voice was too weak. She hadn't even taken off her helmet yet.

Ezren's gaze, dark with guilt, darted to Foster as she moved to the side to reveal the grisly wound in Bex's arm—the muscles barely intact.

"Suns, Bex," Foster breathed, horror turning his stomach. What he'd thought was a minor cut had shredded most of her upper arm. It was no wonder she wasn't moving it—she couldn't. And the blood loss...

Grady looked over Ezren's shoulder and turned away, stifling a gag. "Oh, suns."

"Shiro, is there anything more"—she swallowed—"substantial in the medkit? Bex has lost a lot of blood. I think we need a tourniquet."

Turning his head, Shiro grimaced at the wound. "If you use a tourniquet, she'll lose the arm." Rooting around in the bag beside him, he tossed a larger nanite sleeve. "That's the best we can do until we get her to the ship's stabilizer."

Foster's mind whirled. A wound like that was going to require regen even if she kept the arm, and if they didn't get her to a stabilizer soon, she was liable to bleed out. "We can go back through the tunnel the way we came. The others won't be expecting us to backtrack, and we'll be able to get to our shuttles from there."

"Shut up, Sterling," Bex said between gritted teeth. "This is exactly why I didn't say anything. If we quit now, this will all be for nothing." Her stare met Ezren's. "I won't let this rescue fail because of me. Hart, you have to keep going."

"You have to be fodding kidding me," Foster growled. "There's no way you and Shiro can keep going like this."

"She didn't say that." Grady moved to Bex's side, checking the bandage before carefully sliding Bex's suit back over her shoulder. "She said *you* have to keep going." He turned to Foster with a granite expression of resolve. "I'll take them back. You go with Ezren."

"You can't be serious." Foster's incredulous gaze shifted from person to person. He knew how badly Ezren wanted to do this, but if they were three people down, their odds had just dropped off a cliff. "You said it before. We're not soldiers, and we only have nine hours to get out of here before the real soldiers arrive and shoot us on sight."

"But Ezren's father said there's no terranium here," Shiro said from his spot on the ground. "They're coming in with false information. If I can pass that on to the CIF, we may be able to protect you all."

"And if the planets go to war over terranium, people will die over a lie," Ezren whispered. "Casolla has been at peace as long as the BRR has been in place, and though I hate to admit it, we're one of the reasons that relations are on shaky ground." Her hands fisted at her sides. "If we can do something here to right that, even a little bit, I think we have a responsibility to."

"If war breaks out, Belethea will almost certainly be used as a prize to be captured." Bex's icy blue gaze met Foster's, and on some level, he felt like Bex had somehow known this since she'd first followed Ezren onto Shiro's ship. "We'll lose her to Dreitis or Obrone—or worse, she'll be split between them."

Foster's shoulders slumped, the weight of their arguments settling over him. He knew in his bones they were right, but he also knew, somewhere deep within, that if they continued on this path, there was a palpable chance one of them wouldn't be going back. His hand spasmed, and he clutched it to him. "Is this really our responsibility?"

"You're an ambassador for Belethea, are you not?" Shiro's low voice vibrated through the metal around them. "A royaler who can run, drive, and fight across hostile environments. Don't you think you, of all people, could do this? Maybe that you were even meant to do this?" His dark gaze hardened even as pain edged his uneven breaths. "I wouldn't have brought you here if I thought otherwise."

Ezren stepped forward and took Foster's hand in hers, her expression steady as she kneaded the cramping muscles with practiced movements. "We have the ability, Foster, and we're in the right place at the right time."

He snorted, but a smile curved his lips. "Then why do I feel like we're in the wrong place at the wrong time?"

She offered a bittersweet grin. "Either way, with the opportunity upon us, we can't just turn our backs on Belethea." Her expression grew earnest, and she squeezed his hands. "On Casolla."

He took a deep steadying breath, acceptance finally settling in his gut. As much as he didn't want to, he couldn't look away from everything that had brought them to Otho. Ezren's father, Calderon, the royale... Even he couldn't escape the growing conviction that they were supposed to be here. Called to it. But fodding suns, he hated it all the same.

"Fine." A shared exhalation of relief echoed through the room. "But what do you think we'll find here, if not terranium?" His brows knitted. "Your father said it was worse."

"Yeah, that doesn't give me a warm fuzzy either," Grady said.

Ezren shrugged, looking small in the darkness of the shelter. "I honestly don't know, but when we find out"—she glanced at Shiro—"we need to be ready to blast it to the 'verse."

"We'll be ready." Shiro turned to Grady. "I have a few codes I want you to pass on to your pilot so that we should be able to go directly to CIF along with the masses. Not to mention your VSoc channels. If we hit everyone at once, there's no way whoever's hiding this will be able to smother it."

Bex let out the whisper of a laugh, her eyelids fluttering. "Did I just hear you casually mention hacking into the CIF's comm networks?" She sagged to one side, and Grady moved to prop her up.

"I think of it as non-maliciously pointing out vulnerabilities in their best interest." Shiro smiled.

Forcing his muscles to relax, Foster tugged Ezren to a corner, and the others continued their banter. With a knowing nod, Grady turned his back to give them at least the semblance of privacy. If this was the path they were taking, they were nowhere near close to the end, so Foster had to take the moment while he could—because only the suns knew when they would get another one.

He pulled Ezren into his chest, leaning his cheek against her head. "Why do you always have to be a hero?"

"I'm not a hero, Foster, but I can't look away from this either." Ezren's arms wrapped around his waist, her hair tickling his nose. "It's the right thing to do."

"Yeah, that's what a hero is."

"Says the guy who crossed the system to come after me," Ezren replied, amusement softening her words.

Foster rubbed a hand across her back, seeing the distraction for what it was. Ezren came for her dad, but there were so many other threads tangled here as well. He knew she wasn't impervious to the guilt that the VSoc fritzers and Ambassador

Villegas tried to foist upon them. And he knew the doubts weighed as heavily upon her as they did him.

Would the world be a better place if they'd never run the BRR? If they'd just looked the other way? And would whatever they did here truly atone for the repercussions of their actions, or would this be another regret to add to their list? Another choice they'd be questioning for years to come. Another decision the masses would forever hound them for.

That is, if they ever made it out of here at all.

He pulled away, tucking a tangerine lock of hair behind her ear. "You're sure about this?"

She gave him a tired smile. "Not at all. There's a part of me that just wants to run. To make sure you and the rest of the team get home safe and hope for the best." She looked at him through her dark lashes. "But there are only so many cosmic coincidences I can take before I have to accept that something has brought us to this moment for a reason. Prepared us for it even. There's so many pieces coming together, but I just can't see the full picture yet."

It would've been easier if she was certain. If he was. But he couldn't help but feel the rightness of her words anyway. And now, with time already running out, certainty was a luxury. "Okay. I guess if the 'verse has conspired for us to be here, I at least want to find out why." He leaned down and briefly pressed his lips to hers, savoring the heat of her skin on his. "As long as we're together, we can work everything else out. All I ask is we stay together."

She pressed her forehead to his, the ghost of a smile curving her lips. "Always with you, Foster Sterling."

With that, he interwove his fingers with Ezren's, and brought them to his lips. Then, together they turned toward the door where Grady and the others stood ready to go. His smile fell with the cold reality of the task that lay before them. "I don't like splitting up."

Bex lifted her drooping head. "We'll come back once we're... back on our feet. No chance... we're leaving without you."

"Yeah." Grady tossed one of the packs to Ezren. "The syndicate goons will be waiting out there, so you'll need a diversion to get to the outpost."

Foster's jaw tightened. "Do not do that, Grady. Bex and Shiro are in no shape to make a fast break."

"Don't worry about us." Ezren stepped forward, one hand connecting her to Bex, and the other on Grady's arm. "May the storm winds blow you to the finish. And don't stop till they do."

"Same to you." Grady pulled on his helmet, his goggs glowing teal in the dim light. "We'll see you at the afterparty."

"And remember..." Shiro let out a harsh wheeze, his expression tight as Grady helped him into his helmet. "Don't fight unless you have to, but if you have to, move fast."

Foster let out a dry chuckle. "Trust me, Shiro, you don't have to remind royalers of that." He crossed his arms. "Much less Ezren Hart."

Bex swayed as she stood next to Grady and Shiro, the three of them readying to face whatever was out there once more. "I still don't like the odd numbers."

"I don't know if there's anything we can do about that." Foster slid on his dented helmet and adjusted the rifle strapped to his chest, his body tensing at the thought of what they were about to do. With her helmet on and the bag on her back, Ezren moved to Foster's side. Just the two of them again in a whole new kind of race. One he wasn't sure they could win. "I just hope it's worth it."

It was a thin hope.

CHAPTER 18

8.17.43B: T-minus 6.5 hours until Mt. Aguya's Eruption

EZREN WOULD'VE LOVED to say that the miles flew by, but running through a dark, endless tunnel as the ground quaked around her did not make time go faster. The only pinpricks of hope were the periodic air vents to the surface—some enlarged by small cave-ins that rained ash. Though the chaotic din of violence was never far off, at least these openings presented a viable exit.

Ezren had to force herself to focus on each step as the image of Bex and the others staggering off the way they'd come seared into her memory over and over. She had to tell herself that they were safer this way. That they'd make it back to the ship. But as the tunnel tremored beneath her boots, and the rattle of gunfire echoed from above, a sickening doubt curled through her stomach.

FOSTER: WE'RE ONLY AN HOUR OUT NOW. ARE YOU READY?

Beside her, Foster's chest pumped in time with hers, his long strides matching her short ones, and a wash of gratitude flowed through her, cooling her head. As much as she wouldn't wish this situation on anyone—especially not Foster—she had to admit that Shiro was right. They were their best chance. She just wasn't sure they'd be enough.

Ezren: I... I think so.

Even as she thought it, she couldn't muster up the confidence in her bones. But why? She'd risked her life in the BRR too—with both the planet and the other royalers seemingly conspiring to kill her. Wasn't this the same? Foster's stormy eyes glanced at her from his goggs as they continued to run.

Foster: What's wrong?

Ezren: I don't know. This is no different than a BRR, but I don't feel the same.

Foster: It is different. You have a lot more at stake, our odds are worse, and now you feel responsible for what happens if we lose here.

Each word hit Ezren with such force that she almost had to stop. Because of course, he was right on every account. Though last time she'd technically put Foster in danger, he'd been training for the race his whole life. Now, Bex's arm was shredded, Shiro had a bullet hole in his chest, and they'd already seen the other bodies. If it wasn't for her, they'd be watching this all go down from the comfort of their Petraskis bubble—worrying about war between publicity events no doubt.

Ezren: So what do I do about all that? If I don't get my head right—

The tunnel rumbled around them, sending a piece of metal clattering down from above. Foster shifted them to the wall, covering her body with his own. When he lifted his eyes to hers though, they were the soft green-gray of a sky before a squall. "The first thing I need you to know is that I've run into danger for you before, I'll face death for you today, and I'd do it again tomorrow. I'd do it without a second thought. Chaff, I'd send a hundred people into danger if it meant getting *you* out."

Ezren tried for a smile as they started down the tunnel again. "Well, that doesn't exactly make sense."

"Maybe not. But I don't think there's a soul in the history books who said love had to make sense." His gaze met hers with a burning sideways glance, emphasizing each word. "And while there's so much I don't know, one thing I'm absolutely certain of is that I love you, Ezren Hart."

A desperate warmth filled Ezren, her doubt evaporating as their strides lengthened. "Have I told you I love you?"

His eyes gleamed as he nudged her with his shoulder. "Never enough."

Ezren nudged him back, a smile quirking her lips even while the rumble of an engine echoed down from above, the metal walls vibrating around them.

FOSTER: I AM NERVOUS ABOUT ONE THING THOUGH.

EZREN: WHAT?

FOSTER: DO YOU THINK YOUR DAD WILL LIKE ME?

And for the first time since they set foot on Otho, Ezren laughed.

The deafening clang of metal on metal cut her short as a large vehicle crashed downward into the tunnel behind them, bullets rattling down around it. The quad revved before taking off down the passage, away from its pursuer, who followed quickly after on a jetbike.

Straight toward them.

Ezren's heart kicked into high gear.

EZREN: THEY'RE COMING AT US TOO FAST.

FOSTER: WE'VE GOT TO GET TOPSIDE.

He pushed her in front of him as they sprinted down the tunnel, bullets ricocheting off the metal reinforcements not a stone's throw away. Ezren wanted to be thankful the combatants didn't seem to be specifically targeting them, but she had no doubt they would take the first opportunity to eliminate two unknowns. Most likely in the form of running them over.

FOSTER: FASTER, EZREN!

Chest heaving, Ezren chanced another glance behind her to see the quad accelerating down the tunnel, the driver's goggs glued to them as his passenger fired at the weaving jetbike behind. Cold fear splashed through her. It was only a matter of time before the passenger turned his gun on them. And when that happened, they were dead. She urged her already burning legs faster.

EZREN: I DON'T SEE A WAY OUT!

FOSTER: IT'S COMING.

Ezren squinted, just barely catching the ray of murky light in the distance shining down into the darkness. Too far. They weren't going to make it, and if she waited too long, they'd be out of options. With a clatter of gunfire, the jetbike crashed with a metallic screech, and she knew their time was up. Gathering her strength, she took three more steps before jumping to the center of the tunnel and pulling the pistol from her thigh.

She wasn't as good a shot as Bex or Shiro, but she'd nailed the sims, and now she had the aim-steadying assistance of her topsuit. With her target coming right at them, practically on Foster's heels, there was no way she was going to miss.

The passenger's gun was already swiveling toward Foster when she delivered two shots to his chest, but the driver only got one to the head before their quad veered into the tunnel wall with a deafening crash, flinging both limp forms into the hard metal.

Ezren stared at them lying on the floor. Though her bullets had only stunned them, who knew what kind of damage the impact had done. Had she... had she killed them?

"Ezren!"

She barely registered Foster's shout before he crashed into her, two bullets going just wide of them as they tumbled to the ground. Foster popped to his knees, returning a spray of bullets that caught the injured jetbiker straight in the goggs. With a sizzle of electricity, he collapsed beside his bike. The threat silenced, Ezren's gaze flicked back to the other two forms splayed at unnatural angles.

"Are they dead?" Ezren asked, her voice strangely foreign in the sudden quiet.

"I don't know." Standing, Foster offered a hand to help her to her feet, his breath ragged. "But we have to hurry. There will only be more."

The blood still pounding in her ears, Ezren let Foster pull her from the floor and toward the jetbike. He picked up the bike and straddled it in one smooth motion, bringing it to life with a low purr as she climbed on behind him.

He looked over his shoulder at her, his eyes glinting. "At least they were decent enough to bring us a ride."

Her body was still numb with shock, but there was no time to process it. For the moment, they were soldiers, doing what they had to do to survive. Another clang echoed behind them, and she wrapped her arms around Foster's waist. "Then we might as well see what it can do."

With another growl of the engine, the bike lurched forward as Foster maneuvered it around the bodies and down the dark tunnel. Gunfire echoed behind them, and Foster kicked up the gear while Ezren wired into the mag controls. She disabled the safety limits, trusting in Foster to keep them stable as they hurtled into the darkness, her heartbeat racing along with them.

As much as she loved the running leg of the BRR, she had to admit that driving away from gunfire was preferable to running from it. The jetbike cut their final miles from an hour-long journey to only minutes before they arrived at the heavy steel door at the end of the tunnel.

Foster pulled the jetbike into a smooth sliding stop, and Ezren leapt from the back. Pulling up the entry codes she'd gotten from the last outpost, she projected both the stored fingerprint and the eye scan to open the door with an ominous clank.

"I guess we should all be grateful you use your powers for good," Foster said.

"Breaking into a top-secret lab?" Ezren asked, opening the heavy door and stepping into the airlock. The air cycled and the second door opened automatically, bringing them into a brightly lit hall. "Debatable."

"And not the first time." Foster lifted his rifle as he stepped into the facility alongside her.

Once again, the hallways projected the oddly disturbing, endless fields of grass. Unlike the last one, this research outpost seemed to be intact, the thermal regulator churning out blissfully cool air. Which meant—her body tensed as she opened her mouth to warn Foster, but not before the door slammed shut behind them and something hard jabbed into her back.

"Drop your weapons."

Before Ezren could react, Foster whirled around, his rifle still in hand.

"No, wait!" Ezren shouted, but it was too late.

Foster didn't make a full turn before the butt of a rifle crashed into his helmet with a sickening crack. Ezren screamed as he fell to the floor, the gun falling limply to the ground.

"Don't hurt him!" The muzzles shifted to her, and she dropped her pistol, raising her hands in the air. "We don't want to hurt anyone! We're here to see Dr. Milo Hart."

The two figures paused, and Ezren got a chance to fully take them in. Like the ones that had ambushed them at the South Outpost, these were in full tactical topsuits, but though their armor showed the scuffs of wear and tear, they bore a sleeker, more modern style. It also had a large C with several orbiting moons emblazoned on the chest—Calderon Industries' logo.

Shaft.

The two figures stood locked in some kind of silent debate, unreadable with their black-tinted goggs. Ezren glanced to where Foster hadn't moved on the floor, and her heart ran rampant in her chest.

Ezren: Foster, are you okay?

Nothing.

A cold sweat trickled down Ezren's collar as the seconds stretched, their fate weighing in the balance.

"Please." She pulled off her helmet, her sweat-soaked hair falling around her shoulders. "I'm looking for my dad."

At that, the two figures visibly relaxed, their weapons lowering.

One of them gestured at Foster. "Get him up."

Ezren dropped to one knee and shook Foster's shoulders "Foster, wake up. We've gotta move." She flipped him onto his back, noting the long crack in his helmet. *Oh no.* With the integrity compromised, its functionality would be forfeit if they ever managed to get out of here. She slipped it off of his head and combed her fingers gently through his dark brown waves. "Foster."

"Ezren." He winced, and his eyes fluttered open. "Are you okay?"

"Honestly, been better."

She pushed his goggs into his hand and tugged him to his feet, pulling his arm around her shoulders to keep him steady as one of the guards collected their weapons. Then, with one ahead and one behind, Calderon's soldiers herded them through the long corridors.

Ezren: Calderon Industries has taken over the base.

FOSTER: FODDING CHAFF. BUT I THOUGHT YOUR DAD WAS HERE. DO YOU THINK THEY USED HIM AS BAIT?

Ezren's mouth tightened, a sickening thought creeping in.

EZREN: OR MAYBE HE WAS NEVER HERE AT ALL. THEY COULD'VE FAKED THE MESSAGE. I SHOULD'VE ASKED FOR SOME KIND OF PROOF IT WAS HIM.

She bit hard into her cheek, her confidence withering with self-reproach. Had she really been duped so easily?

FOSTER: BUT THEN WHY WOULD YOUR FAKE DAD TELL YOU TO GET OUT OF HERE? WOULDN'T HE HAVE ENCOURAGED YOU TO COME TO HIM?

The guards prodded them into an elevator, taking them down deeper into the outpost, and Ezren's hope sank with it. "Where are you taking us?"

The guard closest to her tapped her in the stomach with the butt of his rifle. "No questions."

Foster tensed, taking a step forward. "Don't fodding touch her."

The guards raised their weapons again, and Ezren yanked him back.

EZREN: STOP. IT'S NOT WORTH IT. THIS ISN'T A SCRAP, AND THEY'RE NOT GOING TO FIGHT FAIR.

FOSTER: I CAN'T STAND THESE ASSCHAFFS. I'M BEGINNING TO THINK CALDERON'S BEHIND ALL THE EVIL SHAFT IN THE SYSTEM.

The elevator door opened again, and they continued into the maze of corridors that all looked the same. Endless grass fields. Ezren started a tracking app to chart their path in case they had a chance to flee.

EZREN: WE'VE GOT TO WAIT FOR OUR MOMENT. IF MY DAD'S NOT HERE, WE'LL HAVE TO MAKE A BREAK FOR THE

NEAREST SHUTTLE. IF THERE ARE PEOPLE IN THIS OUTPOST, THEY SHOULD ALSO HAVE A WAY OUT OF HERE.

Foster's arm tightened around her shoulders.

FOSTER: IT'S OKAY. WE'LL GET YOUR DAD AND FIND A WAY OUT.

Still, Ezren couldn't help but feel like they were walking to their execution.

The guards stopped at a room with another sentry posted outside it, and something silent passed between the three. They'd arrived at their destination, but she got the distinct sense that whatever waited for them behind the door wasn't good.

She turned to Foster, placing a hand on his chest.

EZREN: I LOVE YOU. NO MATTER WHAT HAPPENS.

Foster's eyes widened with panic, and his hand covered hers.

FOSTER: DON'T SAY IT LIKE THA—

The door hissed open, and the guards shoved them through.

Ezren braced herself for bodies, a cell, a firing squad, and found instead... a control room. Four figures in tactical topsuits stood in front of holos of all kinds while the surface of Otho played across the walls. With the sun now set, Aguya's embers illuminated the ships and vehicles of various manners ranging across the holos as the soldiers went about their work in complete silence.

And Ezren's stomach sank. Whatever this was, there would be no fighting their way out of this one. Each figure had a bulky rifle slung around their chest, and Cs emblazoned on their armor. Why had they brought them here? Was this part of Calderon's game?

"Who the fod is this?" One of the soldiers turned toward

them with a sharp cut of his hand. "What are you doing? They can't see this. Get rid of them."

The man raised his rifle, and Ezren stepped forward, lifting her hands. "We don't want to be here." The gun hummed with charge, and the last week flashed before Ezren's eyes as she scrambled to find the mistake that had led to this moment. "This isn't what we wanted."

And then one of the figures was charging toward her. Foster moved to shield her only to be shoved back by a guard, and Ezren lifted her arms to protect herself from the punishment barreling in her direction. She should've expected Calderon would inflict maximum pain first.

"Ezren!" Foster shouted.

At the last moment, the figure stopped inches away from her.

And for a breath, Ezren only stared.

The man was middling in stature with dirty-blond curls and a bushy beard covering his jaw. His face had a haggard, worn expression to it, and his body moved with a wiry hardness that was completely foreign to her.

But his eyes were impossible to forget.

So dark they looked almost black, they stared at her with such profound awe, it stole her breath away.

Because they were just like hers.

"Ezren." Her name escaped from his mouth like a whispered prayer, his hands hovering inches away, as if afraid to discover she might be a mirage. "Sweetheart."

A sob caught in Ezren's throat, and she threw her arms around his neck. "Dad."

His hands tightened around her, and she was nine years old again, waking from a nightmare. A nightmare that her father had left her behind. Now he was here, stroking her hair, and everything was going to be fine.

"I'm so sorry," he murmured, his voice thick. "Can you forgive me?"

Ezren nodded into his shoulder as she tried to even her breathing, her cheeks wet. "Yes, yes, of course I do." She didn't even know what she was forgiving him for.

The answer would always be yes.

Because he was alive, and he still loved her.

And that's all that mattered.

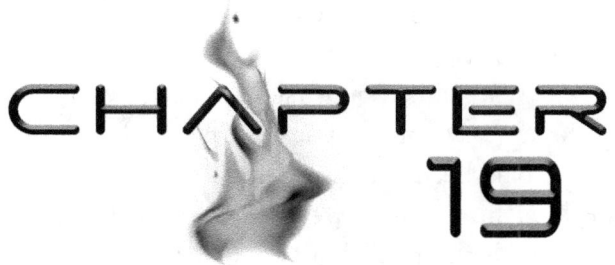

CHAPTER 19

8.17.43B: T-minus 5.5 hours until Mt. Aguya's Eruption

PAIN PULSED between Foster's temples as he struggled to take in the scene before them. They were in some sort of surveillance center staffed by armed men with the Calderon logo emblazoned on their topsuits. And one of them was Ezren's dad. But how was that possible? Shiro said he'd been working for Baxter all these years. While there was a part of him relieved to have found the man they'd come so far to save, there was a much bigger part of him that noticed no one had actually lowered their rifles yet.

"Who the fod is that?" someone barked from the side of the room.

"It's the Prof's daughter, you asschaff," another said closer by. "Don't you recognize her from the holos? And that's her doubles partner, Foster Sterling."

Foster shifted his weight from one foot to the other, not entirely sure if being recognized was in their favor. Would Calderon take this opportunity to quietly get rid of them, or was it better to stand apart from the syndicates' terranium looters shooting up Otho?

Ezren pulled away from her dad, her brow furrowing. "So you're working with Calderon now?" She glanced around at the other guns still pointed very much at them. Surely they wouldn't risk shooting her with one of their own so close. "What's going on here?"

The one who barked out first stepped forward, and Foster resisted the urge to retreat. The man had to be seven feet tall with a shiny bald head and limbs the size of tree trunks. Letting the muzzle of his rifle droop, he gestured to Ezren, his voice almost gentle. "Is this really your daughter, Prof?"

Dr. Hart nodded. "It is, Ferraz."

The man's jaw tightened, and he shook his head. "Lower your weapons."

The others complied without hesitation, but the one who had recognized them, a tiny thin guy with a topknot, held up a hand as if he were in a classroom. "So, I totally get that's his daughter, but how'd she get to this hellhole?" He gestured to the bubbling expanse of lava fields projected on the walls. "And just, why?"

"Yeah." Dr. Hart's face creased into a rueful smile as he glanced around the room at the questioning faces. "I know everyone has lots of questions." He put a tentative hand on Ezren's elbow and turned to Ferraz. "But do you think we can get a minute?"

Ferraz glanced at one of the holos projected from his goggs. "Yeah, but you gotta make it fast. Clock's ticking."

"Of course." Dr. Hart pointed to a side door. "Here, come with me."

"Wait, no." Ezren pulled back against his grip, moving to Foster's side. Her fingers intertwined with his and a wave of relief crashed over him. Her gaze darted to the armed men and back to her father. "I'm not going without Foster."

"Oh, right." Ezren's dad's stare fell on him, and his black eyes seemed to harden as he held out a hand. "I'm Ezren's dad, Dr. Milo Hart, but these guys all call me Prof, short for professor."

Dipping his head, Foster gripped Dr. Hart's forearm, his shoulders tightening with nerves. "And I'm Foster Sterling, Ezren's—" He stumbled over his words. Doubles partner? Not anymore. But then again, boyfriend seemed wholly inadequate for what Ezren meant to him. In the end, Dr. Hart filled in the blank.

"Teammate. I know." Dr. Hart strode through the door with quick, decisive steps. "C'mon, this way."

The three of them filed into what looked like a private office space, the wall divided into a dozen different holos of graphs and data Foster couldn't even begin to interpret.

Dr. Hart leaned against the table, gesturing for them to sit on the two rolling stools. "Okay, we don't have a lot of time, so I'm going to tell you what I can."

Ezren gasped, and Foster whipped toward her, his shoulders tensing. His gaze followed hers to land on the holos projected on the table—there must've been hundreds fluttering by in a huge collage. Ezren, her brother, her mom, from when they were young to even recent photos taken after the BRR.

"You..." Ezren swallowed hard, her eyes glinting in the dim light as her fingers brushed a holo of them in the winner's circle of the BRR. They'd been bloody and battered, but their smiles were pure triumph. "You saw us?"

"Of course I did, sweetheart. I promised I'd never stop looking." A huge smile creased Dr. Hart's weathered face. "I was pulling for you every second of every race—no one could've been prouder of you than me. We even threw our own party to celebrate when you won."

A party? The image of carrying Ezren's limp and bloody body across the finish line flashed through Foster's mind. Something about this didn't add up. He crossed his arms and leaned against the door, ready to grab Ezren and make a break for it if necessary. "So why are you working for

Calderon Industries when you *know* they tried to kill your daughter?"

Ezren frowned at Foster, and then at her dad. "And how'd you get to be here at all?" She moved to the data displays swirling around the circular room. "Everyone's talking about terranium, but from the environment readouts I don't see how there could be any here."

"You're right, there's no terranium on Otho." Dr. Hart scrubbed a hand over his short curls. "But now that VSoc has seized on the suspicion there is, the absence of something is hard to prove." His lips twisted. "Which is especially terrible timing, with Aguya about to blow its top." He enlarged a holo of an aerial map of the volcano with concentric circles radiating out from it and engulfing the bases. "It'll be a death wish for anyone caught on the surface. Even our underground bunkers will be dicey with the seismic activity."

Foster stared at the holo of the volcano, his mind struggling to take in this bad news on top of all the bad news they'd already absorbed. "Does that say a 120-mile blast radius?"

"What? No." Dr. Hart squinted at it. "Ah, that's for complete destruction. It's more like a 200-mile sphere."

Foster locked eyes with Ezren, alarm screaming at him to make a run for it, *stat*. "Um, okay. That sounds really fodding bad." He rubbed at his still pulsing temples. "And when the chaff is that happening?"

"We've estimated the blast will occur in a little over five hours, but the event will start in less than four. You need to be out of here before then."

"And what happens if we don't make it in time?" Ezren asked, her voice soft.

Dr. Hart rolled out one shoulder and then the other. "Assuming we survive, it could be a matter of days or even weeks before atmospheric conditions are adequate for flight."

His tone was so calm, so matter-of-fact, Foster could hardly believe they were both talking about the same thing. "So, let's get the fod out of here." Against all odds, they'd found Ezren's dad. Alive. So what was stopping the three of them from hijacking the nearest shuttle at that very second?

"Wait." Ezren stood, lifting her chin, her own stare unyielding as it met her father's. "Not before you tell us what's going on here."

"Of course, I owe you that much." Dr. Hart let out a sigh, his gaze drifting toward the smoky holo on the ceiling that mirrored Otho's sky. "Originally, I accepted a remote job on Gobrion Station, thinking it was a remote atmospheric study and planning to come home in four years. In truth, it was really a talent appraisal pool for Baxter. After testing my knowledge and skills, I was offered a classified assignment. It was only supposed to last a year, and it promised to pay enough for me to go home with more than enough money to get us through." He shrugged. "It seemed like an easy choice."

"Why didn't you tell us?" Ezren asked, and now that some of her tension had eased, Foster could see the relief and exhaustion playing over her pale features.

"I thought I did." Dr. Hart rubbed his lined brow with a shaking hand. "But it took months before we realized Baxter was reviewing and redacting our communications in the name of security. By that time, it was too late." His face darkened. "I was here, and the only way off was by Baxter's permission."

Ezren leaned into Foster, and he wrapped an arm around her. "Did anyone leave?" he asked.

Dr. Hart turned to meet his eyes, his mouth a grim line. "No."

"But what could possibly be so secret if there's no terranium?" Ezren expanded one of the holos, squinting at the data. "And why is Calderon involved?"

Dr. Hart projected something from his goggs, and the lab floor trembled beneath them. "It's easiest if I show you."

Foster shifted his feet as the floor descended, the air steadily heating around them. The circular walls slid away as the platform lowered into a much bigger area that resembled more of a natural cavern than a man-made space. Strings of bioluminescent lanterns circled the cave, illuminating the rough walls and the crisscrossing rivulets of what looked like steaming, magenta mud. It took a moment for Foster's eyes to adjust to the dim lighting, but when they did, tiny spots floated around his vision. Chaff, maybe he'd hit his head harder than he thought. A lab space occupied the wall closest to him, surrounded by a glass enclosure that walled off both the lab and the elevator.

Ezren's hand slipped from his as she stepped forward, her voice a whisper amid the soft bubbling of the cavern. "What is this?"

Dr. Hart moved to her side and pulled a small dark luminescent tube from his belt. The glove of his topsuit pulsed with a syncopated glow, and a trio of similar floating lights came to life within.

Wait. Not lights.

Foster stepped forward, foreboding and curiosity spiraling together and curling up his spine. Tiny, glowing creatures, no bigger than his fingertip, floated in the air. He could see no eyes or mouths, but they had a myriad of legs floating about their gelatinous body as they emanated a rainbow of colors—purple, pink, green, pink again. Like a soap bubble come to life.

"What is that?" Foster whispered, his voice trembling with an unsettling premonition he couldn't quite identify. If this was the big secret... that meant...

"Is it an animal?" Ezren asked, extending her fingers toward it.

"Yes." Dr. Hart placed the pulsing tube in her hand, and a flurry of the creatures danced inside the glass. "Officially, they're luxopodos, but we call them luxies, and..." He paused, his lips curving ever so slightly. "They're native to Otho."

Ezren whipped her head to Foster, her eyes like two huge headlights.

"But—" Foster's thoughts sputtered as he took in the cavern with fresh eyes. "That'd make this the first complex life-form found in the Casolla system."

Dr. Hart nodded, the kaleidoscope of the luxies' lights playing across his grim expression. "Exactly."

Ezren found her voice in an excited rush. "Then why is Baxter keeping it a secret? Are they intelligent? Rules about planets with complex life are so strict, they're breaking like fifty interplanetary laws right now."

"Why would they risk that?" Foster muttered, pinching the bridge of his nose as he tried to puzzle it out. Somewhere inside his skull, an alarm blared. Baxter had imprisoned dozens of scientists to keep this thing a secret—had killed to keep it a secret. Or was it Calderon? Either way, he and Ezren had now seen it. He felt their chances of escape plummet with his stomach.

Dr. Hart walked up to the glass barrier, watching the luxies float on the other side, his voice as calm as if he were giving a lecture in a classroom. "We're still learning about them, but we estimate their intelligence is somewhere between that of a monkey and a dolphin. They feed off the volcanic fumes here, they're incredibly adaptable, and they live to be around nine hundred years old."

Ezren placed one of the pods in Foster's hand, her face alight with discovery. "How is that possible?"

Foster flinched as the creatures wafted to and fro within the glass, his own thoughts echoing Ezren's question. Though he'd heard of complex life-forms discovered in other systems, most of them were akin to earthen algae, with a few rare instances of aquatic sponges and simplistic crustaceans. No animal he knew of, earthen or otherwise, lived to be half of this creature's lifespan.

Dr. Hart walked over to the lab table, where several of the creatures floated about in various forms of test tubes alongside complex equipment spiraling from the table in mazes of metal and glass. "Their bodies contain a compound which, in preliminary tests, seems to reverse aging."

Foster exchanged a glance with Ezren, hers of awe, his of horror. "So that's—"

"Yes." Dr. Hart turned back to him and crossed his arms. "As lucrative as being the first to discover complex life here would be, it's nowhere near that. These little beings could be the fountain of youth." He pulled a rag from his belt and mopped the sweat of his brow. "Not only that, but we've hypothesized their compounds could hold the key to making humans more adaptable to hostile environments. Quite frankly, the regenerative treatment potential is endless, and I've heard they're already making a fortune on the black market."

"Well, that explains why Calderon is after it." Foster set the tube of luxies on the table and stepped away from it. "The greedy asschaff's on the edge of death himself."

"If Calderon is using the luxies for his personal gain, I'm unaware of it." Dr. Hart took the fluorescent tube and stowed it in his belt. "Since Calderon's taken over the operation, he hasn't allowed any of the luxopodos to be harvested, per interplanetary law protecting alien species. So Baxter has been retaliating."

"Wait." Ezren held up her hands, her brow wrinkled in disbelief. "You're saying Calderon was doing the *right* thing?"

"I don't believe that for a second," Foster scoffed. "He must have ulterior motives."

Ezren's lips twisted as she thought. "Well, if luxies are used to make humans more adaptable, that means we could survive with imperfect terraforming solutions and further human planetary expansion. That's directly contrary to Calderon's pristine planet pitch."

"I suppose your judgment depends on what you believe the right thing is." Dr. Hart swiped a sprinkle of ash from the metal lab table. "Baxter believes they are humanity's savior, dispensing death-defying medicine to the people."

"You mean drugs." A defensive edge hardened Ezren's voice as she looked into the glass case filled with dozens of the creatures. "Untested, black-market drugs."

"I don't disagree," Dr. Hart said. "I'm only saying there are two sides who are both painting themselves the hero."

Foster's eyes narrowed. "If Calderon's such a hero, why wouldn't he tell the CIF about this?"

"He doesn't trust them to leave the luxies alone," Ezren whispered. "There will be vast interplanetary pressure to harvest their regenerative compounds. So he was trying to destroy Baxter's studies, wasn't he?"

"I don't pretend to fully understand Calderon, but that would be my guess as well, Ezzy." He put a hand on her shoulder, and she smiled up at him before he turned to Foster. "I appreciate your reservations about Calderon Industries, and I'm certainly not condoning their actions in the BRR." Dr. Hart ran a hand through his untamed beard, his face smudged with ash. "But that's a million miles from here, and in this case, I'm afraid the enemy of my enemy is my friend. When Calderon first arrived to shut down the operations, we had hope of going home for the first time in years. And when Baxter started the insurrection that killed Calderon's personnel, we knew it was only a matter of time before they buried us as well. So when Calderon sent their second contingent—these equipped for battle—I didn't miss the opportunity when they stormed my lab and offered me a gun." He crossed his arms over his barrel-like chest, his dark gaze scraping the cave. "Though I'm not naïve. My comms are still limited, my movements dictated, and though I'm currently of use to Calderon, my knowledge also makes me a liability. So in some ways, I traded one warden for another." His brow furrowed with a dark shadow. "Though with all of my colleagues—my *friends*—now in body bags, I can't regret my choice."

A silence spread over them, heavy with the weight of Dr. Hart's words. Just how many people had already died here? Rage simmered in Foster's belly as he thought of the other families wondering what had happened to their missing loved ones, just as Ezren had. Never knowing what had happened to them here. Never knowing what Baxter had done to them.

Ezren put the fingers of her topsuit to the glass wall, sending a pulse of light through it, and the luxies responded with a flash of blue and red. "But surely Calderon and Baxter realize it's over now, don't they? The CIF is sending their military here as we speak. And whether they find terranium or..." She gestured to the luxies, and her wide eyes turned to her father, filled with a fear that Foster felt straight down to his bones.

"There's a literal war coming to your gates," Foster finished.

"Yes, they're both trying to sweep it under the rug now. Calderon's only trying to prevent Baxter from shipping the luxies off-planet before the CIF gets here. Either way..." Dr. Hart let out a long breath, his shoulders caving as he shrank in on himself. "At least it'll finally be over."

Despite the heat, a chill curled up Foster's spine. They'd come here to find Ezren's dad, but somehow on the way, they'd stepped into what was promising to be the greatest interplane-tary disaster in Casolla's history. One that could bring wider humanitarian repercussions crashing down squarely on their shoulders.

As Foster watched Dr. Hart hang his head, an icy fear frosted his sweat-slicked skin. Because this man looked like he knew death was coming for them.

And there was nothing they could do about it.

CHAPTER 20

8.17.43B: T-minus 5 hours until Mt. Aguya's Eruption

EZREN HELD on to Foster's hand as if it could keep her afloat while all this new, unbelievable information threatened to drown her. Squeezing her fingers, Foster turned toward her, putting himself between her and her dad.

FOSTER: HOW ARE YOU DOING WITH ALL OF THIS?

Ezren swallowed, looking up at his stormy green-gray eyes, brows drawn low in concern.

EZREN: OKAY, I GUESS. I JUST... WHAT DO WE DO NOW?

Foster blew out a breath, a frown tugging his mouth down.

FOSTER: I THINK WE FIGURE OUT THE SAFEST WAY TO GET OUT OF HERE. WITH THE ERUPTION, THE CALDERON GUYS SHOULD BE TAKING OFF TOO, SO MAYBE WE'LL BE ABLE TO CATCH A RIDE.

But Ezren could see the doubt in the twitch of his lips, the dart of his eyes. He was trying to steady her, to be her rock, but not so far beneath the surface, he was just as unsettled as she was. Foster's gaze flicked between her dad and her.

FOSTER: DO YOU WANT SOME TIME ALONE WITH YOUR DAD?

And Ezren wanted to kiss him right there, because of

course that's what she wanted, but with everything going on she'd almost completely missed it. She squeezed his hand.

EZREN: YES, BUT CAN YOU STAY DOWN HERE? THIS PLACE IS TOO DANGEROUS.

FOSTER: I'LL BE RIGHT OVER HERE. I NEED TO TOUCH BASE WITH DAVIS AND SYLVIA ANYWAY. THEY'RE PROBABLY FRITZING OUT.

With that, he kissed her brow and walked into the far corner of the cavern, a holo projecting from his goggs.

Ezren turned to where her dad fiddled with some sort of measurement device at the lab bench. A strange nervousness fluttered in her stomach as she moved to stand next to him. She'd wanted another moment with her dad for years, but now that it had come, she wasn't sure she was ready. He moved to one of the smaller glass cases holding the luxies and placed his hands into the built-in gloves. The fingers flashed with light, and the luxies bobbed toward them as if he'd brought treats. He pulled something from the small airlock compartment and the luxies swarmed his hands, pulsing in orange and green.

How strange that this was her dad. The man who had raised her for nine years. The man she'd thought dead for four. The man she'd crossed the system to see.

And now she didn't know what to say.

He moved back to the bench, and she stepped to his side, gripping the metal table as if it could anchor her. Her dad cleared his throat, and when he spoke, his voice was hoarse. "I can't believe you're all grown up already."

Ezren nodded, plucking up a test tube filled with what looked like the magenta sludge flowing through the cave. "It's, uh, been a long time."

"They let us get VSoc updates once a month or so, but we rarely got a lot of details." Her dad's gaze flicked to her before returning to his instruments. "How's Sammy doing? Did the regen work for him? And..." His voice caught, and he swallowed. "And your mom?"

A surge of guilt swept through Ezren at the thought of her dad combing VSoc for news of them in the years before her royaler days. She'd never been a big VSoc person, so he would've found next to nothing. Even after she entered the media-crazed world of the BRR, she'd always been reluctant to post anything personal. Those exact details he'd probably been starving for.

Ezren's eyes welled, the work bench blurring before her as the words thickened on her tongue. "They're good, Dad. Sam's perfect. He's fully recovered and going to this ridiculously smart school." She drew in a shaky breath, trying to keep her tone cheerful. "And Mom's one of the lead terraformers on Belethea."

"That's good. Really good." He nodded, as if trying to reassure himself. "Has she... remarried?"

"No, no, nothing like that." Ezren waved her hands back and forth emphatically. "It took her some time to adjust after we lost you, but... she's happy." A sudden thought struck Ezren, and she pulled up the holopros her mom had sent of Sam's first day of school. "Here, have a look."

"Oh, suns," her father breathed, reaching a finger to trace the image of his wife. "She hasn't aged a day, and your brother..." He let out a soft chuckle. "He must be nearly as tall as me now."

Ezren smiled along with him. "He's definitely grown, and look at Waffle. She's so fat now!"

She flicked through the holos of Sam, Waffle, and her mom at home, in the lab, playing in Tuzuno's garden, celebrating on Casolla Day, and he drank it in like a man dying of thirst. After the first three, the tears leaked from his eyes, and after five, a sob racked his shoulders.

"I'm so sorry I missed it all." He covered his eyes with a hand. "The price of a fool's choice."

Ezren stopped and threw her arms around him, the first moment that had brought them here flashing through her. The day Sammy's hand had slipped away from hers. How the speedjet had careened into the crowd. How she'd screamed as her father scooped Sam's limp body from the street, blood everywhere, and ran him to the hospital.

For some reason, coming here, she'd only thought of her own grief of missing her father for years—her mother's and Sam's too. But why hadn't she thought of *his* loss? He'd sacrificed everything for them from that first moment. For Sammy, and her, and the hope of a better life, and somehow they'd managed it without him.

"We would've never made it through those first few years without the money," Ezren choked out, desperately trying to swallow her tears. "We wouldn't have been able to get him through regen without it." She took a deep breath, squeezing him tight as he hugged her in return. "It's going to be okay now though. We're together. We can go home."

"But you shouldn't be here, Ezzy." He pulled back, drying his eyes on the sleeve of his topsuit. "This place is about to explode. How did you even find me?"

Wiping her cheeks, Ezren waved to Foster where he leaned on the far wall, studiously averting his gaze. He walked over, rubbing a sheepish hand along the back of his neck. Stepping away from her father's embrace, she smiled between him and her dad—two people she loved who had always been separated by years in her mind now standing next to each other. Her father's short, heavy-set form contrasting starkly with Foster's tall, broad one.

"Um, Foster hired a P.I. to find you," Ezren said.

Foster's gaze toggled from her to her dad, alarm sparking

through his eyes as he took stock of the conversation. "But I had no idea it would lead us here. Sir, I would never have endanger—"

"I know, I can tell." A wistful chuckle escaped Ezren's dad as he rubbed at a spot on the lab table. "I have no one to blame but myself."

Ezren couldn't let him believe that, and she refused to allow Baxter to steal another second of their precious time. "Baxter's the only one to blame here. They held you against your will. But that doesn't matter anymore. We can just go and leave all of this behind."

Foster edged closer to her side, his sandy complexion practically glowing with renewed purpose. "Our other teammates are bringing an escape pod for us. We can be back on the ship in an hour and get out of here."

Ezren grinned, hope warming her belly. "It'll be like it never happened."

Her father smiled at her, but there was something wrong with the expression. It was sad, not triumphant—the luxies practically dancing behind him in their glass habitat. "No, Ezren."

Ezren froze, sure she misheard. "What do you mean no?"

Her father lifted one of the tubes with two small luxies inside, their many legs swaying in a circle. "There's still work to do here. Baxter is still in control of the Alpha Base, and if we don't get there soon, the evidence of Baxter's crimes here will be destroyed. All of the research we have done, at unfathomable cost, will be wiped. And if we don't stop them, they'll ship the luxies to the stations to who knows what end." He pressed his lips together, rubbing a hand over his beard. "I want people to know. No, people *have* to know what went on here. Who died here. Baxter Research will destroy everything if we let them, and I can't let that happen. I was here at the beginning, and I have to be here until the end." When he looked at her, his gaze was fixed, resolute. "It's my responsibility."

Beside her, Foster scrubbed a hand across his jaw, his expression dark and unreadable.

Ezren's shoulders fell, exhaustion cresting over her in a wave. Suns, would they never escape the burden of responsibility? The tyrannical exhaustion of it? The worst part was, she knew he was right. But why did the right thing always have to be the hardest?

Foster's hand found hers, and she squeezed it hard. "Okay." Ezren sniffed, forcing her shoulders to straighten. One foot in front of the other. "But then we can go home, right?"

Her father smiled, his eyes crinkling in a way she'd once carried only in her memories. "Yes, sweetheart, then we can go home."

The warmth of his presence, his love, filled Ezren's chest, bracing her for the trials to come. And even though she'd crossed the system to get here. Had shot and been shot at in turns. Even though the world was turning upside down. Right then, at that moment, it was all worth it.

CHAPTER 21

8.17.43B: T-minus 4.5 hours until Mt. Aguya's Eruption

FOSTER SHIFTED his weight from one foot to the other as Ezren helped her dad transfer the luxies from their various enclosures into the greater expanse of the cavern. Anxiety spooled in his core as the time ticked away. He understood Dr. Hart's reasoning, sure, but at what point did this become a suicide mission? Already the fantasy of throwing Ezren over his shoulder and dragging Dr. Hart back to the shuttle had cycled through his mind at least half a dozen times. A last resort of course, but one he could not entirely dismiss.

They might never forgive him, but at least they would survive.

His goggs chimed, pulling him from the moment as Davis finally answered his message. Though Foster would never admit it, he'd started to worry about them.

DAVIS: OKAY, SO NOW THAT YOU'VE FOUND DR. HART, YOU'RE READY TO GET OFF THAT PLANET, RIGHT?

FOSTER: I'M WORKING ON IT, BUT THINGS ARE... COMPLICATED.

DAVIS: YEAH, NOT TO RUSH YOU, BUT IT'S GETTING CROWDED UP HERE, AND NOT IN A GOOD WAY.

DAD: AND THEY'RE ONLY GOING TO GET MORE COMPLIcated the longer you hang around down there, so stop tempting fate and get back to the escape pod before you can't anymore.

Foster: Thanks for the pep talk, Dad. Super helpful as always.

Foster's hand cramped, and he clenched it into a fist, turning back to Ezren as she released the last luxie into the darkness. "So, what's the plan then? We've got Baxter trying to defend their operation, Calderon trying to shut it down, the syndicates shooting anything that moves over terranium that doesn't exist, and the CIF coming to wipe everyone off the face of the planet under false pretenses."

Dr. Hart waved a hefty dark cylinder with small luxies floating inside. "If we can get this off the planet, we can prove the luxies' existence to the offworlders." In his other hand, he showed them a small black sphere. "But I also want to get a record of the false imprisonment and murder that's been going on here, along with the accounts of who Baxter has been selling to, and the data we've collected so far. All of those files are kept in the Alpha Base mainframe."

"And neither Calderon nor Baxter wants this to get out," Ezren said.

"But that doesn't make sense." Foster raked an irritated hand through his waves, damp with sweat in the boiling air. "With the CIF rolling in for terranium, they're going to find the luxies and their special compound or whatever."

"Not necessarily," Dr. Hart replied. "While there are a few luxie pockets across the planet, they're not a pervasive species, and Baxter is already attempting to pass them off as a manmade creature."

"Okay." Foster's hand jerked with another painful spasm, and he clamped his other hand on to it. "So what happens when we drop the bomb that it's actually an alien?"

Ezren took his hand in her firm grasp, massaging the pain from each finger in turn. "They would go under intense protection from the CIF, but there's no guarantee that the CIF would honor the extraterrestrial code. They could easily override it in favor of humanitarian gain."

"Which is why Calderon took the operation into his own hands." Dr. Hart's gaze lingered on Foster and Ezren's joined hands, but Foster couldn't read his expression. "With the luxies' long reproduction times, farming them sustainably would be borderline impossible, and that's not even considering the inevitable poaching."

"So we trust the CIF to do the right thing then?" Foster asked, giving Ezren's fingers a grateful squeeze as she released his hand. He thought of Villegas, Calderon, and his syndicate bodyguard standing side by side. *Keep your enemies close.* "What if Calderon's right, and they farm the luxies into extinction?"

Ezren's brow furrowed, her gaze pinned on the rainbow of luxies coalescing in a colorful cloud in the far reaches of the cave. "You're saying you'd prefer it under Calderon's control? Do we trust that his industry will stick to their values over profit?"

Dr. Hart held up his hands to usher them toward the elevator platform. "Ezren, Foster, ultimately, this is too big for us to decide, but we cannot withhold the truth. The people of Casolla need to know. Even those beyond the wormgate. If we don't honor the code, Casolla itself could be subject to consequences from the home system."

Foster let out a low, frustrated growl as the platform took them upward. "Okay, so how're we going to get all of this info out before someone kills us?"

"The summit." Ezren's face brightened under the dim lights. "Foster, it's perfect. Not only will we be able to submit the proof, but we can also lay our case for the luxies to be left alone in accordance with interplanetary law."

Foster stared at her, the platform juddering to a stop under his feet. "You know you're going to give the Never-Terras grounds to call you a hypocrite." A week ago, she'd wanted to run away from VSoc, politics, and the whole circus, and today she was plotting a full-on collision course.

"Yes, and the pro-terraformers will say I'm putting humanity second." Exasperation etched her face at the familiar lose-lose scenario they were encountering more and more often. "I don't care about sides, I just want to do the right thing, even if they hate me for it."

Dr. Hart nodded, his expression creasing with pride. "Okay then." He gestured to the door. "From here, we'll proceed to Alpha Base as planned. The Calderon team doesn't fully trust me, but they have the luxies' best interest at heart, and they need the information to use as collateral. After I get the data I need, we'll use the shuttles to retreat to your ships. This is going to be a delicate and possibly temporary alliance, but they're not a bad lot, so just follow my lead."

With a sharp turn, Dr. Hart opened the door and stepped into the control room filled with Calderon's in-situ soldiers.

"There are no shuttles here, so they'll have to come with us," said the short man with the topknot.

"Fod that." A red-headed man jerked his chin in their direction. "If we take them, they'll only get hurt. They'll be better off making a run for it."

"A run for what?" the short one replied. "If we leave them here, they're going to be roasted in the eruption. I didn't come here to murder kids—especially not famous ones—and it's pretty obvious they're not with Baxter."

The towering bald one, Ferraz, looked the three of them over with hard eyes. "We can't babysit anyone, but numbers aren't on our side." He lifted Ezren's and Foster's weapons from a table in the center of the room and offered one to each of them. "Are you going to be an asset or a liability?"

"I'll vouch for them, Ferraz," Dr. Hart said. "If we're going to break into Alpha Base, we'll need all the spare hands we can get."

Foster stepped forward and took the rifle with more confidence than he felt. "We're royalers. We'll be just fine."

Beside him, Ezren grabbed her pistol and slid it into the holster on her thigh. "Just tell us where to go."

"All right then." Ferraz gave a slow nod, looking for all the world like a man both resigned to his fate and yet ready to fight against it anyway. "Let's go over the plan one more time." He pulled up a holo. "The first objective is to take out their thermal power station. If we knock out their main grid, the base's auto-defenses will be in-op, and we should be able to break in. We only have three tac-Vs on site, so we'll have three guns riding in each. As we learned from the last two bases, it will be heavily fortified, and they'll be raining bullets on us."

Foster took another look at the six imposing figures around him. "Do you know how many people they have?"

"More than us, kid," said the small one with the big mouth. "And more so now that we've lost three."

Foster's blood iced. They'd already lost a third of their crew. His mind involuntarily ran the numbers. If they were looking at the same casualty rate, one of the three cars wasn't going to make it.

"You royalers can drive a tac-V, right?" Ferraz asked.

"Um, yeah," Ezren said. "But we don't have much combat—"

"Don't worry about it." The redhead's gruff voice rasped from his throat as he scratched at his unshaven jaw. "As long as you approve the target, the truck will do the shooting itself."

Ferraz nodded. "The first truck will infiltrate the base from the north, allowing the two others to take out the power from the south. Once we take control, we grab the evidence, wipe the mainframe, and ride the shuttles out."

"What about the terranium looters?" Ezren asked. "They came after us on the way here."

A woman with high cheekbones and a scar down one side of her face looked at Ezren. "Good rule of thumb, if they're shooting at you, shoot back."

"Right." Ferraz moved to a worn, ash-dusted bag against one corner. "Gear up and get to your vehicles. We leave in five."

While we secretly palm a few luxies for the road. Right. Foster liked nothing about this plan. But he'd already rooted around in their base network while he, Ezren, and her dad were talking, so he knew there were no shuttles here, and Alpha Base was closer than the one they'd come from. So basically, this was as good as the plan got.

Dr. Hart handed Ezren her helmet and passed a new one to Foster. "Your helmet had a bad crack in it. This one isn't as efficient as your royale gear, but it has tactical armor and chameleonic skin like the one Ezren's wearing."

"Thanks." Foster took the helmet from him, forcing himself not to ask where it had come from. Apparently its original owner wouldn't be needing it anymore, and he was already feeling too sickened to ask why.

Grabbing his own helmet, Dr. Hart motioned them toward a door. "The vehicles are this way."

Ezren caught his gaze, her eyes round and dark as they walked down the blood-spattered holos of open fields.

EZREN: WHAT ARE YOU THINKING?

FOSTER: I'M THINKING... I'M TRYING NOT TO THINK.

Foster reached out and gave her hand a brief squeeze. He

didn't want to be honest right now. He didn't want to give his fear the opportunity to swallow him, and maybe even Ezren too.

FOSTER: Do you want to drive this leg?

Ezren gave him a tiny smile, the smallest dent in her pale face.

EZREN: I think I can handle that. Were you able to contact the others? Are they safe?

FOSTER: Yeah, but I guess I have more to tell them now.

He shifted the display in his goggs over to Grady's last message

GRADY: We can't send any of the shuttles down to where you are. There's a huge Kalashnik syndicate ship shooting down anything within a five-mile radius of you.

FOSTER: It's okay, we're headed to the central base and trying to get out in their shuttles.

GRADY: Blime, it looks like we have an opening to land a few miles north of there.

FOSTER: No, don't. It's still under Baxter's control, and it's too close to the active volcano. We'll be shooting our way out, and we'll be doing it on the clock.

GRADY: Well, then we'll be scabbed if we're not there shooting our way out with you, kin. There's no chance we're going to miss that action. I mean Bex's arm is barely glued together, and I'm having to hold her back from jumping out the airlock.

FOSTER: Grady, people are dying down here. And Bex and Shiro already got hurt once. There are shuttles at the base we can use.

GRADY: SHAFT THAT. I'M LOOKING AT THE SATELLITE IMAGERY NOW, AND IT'S NOT JUST YOU TRYING TO GET IN THAT PLACE. APPARENTLY, THE SYNDICATES HAVE FIGURED OUT BAXTER'S HIDING SOMETHING IN THERE TOO. IT'S LIKE A FODDING WARZONE. WE'RE COMING.

Foster took in a breath through his nose, knowing there was no way he could force Grady to do anything once his mind was made up.

FOSTER: YOU'RE A REAL PAIN IN THE ASS, YOU KNOW THAT?

GRADY: YEAH, WELL BE GLAD I LEARNED SOMETHING FROM YOU.

FOSTER: THANKS, GRADY.

GRADY: JUST REMEMBER TO SAVE ME A SEAT IN THE AFTERLIFE.

Foster looked up from his messages just in time to see Dr. Hart pause in front of the thick exterior door. Calderon's six soldiers had joined them too, checking topsuits and weapons.

Foster turned to Ezren and ran a visual check of her suit, looking for tears and dings. Thankfully, despite the damage it had taken, its functionality hadn't been compromised. Yet.

"Your suit's at 95% with the new helmet." Ezren ran a finger along a shallow tear in his sleeve. "Should be enough to weather a few dozen miles."

"Your suit's good too." Foster put his hands on her shoulders, noting her dad subtly peeking in their direction. He still couldn't get a solid read on whether or not the man approved of their relationship, but he tried not to let it unbalance him. With a battlefield ahead of them, he couldn't afford to. "Are you ready?"

The short Calderon man laughed from his spot by the door. "Kid, no one is ever ready for this type of thing. Chaff's going to go sideways the minute we step out the door, and old Ferraz's plan will instantly be shafted."

The bigger redhead smirked. "What'll you do then, sporty boy? There are no rules to save you here."

Foster straightened, his muscles tensing beneath the familiar grip of his topsuit. "I don't know what we'll find out there. But when I step on the surface, I never do." He looked at Ezren and her dad. "I've survived people trying to kill me with their fists, wheels, and now bullets, and I've stared a dead friend straight in the face." The men shot furtive glances at each other, and Foster's resolve only rose with his words. "Royalers know how to run when we can and fight when we have to. Ezren and I can outdrive any one of you fritzers, and we'll outlast you in these topsuits for days." He gazed at the helmet in his hand and thought once again of its unlucky owner. "I don't want to be a soldier, but I will if that's what it takes to get my family off this fodding planet."

Dr. Hart's dark gaze speared him with an unreadable look, but if anything, Calderon's men seemed to relax.

"Well said." Ferraz charged his rifle with a low hum. "The first royalers were soldiers after all. Explorers. Survivors. I can see now why Calderon speaks so highly of you. The spirit is strong still."

Foster didn't have time to react to this before bigmouth spoke up. "Chaff yeah, it is. What is it that the Belethea royalers say before racing?"

"It's a Belethean prayer," Ezren said softly, pride glowing in her eyes as she looked at Foster.

"But Otho has her own," Dr. Hart said. "We've buried enough here to need one." Clearing his throat, he closed his eyes as he bowed his head. "While the smoke may blind our eyes, the air choke our lungs, and Otho, herself, rage beneath our feet, we shall never waver. Never blink. Here in these flames, may we forge ourselves anew, as we go into the fire."

Instinctively, the crew answered as one. "Into the fire."

And as they walked out into the bullet-rattled inferno of Otho, the smaller soldier clapped Foster on the shoulder. "Don't sweat it, kid. We're a rough group, but we've got your back."

With those words, Foster realized they were, if only for a brief time, on the same side as Calderon Industries. And the coil of dread tightened around his chest.

CHAPTER 22

8.18.43B: T-minus 4 hours until Mt. Aguya's Eruption

EZREN SLID into the seat of the tac-V, securing the harness and connecting her chip to the holodash. Even inside her topsuit, sweat slid around her goggs.

"Is it just me, or is it getting hotter?" Even as she said it, she consulted her data collection. Holy shaft, it *was* getting hotter. A lot. She turned to her father and sent him the data she'd been analyzing. "Is this temperature spike normal?"

Her father buckled into the webbing of the backseat to one side of the turret as he squinted at the data. "Normal? No. But we are experiencing a once-in-a-lifetime volcanic event. While we have projections for nominal conditions, we have no real data to support the current anomaly."

Ezren winced as she noted the strain in her dad's eyes. Topsuits could only be worn indefinitely by those under the age of twenty-two. After that, if used too long, the strain could inflict permanent damage on the wearer. "Dad, the topsuit... will you be able to—"

"I'll be fine, Ezren," he said, his tone brooking no argument. "I've been surviving here for years. I know my limits."

Foster's gaze met hers as he slid into the front seat beside her, a bristling weapons holo coming to life before him. "Well, between the volcano and the looters, it seems like this place is *trying* to kill us at this point." He flicked through the holo controls, showing different firing and targeting options. "Will the native luxies be able to survive this?"

"Historical evidence suggests they'll adapt and regenerate," Ezren's dad replied. "But even if it's too much for those at the epicenter, the more distant colonies will be fine."

Ezren reluctantly faced forward, her lips twitching as she connected her goggs to the HUD and extrapolated the data she'd collected from her algorithm. With the limited instrumentation she'd brought along with her, it was rudimentary at best, but it was all she had. "Based on these predictions, we have about three hours before the temperature on the surface becomes unsurvivable even in our topsuits."

Foster gave her a sideways glance, and she knew they were thinking the same thing.

They would have three hours, but the others were above the recommended age for indefinite use. Their older bodies wouldn't be able to endure the incredible drain the topsuits would extract as they tried to compensate for the deadly conditions. But she didn't have an equation to calculate their reduced time.

"What about the tac-V?" her dad asked from the backseat. "How long will it withstand the increasing heat?"

Another excellent question. Ezren turned to the controls once more, searching the specs for a maximum temp. Unfortunately, the thermal regulator would be the first thing to burn out, and it wouldn't take long. Ezren flew through the calculations and grimaced. "We'll have to gun it."

Foster watched her closely as she synced their vehicle's channel with the other two.

"Ferraz, are you there?" she asked.

"Present and accounted for." Ferraz's deep bass echoed through the truck's cab. "You ready, royale-girl?"

"Listen, if you're going the long way, you're going to have to average sixty miles per hour to make it before your thermal regulator fails and the truck turns into an oven. At these temps, it won't be long before you cook even with your topsuits."

A silence stretched over the line. "Did you say *cook*?" the smaller one said.

"Yeah... not to put us on a clock or anything. But in three hours, going onto the surface with anything other than an exo-atmospheric vehicle will be suicide."

"Well, then we'd better get this party started," Ferraz said. "Santino, watch out for the kids, will ya? I really don't want to have to explain that to the boss." With that, the engine of his tac-V revved, and he peeled away from the building in a spray of ash.

"You lead the way," her dad said from the backseat.

Ezren started the tac-V with a command from her chip, cocking her head. If the boss was Calderon, that seemed to imply that he wouldn't be happy to see them dead. Then again, there was probably a long chain of command to get to the top. So perhaps Calderon Industries wasn't rotten all the way down. At least that was one reassuring thought.

"You know." Santino's engine revved beside hers, and she could see him peering at her through the window, his beady eyes glinting. "When I was a kid, I always wanted to be a royaler."

Foster glanced at Ezren, a smile in his gaze behind his goggs. "Is that right?"

"And wouldn't you know it," Santino continued, "now I get to drive with the champs."

"Shut up, Santino, and start driving already," the gruff redhead chimed in through the comm.

"I'm just saying, I think this is the perfect time for a little race," Santino said.

Ezren's dad shook his head. "Racing is not a tac—"

But Ezren had had enough of the tension and the talk of doom and gloom. They were on the clock, and she outright refused to spend it in fear. If this was going to be the last drive of her life, she was going to enjoy it.

"You're on." She slammed on the gas, and they rocketed away from the research outpost.

A wild, raucous laughter drifted over the comm. "Fodding blime!"

Ezren couldn't help joining in with her own hysterical giggles even as she wove around Otho's hot patches, lava and embers transforming the night into a copper dusk. Beside her, Foster boomed out his own belly laugh. A sound, Ezren realized, she hadn't heard in a very long time. It vibrated in her bones, the buoyancy of it threatening to lift her out of her seat. When they got home, she resolved to make sure she heard it so much more.

"Ezren!" Her father bounced in his rigging as she launched off a rock formation. Though the cab was already too hot, it was an incredibly rugged vehicle—engineered perfectly for this terrain. While they'd trained on similar storm trucks often in the BRR sims, they were very rarely used in royales. Some argued they were too safe or gave too much of an advantage. But out here, they certainly couldn't get enough of that.

"Yes, Dad?" Ezren said in her sweetest, most innocent voice. A tone she hadn't used since... well, maybe since he'd left. It made her feel younger somehow.

"This isn't safe," he protested. "With the terrain and the—"

A spray of gunfire rattled down on their right, and Ezren banked a hard left.

"The looters?" she asked pleasantly. She swerved again, her

brow furrowing as she focused. "Seriously, Dad, with the volcano, the bullets, and the CIF bearing down on us, we can't afford to slow down. We might as well make it fun while we can."

"Hey royalers," Santino called over the comms as a boulder shattered on their left. "Why the chaff aren't you shooting back at these fodders?"

"The target's set for the power center at the base." Foster whipped through the holo as the vehicle pitched a hard right to avoid a pool of smoking lava.

"Well, set it to return fire already," Santino yelled, their own guns chattering almost nonstop behind them. "We have to get to the base first."

"I think you're just trying to slow us down," Ezren said, the tac-V careening into a ravine to narrowly avoid a low-flying craft. What the chaff was that?

Santino's laughter echoed over the channel. "Look, girlie, I'm just happy to be here."

"Well, that makes one of us," Ezren's dad grumbled from the back as they jostled violently across the uneven terrain.

Ezren swerved again as they nearly ran into what looked like a small encampment of at least three quads.

"There are people everywhere now," Foster said, the vehicle vibrating as their own guns swiveled to return the fire of the quad-riders. "And I'm really getting tired of them shooting at us."

"They're trying to lay claim to the land we're crossing," Ezren's dad said from the back, his tone dark. "We're a threat to their terranium."

"It's a tale as old as time," the scarred woman laughed over the line. "Shoot the competition, and suddenly, there's no more competition."

"It's also why they outlawed weaponry in the original race to the terranium on Belethea," said the redhead, and Ezren had to wonder if these people knew the roots of the BRR better than she did. Was that like a Calderon Industries requirement?

"This is stupid." Ezren's gaze swept the terrain, now taking in the sheer number of ships and vehicles. There had to be over a hundred headlights spread out across the dark mud flat while Mt. Aguya spewed ash not fifteen miles off. "They're all going to die here."

"Um... good?" Santino said. "These are murdering, terranium-thieving syndicate thugs we're talking about here."

"Yeah, and I'm not going to have them on my conscience for the rest of my life." Ezren looked sharply at Foster, her patience dissolving under a new ferocity. "Open a wide channel."

Foster didn't move. "Why?"

"So I can tell them," Ezren said just as their car skidded down a sharp incline, the ground shifting beneath them with the groan of an earthquake.

"Ezren, if you do that, Baxter will know we're coming," her father said, leaning forward.

Ezren barked out a dry laugh, but it was Foster who answered. "Everyone already knows we're coming."

"Right." Ezren nodded, praying to the elder suns that Ferraz had made it to the other side. "Our only chance is that the other tac-V knocks out the gunners from the inside first." She really didn't want to think about what would happen if they didn't, but it involved a hard U-turn under a flurry of bullets they almost certainly wouldn't survive.

"And this might help to draw attention away from them." Foster stared at her a moment, before flicking through his holo to the open channel. "You're sure?"

"Yes." Ezren couldn't afford to overthink anymore. They didn't have the seconds to spare.

Her goggs dinged with a private message.

FOSTER: HAVE I TOLD YOU THAT I LOVE YOU YET?

He squeezed her knee, and Ezren blushed hot under her helmet.

EZREN: TELL ME AGAIN.

"All right," he said aloud. "You're broadcasting to everyone in a two-hundred-mile radius."

"Turn on our holo cam too." Ezren took a deep breath. There'd be no coming back from this. But she refused to let anyone die when she could do something about it. She wasn't Calderon after all.

"You're on."

Well, here went nothing. "Otho, listen up, this is Ezren Hart, Belethean Royaler and athlete ambassador. I came here to rescue my father from Baxter's illegal operations, but I know most of you are here for the alleged terranium." She swallowed. "You were lied to. There's no terranium here, and the temperatures are rising with Mt. Aguya's impending eruption. In less than three hours, your topsuits won't be able to compensate, and you *will* die. That is if the CIF doesn't kill you first for trespassing. Get off the surface while you can or start digging your graves here." She looked at Foster, the bullets snarling from their tac vehicle. "End broadcast."

The holo terminal flicked off, and she let out a long breath. "Did I miss anything?"

"I can think of one or two." His eyes curved into half-moons behind his goggs, and he squeezed her knee again. "But they're on a need-to-know basis."

"Ezren," her dad breathed from the back, astonishment lining his words. "Do they teach you royalers to do that in school or something?"

Ezren laughed. "I'll make sure to let Sylvia know you were impressed."

"You did good." Foster's attention flicked back to the weapons monitors. "If they don't leave now, it's on them."

"Yeah, that was a nice testimony," the redhead said over comms, an explosion crackling in the background. "Might want to put that in your will too."

"Feel free to leave everything to me," Santino chimed in.

Foster stiffened beside Ezren, his face going dark as he whipped toward her. "Ezren, there's something I need to tell—"

A truck crashed into their tac-V, and they rolled before Ezren righted them again. The mag-controls whirred as they tore away from their pursuer. Her ears rang, and something exploded just behind them. "Tell me you're joking."

Holding on to the brace bar, Foster leaned closer. "Dead serious."

"Is this a great time?" While a few ships were taking off into the atmosphere, it looked like her message had only drawn more of the looters to them. Were they really here for the terranium at all?

"Suns, please tell me you're proposing," Santino rang in. "I want to be able to tell my future grandchildren I was there when it happened."

Ezren couldn't help but laugh. Apparently, Santino was a proper belroy fanboy. She'd have to remember to introduce him to Micah, the de facto head of the Belethean Royale fan club, after they got out of this. "Foster, I love you with every cell of my being." She swerved hard. "But now is not the time."

He seemed to relax, something in his expression shifting. "But what if we die here?"

She raised a brow at him. "Are you doubting my driving skills?" She released the grav controls as they flew up a ramp-like incline, and the tac-V went airborne. Foster punched the jet drive and they rocketed through the air, narrowly missing a low-flying ship.

"I didn't come all the way to die here." Ezren's voice softened, her hands tight on the steering wheel. Whatever Foster was going to say, she had a feeling it wasn't going to be good, and she could not handle one more word of bad news. If they weren't careful, they'd drown in it. She strove to keep her voice light. "Whatever it is, there'll be time later."

"I'm beginning to wish I'd chosen a different car," her dad said from the backseat.

They bounced along the ground as they landed, and a bullet cracked their windshield. "Not you too, Dad." She slapped Foster lightly on the shoulder. "You're giving my dad the wrong idea. Tell him I'm a good driver."

"It's not that," her dad groaned, eyeing Foster's hand on her thigh. "It's all this mushiness coming out of my teenage daughter."

Ezren burst out laughing, but Foster ignored her dad, facing Ezren instead.

"Nope. It can't wait." He took a deep breath as if steeling himself. "Calderon asked me to work with him and be a part of the BRR council."

"What?" Ezren jerked the wheel around a steaming pool of lava. "And what'd you say?"

"Fod off."

Ezren smiled at the picture, but confusion still scrambled her thoughts. "Why would he do that?"

"Calderon is a man who will keep his friends close and his enemies closer," her dad said from behind them. "A timeless strategy, but not a bad one. Especially when you have a common enemy."

"Yeah, he did say something along those lines," Foster said

over his shoulder, gripping the brace bar as they took a leap over a rock shelf. "But I told him we do everything as a team, so I wanted to talk to you about it first. It could give us some protection, but it's a risk."

"Everything's a risk," Ezren muttered, her head threatening to spin off its axis. "And I'm beginning to think we have enemies everywhere. It's starting to get crowded." Before this little adventure, she would've rejected Calderon's truce on the spot. But now? Now, she didn't know who to trust, and Baxter had officially taken over as enemy number one. "I don't—"

She didn't have a chance to finish the thought before a growl of bullets interrupted the moment.

"Watch out, they're locking on to us. Foster, where's the return fire?"

"They're jamming it." He swiveled and pulled up a targeting holo. "Taking it to manual." In another storm of bullets, something detonated in a billow of flames, the force of it pushing them to the side.

"Nice shot, kid," Santino said.

Ezren maneuvered around the smoking remains of a vehicle and studiously tried not to think about what had happened to its operators. Fumbling for safer thoughts, she glanced back at her dad. "By the way, did you seriously just call us mushy? Honestly, Dad, I thought you'd be more protective."

"I am protective." He ducked as another blast shook the car, and Santino whooped over the radio. "I just think we have more to worry about than your boyfriend right now."

Foster turned in his seat to lock eyes with her dad, his shoulders tense. "Ezren's more than a girlfriend."

Her dad held his gaze, something serious passing between them, and then it was Ezren's turn to shift awkwardly in her seat. So much for safer ground.

"Then we'll have to make time to talk about that later too," her dad said.

"We're nearly there," Santino said over comms. "Be prepared for a barrage. Charge weapons for the power shot and put the rest of your energy on shields."

"Until then, I don't want any of that doubt talk." From the back, her father gripped their seats. "You have to create your own certainty and hold on to it with everything you have. The slimmer the hope, the harder you have to hold on to it. It's the only way to survive this planet. Every day was hell, but I knew I would come out on the other side." He caught her gaze. "I had too much to live for."

The words nearly punched the breath from Ezren's lungs. Because at some point, she *had* lost hope. She'd stopped looking for her father in the night sky, abandoning him on every level, while he, alone on this boiling moon, had never once given up on her.

Ezren sniffed, shoving away all the emotions she didn't have time to feel. *Don't let the them in. Not yet. Keep it light.* "Yeah, well, you know it's my birthday in a few months, and Foster did promise me a three-tier coffee cake, so it's not like I'm going to miss out on that for a fiery death."

"That's a girl after my own heart there," Santino said.

"Back off, Santino, she's my girl," Foster replied. "And after this, I'm making it four tiers."

"And I'm not sharing with anyone." Ezren laughed. "Besides, Santino, you need to focus on driving before you fall even more behind."

"Okay, listen, if I lose, I should at least get a consolation royaler lesson, right? I mean, there's obviously some magic you're putting in that truck, and I've gotta know what it is."

"Sure, Santino," Ezren said. "When we get back."

Ezren and Foster laughed along with Calderon's crew as

they bantered on the channel, the ground flying under their wheels, and the sky on fire above them. And even though they were surrounded by death, her dad was in the backseat, the love of her life was beside her, and she'd never felt more alive.

But no sooner had she thought it than everything around her ignited with a wash of flames.

CHAPTER 23

8.18.43B: T-minus 3.5 hours until Mt. Aguya's Eruption

CIF Warning: Heightened syndicate hostilities in Otho atmosphere. Remain vigilant.

A DEAFENING EXPLOSION nearly shattered Foster's eardrums as the tac-V hurtled hood over bumper. The world blurred before his eyes, the netting constricting his chest while the truck rolled at what seemed like an impossible rate. Someone was screaming, but he could barely hear it over the roar of gunfire.

"Ezren!" he yelled through clenched teeth, the vehicle still tumbling. "You've got to get control. In the low G—" Another explosion hit them from the side, and his body jerked, his suit compensating for the impact as the vehicle tore in a different direction.

"What's hitting us?" Dr. Hart yelled from the back.

"It's the base." Ezren's breaths came in short gasps, the mag controls whirring and alarms blaring on the HUD. "They're not distracted. Ferraz isn't there."

"Fod it." Foster grappled for the gun controls. "We're not in range yet for the power shot."

Another explosion rocked the vehicle, but this time, Ezren managed to get their wheels back under them.

"Our shield won't last long under this," Dr. Hart said. "Santino, what do you want us to do?"

For a beat, there was only silence on comms, and Foster's bones crystallized to fragile ice. "Santino?"

Finally, a crackle came over the line with a thick cough. "Hey royalers."

A wave of relief rushed through Foster. "Santino, what happened? Are you hit?"

"Yeah, kin," he rasped. "I don't think it's looking good for us."

Foster whirled their rear cam to get a close-up on Santino's vehicle, and his chest turned to lead. Their tac-V was in three pieces, two bodies lay on the ground, and one hung at an odd angle from what was left of the interior. Only one was showing vitals, and even from afar, the holo captured the blood seeping through the cracks in his topsuit.

"Shaft," Foster breathed, his limbs turning to stone.

Ezren glanced at the image with a gasp. "Hang on, Santino, we're coming t—"

"Oh no, girlie, Otho's going to get me before you even get close." His chest rattled. "Just wanted to say it was a pleasure driving with you. A real dream c—"

Another detonation rattled the line, and Santino disappeared in a plume of flames.

Ezren screamed, and Foster banged his fist against the brace bar. "Mother suns."

But they didn't have time for grief.

"Dad!" Ezren shouted, desperation cracking her voice while rock and lava spewed around them with another rain of fire. "Our shields are at ten percent." The vehicle vibrated with another earthquake, and still Ezren drove on. "And this tac-V isn't going to survive much longer. Is there anywhere we can take shelter?"

"I brought my daughter here." Her dad stared out the windshield in a dazed stare, blood dripping down the bridge of his nose from a cut beneath his goggs. "We must turn around."

"Too late now, Prof," Foster snapped. An alarm blared as the base's guns locked on them from the cluster of low-lying buildings. "We need an Othonian miracle in two seconds, or we're going to be another scorch mark."

Dr. Hart shook his head, his dark eyes still unfocused. "There's nothing out here. The base is the only—"

"Then I'm deploying everything we've got," Foster said. "Ezren, are we in range?"

Rocks showered across the vehicle as another blast narrowly missed them. "We are now."

"Shoot first, questions later." With that, Foster sent off a silent prayer and punched "deploy all."

The tac-V rocked backward as the munitions exploded from their vehicle toward the base. Sweat beaded on Foster's brow as the power cells disappeared from view in a billow of white fire.

"Got 'em." Ezren serpentined the tac-V toward the base. "Thank the suns."

But Foster's eyes were still glued to the holo, and his stomach sank. "No."

"What? What's the problem?" Dr. Hart leaned forward, his eyes refocusing.

Foster's mind spun as their alarms whined, announcing the enemy's guns locked on them once again. "We didn't break through their shields. We needed both vehicles to unload."

Ezren glanced sideways at him. "So that means…"

He looked at her and shook his head as the launch signal alerted. "We've got nothing left."

Ezren swallowed, and her hand grappled for his. "I'm s-sorry. I'm so sorry. I didn't want—"

"Don't." He squeezed her fingers. "For you, I would do it all again."

Ezren's other hand found her dad's as the telltale whistle of ordnance hurtled toward them. Foster closed his eyes tight, bracing for the end, when another blinding explosion rocked the vehicle.

But there was no pain.

A familiar voice crackled into their channel. "Shaft, that one was close. You okay down there?"

"Grady." Foster's eyes shot open, and he sent their target to the military-grade fighter hurtling through the fiery night toward them. Suns, where did he get that? "Grady, I need you to take out that power cell."

"Please, don't trust Grady to shoot things."

"Bex!" Ezren said, her voice high with some cross of elation and fear.

"Check off the power cell." Grady had barely said the words before it erupted in a blinding inferno. "But you need to get the chaff under cover, cuz there's more guns—" Another explosion went off in their comms.

"No!" Ezren screamed, still maneuvering the truck toward the base.

"Grady! Bex! You there?" Foster swiveled the cam once again to spot their ship coming in hot, one wing burning.

"We're here," Grady said, voice tight. "And landing a little sooner than expected. Meet you at the door I guess and really hoping you have a different way out of this joint."

"We do," Ezren's dad said before turning to Ezren. "Those are friends of yours, I assume."

Her voice trembled, but Foster could hear the smile in it. "The other half of the team."

Foster sucked in his own shaky breath, his body tingling with adrenaline and relief. He'd almost died many times, but that was the closest he'd ever come to darkening the door of the afterlife. And they still weren't out yet. "Do we even want to go in there? If Ferraz and the others didn't clear it, we could be walking into a trap."

Ezren enlarged her holos tracking both the weather and the tac-V's integrity. "We don't have a choice. The cab's already cooking at 193 degrees, and the tar is degrading our tires. We'd never make it back." She maneuvered the vehicle to the door in the low building and turned to her dad. "I assume the main-frame has some tight cyber security. You do have the access codes to get in, right?"

"That's something we should've asked before we left," Foster muttered, sweat trickling down his temple inside his helmet.

"I do." Dr. Hart unbuckled his restraints. "But let me worry about the data. You and your friends need to go directly to the escape pods. I'll follow behind you."

"Oh please, don't get all protective on me now." Ezren ripped off her netting and swiveled around to glare at her dad. "Royalers don't go alone."

She opened the door just as Grady's fighter skidded to the ground next to them, one of the engines alight. *Not again.* Foster rocketed out of the tac-V to the ship, ripping open the exterior door before Grady and Bex stumbled out, coughing.

"Suns, kin." Foster clapped Grady on the back, the growing heat distorting the air around them in vicious waves. "I thought you said you couldn't fly space craft."

"Well, Davis did attempt to teach me this past week." Brushing an ember from his topsuit, Grady gestured to the wreckage with a dry laugh. "But I didn't lie."

Foster turned to Bex, his eyes scraping over her wounded arm, but her torn topsuit revealed none of the damage that might've remained beneath. "Are you two okay?"

Bex adjusted the med-bag on her shoulder, shifting her arm behind her in a way that did not inspire confidence. "A couple hours in the med bay. It'll keep till we get home."

"Shiro, on the other hand, needed more time to bake," Grady added. "But maybe he can keep Sylvia from fritzing out. Big maybe."

Bex turned to where Dr. Hart emerged from the tac-V, a black bag on his back that Foster knew contained both the data sphere and the portable luxie habitat tube. "So you found your dad then?" Bex asked.

Ezren nodded. "Bex Gunderson, Simon Grady, this is my dad, Dr. Milo Hart."

"I guess all of you royalers must be crazy drivers." He arched a brow at the fire spreading from the engine to the fuselage.

Bex raised the pistol in her good hand. "Just wait till you see us fight."

Grady took in the metal outpost built into the side of the obsidian cliff. "So, remind me, what is it about this base that's so important?"

"Later." Foster shifted, his suit already scorching against his skin as the building fatigue from its energy-draw tugged at his bones. "We need to get inside before we cook." He hurried them toward the door where Dr. Hart was already opening the airlock. "Grady, you got your hovercam on you?"

He pulled one from the nutripack on his back. "Always."

"Send it in ahead of us so we can see what we're dealing with," Foster said.

The metal door swung open with a heavy clank, and Dr. Hart stepped into the cool darkness first, followed closely by the others. Foster took one last look at the molten world around them, spacecraft strafing the unnatural dusk and gunfire roaring in the distance, before closing the door.

With the main power cell destroyed, blackness enclosed them in the small space of the airlock, illuminated only by the glow of their topsuits. Grady opened the inner door and threw his cam into it. Quietly closing the door once again, he projected a holo from his goggs with the hovercam's feed.

Bex flexed her bad arm with a wince as the rest of them crowded around the image. "So, what's the plan if there's a bunch of guys waiting to kill us?"

"Oh, you mean since all of our ground vehicles have turned into kilns?" Ezren said with faux-cheer, her gaze intent on the empty halls unfolding before them.

Dr. Hart cleared his throat. "The emergency evacuation vehicles were kept here. They were under maximum security, but if the guards have been taken out, we should be able to access the bays without a problem. They and the mainframe will still be on the emergency power cell."

"And what happens if the Baxter asschaffs already took off in them?" Grady asked as the first body appeared on the holo.

"Zoom in, Grady." Foster leaned closer. "See if you can identify if it's Baxter or Calderon."

"If the pods are gone, we'll have to put out a mayday call and hope there's time for rescue," Dr. Hart continued.

"It's one of Calderon's," Ezren whispered.

Fodding suns. Foster would've never expected he'd be agonizing over the death of one of Calderon's people. "Hope. Right." He scowled.

"I'm not going to tell you again." Dr. Hart turned, something dark in his expression. "Do not underestimate hope. It's the foundation of everything we build—progress, courage, change. It's the one thing that's kept me alive in the face of immeasurable loss, and I refuse to let any of you let it go when we need it most."

Foster held his gaze, the man's fierce determination coming

off in hot waves. Or was it desperation? Either way, he got the distinct impression that he was on the edge, hope or no. "Sure." Foster turned back to the holo-feed. "No way to go but forward."

The cam caught a glimpse of a knot of soldiers lined along the side of the hall, bristling with weapons, but before Foster could identify them, the feed went dead.

"Well, that wasn't polite," Grady said.

Ezren straightened, shifting the pistol in her hands. "That was Ferraz and his crew. They must've gotten here late." She took a step forward, her hand on the manual latch. "We have to help them."

"No," Foster and Dr. Hart said at the same time.

Foster looked at him, and they exchanged another tense glance, but Dr. Hart continued, "The Calderon team is doing their job, and now we at least have a distraction. We need to make it to the main server room to get the data, and from there, run to the escape pods."

"We're just going to leave them to die?" Ezren's eyes rounded, and Foster was strangely glad he, at least, wasn't on the receiving end of her plea this time.

Dr. Hart pulled the data sphere from his pack, brandishing it in his hand. "It's bigger than that, Ezzy. They know it, and we have to honor their sacrifice for what it is."

Foster primed his rifle. "Do we know where we're going?"

"Yes." Dr. Hart pulled up a schematic in his goggs and projected it in front of them. "Unfortunately, the server rooms and the escape pods are nearly on opposite ends of the compound. We should guard the escape pods now, just in case someone else tries to commandeer them."

Something hard knocked against the exterior door, and Foster peered out the viewport to see three quads pulling up alongside their wreckage. "Great. The looters are here." He slid the manual bolt into place just as a hailstorm of shots impacted the door. "And by the look of their weaponry, it won't be long before they're inside."

Bex lifted her rifle with her good arm, bicep bulging in her form-fitting suit. "Grady and I will secure the pods and hold them until you get there."

"Okay. Foster and I will go with my dad, and we'll rendezvous at the pods." Ezren opened the interior door, and the four of them slipped through, bolting it behind them. Ezren held out an arm to Bex. She grabbed it and their heads knocked together.

"Odd numbers," Bex whispered.

Grady put his arms around them in a makeshift huddle. "Just like we're back on Belethea." He reached out and pulled Foster into their knot. "Be strong. Be swift."

"But there's no finish line," Foster said. "No race."

"We're always racing against time," Bex answered, her ice-blue eyes like cold stars. "And may we always be faster."

"Belethea, mother of mountains and skies," Ezren whispered.

"Protect us," they said together, another explosion reverberating through the metal walls.

Unlinking, Grady and Bex turned down the hall, and Grady gave one last wave. "When we get back, the first round of umbrella drinks is on me."

Foster's stomach lurched. The last time they'd said that, Grady and Bex had nearly died. "Seriously, Simon," Foster said, the words laced with exhausted urgency. "Be careful."

Grady waved him off. "Oh, c'mon, kin, I'm as careful as it gets. Come find me when you need a getaway driver." Then they were around the corner and gone, and Foster's chest squeezed with the realization that it could be the last time he'd ever see them.

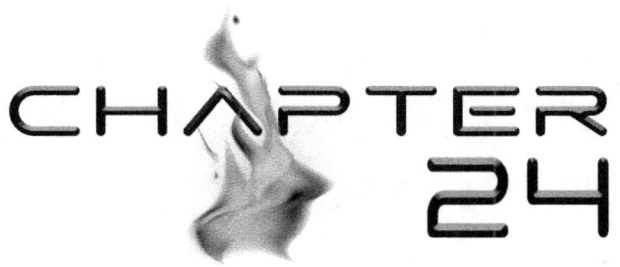

CHAPTER 24

8.18.43B: T-minus 3 hours until Mt. Aguya's Eruption

Warning: Evacuate Immediately. This is your last notice.

IN THE ENSUING silence of Grady and Bex's departure, Ezren's dad gestured down the opposite corridor. "So those were your friends?"

Ezren's heart swelled in her chest as she fervently sent up a prayer that Casolla would keep them safe for just a little while longer. "More than friends, Dad. Family."

"Seems like you have a lot of that on the team." He led them through the dark corridors, and Ezren was almost glad the main power was out so they didn't have to look at the disturbing field holos.

"How long do you think it'll take us to get to the servers?" Foster asked, his gaze on a constant swivel as he looked up and down the corridor.

"At this rate, five minutes to get there, and then perhaps ten minutes to download the data," Ezren's dad answered, his footfalls too loud in the eerily deserted halls.

"Then another ten minutes to get to the escape pods." Ezren strained her ears for the Baxter and Calderon soldiers she knew stalked the warren of a base. "There should be a lot though, right? I mean there had to be at least fifty of you stationed here."

Her dad let out a dry laugh, shifting the data sphere in his hands. Behind them, a boom echoed through the hall, followed by the clatter of the interior door blasting off its hinges. "You're assuming that they would've evacuated their scientific prisoners."

Ezren's skin prickled beneath her topsuit, a chill scraping her neck. If they had fifty scientists, they probably would've only needed a dozen or so armed guards to keep them in check. That didn't bode well for the number of escape pods. They paused at a metal door, and her dad's goggs connected to the security code with a satisfied chime before it slid open.

Gunshots erupted from the room, but Ezren and Foster were ready. The gun vibrated in Ezren's hands as her topsuit steadied her aim, and she squeezed off three shots at the single shooter in rapid succession before retreating. For a moment, they stood silent, but no other sounds came from within.

"Good response time." Her dad scanned the room, but when no gunfire erupted, he stole inside. Ezren and Foster followed the red glow of his topsuit wordlessly as he stepped over the unconscious man and sat down at his seat. "Here, take one of these in case we get separated and you have to make a run for it." Her dad drew one of the dark canisters from his bag and handed it to her, a dozen octopus-like creatures glowing within.

"It's one of Baxter's." Foster kicked the shooter's gun aside, and her dad passed him the restraining rings from within his supply bag.

The holo flickered to life in front of her dad. "We're lucky there was only one. Keep an eye on the doors. There'll be more."

"So this place is run on some kind of emergency power

grid?" Ezren eyed the towering server stacks dubiously and shifted the gun in her grip.

Her dad nodded, his gaze focusing on something in his goggs. "Yes, with all the volcanic activity, power outages are normal, so there's several backups for crucial systems." He let out a breath as he projected a holo in front of him, hacking through the system with a speed that floored Ezren. "Unfortunately, it will take me a few minutes."

The clatter of footsteps rang through the hall and Foster moved to the door. "I don't know if we have a few minutes."

Ezren circled the perimeter of the room only to find four more entry points. "What the chaff? Why are there so many doors?" There was no way she and Foster would be able to hold the room alone.

"This room is in the center of the base. Mostly for protection—from both the elements and intruders. When this place was fully manned it would've been nearly impossible to enter without someone seeing you."

"So, where are all the people now?" Foster asked, backing closer to him with his rifle raised.

"When Calderon started attacking the outlying structures, Baxter sent reinforcements to try to extract or silence the scientists." He glanced at Foster. "Many of them didn't make it."

"How many of Baxter's reinforcements do you think are left?" Ezren asked.

"I have no idea, but I imagine Calderon must've taken out most of them if they only left one in here. The others will be addressing the Calderon intrusion, but after that ruckus at the door, they're certainly on their way here now." Her dad said this all with complete calm, as if he wasn't talking about a life or death situation.

Ezren connected her goggs to the doors, but they were already locked with the manual bolts engaged. Which would buy them all of two minutes. "So what are we going to do?" Her heart fluttered in her chest as she edged nearer the center command station, putting her back to Foster's.

"If they breach the door, you're going to make a run for the pods," her father said, shadows playing across his blond beard as he continued to scrub the data. "I should be able to buy you some time."

"Dad, this data isn't worth your life," Ezren said. "You have to come with us."

"Without a distraction, the three of us won't have a chance," her dad replied.

Ezren's goggs lit up with a message from Sylvia.

Sylvia: Ezren and Foster, the CIF has arrived, and they've officially given an evacuation mandate with a ten-minute warning. After that, they're declaring Otho a no-fly zone.

Shiro: And with odds of syndicate compliance at zero, it'll only escalate from there. They'll take any excuse to bite a chunk out of the other, and if you get caught in the middle...

Ezren exchanged a tense look with Foster, but there was nothing to say. Their reality was too precarious for words.

Ezren: Copy. We're securing escape pods now.

Sylvia: Hurry the fod up please, things are getting fritzing suicidal up here. I've told Davis to leave with the other ship, but they're refusing to go without you.

Davis: Of course we're not leaving. But I whole-heartedly second the hurry the fod up please.

Unknown: We're past *please*. Just stop talking and move already. I thought you royalers were supposed to be fast.

Ezren glanced at Foster, cocking her head at the unknown sender, but Foster only rolled his eyes.

FOSTER: GRADY AND BEX, WHAT'S THE STATUS OF THE PODS?

SIMON: THE GOOD NEWS IS, WE FOUND THEM.

EZREN: NEXT TIME START WITH THE BAD NEWS.

BEX: GRADY'S BEEN SHOT, AND THERE ARE ONLY FOUR SINGLE-PERSON CRAFTS LEFT.

SIMON: SHOT IS A STRONG WORD. MY SUIT TOOK THE BRUNT OF IT. WHICH I'M COUNTING AS MORE GOOD NEWS.

Ezren's stomach twisted, her brain going into hyper drive.

EZREN: THAT SHOULD BE FINE. SINCE IT'S A SHORT FLIGHT, WITH SAFETY MARGINS, WE SHOULD BE ABLE TO FIT TWO IN EACH NO PROBLEM.

As long as the CIF didn't shoot them down first.

FOSTER: IF WE'RE NOT THERE IN FIVE MINUTES, THE TWO OF YOU TAKE A POD AND LEAVE WITHOUT US. I'M NOT FODDING AROUND.

Teeth grinding, he started a shared timer in their goggs.

10:00, 9:59, 9:58...

Something knocked into the door, and shouts echoed down the hallway along with the rattle of gunfire. "Dad, tell me you're almost done." An earthquake rocked the floor beneath their feet, and Ezren nearly choked on her spasming heart.

"One more minute, and we'll be out of here," he said, his body tense as the numbers in the holo flashed faster than Ezren could take them in.

Another door banged with a dull explosion, and Ezren flinched. "They're coming at us from both sides."

"Worse than that." Foster ducked as another ringing detonation shook the wall behind them. "They're surrounding us before they come in." He charged his rifle. "Which means it's Baxter."

Ezren's heart raced, and her grip tightened on the luxie cylinder as she turned to her dad. "There isn't another way—"

"I've got it." Her dad ripped the data sphere from the dock and stuffed it in his bag. "Now let's get—"

The doors imploded simultaneously in a flash of flames, and six gun barrels glided into the room, the soldiers moving with smooth, measured steps. "Dr. Hart, put the data sphere down."

The blood drained from Ezren's face. They were totally chaffed.

Ezren's dad stepped in front of her. "It's already over, you know. The CIF are on their way. There's still time for you to get on the right side of history."

"You know it's too late for the CIF," one man sneered. "In a couple hours, that mountain is going to erupt, and all the evidence will be burned to dust. Then we can start over."

"After all," said another, "if Calderon can get away with murder, then we can certainly get away with this."

"If you give us the data sphere, we'll let you come with us," the first said. "And you can continue the work you started."

Ezren's hands tightened on the luxie cylinder. "My dad doesn't belong to Baxter. Not before and not now either."

The soldiers only edged closer, one glancing at the other. "And who's this?"

"A complication," his companion replied.

The other lifted his rifle. "Understood."

Her father raised his own gun, and Ezren's hands tightened on the trigger of her pistol when a man hurtled into the room, charging into one of the soldiers on their right. With a chorus of yells, a raucous group of ragtag figures burst through the doors after him. They'd pulled off their helmets to reveal bloody and ash-smeared faces, crimson horses running in tattoos across their cheeks.

Their eyes locked on the cylinder in Ezren's hand. "Hand over the terranium."

"It's not terr—" Ezren was cut off as the Baxter soldiers opened fire on the looters.

The syndicate crew returned the bullets in kind, and one of them lunged toward Ezren with outstretched fingers. Foster beat him back with a swing of his rifle, and Ezren backed into a corner just as another explosion tore open the whole right side of the room, knocking them all to the ground.

Ferraz's voice boomed through the ringing of her ears. "Prof, you in there?"

Her father called out, his voice sounding far away. "Yes, we're here!" He lurched to his feet and yanked Ezren up while Foster staggered beside them. "C'mon, we've gotta move."

No sooner had the shooting stopped than it started up again in a blur of flashes.

Ezren ducked low but couldn't avoid one of the looters as he barreled into her, trying to smash the cylinder against the floor.

"No!" she screamed, the cylinder rolling just out of her grasp.

Foster yanked the man off of her and shot him in the chest for good measure. "Forget the tube, let's go."

But Ezren was already scrambling for the rolling cylinder. "It's too important."

"I told you it's terranium," one of the looters shouted.

Ezren's hand closed around the smooth metal when a gun stock slammed into her chest, knocking the breath out of her. "Destroy the container!" one of the Baxter guards called.

Time slowed as all the barrels swiveled to her, and Ezren barely got a chance to right herself before a shot rang through the air. The bullet only grazed the cylinder before ripping through her suit and tearing into her side. A bolt of pain dropped her to the ground.

"Ezren!" her dad shouted as Foster reached for her.

Pain ripping through her middle, Ezren looked blearily down at the scorched container in her hands. The blast had forced it open, and the luxies were floating upward into the air. Head spinning, she slammed the cylinder shut as three of the escaped octopi-like creatures pulsed in the dark room.

The gunfire ceased, all eyes on the small, colorful life-forms.

"What the fod is that?" said one of the looters.

"That, gentlefolk, is the first complex alien life-form found in the Casolla system, and the fifth in the history of humanity," Ezren's dad said, resignation weighting his words. For a moment, they watched as the creatures' pulsing light slowed, their lights dimming.

"What's happening to it?" said a female voice—one of Calderon's soldiers.

"They're dying," Ezren's dad said. "Without the simulated heat and pressure of their environment, they cannot survive. The sudden change is too traumatic on their small bodies."

At the sight of the suffering creatures, something in Ezren hardened, and she got to her feet, her back straight. "According to interplanetary law, this is a land of complex life, and there can be no human claim or activity here." She swallowed, the pain like fire in her side. "Because if there is, we might as well kill them now." The truths Calderon had volleyed at them in the Churn Belt a year ago rang through her ears:

I have yet to see humanity resist any temptation that saves money or effort.

They'll suck the planet dry and erase its beauty faster than you can snuff out a candle.

And deep in her core, she knew that in part, Calderon had been right. Even then, he was facing Baxter's insatiable greed. A greed that would doom the luxies, and potentially, any other alien life they came across. As if to emphasize her thoughts, the luxies' light faded to gray. With a soft mewl, they stilled, and then, ever so slowly, drifted toward the ground.

"So sad," a soldier drawled, whatever spell they'd been under broken. "That's Baxter property, girl." He lifted his rifle just as Foster covered her with his body, but it was Ezren's gun that fired the shot. A percussive blast rippled through the air, and the soldier dropped to the ground.

With that one bullet, the room exploded once more, and Foster bodily heaved her from the room as Ferraz's voice rang out over the clamor. "Run, Prof, we'll hold them off. Get the word—" A shot hit him in the chest, and Ezren screamed, raising her pistol only for another of the Calderon soldiers to push her forward.

"Go! Now!"

And as Foster dragged her out of the room, her dad pushing her from behind, a message dinged in their goggs.

Ferraz: Protec

Ezren waited for the last word, but it didn't come. Tears streaked down her face as they ran away from the death and screams. When they finally got out of earshot, Foster paused to scout their path, and Ezren looked at the cylinder in her hands.

Of the twenty luxies that had been contained within, nine had escaped, and another eight floated dead inside. Only three continued to pulse with light, and when she put a glowing finger to the glass, they pressed their bodies to the contact.

Her dad squeezed her shoulders from behind. "It's going to be okay, Ezzy. You have to believe that."

She swallowed, nodding, as Foster ran back to her. A

sudden dizziness rocked her from her boots to her scalp, and she sagged against the wall, the world tilting.

"What's goin—" Foster caught her just as she fell. "Ezren, what's wrong?"

Ezren put a hand to her side, and it came away red.

"Ezren," her dad breathed.

"It's okay, I've got you." Foster lifted her into his arms. He glared at her dad, and Ezren didn't miss the blame in his eyes. "She's lost a lot of blood already. We need to move fast."

"I'll be... okay." Her dad had said so, right?

Her dad pressed ahead. "I'll lead the way."

"Hold on, Ezren." Foster held her tighter, his gaze boring into hers. "You're not allowed to leave without me, remember? We've talked about this."

As a warmth spread across her middle, and he sprinted through the corridor, Ezren touched a hand to his cheek. "If I do, you can't come get me this time," she whispered, a strange fatigue coming over her.

"Stop it," he growled. "I will go to hell and back for you if I have to. I swear it on the sun."

And a cold sort of acceptance came over Ezren with the certainty that no matter what happened to her, at least Foster could get her dad and the luxies out.

For her mom and Sammy. For Casolla.

And then everything would be okay, because that's what she'd come to do after all.

A smile curved her lips at the thought, and she slid into blackness.

CHAPTER 25

8.18.43B: T-minus 2.5 hours until Mt. Aguya's Eruption

Warning: Otho atmosphere is now under CIF control.
ALERT: CIF craft taking fire.
ALERT: Trespassers will be shot on sight.

FOSTER BURIED the urge to shove Dr. Hart out of the way as he stopped at every single hall crossing to check around the corner. He wanted nothing more than to push past him and sprint to the pods, but with Ezren dripping blood in his arms, he was defenseless. And then she went limp.

Shaft. Shaft. Shaft.

"I'm losing her," Foster barked. "How much farther?" Dr. Hart came screeching to a halt, and Foster ran into his back with a curse. "We need to—" He brushed past, and Dr. Hart caught him by the arm, yanking him back.

A spray of bullets hurtled down the cross hall, and Dr. Hart returned fire before tugging Foster along with him again. "I know we're short on time, but you have my daughter in your arms, so you'd better be fodding careful with her."

"*I'd* better be careful with her?" Foster spat, the bitter words spewing from his mouth. "You're the one that left her behind on Obrone when she was nine years old."

Dr. Hart cast a glare over his shoulder. "It was the last thing in the 'verse I wanted to do."

"But you did it anyway," Foster yelled, a part of him knowing he wasn't being fair and not caring. "I would never have left her."

Another shot whizzed from behind them, and Dr. Hart pulled them low before returning fire and turning them down a different hallway. "Because I had to leave my family behind so I could save my youngest from dying." His eyes blazed under the glow of his topsuit. "And I hope to suns you never have to make the same choice."

"Yeah well I hope your data was worth this," Foster said, clinging to his anger to keep the despair at bay.

"I'll take the blame if I have to." Dr. Hart's gaze softened as he looked at Ezren's limp form cradled in Foster's arms. "Because this is larger than any of us, and Ezren recognizes that. She's always been a big thinker."

"Yeah, fat lot of good that's done us," Foster scoffed. The VSoc hate, the protests, the violence, and now this. "Life would've been a lot chaffing easier if we just focused on something smaller than, you know, the whole fodding 'verse."

Dr. Hart skidded to a stop at a large door. "Are you really that selfish?" He turned to him sharply, his gaze as hard and dark as Ezren's. "When you're capable of so much more?"

But Foster didn't back down, his panicked fury threatening to consume him. "I could care less about the 'verse if I have to sacrifice Ezren for it. And if that makes me selfish, then I don't give a shaft."

For a moment, the two of them stared at each other, then Ezren let out a low moan, and Dr. Hart shouldered into the escape pod bay. He didn't make it half a step before two rifles were directly in his face with Bex and Grady looking down the barrels.

"There's more behind us." Foster brushed past Dr. Hart to lay Ezren on the ground and looked up at Bex. "Please tell me you still have that med bag."

Bex's eyes caught on Ezren's stomach wound, and she practically shoved him aside. "Hart, what happened?" Ripping open the bag, she grabbed a diagnostic chip and attached it to Ezren's neck before pulling out a length of nanowrap.

"Is she going to be all right?" Foster asked.

"We can keep her going with nano stimulants for now and the bandages will stop the bleeding." Bex glanced at the chip's small output holo. "But she'll need a longer stay in the paramedic chair when we get back to the ship."

"I can live with that." Foster glanced at the vessels, counting four, and let out a sigh of relief. "Looks like you all were able to hold the pods." He glanced up at Grady. "Are we ready to go then?"

Grady stared at him, leaning heavily on one leg, his expression unreadable. "About that..." He glanced up at the clear observation ceiling above them.

Foster followed his gaze, and the cautious hope he'd been clutching evaporated. Ships streaked across the ash-choked darkness only to be shot down in green pulses of light. Foster looked at the time in the corner of his goggs. Forty-one seconds remaining. "But how could that be? Our time's not up yet."

Dr. Hart looked up at the ember-dusted darkness. "It doesn't make sense for the CIF to cleanse the planet this ruthlessly. Baxter has to be behind this somehow. They don't want the witnesses getting out."

Foster's gaze flicked back to his goggs. In his rush, he hadn't even seen the messages from Sylvia and Davis.

DAVIS: WHAT IN THE SIX SUNS IS GOING ON DOWN THERE? THIS PLACE IS TURNING INTO A SHOOT-OUT. SCRATCH THAT. I DON'T CARE WHAT'S GOING ON, YOU GUYS

NEED TO GET BACK *NOW*. WE CAN'T HANG HERE MUCH
LONGER.

SYLVIA: THE STATIONS HAVE ALREADY STARTED SHOOT-
ING, AND SHIRO'S LOOKING AT OPTIONS. SPOILER, THEY'RE
NOT GOOD. IS THERE ANY WAY YOU CAN SHELTER IN PLACE
UNTIL THIS DEATH MATCH DIES DOWN?

Panic scrabbled at Foster's chest, and he stumbled to his
feet. "What do we do now? Is there a bunker we can lie low
in?" Beside him, Bex injected something into Ezren, and her
body jolted.

"There is, but even if it survives Aguya, we'll never get
through Baxter to make it there." Dr. Hart took a slow breath
through his nose. "We're going to need the air defenses in the
next bay over."

Foster snorted. "You mean the ones we disabled when we
blasted in here?"

Dr. Hart turned to him with the familiar challenge in his
eyes. Yes, Ezren was definitely his daughter. "We can still work
the guns manually." He gestured to the skies above them. "When
the CIF's already dealing with this level of smoke and atmospheric interference, there's no way their shots are accurate."

Grady gestured to the egg-like craft. "But these things don't
have any guns or evasive maneuvers."

"No automatic maneuvers," Dr. Hart corrected, shifting
the bag on his shoulder. "And I believe as the wheels, you're
familiar with manual evasion. They also have basic shields and
defensive expendables."

Foster shared a look with Grady, but there was nothing to
say. No choice to be made, and with every moment they hesitated, seconds slipped away. "I'll check with Shiro to see if they
can lend a hand."

FOSTER: SHIRO, WE'RE GOING TO MAKE A BREAK FOR

IT; WILL YOU BE ABLE TO LAY SOME COVERING FIRE FROM ABOVE?

SHIRO: IF YOU CAN MAKE IT THROUGH THE LOWER ATMOSPHERE. OUR RANGE ISN'T AS GOOD AS THESE BATTLE-SHIPS BY ANY STRETCH.

Foster turned to Dr. Hart. "If the manual guns can get the ships to the upper atmosphere, our getaway ship can take it from there."

Ezren coughed on the ground, and Foster bent to help her sit up. Her topsuit hung from her small frame in tatters, and nano tape bound her waist. "Foster," she rasped, her blood-streaked fingers reaching for him.

"I'm here." He hugged her close, pressing his lips to her temple.

Her eyes fluttered open. "Where are the luxies?"

Retrieving the cylinder from beside her, he pressed it into her hands. "They're safe and we're getting you out of here."

Bex straightened, her ice-pick stare skewering the three of them. "So if we need the guns to make it to the outer atmosphere, who's going to man them?"

"It has to be me," Foster cut in.

Grady snorted. "Like chaff it does. That's a suicide mission."

"If we put two in one pod," Dr. Hart cut in, "whoever stays to man will still have an escape route. They'll just have to run from the gun bay."

Grady crossed his arms, his hazel eyes narrowing beneath his goggs. "You mean *if* the others haven't taken it yet, and *if* they're able to get through the lower atmosphere without cover fire, and *if* the fodding planet hasn't exploded yet."

"C'mon, Grady," Foster said. "I'm the only one who doesn't have an injury slowing me down. I'll be the fastest." He helped

Ezren to her feet. "Besides, we all know you're going to be the best at this manual evasive maneuver thing."

"It can't be you, Foster." Ezren shook her head, her gaze half-lidded. "I brought us here. It should be me."

Foster barked out a dry laugh as he turned her toward him, still holding her up. "As I recall, you didn't bring us anywhere. We're here because we chose to be." He held her gaze, his hands gently running along her arms. "And I choose this." He leaned his forehead against hers. "If it's what I have to do to protect my family, it's what I'll do." And suddenly, he completely understood Ezren's dad and the decisions he'd made. Sometimes, the only choices were bad ones.

Ezren pulled back, straightening with the strength of the stimulants flowing through her. "But we're partners. We're supposed to do things together."

"She's right, Foster," Bex said. "I'll come with you. You need a double in this."

Foster eyed the crimson bandage now wrapped around Bex's arm where the blood had seeped through from the damaged fabric. Her topsuit wouldn't last much longer either. He squeezed her shoulder. "We *are* doing this together, Bex. Sacrifice is part of being a team."

Grady lowered his gaze from the laser-strafed sky. "Forget the guns. We should take the risk together. All of us."

Foster shook his head as he backed toward the door. "You know that's the wrong move, Simon." He looked to Dr. Hart, staring at him with an unreadable expression. "I need the map, the code to get in, and instructions to man the guns. I'll send a message when I'm in place."

Dr. Hart's goggs flashed so quickly, Foster knew he must've anticipated the request. "Sent your way."

Foster held out a hand to Grady. "I'll see you back on the ship."

"You'd better, or I swear I won't forgive you this time."
Grady gripped his arm and pulled him into a tight hug with a
rough slap on the back.

"And we were just starting to get along." Foster chuckled.

Bex stared at him coolly. "I refuse to say goodbye to you."
Her gaze swiveled to Ezren and Grady. "To any of you," she
added, stalking off into one of the pods. "I'll see you on board
the ship."

Grady nodded. "Guess I'll be going too." He turned and
limped to his own shuttle, pausing at the door to glance at them
with a wistful gleam. "Last one to the ship buys the first round
of umbrella drinks."

The door hissed behind him, leaving only Foster, Ezren,
and Dr. Hart.

Foster walked Ezren to the pod, her dad following a
respectful distance behind as he set her in the padded seat. Her
gaze was still glazed with shock as he strapped her in with
quick hands, realizing that it would be a tight squeeze for her
dad to fit as well. The shuttles really were meant for one. It was
a good thing she was small.

"Foster," she whispered. "How did we get here?"

He smiled at her, keeping his voice light as he set the pod's
destination along with some pre-programmed evasive maneuvers. Ezren wouldn't be in any state to do them herself, and it
was highly probable her dad would lose consciousness without
being strapped in. "Well, it started with me hiring a P.I. to find
your dad, and then you came after him, and then I came after
you."

"And now I'm leaving again." Ezren's brow pinched over
her sickening pallor. "This doesn't seem right."

"I know. But it's going to be okay." He swallowed, Dr.
Hart's words echoing in his head. *Don't underestimate hope.*
"People leave, but you and I, we're forever. So no matter how

many times the 'verse separates us, it's never far and never for long." The truth of his own words hit him as they left his lips, and the calm of acceptance sank into his bones.

"Then why is it so hard?" Ezren sniffed, wiping at her eyes.

He smiled ruefully. "I guess it's part of being in love."

Ezren's lashes fluttered again, her lips trembling. "I'm not ready to say goodbye yet either."

Foster's eyes filled as the odds of their predicament weighed on his shoulders. "You don't have to, Ezren."

"I love you, Foster, too much for the 'verse to hold." She looked up at him, her eyes huge and dark. "Promise I'll see you again."

Foster's chest squeezed so hard he thought it might suffocate him. "I'll do everything in my power to make it back to you."

"No." She shook her head defiantly. "That's not good enough."

"It's all I have." He pressed his lips to hers, tasting the salt of her tears as he kissed her with everything he had. Like one kiss could fill a lifetime. Like it could be the last. Untangling her fingers from his hair, he pulled back, enfolding her hands in his. "No matter what, know that I love you with everything that I am."

"No, Foster, don't—"

Tearing his hands away, he turned and ran out the door, Ezren still screaming his name as he nodded to Dr. Hart. He shoved on his helmet and stepped out of the shuttle bay. He would make sure her pod got off the ground.

And he would make sure it got the rest of the way.

Because his heart was in that pod, and if it didn't escape, then it didn't matter if he made it off this death planet or not.

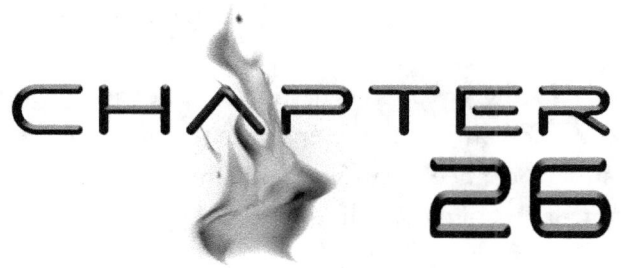

CHAPTER 26

8.18.43B: T-minus 2 hours until Mt. Aguya's Eruption

TRAPPED in the snare of the escape pod's safety netting, Ezren tried to think of the last time she'd watched Foster run away from her. But for some reason, it wouldn't come to her fuzzy mind. He'd always been running with her. Running towards. And even as the taste of his kiss lingered on her lips, it killed her that his retreating back might be the last she'd ever see of him.

The door to the hangar opened and shut as he ran out to man the guns in the adjacent bay, and tears streaked down her face. Furious, desperate, scared tears.

Then her dad was leaning in the door with a soft smile. "I wasn't sure he'd actually leave."

Ezren wiped at her wet cheeks, trying for a smile that failed miserably. "Yeah, me neither." She adjusted the luxie cylinder in her lap, making sure the three survivors were still pulsing happily within. "But it's going to be fine. He'll be in the last pod, and we'll figure out where to take the luxies from there."

"Yeah." Her dad ran a hand over his scraggly beard. "You know, I probably shouldn't say this, but I'm so glad you came, Ezren."

"Yeah?" She smiled up at him, even as the pain pulsed through the wound in her side, the tears still heavy in her lashes. "You would have probably gotten out just fine without me."

Her dad tugged on the netting around her. "No way. I think you and your royaler friends are the only ones who ever really stood a chance of surviving this place." He looked up at the flame-laced night swirling across the translucent ceiling. "Something about the way you keep leaning forward no matter what's ahead." He locked eyes with her, unmistakable pride glowing from his coffee-dark eyes. "I can see why you win."

Ezren pressed her lips together to keep them from trembling and she reached for his hand, his rough palm dwarfing hers. "It was just the one time."

"Please." He scoffed. "I saw the holos. Of the race, of the aftermath, and all the struggle before." His gaze softened. "I never doubted you for a second, but still, I wish I could've been there for you."

"No, you don't. It was too stressful." Ezren shook her head, her vision swimming with painful sparks. "Mom says the royale business has turned her hair gray. Better now that it's over."

"Oh, I don't know if anything's ever really over." He twisted his lips in a wry, bittersweet grin. "But I want you to know I'm so proud of you, Ezzy. For all of it."

Ezren snorted, a sob on the edge of her voice. "But everything's going wrong, Dad. The terraforming movement is a mess, Calderon is a murderer but also allegedly saving the luxies, the CIF is shooting everyone, the people I love most are in the middle of a firestorm, and we don't even know if we're going to be able to get off this exploding rock."

His grip tightened on hers, his face darkening with gravity. "Ezren, things will always go wrong; that's out of our control. But it's now, when the world is at its darkest, that we find out who we really are, and what truly matters. I know you're scared, but it's when you're at the end of your rope that you have to fight the hardest to hold on."

For a moment, Ezren could only stare in awe of her father, trapped at the end of everything for four years and still fighting.

Their goggs chimed as Foster's message came in:

FOSTER: OKAY, I FOUND THE GUN BAY, BUT THIS PLACE LOOKS LIKE IT'S ABOUT TO CRACK OPEN. MAKE SURE YOUR LAUNCH PROTOCOLS ARE READY.

SIMON: LET'S GET IT STARTED THEN.

BEX: MAY THE STORM WINDS BLOW US HOME.

With those words, the two pods rumbled next to them, their takeoff sequence initiated. Ezren's dad tucked the data sphere into the safety netting around her.

"Close the door, Dad." Ezren shifted to one side to make room for him. "We want to take off at the same time so we can divide their attack as much as possible." Her father pressed a kiss to her head before stepping back, and her heart skipped a beat, her body a step ahead of her sluggish brain. "What are you doing? It's time to go home."

A sad smile tugged on her father's lips beneath his beard. "I'll catch the next one, Ezzy."

"Wait, no." Ezren flailed against her restraints, but they were already locked in, her takeoff protocol already started. "You can't both get in the last one. There will be no one to lay cover fire for you. It's too much of a risk." He took another step back, and the door closed as she screamed her frustration, the luxie cylinder cutting into her hands. "This wasn't the plan! I can't lose you and Foster at the same time."

DAD: TWO GUNS ARE BETTER THAN ONE. BESIDES, I'VE GOT TO MAKE SURE SOME KID DOESN'T DIE FOR MY MISTAKES. NOT WHEN MY DAUGHTER'S IN LOVE WITH HIM.

He put his hand to the viewport window, and it was all

Ezren could do to press her palm to his, the glass still separating them. Her dad's eyes glistened, and Ezren sucked in deep breaths to keep the racking sobs at bay.

Ezren: I can't do this.

Dad: You can. Just promise me, no matter what happens, you'll get the luxies to the ambassador summit.

Ezren swallowed.

Ezren: I promise.

Dad: I love you, Ezren. Be safe.

With that he turned and left out of the same door as Foster.

Ezren: I love you, Dad.

Then the door closed on her father, and Ezren let the sobs go. When she was fourteen, Ezren once thought there was no grief like thinking her father had walked away from her.

But she'd been wrong.

CHAPTER 27

8.18.43B: T-minus 1.75 hours until Mt. Aguya's Eruption

Warning: Report to your designated emergency shelter immediately

THE BURNING AIR shimmered around Foster as he sprinted from the escape pod hangar to the guns bay some fifty meters away. The ground shook beneath his feet, and overhead, aircraft and guns screamed through the thickening smog. Barely able to see the bay on the ridge ahead of him, he ran blind, his topsuit giving off three different warnings about heat, air quality, and structural integrity.

But though his skin burned, and the air tasted sour on his tongue, he pushed himself forward. Because if he didn't, his team would be dead in the air. Otho's blistering surface undulated under his boots, throwing him to the ground as the rumble of a rockslide crashed to one side of him in the smoke. Forcing himself to his feet, he almost ran smack into the guns bay door. He ran the code Dr. Hart had given him and the panel gave an unlocking chime, but it didn't hiss open.

No. Foster pressed his shoulder against the metal, but the door's thermal sealant had melted to the frame. Digging his fingers into the seam of the door, he heaved again, but it only gave a whine of protest. He needed a crowbar, but he had no idea where to find one. And even if he did, it would waste precious time he didn't have.

He aimed his rifle at it in desperation, but the bullets only further scorched the sagging metal.

"Mother fodding shaft it." He kicked at the door once, twice, three times. Sweat cascaded from his brow, stinging his eyes—the heat nearly unbearable.

"Stop wasting your energy."

Foster whipped around to see Dr. Hart coming toward him out of the smoke, his chest heaving.

"Dr. Hart, you shouldn't be out here." He gestured back to the hangar. "You need to be ready for takeoff, and that topsuit's going to shred your body in these conditions."

"Aren't you the mother hen?" Dr. Hart pulled three circular devices from his bag and attached them to the door. "A mother hen that did not come prepared." With a chime from his goggs the devices detonated, blowing the airlock door inward. "C'mon then," he rasped, beckoning Foster as he stepped into the airlock.

"What are you doing?" Foster asked, the pieces not fitting together in his head. Was it the poison in the air? Was he seeing things?

Dr. Hart opened the interior door with another chime. "I'm saving my daughter's life."

Foster followed him into the weapons bay, the door hissing shut behind them. Three pairs of huge double-barreled laser cannons peeked out through the ceiling on the ridge toward the smoky sky above. "I thought we decided that I was the best choice for the gunning job."

Dr. Hart shrugged as he sat at one of the cannons, his goggs connecting to its targeting holo. "And then I decided that you might need some help."

Foster sat down at one of the other guns, changing the settings to the swarming chaff and flare per Dr. Hart's directions. They were the ammunition that wouldn't necessarily hurt aircraft but would certainly throw off their guided missiles and bullets. And hopefully prevent the big guns from turning to blow them to pieces.

"So you didn't trust me?" Indignation swelled in Foster's chest. All he wanted to do was get Ezren and her dad off this melting planet. That had been his singular goal since setting his boots on the ground, and now here, in the eleventh hour, her dad was being chaffing difficult.

"You can drop that chip on your shoulder," Dr. Hart said. "They'll have a better chance with two gunners than one, and that's all I really care about. Especially since I'm the reason my daughter walked into danger in the first place."

"You and Ezren really need to drop that line. It's seriously starting to piss me off," Foster said. "One person is worth it if you love them enough."

For a moment, Dr. Hart held his gaze. "Agreed." He turned back to the aiming holo glowing in front of him. "Now, are you ready? Give them the signal."

"Fine."

FOSTER: LAUNCH.

The three pods reacted immediately, bursting out of the hangar in a flash of white fire, and Foster squeezed the trigger on the massive cannons, covering them with a net of distractive ammunition.

"You cover the rightmost, I've got the left, and we both get center," Dr. Hart commanded as his cannon bellowed out deep, bone-vibrating blasts.

On his display, the range of the obscurants covered the three pods as they zoomed upward, but Foster could also see the volley of bullets and missiles headed toward them.

FOSTER: LOOK ALIVE, YOU'VE GOT HEAT INCOMING, MAKE SURE YOUR SHIELDS ARE UP AND EVADE.

Foster willed the escape pods to go faster on his holo, wincing as one of the bullets ricocheted off their pulse shields. Yet all he could do was keep his aimpoint on them as he sent out more radiators to throw off the deadly shells.

"So, what are your intentions with my daughter?" Dr. Hart asked as he swiveled to keep his aimpoint on the escape pods screaming toward the sky.

The building shook around them—with the force of ammunition or an earthquake, Foster couldn't tell—and he gripped the cannon to try to keep from falling out of his chair. "Is this really the best time to talk about that?"

"Kid, I'm not sure there's going to be a better time." Dr. Hart's face lit up in a wash of blue as he shot a shield replica into the heavens.

Foster's jaw tightened, sensing this was more like an interrogation than a friendly conversation. "I intend to spend the rest of my life with her and make her as happy as I possibly can."

"And you think you're qualified to do that?" Dr. Hart volleyed back. "You think you deserve her?"

Foster's annoyance only boiled in his stomach with the rising heat. Was it not enough that he'd come to try to save Ezren from this place? Was it not enough that he was sitting here right now, trying to protect her with his last breaths? Seriously, what did this guy want from him? "No," he said through gritted teeth. "Ezren is brave and honest and she throws her whole self at everything that comes her way. She's beautiful and smart and the strongest person I have the privilege to know. I doubt there's anyone in this 'verse that deserves her, but I'm trying with everything that I fodding have."

Something exploded next to one of the pods, and Foster's

heart froze in his chest, the image obscured by the lingering heat. He waited—one second, two, three—his mouth dry. Had they lost them? But there they were. The three pods breaking free from the rubble.

Foster sagged in relief, falling back into his chair, fully reclined as the cannon pointed through the opening in the ceiling, now constantly rumbling with the force of the quakes. "And I also wake her up with a cronut and one of the dessert-coffee drinks she likes."

Dr. Hart barked out a laugh. "So I guess she still has the sweet tooth, huh?"

Foster's cannon beeped irritably, signaling his target was out of range, but he fired anyway. "You have no idea."

FOSTER: SYLVIA, SHIRO, THE ESCAPE PODS MADE IT OUT OF OUR RANGE, SO YOU'VE GOT TO COVER THEM NOW.

SHIRO: GOOD WORK. WE'VE GOT THEM FROM HERE.

SYLVIA: NOW YOU GET OUT OF THERE TOO, FOSTER YUNIN-STERLING, BEFORE I COME DOWN THERE AND KILL YOU MYSELF.

"Okay, they're away." Dr. Hart rose stiffly from his seat. "We need to get the fourth going before this place crashes around us."

"Right." Foster looked up again, just as another looter craft was shot from the sky in an explosion of sparks. This time, as they crossed the short expanse to the pods, they said nothing. Foster tried not to think about what dying in the pod would feel like. At least it would be a quick death, better than slowly melting on the surface. If only he could tamp down on his racing heart threatening him with hyperventilation in the foul air.

Thankfully they ran into no one else as they got to the last pod, and Foster had to wonder if they were all already dead, or if perhaps they were taking their chances in a bunker somewhere. But by the way the temperature already seemed to have leaked inside, he didn't take their chances lightly. "Do you want the netting or no?" he asked.

Dr. Hart gestured for him to enter first, his barrel chest heaving with the strain of his suit. "Brawn before brain."

Swallowing, Foster leaned against the padded wall, directing the netting to ensnare him with a message from his chip. Dr. Hart stuffed his bag in the mesh, and Foster sized him up—there was room, but it wasn't going to be a comfortable squeeze for either of them. Not that it really mattered if they were going to be blown up in the next thirty seconds.

But Dr. Hart wasn't getting in the pod. Instead, he punched the take-off protocol and sealed the door after him.

"Hey!" Foster yelled, straining against the netting. "What the fod are you doing?"

"You still need someone to cover for you," Dr. Hart called through the window. "You and I both know if we launch out of here without a defense, we'll be dead in seconds."

Foster's gaze narrowed, panic scuttling along his spine. "You've been planning this since Ezren's pod took off."

"I do like to think ahead." Blood leaked from Dr. Hart's dark eyes, the skin beneath his goggs splitting from the topsuit's steep toll. "You should try it sometime."

Foster punched the side of the craft, rage and helplessness cascading through him in turns. His chip scrabbled to override the launch protocol, but Dr. Hart had managed to lock it somehow. "Why'd it have to be you?"

"It was me from the moment I left Obrone nine years ago." Dr. Hart's gaze softened, his shoulders falling a touch. "But seeing my daughter one more time was a gift I didn't expect to receive. So at least now, I can die a happy man." A message dinged in Foster's goggs from Dr. Milo Hart. "I've explained it to my family in the messages. And in the bag, you have a spare luxie cylinder and a copy of the data sphere with the most pertinent information." When had he made that? The man was certainly prepared.

Foster's eyes stung with twisting relief and shame. He didn't want to be relieved—he wanted Dr. Hart to get on the ship and haul his ass back to Belethea.

"Don't do this," Foster pleaded. "She won't be able to live with this." Shaft, he wasn't sure *he* could.

"She's lost me before, and she'll be able to weather it again." Dr. Hart lifted his chin. "We both know she's strong enough."

"We agreed it would be me." Foster shook his head, denial his only refuge as Dr. Hart programmed in the evasive maneuvers. "And what about that talk we were supposed to have?"

At that, Dr. Hart grinned at him, his round face transforming with it, and for a moment, Foster saw the father that had once shown Ezren her first terraforming lab. "I think you would've been a really annoying son-in-law."

"Wow." Foster let out a dry laugh, even as the tears gathered in the corners of his eyes. "Thanks."

Dr. Hart took a step back, his voice catching. "But I would've loved you anyway."

"Suns, Milo, please don't do this. I'm begging you. There must be another way." Foster's voice broke on the last words, the lie obvious even to him as the walls cracked around them.

Milo Hart smiled one last time as he backed toward the bay doors. "Take good care of my daughter, Foster."

And in the end, all Foster could do was nod, because that was a promise he could keep. "I will."

With that, the door hissed shut on Dr. Milo Hart.

CHAPTER 28

8.18.43B: T-minus 1.15 hours until Mt. Aguya's Eruption

EZREN'S BODY wrenched into a hard knot, every muscle fighting the Gs as the escape pod zigged and zagged. Exactly what kind of course had Foster plotted into the thing? The cacophony of explosions deafened her, skewing time into an indecipherable snarl as the small craft shook with every percussion, the near misses too many to count as she rose above the smoke layer.

EZREN: SYLVIA, WE'RE CLEAR OF THE ATMOSPHERE. WE'RE GOING TO NEED SOME HELP HERE.

SYLVIA: I SEE YOU. DON'T WORRY, WE'RE ON IT.

EZREN: SIMON AND BEX, YOU STILL THERE?

SIMON: NO SWEAT, E. YOU THINK THEY CAN CATCH ME?

BEX: HERE.

Ezren blew out a tightly controlled breath, the nanites and adrenaline scrambling her brain. There was an almost uncontrollable part of her that wanted to ask about her dad and Foster.

But if the news was bad, she knew she wouldn't be able to press through whatever came next.

BEX: YOU OKAY, HART?

Ezren checked in her goggs for her blood levels. Not great. Well... objectively terrible. But she would stay conscious. Hopefully.

EZREN: FINE.

DAVIS: SIMON, EZREN, IS THAT YOU?!

Ezren's eyes shot wide. She had almost forgotten about Davis.

EZREN: WHAT ARE YOU DOING HERE, DAVEY? YEAH, SIMON AND BEX ARE WITH ME.

UNKNOWN: THIS IS GERARD Y. WHERE'S FOSTER?

If Ezren had the energy to be shocked, that would've knocked her clean into the stars. Foster's dad was here too? How had she missed that?

EZREN: HE'S COMING UP ON THE LAST SHUTTLE.

SIMON: BUT IT'S NOT LOOKING GOOD. THAT PLACE IS FRITZING APART.

DAVIS: YEAH, WE'RE WATCHING IT.

Ezren's holo blinked with an incoming missile, and she deployed her last flare swarm to distract it. Another one hit her side-on, and an alarm blared as her shield failed.

EZREN: I'M ALL OUT OF DEFENSIVE EXPENDABLES. SYLVIA, SHIRO, CAN'T YOU EXPLAIN WHO WE ARE AND GET THEM TO STOP SHOOTING AT US?

SYLVIA: I'M TALKING AND SHIRO'S SHOOTING, JUST HOLD ON.

BEX: I GOT YOU.

SIMON: BEX, WATCH YOUR*SELF*, GIRL. I JUST SAVED YOUR ASS AGAIN.

BEX: GOOD FOR YOU, I'LL BUY YOU ONE UMBRELLA DRINK.

EZREN: SIMON, YOU'VE GOT ONE COMING FROM UP HIGH.

SIMON: THANKS FOR THE HEADS-UP. BEX WAS DISTRACTING ME WITH UMBRELLA DRINKS.

SYLVIA: I'M GOING TO WATERBOARD YOU WITH UMBRELLA DRINKS IF YOU DON'T SHUT UP AND FOCUS RIGHT CHAFFING NOW.

Another blink with an incoming missile, and Ezren held the luxie cylinder tight to her chest as she braced for impact, hoping it would kill her quickly. The last thing she wanted was to gasp for her final breath while hurtling through empty, cold space.

An explosion racked her pod, throwing her off course. But her shuttle held, structural integrity alarms screaming.

SHIRO: SORRY ABOUT THAT ONE, EZREN, A LITTLE TOO CLOSE.

SIMON: I'M DOCKING NOW.

BEX: AND I'M COMING IN STARBOARD SIDE.

SYLVIA: EZREN, WHERE ARE YOU?

Ezren's stomach flipped as she battled nausea to regain control of her ship. Sweat slicked every inch of her skin under her suit, her body completely and utterly drained. If she didn't make it in the next thirty seconds, she would pass out, and that would be the end of her. She looked down at the luxies clutched in her grip. The ones so many had died for. The ones her father had pressed into her hands. Entrusted to her. She had to hold on.

EZREN: I'M COMING.

Forcing the pain down, she punched full acceleration even as the pod cracked around her. She charted through the incoming long-range bullets, her teeth grinding as the Gs tried to tear her muscles from her bones—her topsuit just barely holding her together. But there was Shiro's sleek stolen military vessel. Straight ahead and drawing closer.

With black edging her vision, she accepted the request to dock, and an explosion rocked her from behind. She initiated the topsuit's resuscitation protocol simultaneously with a hard deceleration. This time, she blacked out instantly, only to come blinking back with a series of electric jolts that tore a scream from her throat.

EZREN: How long was I out?

For a second, no one answered her, and Ezren retched with the toll of the nanites destroying her body. *Suns, don't let them be gone. They have to be there.*

But then the door of her ship hissed open, and Simon's silhouette leaned over her.

"Chaff, E, you've got some stones, girl. That was fritzin' nervy." He released the netting, and half-dragged her out of the egg-like pod. "Let's get you to the regen room before you really do die on us."

Pulling one of her arms around his neck and looping a supportive hand around her waist, Simon practically hauled her through the halls that someone had programmed to look like the mossy, mauve spires of Belethea. Had that been her? She couldn't remember. Her mind was so fuzzy, if she closed her eyes, she could almost smell the tangy petrichor of Belethea's surface.

"Ezren!"

With a herculean effort, Ezren lifted her impossibly heavy eyelids to see Sylvia flying toward her, curly hair wild and eyes huge. "Why are you always trying to die on me? I'm fritzing out over here."

One corner of Ezren's lips curved up. "I promise I'm not trying."

"If this is what she can do without trying, imagine what she could do if she did," Shiro called from his seat at the controls where Bex leaned over him. "She could probably die and come back like three times."

"You hush. I am on my last nerve, and you do not want to see me without it." Sylvia pointed at the satellite feed of Otho's red-hot surface. "Have you got a lock on the last escape pod?"

"Not yet," Bex said, her holo projecting the upper atmosphere of Otho in what looked like a graveyard of ships and detritus amid the smoke-obscured troposphere.

Sylvia's rainbow brows knitted as she turned back to Ezren, Turnip brushing by her ankle. "Don't you worry. We'll get him out. Now you"—she shooed Simon toward a metal door—"get her to the med bay already."

"Everyone buckle in," Shiro said from the front, his words strung taut. "We have a complication."

Sylvia snatched Turnip from the deck. "What?"

"We've now been identified as looters with illegal materials on board," Bex said. "A CIF ship is coming after us."

"Well, they can try." Shiro looked at Simon, the muscles in his jaw ticking. "Strap Ezren in the med bay, quick. And Sylvia, babe, for the love of suns, sit down."

Ezren didn't have time to trip over the word "babe" before Simon hauled her off into the adjacent room and belted her in the nanite-coated paramedic chair. Simon fell into the seat next to her, the netting constricting around them just as the ship lurched to the side.

"What about Davis's ship?" Ezren asked as the nanites pooled across her, the relief nearly instant as they flooded her system with a blood transfusion. "Have you heard from him?"

"They went dark right after the update on Foster." Simon glanced at her face and then rushed to add, "But they're probably just trying to avoid the CIF like the rest of us. Maybe they left already."

Ezren supposed that should've relieved her. At least that

meant two people were out of danger—maybe—but at the moment, she could barely find the energy to feel anything. Her thoughts were limp, as if she had reached maximum capacity on emotions and couldn't find the bandwidth to process anything else. She looked down at her hands to see only two luxies staring back at her, the third floating gray beside them. Her heart squeezed with guilt. The Gs had been too much.

C'mon, I know it's a lot, but you have to hang in there. If we make it out of here, I swear I'll shout your story to the 'verse. If there was a reason she had a voice, surely it was for this. The ship wrenched again, and she called out to Sylvia. "Can we open a channel?"

"I like where your head's at," Sylvia's voice echoed through the open door. "Simon, you got the cam?"

"Don't say anything that's going to make them shoot us," Shiro yelled. "All the guns are tracking us now."

"On it." The red dot flickered on Simon's goggs. "You're a go, E."

Ezren took a deep breath, not wanting to think about the blood, sweat, and ash coating every inch of her. "This is Ezren Hart of Belethea addressing the Casolla Interplanetary Federation. Lower your weapons. We don't pose a threat, and we have crucial information concerning Baxter Research's illegal activities."

A grating, unfamiliar voice cut through her goggs:

"Ezren Hart, this is Commander Yao of the CIF. You are guilty of trespassing on Otho against explicit instructions and suspected of theft of CIF resources."

"This is a giant misunderstanding," Ezren continued. "I was on Otho to find my father, and if you're talking about terranium—"

Ezren flinched as a long tone screeched through her ears. "What's happening?"

"They're jamming our comms," Bex said.

"And their guns are still pointed at us, by the way," Shiro added.

"No, no, no, no." Ezren put her fingers to her temples. "What do we do now?"

A different voice shot through her goggs:

"Ezren Hart, this is Ambassador Oliver York from the Delegation of Stations. Looks like you got yourself in another bind."

It took Ezren a moment to dredge up the familiar name in her spinning head—the PR event where she'd met York now seeming like years ago. "Ambassador York, yes, we need any assistance you can provide."

"You got it," he said easily. "We believe the information you hold is crucial to resolving the situation, and we're willing to offer you safe harbor aboard our ship until we sort this all out."

Ezren sagged with relief. "Did you hear that?"

"More than heard it," Shiro practically growled, tugging at the bandages still encasing his shoulder. "The ambassador's ship is inviting us to dock."

"Why do you sound like that's bad news?" Simon cocked an eyebrow. "That ship is the size of half a station. Seems pretty crisp to me."

Shiro limped into their doorway. "Because we don't have time for detours."

"We also don't have time to be arrested or blown to pieces by the CIF." Sylvia popped her head in after him. "Are you ready? They're going to want to see you right away."

Ezren nodded. Though the healing interface indicated she was still in poor condition, there was a huge difference between being an inch from death and half a foot. "I'm fine. And we have all the proof we need." She lifted the data sphere in one hand and the luxie tube in the other.

Bex supported her injured arm with her good one as Ezren walked to the docking door. "I don't like this."

"Good." Shiro clapped her on her intact shoulder. "You and Simon stay on the ship and stay out of sight. They don't know how many of us are here."

"Oh, c'mon." Ezren tried for a smile but didn't quite make it, the ship whirring as it sealed the docking hall. "I met this guy at the BRR announcement. He's a fan."

Sylvia's lips twisted as Bex and Grady quietly disappeared into the back, Turnip trailing after them. "This is literally one of those any-port-in-a-storm moments. As long as no one is shooting at us, I'll take it as a win."

Shiro smirked at her. "You really need to raise your standards."

"Oh, believe me, that's recently come to my attention," she shot back, and the ship chirped with a solid air seal, as if agreeing with her.

The door slid open to a pair of guards that made Ezren's heart quail. She'd hoped she was past this part, but apparently, the DOS had come prepared for violence, just like the rest of them.

"This way." They led her through the holos which looked eerily like the ones she'd seen on Otho. Never-ending green fields. What was the deal with those things? After a series of turns, they stopped at a nondescript door, and the guards gestured to Shiro and Sylvia.

"If you two will wait here, this is a classified meeting for Ezren Hart only."

Shoulders back, Shiro gave a curt nod, and Sylvia gave him an uncertain sideways glance. Ezren shrugged, and the guards delivered her into what looked like a large boardroom with a holopro of Otho's near-space taking up one side. Ezren's legs jellied with relief when she saw Ambassador York in a bright spacer's suit of dancing holo flames on the other end of a long table with his signature broad smile.

"Ezren, seems like you've certainly been up to quite the adventure."

Ezren bobbed her head into a bow. "Suns, Ambassador York, you have no idea." She offered a shaky grin but couldn't quite get it to take. "We've got to get them to stop shooting. My dad and Foster are still trying to get off the planet, and they have nothing to do with the looters."

"Oh my." York raised his brows, his twinkling smile unfaltering. "And what did you say you were doing on Otho?"

"This is going to sound crazy, but Baxter was keeping my father there against his will to study the *first complex lifeforms* in Casolla." Ezren raised the cylinder as proof, not hiding the shock on her face. She could hardly believe what she held herself.

"And they're in there?" York's jaw dropped, two pink patches appearing high on his pale cheeks "What's in the sphere?"

Ezren nodded, regarding both the cylinder and the data sphere in her hands. The items her father had risked everything to get out. "Yes, I know it's hard to believe, but we were able to download all the data files, and we got a few living specimens out in one of these environment emulators. If we get this evidence to the Casolla summit, we can bring Baxter to justice, get the creatures the protection they need, and stop everyone from going to war over terranium that's not there." Ezren waved a hand to the side of the board room that showed a holo of the chaos still orbiting Otho. Warships from Obrone, Dreitis, and the CIF loomed like circling sharks in the darkness.

"That is truly a wild story." York's lips pursed thoughtfully. "But I suppose with enough proof, you could certainly bring it to life." He reached for the cylinder in her hand. "May I?"

Ezren placed the container in his palm, and he lifted it to his eyes, the two luxies dancing within in red and purple.

"Remarkable." He looked at her. "Do you know what this discovery could mean?"

Ezren shook her head, her legs trembling beneath her as she longed to sit in one of the chairs. "I couldn't even begin to—"

"It will take the sails out of your terraforming movement," he said conversationally. "And once the home system gets wind of it, the arks will come here en masse, vying for already scarce resources among the stations. There will be so much oversight from the Humanitarian Collective, you won't be able to breathe without approval."

Ezren's brows knitted, not quite following. "But the mere existence—"

"Then you can't forget the research in the anti-aging properties."

Ezren went rigid at those last words, but the guards' hands were already on her, gripping her arms. "You know?" Distantly, Sylvia gave a yelp from the hall, and Ezren whipped toward the door.

York let out a warm laugh. "I more than know."

"But I saw you with Calderon."

"Indeed." York rolled his eyes indulgently. "He and I go back decades."

Ezren's eyes went wide. Decades? But York didn't look any older than thirty. That meant... the anti-aging was for *him*.

"He's like an annoying older brother. Always trying to keep an eye on me. But I don't think it's going to work out for him this time." York connected his dark half-visor to the cylinder, unlocking it.

"Wait!" Ezren screamed, struggling against the guards. "If you do that, they'll die."

York fixed her with a quizzical look, some mixture of

curiosity and boredom... and something darker. "Well, yes. That's the point. But don't worry, their compounds can still be harvested post-mortem." The canister opened with a hiss and Ezren screamed as the final two luxies floated out, their colors fading almost instantly.

"You selfish asschaff." She bucked and kicked, but the guard plucked the data sphere from her hand and passed it to York. Ezren could only watch as he erased the data in front of her eyes. "Don't you have a conscience? If the luxies continue to be harvested, you'll drive them to extinction. They deserve a chance to evolve in their home environment. Not to mention starting an interplanetary war over a lie. What's the matter with you?"

"I'm sorry," York said, his tone still light. "I missed the part where that's my problem. I'm here to do what's best for the people of the stations. The creds from the luxie trade will finally allow us to compete with the titans of Obrone and Dreitis."

"You just want to line your pockets," Ezren shouted, her rage too huge to contain. "I guess that's why you've got one foot in the underground." Her brow furrowed as the other pieces slotted into place. "You're the one who spread the rumors of the terranium." Her eyes widened. "And that was just the excuse. You *sent* the syndicates there specifically to kill us."

York spread his arms wide and took a self-satisfied bow. "Calderon did say you were smart. Too bad you were just a little too slow this time. Sewing confusion really does work wonders, but I'm afraid we still have more work to do here." He turned to the guards. "If you see any more escape pods, shoot them on sight."

"No!" Ezren screamed.

"What are we going to do with the girl and the others?" the guard asked.

York tapped his cleft chin theatrically, the smile still playing across his lips. "I haven't completely decided yet. Do I want to frame and discredit her on a world stage, or just nip the problem in the bud now and be the first to grieve that they never made it off Otho?" He clicked his tongue. "Tell you what, let me talk to the PR team for their opinion, and I'll get you an answer in fifteen. Until then, keep them contained."

This time, Ezren didn't fight the guard's grip. Instead she stilled, staring straight at York. "You can do whatever you want with me, but Calderon's not going to let you do this."

York only leaned closer. "Calderon is an old man. I don't think anyone would be surprised if he passed away any day now. Completely of natural causes of course. And who do you think will be poised to take over your little race? I think I could make an excellent compromise between Obrone and Dreitis, especially if they're at war. After all, it's not like they see us as a threat. Then with the luxies and terranium at my disposal, I'll create a paradise among the stars the likes of which has never been seen. Like the garden of Eden, a burbling fountain of youth with me as its god."

"As if anything would ever be enough for you," Ezren spat as they dragged her from the room. "Your hunger will only eat you from the inside, and you'll always be empty."

York flashed her one last sharp-toothed smile. "My dear, when time and the universe are infinite, nothing is ever enough. This system will only be the first. Who knows what other treasures lie in the expanse to be harvested. This world exists only to test me, and I'll gladly rise to the challenge."

With that, the door hissed shut on his smug face.

But apparently, they'd already shuffled off Sylvia and Shiro, because the hall outside was empty and quiet. As the guards walked Ezren down the corridor of boundless fields stretching on either side, her imagination involuntarily conjured a universe of immortals, ever destroying and consuming as they made their way through the galaxies, with York at the head of it. Anthills of humanity swarming every star, harvesting the life from every planet before it even got a chance to begin.

And she'd never felt such fear.

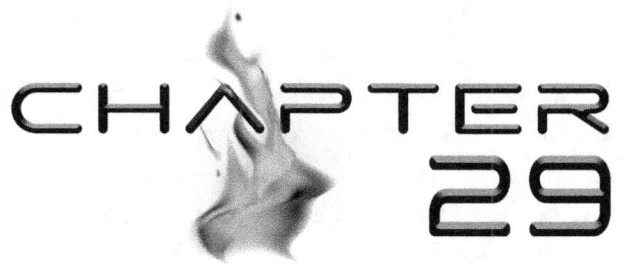

CHAPTER 29

8.18.43B: T-minus 1 hour until Mt. Aguya's Eruption

THE LAUNCHER SHOT Foster's escape pod out with such speed, he thought his skin might rip from the bones of his face, the wound in his ribs screaming with pain. Even as he went through the motions of evasion on his ascent with Dr. Hart's suppressive fire lighting up all around him, his mind still hung on the what-ifs. Maybe Dr. Hart could find shelter in the bunker, and then they could come back for him. As his craft climbed, he mentally dictated a message.

FOSTER: I'M ALMOST THROUGH THE THICK OF IT. FIND SOMEWHERE TO SHELTER IN PLACE.

Somewhere not far from them, a cloud of ash billowed into the atmosphere, and Foster watched in horror as aircraft disappeared on his radar before it. But with still an hour until the eruption, this was just the warm-up.

DR. HART: SORRY, KID, BUT WE CAN'T ALL BE CHAMPION ROYALERS. I'M AFRAID MY BODY HAS HAD ENOUGH. I WON'T BE LEAVING THIS SEAT.

FOSTER: You CAN, DR. HART. YOU'VE GOT TO TRY.

DR. HART: MY TOPSUIT'S ALREADY GASPING ITS LAST. IN ANOTHER MINUTE, THE GASSES WILL GET TO ME.

Foster tried to imagine staring death in the face like that.

Tried to imagine the pain. But the fear and despair threatened to overwhelm him, flooding his senses with the buzz of desperation. He swiveled his cam to zone in on the gun bay where Dr. Hart sat behind the cannon, his vitals impossibly weak.

DR. HART: OH, DON'T GET CHOKED UP, KID. I'VE ALREADY GOT ALL THE PAIN MEDS I NEED. IT WILL BE MERCIFUL, SO LET EZREN KNOW I DIDN'T SUFFER.

Suns, he'd even prepared for this moment. How long had he known it was coming?

FOSTER: I WILL.

Foster's mouth went dry, searching for something, anything he could offer the man who'd traded his life for Foster's own.

FOSTER: THANK YOU, DR. HART. I'M GLAD I GOT TO MEET YOU.

DR. HART: LIKEWISE, FOSTER STERLING.

Foster got a warning that he was going out of range, so he tried for one more message.

FOSTER: MAY THE STORM WINDS BRING YOU HOME.

Another cloud erupted from the volcano—a blasting plume rippling across the surface—and the entire gun bay collapsed before his eyes. In a blink, Dr. Hart's vitals dropped to zero, and the unmistakable tone of a flatline buzzed in his ears.

Gone.

He severed the connection with a choked gasp, slamming his fists into the side of the pod. Ezren's dad was gone, and he died protecting Foster. The thought threatened to shred him from the inside out, and an agonized sob racked his body. But he didn't even have the luxury of dwelling on it when he had other problems to face.

Namely, the warships that were now bearing down on him in the stratosphere. He swallowed down the agonizing grief, tucking it away for a later he could only hope to see.

Foster: Sylvia, I need cover fire. These guys look like they're about to blow me back down to the surface.

No answer.

Foster: Shiro, are you at the controls?

No answer. Cold sweat trickled down his temple. Had something happened to them?

Foster: Ezren? Grady?! Anyone!?!

Something exploded against his hull, and Foster swore as a crack raced through the exterior. Dr. Hart had not sacrificed himself so he could make it this far and die here. No way.

Foster: Davis, where are you?

Davis: Foster! We've been waiting for you. Just hang on.

Another blast rocked the pod.

Foster: Davis, I'm in bad shape here, where are the others? I need cover fire before I get torn apart.

Davis: I'm not sure. There was drama, and now they're docked with a DOS ambassador's personal ship.

Dad: And we don't have a good feeling about it. Things are deadly tense here.

Foster resisted the urge to roll his eyes. He'd nearly forgotten his dad was there too. The alarms on his pod started to whine through his goggs, warning of oxygen depletion. Fod it. He grabbed the emergency oxygen supply and strapped it to his suit, his heart pounding.

Foster: Well, I'm about to be space chaff here in a second, and I'm not exactly sure how long my topsuit will be able to hold out.

Technically still in the outer reaches of Otho's atmosphere, he hadn't quite yet made it to space, but he wasn't sure if that would help or hurt him.

DAD: YOU JUST NEED TO HOLD FOR 60 SECONDS.

The pod rattled again, the crack spreading, and Foster gripped Dr. Hart's bag to him. At this altitude, it wouldn't be long before he burned up in the atmosphere.

FOSTER: DON'T KNOW IF I HAVE 60 SECONDS.

DAVIS: 45 NOW.

FOSTER: OKAY, LISTEN, EVEN IF I DON'T MAKE IT, JUST KNOW I HAVE A DATA SPHERE AND A BOX ON ME THAT YOU NEED TO GET TO EZREN.

DAD: FOSTER, STOP IT. WE'RE GOING TO MAKE IT.

DAVIS: 15 SECONDS.

And then the world exploded around Foster. He clutched Dr. Hart's work to his chest for dear life as he went hurtling through space, screaming into his helmet as he spun head over feet, every siren in his goggs screaming.

But then as quickly as it began, someone grabbed his wrist. He flailed as his spinning stopped, and another hand closed around his elbow. Though he was certainly still flying through space at speed, he wasn't spinning anymore. Instead, he was looking directly into his father's face through a space-exposure suit, and for perhaps the first time in his whole life, he was happy about it.

DAD: GOT HIM AND PULLING HIM IN.

His dad yanked him through the top hatch of the ship and the access panel slid shut behind him. Foster shivered uncontrollably, his suit unable to compensate for the extreme cold he'd just experienced. It was as though the sweat that had coated his body had frozen to ice. If he'd stayed out there even a few seconds longer, he would've been dead. His body trembled violently as he opened his mouth but no words came out through his chattering teeth.

"Foster," his dad breathed. "You scared the chaff out of me." Gerard pulled him into his chest, wrapping his arms around him, and Foster wasn't sure if it was to share heat or affection.

Either way, it was weird. His dad was not a hugger. "H-how'd y-you g-get here so f-fast?" he managed.

"We've been tracking you since you launched." With an arm still around his shoulders, Gerard ushered him down a ramp to the command center where Davis stood surrounded by holos.

He glanced over his shoulder at them with a relieved grin, wearing his own space exposure suit. "Suns, kin, that was a close one. Glad we were able to snatch you." He turned back to his holo as something detonated way too close. "The original plan was to open the bay doors and try to grab the whole pod, but when it cracked, we had to scramble."

For a moment, Foster just stared at him, trying to comprehend the amount of calculation or luck that had gone into that rescue. They would've had to match his speed while flying only inches away from his out-of-control body. "Shaft, that was some good flying, Davis."

"Yeah, well." He grimaced, rubbing at the back of his head. "Hopefully I haven't peaked yet because we're not out of this storm by a long shot."

Gerard pushed Foster into a seat, strapping him into it like a child before taking his own.

"What about the others?" Foster asked, the warmth finally returning to his tingling limbs. "You said there was drama."

His dad exchanged a glance with Davis, and agitation spiked through Foster. "What? Tell me. Now."

"Calm down." Gerard's brows pulled even lower. "The

truth is, we're not sure what to tell you. They were taking heavy fire, but now they're currently docked with a station ambassador's ship, and we're not sure why."

Foster frowned, remembering the young, smiling ambassador with the thick head of auburn hair from the event. "Wait, is it York's ship? Why would that be a bad thing?"

"You know him?" His dad barked out a laugh. "So you know of his connections with the Kalashnik, the biggest organized crime syndicate in Casolla?" Gerard's gaze hardened and for a moment, he almost looked like a typically stern father figure. "I really hope the answer is no."

Foster froze as all the connections clicked into place. The looters coming after them. The luxies on the black market. York's strange youth. The syndicate thug that had been in the police station... he'd been working with *York*—not Calderon.

"Wait, was that common knowledge?" He shot a look at Davis. "Did you know this?"

"Not till your dad told me." He flinched as another shot rattled their shield. "I know you don't think highly of me, but crime syndicates aren't really my scene."

Foster accessed the exterior holocams with his goggs, searching for York's ship. "Then we have to go get them. If they find out Ezren's carrying evidence, they'll kill her."

The incoming munition alarm rang through the cabin, and their three heads shot up simultaneously.

"No offense, but I think we have our own problems." Davis looked at Gerard, his normally olive complexion pale. "It's locked on; we won't be able to avoid it."

"We didn't even get a warning hail?" Gerard grabbed the integrity breach kit from the wall along with another exposure suit.

Foster struggled out of the webbing of his seat, his fingers still not quite working properly. Hopefully it was just shock and not permanent damage. "Does this thing have any defenses?"

"Does it look like a fighter to you?" Gerard threw the exposure suit at him before turning to the HUD. "How long do we have, Davis?"

Davis flicked through his holos, the ship rattling with small fire. "Two minutes."

"The escape pods then," Gerard said with an air of command in his voice that Foster wasn't at all used to. "Davis, leave now in the first one and aim for the nearest station. We'll take the second."

Foster struggled into the exposure suit. "Why is Davis going alone?"

"Didn't anyone ever tell you not to put all your eggs in one basket? We have two pods left, and we're taking both."

Dr. Hart's words rattled back to him, and Foster made sure the data sphere and luxie cylinder were secure within his exosuit.

"Right." Davis didn't hesitate as he vaulted into one of the escape pods. "Guess I'll see you when I see you."

"Davis, wait." Foster lurched forward, offering a hand. Though he was wasting precious seconds, he knew too well he might never see him again. "Thanks, kin, we wouldn't have been able to do this without you and... you really saved my ass."

"The Harts are family. I was glad to help." Davis's sure smile faltered. "See you on the other side?"

Foster's mouth tightened—he didn't have time to think about that yet. "If it's the same to you, I'd rather it be this side."

"Right." Davis snorted and he gave a small salute to Gerard. "Sorry about your ship, she was a pleasure to fly."

Gerard clapped him on the shoulder. "Thanks for getting us this far."

"See you back on Belethea." With a wink, Davis shut the door and punched the launch, his pod away.

Gerard practically shoved Foster into the second one.

"I'm going," Foster snapped. "I think I can make it the last few feet to the pod on my own."

The door sliced shut behind them. "For a royaler, you're not moving very fast." His father secured the helmet of Foster's exposure suit. "Check your seals."

"Dad, we're running out of time. Just punch already!" But even as he said it, Foster tightened the connection between his suit and his helmet.

His dad hesitated only a second before launching them into space. The force of it knocked Foster into the wall of the pod, but although the craft was tiny, it was way more cushioned than the spartan one-seater he'd just escaped, and, he hoped, sturdier. For a moment they were silent as their bodies acclimated to the acceleration, distance stretching between their ship and the pod. Though there was enough space inside for four, their knees still touched where they sat across from each other. Foster checked his goggs and Davis's trajectory, and then saw to his horror the missile hurtling toward his dad's ship, and they were nowhere near far enough.

"Brace for—"

Foster didn't get the words out before the missile tore through the ship, a plume of silent fire expanding toward them. The viewport went bright orange as it enveloped them, heat alarms firing as the force propelled them forward once more. His father's hand found his arm, and he squeezed tight. Everything heated around them, the steel exterior groaning, and Foster inwardly swore if he survived this, he was planting his boots on Belethea and never leaving again.

But then, in a slow-motion miracle, the fire receded.

Gerard looked out the viewport at the wreckage of his ship

now just a speck in the distance. "Do you usually have this many close calls in the BRR?"

"Not like this," Foster said hoarsely as he extracted his arm from his father's grip. "Don't celebrate yet though, they could still home in on us."

"All the more reason to get out of here." Gerard pulled up the nav holo, and Foster braced for the rumble of the engines again, but the holo only flashed red. His father swiped it away with a scowl. "Fritzin' piece of chaff."

Foster let out a sigh, fatigue threatening to overtake him. "Let me guess, more bad news?" Foster checked his goggs again, but it looked like Davis had made it safely out. At least there was that.

"The blast fried our engines," his dad said.

Foster banged his helmet against the padded wall in frustration. "So, now what do we do?"

"Now we wait and hope they think we're just wreckage debris." Gerard shrugged and took off his helmet. "Between the suits and this ship, we have enough air for three days. We'll wait for this to blow over, and then call for help."

"What about Ezren?" Foster asked through gritted teeth. "She could be in trouble. She needs us."

Gerard lifted his hands in mock surrender. "If we call for help now, they're as likely to kill us as to rescue us. As it stands, the only thing you can do for her is survive."

Foster's hand spasmed, and he looked away, massaging his twitching fingers as his mind searched for alternative solutions.

His dad leaned forward, his expression softening. "From what I've heard of her, that girl can take care of herself. And she has plenty of help. If anyone can make it out of this, it's her."

Foster's jaw set, not quite willing to admit that his dad's words were, in fact, reassuring.

Gerard rubbed his hands together, his gaze drifting to the metal floor of the pod. "I'm guessing you didn't find Ezren's dad?"

Foster pressed his lips into a thin line, but his voice broke anyway. "No, we found him."

"Oh." Something like empathy softened his dad's face. "I'm sorry, Foster."

Foster balled his hands into fists as the last twelve hours sank in. "Thanks, for coming to get me." He rolled out his shoulders, each word tightly controlled. "And I'm sorry about your ship."

"It's okay. It was just a ship." His dad tapped his fingers against his knees. "I know I'm probably the last person you want to float through space with for the next who knows how long, but I'm glad I was able to be here for you."

Foster swallowed the massive knot in his throat. How strange a universe was it that Gerard, the last person he'd ever counted on, had been there when it counted most. Was here now when everything fell apart. Was looking at him like... like a father. "Me too, Dad."

Gerard held his gaze. "Do you want to talk about it?"

And Foster let out a long, exhausted breath. While a part of him wanted to sleep, after narrowly escaping with his life, another part of him wanted to do anything but. And he wasn't sure if he'd even be able to rest with all of this weighing on his chest—with Dr. Hart's face ready to haunt his nightmares right alongside Vieve's.

"Sure. I mean what else are we going to do?"

CHAPTER 30

8.18.43B: T-minus 0.75 hours until Mt. Aguya's Eruption

EZREN ARGUED with the guards as they walked her down the length of the ship. "Listen to me, just leave Foster Sterling's shuttle alone. The only reason he came to Otho was to get me. He doesn't even know anything about the luxies or Baxter or anything." While, admittedly, lying was not Ezren's strongest gift, she'd be chaffed if she didn't try. She stared up at the guards' hard faces but they didn't so much as flinch. "Besides, he's the son of Gerard Y and Greta Sterling. Do you really think they're not going to investigate what happened to him? I mean, all the eyes in Casolla are on Otho right n—"

Finally, one of the guards sighed and stopped them in the hall. "Okay, look, girl. I was always a BRR fan, so I'm going to be straight with you. The good news is, Sterling made it off the planet, and he even got picked up by some other random ship. The bad news is, we blew it up."

Ezren's brow furrowed as she took in his stony, unmoving face. "You're lying."

He glanced at the other guard before projecting a holo in front of him. "Unfortunately, I'm not."

Ezren watched in horror as she saw the escape pod hurtle out of Otho's smoky atmosphere, only to break apart and send Foster hurtling into space. Miraculously, a small, posh ship managed to pull up adjacent to him, and someone in an exosuit popped out of the top to pull him in a hatch. The footage fast-forwarded until three minutes later, when the ship erupted in a blast of fire.

"Guess you can only cheat death twice before reality comes due," chuckled the other guard.

And whatever shock and grief Ezren was experiencing curdled into pure, unadulterated fury. Wrenching out of their lax grip, she drove her fist into the guard's belly and then delivered a solid uppercut to his jaw. The other tried to grab her before she kicked the feet out from under him and then stomped savagely on his ribs. She reached for his gun, only to be seized in a bear hug by the first and lifted from the ground, still lashing out. "How dare you say you're a fan," she spat. "You just killed Foster in cold blood."

The guard hauled her bodily down the hall while the other one got to his feet. "You're not really a BRR champion if you have to cheat to win."

"That's such fodding shaft," Ezren screamed, jabbing her elbows and feet into any part of him she could find. "You're all chaffing monsters."

"Suns, someone stop the shrieking already," said the first. "My head's already aching."

A door slid open, and they threw her into a dark room. With a hiss, Ezren turned and ran for the already closing door, kicking and banging on it before letting out an ear-piercing screech of rage. Chest heaving, she replayed the footage in her mind, and the fight slipped out of her in a rush of air as she realized her dad hadn't even been on board the shuttle to begin with.

He hadn't made it off the planet, and now neither of them would ever come home. She hugged her knees to her chest, her body trembling. She'd lost them both. For nothing.

The luxies were gone, and the ambassador had well and completely caught her in his web.

Where could she possibly go from here?

"Ezren." A light touch on her shoulder jerked her head up to find Sylvia kneeling next to her.

"Sylvia!" Ezren threw her arms around her with a choked gasp.

"Ezren, are you okay?" Sylvia stroked her hair soothingly. "Did they hurt you?"

"No." Ezren shook her head, wiping away the tears. She couldn't fall apart yet. Not now. Not here. "But my dad... my dad and Foster are gone."

"Foster could still be alive." A muffled voice echoed through the wall, and Ezren nearly jumped out of her skin.

"Shiro's locked in the room beside us," Sylvia explained in a whisper.

"But I saw their ship get hit," Ezren said.

"Yeah, but what fritzer sees a locked-on missile and doesn't use the escape pods?" Shiro asked. "I know they had two. They could've gotten away."

Sylvia nodded. "These guys are asschaffs, but they're over-confident asschaffs. From what we can tell, they haven't found Simon and Bex yet either." Her teeth sank into her full bottom lip. "But I am sorry about your dad."

The relief of Foster's escape twisted with the grief for her father in a festering tangle of emotion. But she couldn't deal with that now. Shiro, Sylvia, Bex, and Simon were still alive and fighting here with her, and she couldn't let them down. She wiped at her soggy cheeks.

And Foster could be out there. Alive. She could hold on to that hope. It was the hope her father had entrusted to her, even after everything he'd been through. And there was no way in the 'verse she would ever let it go again.

"So how're we busting out of here?" Ezren whispered.

Sylvia smiled with a pat on Ezren's cheek. "There's my spitfire girl."

"Well, the bad news is they took our goggs and our weapons, so we're limited to what we can use in here until Simon and Bex find us," Shiro said.

Ezren nodded, the gears in her brain starting to turn once again. "So what's the good news?"

"The good news is, *I* am always prepared." Sylvia pulled a purple half-visor from somewhere deep in her jumpsuit.

Ezren let out a sharp laugh. "I hate to ask, but why did you have that in your cleavage?"

"When I knew we were coming aboard a station ship, I didn't want to stand out, so I brought it in case." Sylvia held it out to her with a prim sniff. "But will you be able to—"

"Already on it." Ezren connected her chip to the visor, and in a minute, hacked into the door control panel in an override that was embarrassingly simple. This wasn't a jail cell. They were literally in a single-stall bathroom.

"Shiro, I can get us into the hallway, but there's going to be a guard there." Ezren pressed her ear to the door. "Maybe even two."

"Open both doors at once and let Sylvia run down the hall to distract them," Shiro said. "Then we'll have our own little royale brawl."

"Are you saying I'm the bait?" Sylvia's lids lowered, clearly unimpressed with this plan.

"The most beautiful bait," Shiro replied smoothly.

"Oh, stop it." Sylvia bounced from foot to foot. "I'm ready."

Ezren's lips quirked, but she didn't have time to do anything but roll with it. "You're a go."

With a command from Ezren's visor, the doors hissed open,

and Sylvia burst out with a hard right turn. "Oh, suns, I really should've stretched."

"Hey!" one of the guards shouted as they instinctively lunged for her, catching her in two steps. Ezren was about to surge forward when Shiro beat her to it, capturing one from behind in a perfect headlock.

"Hands off, asschaff."

The other guard raised his gun toward Shiro, but Ezren was there first, knocking the weapon from his hand and landing a jump kick straight to his chin that would've made Bex proud. Another side kick sent his head into the metal wall with a hollow clang, and he dropped to the floor in a stunned heap. Ezren snatched the gun from his hand and whipped it across his temple, sending him into unconsciousness.

"Not exactly a grade-A plan," Sylvia said from the ground.

"It worked, didn't it?" Shiro offered her a hand and tugged her to her feet, eyes gleaming.

Sylvia pressed a brief, hard kiss to his mouth. "I guess it passed."

He smirked, his gaze lingering on hers. "I'm going to be very disappointed if we don't get to spend more time together when our lives aren't in danger."

Ezren started to pick up the guns, but Shiro waved her off. "Those will be coded to them."

"But these won't."

Ezren turned to see Simon and Bex behind them, their own rifles in hand, and she flew toward them, wrapping an arm around each. "How'd you know the ambassador was rotten?"

Bex threw a gun to Shiro. "If the ex-CIF agent has a bad gut feeling, that's something I can trust."

Simon lifted his rifle and glanced over his shoulder. "And basically, we decided that forgiveness might be a better bet than permission."

"So you're saying you got lucky." Sylvia plucked her own pistol from his waist. "As usual. What now, then?"

"We get the chaff out of here." Ezren projected the map of the ship from Sylvia's spare visor. "There are a dozen escape pods, but they're equally spaced on both sides of the ship."

"Can you deploy them from afar?" Shiro asked.

Ezren frowned. "Yeah, but we want to be on them, right?"

"Not if I can help it," Shiro scoffed. "What other ships are docked here? I saw at least one."

Ezren continued her scan. "There are two personal transports of some kind in the docking bay. Luxury by the look of them."

"Bingo." Shiro grinned and stooped to slip a small device out of his boot. "This will jam the cams, and those will be your ride out of here."

"What about you?" Bex asked.

"I have a stealth ship, and you can bet your ass I'm going to stealth my way out on it." Shiro tilted his head to one side. "Plus, my cat's still on board."

"Wait, are you saying we're going to split up?" Simon's shoulders tensed, and he shifted the gun in his hand.

But Shiro was already limping down the corridor, blood seeping through his one-piece from his not quite healed wounds. "That's exactly what I'm saying."

"We want to stay together," Bex said as Ezren directed them toward the first pod.

"Cute." Shiro shoved his messy dark hair out of his eyes with a hand. "But I want you to stay alive. Where's the luxury bay?"

"Not far," said Ezren. "They're all on the port side."

"Excellent." Something like excitement lit Shiro's face as he fiddled with his rifle. "Shoot any and every chaffer we see before they get the chance to set the alarm." His gaze strafed them all before he nodded with satisfaction. "Let's go."

Ezren led them through the corridors with Shiro's rifle practically hovering over her shoulder. True to his word, all were shot on sight, but it didn't take three minutes before someone noticed their unconscious crewmates, and the siren went off.

Ezren froze, her heart hammering in her chest, but Shiro only grinned wider. "Deploy the pods."

Ezren punched in the command for immediate release, and Simon pressed his face to a viewport. "Holy shaft, it worked. They're all taking off out there."

"Where'd you send them to?" Bex asked.

A satisfied smirk curled Ezren's lips. "Twelve different space stations."

"All personnel to the command room immediately." A robotic voice vibrated through the comms.

"Stop standing around congratulating yourselves." Sylvia snapped her fingers impatiently in front of Shiro's grinning face. "What do we do now?"

Shiro enclosed her hand in his and squeezed. "Time to run."

"Now we're talking," Simon whooped.

From there, they tore down the halls, shooting another three guards before gaining access to the docking bay where two shiny new ships awaited them.

"Royalers, your carriages await," Shiro announced.

"I've got the one on the right," Ezren said, choosing the sportier ship with the larger engines.

"Who said you get to pick?" Simon protested.

Bex crossed her arms. "Or go alone."

"I'm not really going alone." Ezren met their gazes, her voice hard. "I'm going to pick up my doubles partner." She looked at Sylvia, all her doubt replaced by furious conviction. "And then we're going to that ambassador summit."

Bex nodded, approval shining in her eyes. "We'll meet you on Obrone then."

"Us too." Sylvia wrapped her in a tight hug. "But please try to at least wash the blood off before you get there."

"I don't know." Shiro winked. "I think it adds character." A shout in the corridor turned their heads, and he offered a quick wave before tugging Sylvia back into the hall.

"You'd better take care of her, Shiro," Simon yelled after him. "We only have one manager."

"With my life," Shiro called back.

Then Bex and Simon were running to their ship, and Ezren was sprinting to hers.

"Race you there?" Simon asked, a heavy limp to his stride as their boarding ramp lowered.

And Ezren couldn't help letting out a laugh. Her craft was obviously faster, but since she was making a detour, he might stand a chance. "I thought you didn't fly spacecraft."

"Neither do you," he volleyed back.

"Then I guess you're on." Ezren pulled herself into the small command cockpit of the ship. This was certainly no lunar hopper. With only two seats, this craft was obviously built for speed.

As the engines rumbled to life, she couldn't help the grim smile that tugged at her lips. She had no idea what she was going to say at the ambassador summit without proof, but she sure as chaff was going to get there before York.

After all, she was here to win.

CHAPTER 31

8.18.43B: T-plus 0.5 hours since Mt. Aguya's Eruption

SURVIVORS: o

Notes from observing Baxter scientists in orbit:
No man-made structures remaining below or above surface.
Ash ground layer up to sixty feet deep with global ash cloud
dispersion.
Luxopodos activity detected seventy-three miles from eruption.
Otho has been swept clean.

The horrors of the past twelve hours didn't truly hit Foster until he unfolded them before his dad. Surviving the first ambush at the outpost, the pursuing looters in the race across the planet, the discovery of the luxies, the loss of Santino, the stand-off in the central command post, and of course, Dr. Milo Hart's final sacrifice. Though none of them had escaped unscathed, looking back on it now, he could see how miraculous it was that he and the others had survived at all.

Well, that is, if they made it off York's ship.

And through the whole gritty telling, even as Foster stopped and started, his voice cracking with emotion, Gerard sat still, his attention intent on Foster. When Foster finally managed to get through the entire tale, his gaze strayed to the depths of space, searching like he might be able to see whether or not the others had made it. Because as much as he wanted that to be the end of the story, they weren't safe yet. Not by miles.

"And now I guess we cross our fingers and hope that someone doesn't pick us off before we catch a ride out of here." Foster frowned, fatigue weighing on every part of his body. "It would be a shaft way to go after all that." And Ezren would never know what happened to him or her dad. Baxter would continue to exploit the luxies, and all those people on Otho would've died for nothing—Milo Hart included.

Across from him, Gerard nodded, rubbing a hand over his trim beard. "And I thought watching the royales was stressful."

"How would you know?" Foster snorted, probing the reopened injury in his right side. Luckily the pressure of his topsuit had already stopped the bleeding. "You were never a fan."

"And that's why," Gerard replied with a dry laugh. "I couldn't even watch them without my hands starting to sweat." He rubbed his fingers together as if they were sweating now. Maybe they were. "Watching those kids risk their lives over and over again—some dying..." He shuddered. "I don't know how people can watch that. When their goggs cams go out, and they flatline, and you know you just watched a kid die. Watched their last moments through their own eyes. It's wrong, all of it."

"And yet you were with Mom, a royaler legend, for what? Ten years?"

"But she wasn't royaling by then." Gerard tunneled a hand through his long hair. "Then you got into royales, and I could see the writing on the wall. You were always good, even when you were a kid in those ridiculous training camps." His lips twisted in a grimace.

And so you took off, Foster thought. *Great excuse.*

"It about drove me mad with worry. I tried to distract you from it all. I took you on tour, hoping you'd get into music instead, but you were already crazy about royales."

"Wait, what?" Foster's brow furrowed. "You never took me on tour."

Gerard's eyes widened. "Holy chaff, yes, I did. I carried you around with me for a solid three years straight. Age five to seven."

Foster cocked his head. "You're fritzing me. I don't remember that."

"That's because all those blows to your head have fried your brain." Gerard pulled up a holo montage in his goggs and sent it to Foster. "Here, look."

There were all kinds of holos of a pudgy five-year-old kid peeking out of a curtain at his dad's rock show. Six-year-old him at some ridiculously fancy dinner party. Him bouncing along on stage with his dad. He and his dad playing pool aboard the very luxury spaceship they'd just blown up.

"Is it coming back to you now?" Gerard smirked.

Foster pursed his lips as vague memories of lots of people and loud music filled his mind. "Maybe."

"It's probably because you hated it. Despite my best efforts, you never had a passion for the music, and you hated the publicity." His dad shrugged. "So I let you off the hook."

Foster stared at his dad, trying to weigh the truth of this account. "I thought you did it because the rock star life wasn't conducive to having a kid around."

"Please," he scoffed. "I always wanted you around; you just never took to music. And I just about pass out every time I watch you race in a royale." He shifted in his bulky exosuit. "But maybe I should've tried harder to find common ground."

Foster stared, his over-wrung brain struggling to process. Was his dad apologizing for not being around when he was a kid? Or had he fallen into some bizarro-world? The bizarro-world seemed more likely. "Well, you got it. Now our common ground is this pod and our near-imminent deaths."

A startled laugh rang out from his dad. "Your mother is going to murder us when we get out of this."

Foster chuckled, fiddling with the exo-helmet in his lap. "Nah, she's so used to the near-death thing, it won't even faze her." He winced, his hand spasming again. "Though I do hope word hasn't already gotten out. If she knew we were here, she'll be charging into the fray now to get us." Foster looked out the window as if his mother's face might appear at any moment.

"Seriously though, Foster," his dad said. "When we get out of this, I don't want us to go back to being strangers."

Foster eyed him carefully. While his dad seemed sincere, one day of warm fuzzies didn't undo a dozen years of inconsistent calls. "Well, I still hate crowds and all that."

"Which is ironic, because now you have more of it than I do." Gerard chuckled, his age finally peeking through the crow's feet creasing his face. "Kind of nice that's not my fault anymore." He looked at Foster, affection softening his gray eyes. "Just remember that while fame may often feel like a curse, there's still so much good you can do with it. Don't spite yourself by missing the opportunities it gives." His rock star grin nearly lit up the pod. "But you know, I do have three decades of experience navigating that chaff if you want some tips."

Foster barked out a laugh. "Which reminds me, *you* haven't been taking any black-market youth regen treatments, have you?"

"Ha." His dad framed his jaw with a hand. "You'll be happy to know my youthful good looks are all natural. Though if you're not careful with these death-defying stunts, my amazing genes will be wasted on you."

Foster's shoulders relaxed with a chuckle. "Yeah, yeah, well, maybe once we get back, you can give us some of those tips over that dinner we were supposed to get." After watching Ezren lose her father, he felt like he had lost one as well, but the truth was, his dad was right here in front of him, extending an olive branch. And after everything he'd been through in the last two years, Foster would be chaffed if he wasn't going to take it.

"You know—" The squeal of an alarm interrupted Gerard, and Foster scrambled to bring up the command holo.

"Fodding shaft it," Foster swore. "Someone's locked on to us."

Gerard swiveled to look out the viewport. "Guns? Missiles?"

"It doesn't say," Foster said. "But either way it doesn't matter. We don't have any anti-weapon defenses."

"That's because people don't typically shoot at civilian escape pods," Gerard said, his voice taut with something that almost sounded like rage. "Shaft. I can see it now. It looks like a DOS space fighter. Open a channel."

"And say what?" Foster said. "Please don't shoot us?" His mind was already spinning way past that. If York had sent a fighter to finish them off, who knew what had happened to Ezren on board.

"Just do it," Gerard snapped.

Foster attempted to access the shuttle's comms, but whatever capability it held had been stripped by the blast. "It's not working." He swiped away the string of error messages.

"They're coming in hot," Gerard said, as if there was something Foster could do about it.

"And we're basically sitting in a useless steel ball. What do you expect me to do?"

"I expect you to not give up." Gerard scowled. "Didn't your royale time at least teach you that?"

"Right, so I'll just start making hand signals."

"Yes." Gerard's eyes widened with a sudden idea. "That's exactly what I mean."

He ripped off his goggs and shoved them against the window just as they started to flash in what Foster belatedly recognized as Morse code. His goggs automatically translated.

S.O.S. Don't shoot. No comms. No engine. Gerard Y on board. S.O.S.

Foster raised a brow, begrudgingly impressed at this thought. "You're not going to mention me?"

"If you haven't noticed, you're a bit of a persona non grata."

"And you aren't?"

Gerard flashed him a smile that looked disturbingly like Grady's. "Hey, you never know who's a fan."

Foster jammed on his exo-helmet, his heart pounding in his chest despite their banter. "It's still coming closer."

"But it's slowing down," Gerard said. "I think they're going to help us."

"Or maybe they're just trying to avoid any possibility of escape by shooting at point blank range," Foster grumbled.

His dad shoved on his helmet. "The pessimism really doesn't help."

"Neither does the optimism." The fighter's glowing orange patterns began to flash back. "Wait, what are they saying?" Foster held his breath, waiting for his goggs to translate. Though he was fairly sure now the pilot wasn't here to kill them on sight, it was still a coin flip whether they would detain them or not. And their decision might change when they saw it was Foster on board and not just Gerard. His goggs finally relayed the Morse code.

Can you dock?

Gerard flashed one word. *No.*

In exosuits?

Sweat gleamed inside Gerard's helmet. *Yes.*

Matching speed. Will open airlock.

Gerard smirked triumphantly at him. "Looks like we've got a ride."

"If we can get out of this thing and make it in there." The thought of spinning through space again twisted Foster's stomach.

Gerard snorted, checking Foster's helmet seal. "You've done a hundred more dangerous things than this in the past twelve hours, and a little space hop is what's getting you down?"

"I don't like space." In fact, Foster was going to chaffing hug solid ground once they landed on a planet. At this point, he didn't even care which one.

"Hold on to something while we depressurize." Gerard punched the emergency exit valve, and the door separated from the vessel, sucking the air out with a cold whoosh and a shriek of sensors. An icy sweat ran down Foster's cheek as he prayed his exosuit would hold, and he was belatedly grateful his dad had double-checked it. The small space equalized, and Foster could make out the fighter hovering at an angle immediately above them, its airlock door open.

"Are we sure we want to do this?" Foster felt for the luxies and the data sphere still secure inside his suit. "We have no idea who's picking us up here."

"Yeah, but c'mon, when I'm offered an upgrade, I don't usually turn it down." Gerard extended his hand to Foster. "We're going to want to take the jump together though. The pod's going to spin when we push off."

"Right." His muscles tensing, Foster grabbed his dad's arm, and then together they leapt into space.

The seconds stretched as they floated through the empty expanse, and Foster's lungs pumped in and out as he struggled to control his anxiety. They were canting too far to the left.

"We're going to miss the airlock," he gasped out, his mind already spiraling with panic at the thought of floating through the empty abyss.

"Nah, I've got it." Gerard reached out and just barely caught the edge of the airlock by his fingertips.

Foster crashed into the side of the fighter, righting himself while he kept the death grip on his dad. "Can you pull us in?"

"In zero-G? Give me some credit." Obviously unbothered by the endless void, his dad laughed as he heaved himself into the airlock, hauling Foster along behind him. Foster scarcely cleared the lip before the door slid closed, and the tight airlock hissed with pressurization. He held on to a brace bar for dear life, and his father looked closer at him. "Are you sweating?"

Foster's chest heaved. "I don't like space walks."

"Well, I suppose that should be reassuring that even the great Foster Yunin-Sterling fears something. Good to see your sense of self-preservation is still in there somewhere." He clapped him on the shoulder. "Don't worry, I won't tell anyone."

Foster glared at him, loosening his helmet as the oxygen reached breathable levels. "So what do you think the spacers want here?"

"I figure they're either here to rescue or ransom us." His dad looked at the hatch into the cockpit. "If it's ransom, they won't open the door."

Foster's hands balled into fists. "But if they do, I'm commandeering the ship and going to get Ezren."

His dad took off his helmet and shook out his long hair. "The odds of winning there are slim. You're better off flying to Obrone with this." He patted the bulky lump in Foster's suit where the luxies sat. "You know that's what she would want. And if you miss the summit, you're going to lose your chance."

"But what if she's—"

"If they haven't killed her yet, they won't."

"That's *not* reassuring."

"I thought you wanted the truth."

Foster gritted his teeth, the rage bubbling up in him again. He knew his dad was right, but that didn't mean he liked it. He yanked off his helmet and drove a fist into the hatch. "Why isn't this fodding door opening?" Because if they were detained, then they were just as chaffed as Ezren was. "Open the door!"

"Wow, not even a please?" Gerard crossed his arms, looking way more casual floating in zero-G than he had any right to be. "I don't think that's going to help."

But Foster didn't care. He was about to knock on the door again when it retracted into the wall, and a familiar voice carried out.

"Sorry, the pressure sensor release was taking forever to equalize, and I've never piloted a space—"

Ezren froze when she saw him, her dark eyes wide as she hung suspended in the weightless cockpit. A bruise darkened one side of her face, shadows smudged the underside of her lashes, and the nanowrap still encased her waist. But she was alive, and she was *here*.

"Ezren." Her name sounded like a whispered prayer on his lips.

Then he was reaching for her, and they were crashing together, his arms drawing her to him as she buried her face in his neck. Pure relief rushed through him, pulling his frayed edges back together, drowning him in euphoric peace. He clutched her to his chest, pressing his face in her hair, drinking in the warmth of her skin—trying to convince himself that she was real. This moment was real. They were alive—her touch rekindling his dying hope into a blazing fire.

"I wasn't sure if you'd made it off your ship," Ezren said, her voice muffled against his jaw. "I saw them destroy it, and the pod didn't look big enough for two."

"It's okay. We're okay, and Davis got out too." But then he remembered that it wasn't and pulled back, his hands cupping her face. "But Ezren, your dad, he's... he's gone."

"I know." Ezren's face fell. "They had footage of you escaping the atmosphere, so I knew he wasn't on the escape pod." She pressed her palms to her eyes, her voice shaking. "But York killed the luxies and wiped the data, I don't—"

"Wait." Foster unzipped his suit to reveal the five luxies still dancing within the cylinder against his chest. "It's okay. Your dad gave me everything."

For a moment, Ezren only stared, eyes still swimming with tears. Then she took his face in her hands and kissed him. They tangled together in the zero-G, holding on to one another as if they could crush out the grief that threatened to drown them. Her lips were warm and soft on his, the familiar taste of her like a balm for the fear still rampaging through him. And even though beyond this moment, everything was still so wrong, they were together—and for now, that was all that mattered.

"Um, so..." Gerard coughed in the corner. "This is your girlfriend then?"

"Oh." Foster rasped out a laugh, full of joy and pain and life. "I guess you haven't met. Ezren, this is my dad, Gerard Y, and dad, this is Ezren Hart." He looked at her flushed face, warmth suffusing his every cell. "She's my... everything."

Gerard nodded to her. "I've heard a lot about you, Ezren."

"A pleasure to finally meet you." Ezren dipped her chin with a bittersweet smile. "And thank you so much. I saw how you saved Foster."

Something swelled in Foster's chest as he looked from his dad to Ezren. Like something right was finally coming together. And then he realized with sudden clarity—it was his family.

"What about the others? Grady and Bex?" Foster asked.

"They're all fine." Ezren wiped her face again, then tugged him into the tiny two-person cockpit. "But we've got to get out of here before York finds us."

"Right." Gerard smiled as he followed them. "We have an appointment on Obrone. And since I heard you say you don't pilot spacecraft, I'd be happy to."

Ezren cocked her head. "You can fly?"

"Well, I'm no royaler." Gerard slid into the first seat, and the holos flickered to life around him. "But space control I can do, as long as I've got a copilot." He glanced over his shoulder at Foster.

"Looks like you've got two copilots." Foster moved into the seat behind his dad and shot a roguish grin at Ezren. "Guess we'll have to share."

Her lips quirked up as she pulled herself into his lap, knotting her fingers around his neck as the netting enshrouded both of them. "Never thought I'd actually want to go to the ambassador summit."

"Me neither." Foster checked the netting around her. "But we're going to have to gun it to get there first."

Gerard smirked over his shoulder, the course unfolding before him in his holo. "Do you doubt us?"

Ezren looked straight at Foster, an earnest expression on her battered face. "Never."

And for her, Foster knew he could've done anything. But his eyes caught on the dark bruise marring her pale skin, and his fury resurged, burning from his fingers to his scalp. "Who hit you?"

Ezren wrinkled her nose. "One of York's syndicate thugs.

Apparently he was working with Baxter and the Kalashnik the whole time."

"Yeah, we put that together on our end too." He couldn't help but picture beating the smug ambassador into the ground. "Did you get even?"

She flashed her teeth with a tense ferocity. "Of course."

"That's my girl." He leaned his head against hers, pulling her more tightly against him as the ship accelerated. "But that's not going to stop me from beating the fod out of York the next time I see him."

"I'll be right beside you." Ezren nestled her head in the crook of his neck with a soft sniff. "It'll be VSoc gold; Sylvia will love it."

"Well, if that's what being an athlete ambassador is about, I can get behind that." Foster rested his cheek on her hair, breathing her in. "Now I'm practically looking forward to this PR event."

"See, I knew you'd come around to the fame thing," his dad laughed.

But though their banter was light, Foster didn't miss the covert sweep of Ezren's hand across her face. She snuggled closer to him, and he bent his lips close to her ear. "It's okay, Ezren. You can let go now."

"I can't fall apart yet." A choked sob rippled through her. "Not till after the summit."

"You can always fall apart here." Foster pressed his lips to her hair, his arms tightening around her. "I'll hold you together."

"I'm counting on it." With a shaky breath, Ezren straightened, her tear-stained face trying for a wobbly grin. "Just not yet."

And with that, they took off toward the aqua-blue dot that was Obrone, and whatever lay in wait for them there.

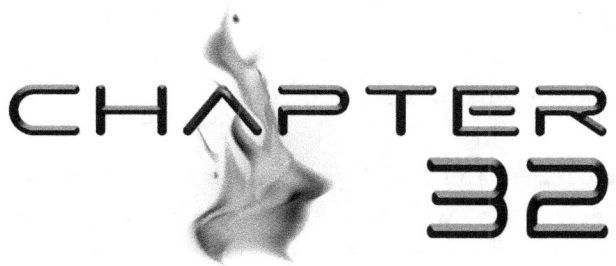

CHAPTER 32

8.18.43B: T-plus 4 hours since Mt. Aguya's Eruption & T-minus 1 hour until the Casolla Ambassador's Summit

FOUR HOURS LATER, the force of their continuous acceleration still pressed Ezren against Foster's chest as the stars streaked away from them. Foster linked their comms to the broad channel and projected a holo from his goggs with their course to Obrone along with the scattering of warships between them and it. Thankfully, Obrone's and Otho's orbits were adjacent, and with their current alignment they were about as close as two of Casolla's moons could be. With their current speed, assuming no interference, they would be there within the hour. "I guess we're not being sneaky anymore?" Ezren laughed, the thrill of their escape still singing through her.

"No way," Foster said. "Now it's all about speed."

"I prefer it that way." The image of Simon's beloved jetracers crossed her mind, the rush of the land blurring outside the windshield. Even from her brief, fumbling stint in the seat of this craft and Shiro's lessons, she knew for a fact piloting was a lot different from driving. "But you are going to give us enough time to decelerate, right?"

"Of course, have a little faith." Gerard's gray eyes flicked to something lighting up his holo. "Heads-up, incoming hail."

Foster adjusted course for the obstructions in their path. "Do we accept?"

"It could be Bex or Sylvia." Ezren eyed the accept option on the incoming call. "And even if it's the asschaff, at least we'll want to know what we're dealing with."

Gerard nodded, and with a thought, accepted the call. "Star-racer here, this is Gerard Y, your captain speaking."

"Gerard Y." Ambassador's York's familiar lilting voice flowed through the cockpit, and Ezren scowled. "I assume you're harboring CIF fugitives Ezren Hart and Foster Sterling?"

"Assumptions are dangerous," Gerard replied, matching his light tone. "But why would two champion royalers be fugitives?"

"For trespassing on the CIF-claimed planet of Otho and the theft of my star-racer, which you are currently piloting, to name two, but I'm sure there will be other charges."

"Pfft," Gerard scoffed. "So they walked somewhere they weren't supposed to and pinched a toy. That's got nothing on your laundering, piracy, murder, and alien exploitation hobbies."

York's voice pivoted on a dime, his words frosted and brittle. "I'm giving you one chance to return the jet with the fugitives or we're blowing you into the void."

Foster raised their speed with a pointed look at his father.

"Well, you can try," Gerard said, and Ezren gritted her teeth as the Gs increased. "But you know, tensions are pretty high right now, and I'd hate to have a spacer missile detonate in the Obronian sector if I were you." He grunted with the force of their acceleration. "They're a little touchy about that."

A heavy pause blotted the line, and Ezren almost thought York terminated the transmission before his snarl raked the silence. "You think you're fast, but I was a royaler too, and there's no way in the Casolla system that you're going to get there before me."

"You're on, old man!" Ezren shouted.

With a bark of a laugh, Gerard cut the line. "Okay, time to be real, we're not quite to Obronian space yet, so they still have a chance to blow us away. Foster, are you tracking them?"

"Yeah." Foster pulled up the image of the monstrous ship not three clicks behind. But Ezren's attention slipped as they passed the blur of another vessel.

"That was Bex and Simon," she shouted, pointing to the luxury liner. "I'm hailing them." The holo flashed green, and Ezren pushed the words out even as the Gs weighed on her chest. "Simon, Bex, you there? You okay?"

"Chaff, E," Simon said. "Was that you that just blew by us?"

"We're here," Bex cut in. "And we're fine. Did you find Foster?"

"Team Belethea all accounted for," Foster said, his gaze still pinned to York's ship.

"And that was actually me that blew by you," Gerard added.

"Thank the suns. You all scared the shaft out of us," Simon said. "I told you we should've taken the faster one."

"It's good to hear your voice," Bex said, her voice low.

"Same," Foster replied, his face softening with barely veiled emotion.

Ezren laid her hand onto his. "But York's onto us and tossing threats, so watch out."

"Don't worry about us. You're drawing his whole attention," Bex said. "Sylvia and Grady are telling everyone they can think of what's going on, but there will be a comm delay across the distance. Shiro says when you get to the ambassador summit ask for Commander Liassidi, and tell him Agent Shiro Tanaka sent—"

"They're firing on us!" Gerard interrupted. But no sooner had the alert chimed than it went black again.

"What just happened?" Fear hurtled through Ezren's veins. "Did it go dark?"

Simon cackled over the line. "Nah, that'll be Shiro shooting them down. He's got your back. You just get to the summit."

Ezren and Foster sank back with twin expressions of relief, and Ezren leaned her head into his chest. "Right. Can I just say, after this, I'm throwing a big party."

"The occasion?" Bex asked.

"To eat cake of course," Ezren said. "Every near-death experience deserves a cake."

"We're going to need a lot of cakes," Foster rumbled against her ear.

"Perfect," she replied.

"They're firing three more," Gerard said. This time two exploded, but the third kept on coming. "We're going to have to outmaneuver it." The restraint webbing retracted from his shoulders. "You two take over the controls."

"Where are you going?" Ezren asked, her attention locking on to their virtual track.

Gerard rolled from his chair, only to be immediately thrown to the rear of the cabin. Grunting with the impact, he opened the inner airlock hatch. "There's gotta be something we can throw out that it'll home in on. Maybe we can toss out one of these chairs."

"No, it doesn't have to be large, just electrical." Ezren frowned and then tossed him Sylvia's visor that she'd tucked into her nanite bandage. "This might work."

"Good thought." Gerard took off his own goggs, and threw both items into the airlock. The door hissed shut, and with another punch, they were sucked out into space.

"Dad, you've got to strap in, we're going to veer hard," Foster said.

Gerard pulled himself hand over hand back into his seat, his eyes bulging from his head and a vein pulsing in his temple with the strain. "Got it."

Foster swerved directly toward a DOS ship, and Ezren nearly screamed. "Foster, you're going to hit them."

"Not quite." He broke a hard turn at the last second, back toward the ever-growing sphere of Obrone. Ezren rotated the cams just in time to see the missile home in on their goggs and visor, way too close to the space ship. "What are you thinking?"

"Just trying to give them a few obstacles," Foster said as the missile went cold, disarmed from afar. "And now that we're in Obronian airspace and the other spacers are sparking pissed, we should be good." He expanded the command holo from his goggs. "But we're about to go through the atmosphere, and we're still going way too fast."

"There's no way this is an authorized approach," Ezren cut in, panic fluttering wildly in her gut.

Foster and his dad both looked at her with matching incredulous expressions. Wow, they really were related. "I think authorization is the least of our worries," Gerard laughed.

"What about landing?" Foster asked, his fists tight as he tracked their course and the vast blue of Obrone's oceans filled their windshield. "I have concerns."

Gerard's hands flew through the holos, fine-tuning their approach and initiating atmosphere entry protocols. "The summit is supposed to convene in thirty minutes. We don't have time to land."

Picking up his meaning, Ezren scanned the cockpit before spying the storage drawer on one side with *emergency* scrawled across it. "Your dad's right. If we do, they're going to apprehend us immediately, and who knows how long it'll take us to get out—"

A voice blasted through their comms. "Star-racer 4351. Your ship has been identified as stolen. Decrease your speed and report to spaceport 413J, hangar 31C. If you fail to comply, we will send an escort."

Foster let out a hiss through gritted teeth, his muscles tensing beneath Ezren. "This seems like a really bad idea all of a sudden."

Gerard reached forward and pressed the button, his voice honey-sweet. "This is Gerard Y from Badditude with Foster Yunin-Sterling and Ezren Hart on board. We're dealing with an emergency CIF situation. No escort required."

Ezren leaned forward as they cut through the silver cloud layer and the brilliant sapphire ocean appeared beneath them. Ahead she could just make out the skyline of buildings on the horizon. Her throat closed with bubbling memories of her Obronian childhood—her father's booming laugh as she clutched his hand—and she forcibly shoved the images away. Not now. Right now, she just needed to stall long enough to get close to the summit.

"This is Ezren Hart here, and we're under direct orders from Ambassador Villegas and Commander Liassidi to report to the summit with crucial evidence to present in an ongoing interplanetary case." It was... plausible, though she had no doubt wherever Villegas was at the moment, she was mentally murdering them.

"Look, we're all about returning the ship if that's the problem." Foster flicked through the holo until he pinpointed the landing strip closest to their destination. "But we'll be landing it at Caraff spaceport."

A long beat of silence stretched in the cabin before the

voice finally answered. "Copy that. Report directly to Caraff, and we will take you in for questioning."

"Fantastic," Gerard replied. "We appreciate your cooperation."

The line cut out, and Ezren wriggled out of the safety webbing. "But we're not landing, right?"

"Well, *you* aren't," Gerard answered. "But I like to plan ahead."

"Why do I get the feeling it's a bad plan?" Foster practically yelled, the ocean spilling out beneath them as they raced to the gleaming city rising in the distance.

Ezren tapped into the control holo with her chip. "I'm directing the ship to slow down to survivable exit levels two miles from the summit, but we're only a few minutes out now." She turned back to the storage locker. "Gerard, you're going to have to fly us in low."

"Okay, wait." Foster untangled his long limbs from the safety webbing and stooped down next to her. "I think I missed part of the plan."

"We're going out the airlock." Ezren lifted out two backpacks from the emergency hatch. "With these jetchutes."

"Into an urban environment?" Foster's jaw flexed. "Ezren, there's going to be so much air traffic and buildings and—"

"It's the only way we're going to get there in time." Ezren slipped on the backpack, the racer already slowing, and Obrone's gravity weighing heavy on her shoulders.

With a reluctant growl, Foster took the other backpack from her as she punched open the interior airlock door. "Are they even going to let us in this place once we taunt the reaper to get there?"

Ezren looked at Foster—blood and black grit coated his face, a baggy exosuit hung from his frame, and his brown waves stood in a wild, untamed mess. She knew she probably looked even worse. Sylvia would absolutely die. "Well, we *were* invited."

"Right." Foster scrubbed a hand over his jaw and glanced back at Gerard. "Well, Dad, thanks for the ride. Don't wait until the next time someone's trying to kill us to drop by."

Ezren frowned thoughtfully. "But that could be pretty soon."

"Don't worry, we'll definitely get that non-life-threatening dinner we were planning." His dad waved to them over his shoulder with a twitch of his fingers. "And Ezren, it was a pleasure to finally meet you. Take care of my son."

"Always." Ezren smiled at Foster, and he rolled his eyes as she jumped into the airlock.

Foster followed her, checking the fit of the straps on her pack. "Okay, but how do we know these things work?"

"This ship is top of the line, it can't be more than five years old, but in case the jets have a technical malfunction, there's a backup chute."

Foster stomped on the exterior airlock door beneath their feet, and it turned translucent, Obrone's white-capped waves seething beneath them. "Looks like this place is on the coast, and seeing as the last time we landed in the water didn't go so well"—he gave her a knowing look, calling back the dark memory of them crash-landing in the oceans of Belethea's churn belt—"I'd greatly prefer to end up on land."

Ezren shrugged, linking her chip to her pack. "You're the only one with the goggs, so you're going to have to—"

The star-racer lurched to one side, and Foster's arms folded around her as they slammed into the wall of the airlock. Ezren gasped in a sharp intake of breath, only to smell the acrid tang of smoke.

"Dad!" Foster yelled. "What happened?"

"Someone shot out one of our engines," he yelled. "I'll need to glide it in, but you're going to have a better chance if you jump now."

"What about you?" Ezren yelled, the smoke thickening.

"Don't worry," he called. "That's why I have two engines. Go while you have altitude."

Fear curdled in Ezren's belly. "This is bad." Without hesitating, she shucked off her pack and threw it into the cockpit. "I'm leaving you the other chute."

Foster's jaw fell open, but a spluttering cough killed any protest he may have had.

She returned his stare with bold confidence and wrapped her arms around his waist. "We can share."

Foster's lips tightened, and he yanked her to him, his arms like vices around her before calling up through the open airlock. "You'd better make it out, old man." He punched the exterior door release. "Because you still owe us dinner."

If his father responded, his words were lost as the floor sliced open beneath them, and Foster and Ezren plunged into the atmosphere.

CHAPTER 33

8.18.43B: T-minus 15 minutes until the Summit

AS THEY PLUMMETED to the ocean, the smoking star-racer curved along the shoreline toward the spaceport and Foster hoped his dad wouldn't hesitate to use the chute. His grip around Ezren tightened as he looked toward the glass skyscrapers lining the shore not a half mile away, the air whistling by his ears while the jetchute rumbled to life, supplying downward force to slow their descent.

Unfortunately, it was still bringing them straight down toward the wind-whipped waves below. He checked the ticking time in his goggs. If they were forced to swim, they'd never make it.

"Ezren," he called over the roaring wind. "I think we're going to have to deploy the chute and use the thrusters to get us closer to the shore."

"Do you think we'll have enough control?" she yelled, her arms knotted around him.

"We'll have more than we do now. Can you reach the cord?"

Ezren didn't hesitate as she ripped the manual cord from the pack and the old-fashioned parachute yanked them upward. With her legs locked around Foster's waist, Ezren unbuckled the decelerator and pointed it behind them.

"You'll need to adjust its deceleration levels through your goggs."

Foster hooked into it with his chip, the time slipping away in the corner of his holo. He powered the jets to full thrust and they launched toward the buildings. He shifted Ezren in his arms, allowing himself a tight smirk of satisfaction.

"So I have good news and bad news," Ezren said, her cheek pressed against his.

"What's the bad news?"

"Looks like your dad made it to the runway."

Foster frowned, his gaze trained on the ever-nearing land. "That's the bad news?"

"No, I just thought we've had plenty of bad news already, and I wanted to break it up with the good stuff first."

"Ezren," Foster said, his voice pitching. "What's the bad news?"

"York's ship is coming in too."

"Shaft." Foster couldn't turn to get a visual, but he felt the added pressure like a pair of eyes on his back. "We're still two miles away from the summit, and it's closer to the runway." He squeezed her tighter as he aimed for the crowded dock.

"Watch out!" someone yelled, and the rapt throng parted with a chorus of shrieks and gasps, dozens of recording red dots pointed at them.

"Is that Sterling/Hart?" another onlooker shrieked, and the mob erupted in an excited clamor as everyone jostled to get a better look.

"Holy chaff, it is!"

Foster braced for impact, but at the last minute, Ezren detached the chute and pointed the decelerator toward the ground, where its proximity sensors took over, setting them down almost gently.

The crowd, dressed in the barely-there shorts and translucent shirts of Obronian fashion, erupted into applause, and Foster let out a long breath, wishing that was the end of it and knowing it wasn't. Would this marathon ever end? "Definitely one of our better landings."

"I'll take it." Ezren smiled at him. "Ready to run?"

Foster eyed one of their gaping spectators balanced atop a jetbike. "To be honest, I'd much rather drive."

Catching his eye, Ezren jogged up to the biker in his gauzy tank top with a big, Sylvia-approved smile. "Hi, my name is Ezren Hart, and we're late for a super important meeting. Could we borrow your jetbike?"

The young man stared at her with a slack jaw, star-struck, and Foster ran up next to her, putting his hand on the handlebars. "We'll buy you a better one later, I swear."

Foster was about to wrench the bike from him when the boy came back to himself and stepped away, head bobbing. "P-please, take it."

Even through the blood and ash, Ezren's smile practically sparkled. "Thank you."

Foster straddled the bike, and Ezren followed suit, slipping her hands around his waist. "Clear the way!" he shouted.

Obediently the crowd parted, and Foster revved the engine once before taking off down the dock and onto the street. The familiar feel of a jetbike on smooth pavement was practically comforting as Foster swerved around traffic, his goggs highlighting the fastest route. This, he could do. This, he had trained for. With the wind in his hair, Ezren's arms around him, and the ground beneath their feet, Foster felt almost normal.

They were going to make it.

Then something tore through his arm, and the now all-too-recognizable rattle of gunfire ripped through the air. Behind him, Ezren screamed and pedestrians ducked for cover as he swerved onto a side street.

"Ezren, are you hurt?" Foster said, ready to break and duck for cover.

"No," she yelled, her breaths coming out in gasps that spoke otherwise. "Don't slow down, they're coming after us. Out of the way!" she yelled as they burst onto yet another busy road, speedjets and autocabs congesting the street on a three-dimensional level.

Foster tightened his grip and gunned to full speed once again. But there was no straight path as he wove between winged and wheeled vehicles alike, zigzagging through the clogged motorway while Ezren leaned into the curves with him.

Another explosion of gunfire popped way too close, and Foster turned again, maintaining their general direction. Four minutes and thirty seconds left. "It's going to be close."

"And York's going to be waiting for us," Ezren said. "We can't stop for anything, Foster."

Warmth oozed down his injured arm, the adrenaline masking the pain, and Foster nodded with grim determination. "I know."

"I'm going to connect the data sphere to your goggs so as soon as we get in there, you can project it for the council."

He just barely missed a pedestrian, and Ezren gasped in his ear with a low swear. He was only one street over now. They were so chaffing close. "Do you think they'll shoot us if we bust in?"

"They're already shooting at us." Ezren coughed out a dry laugh. "But it might help to broadcast who we are. Can you project a holo of the Belethea Royale crest and stream live?"

Foster sent a mental command, and the lightning bolt shield popped above them along with their racing name: Sterling/Hart. A little red dot lit up his goggs as he recorded through his eyes. "And we're live."

"This is Sterling/Hart from team Belethea returning from Otho. And yes, someone is shooting at us while we make our way to the ambassador summit with a world-changing message for the humanitarian council." Ezren said this all in a smooth, hololog-worthy broadcast voice.

With another turn, the huge emerald glass of the towering auditorium came into view through the narrow alley. A packed street stood between them and it with a wide staircase crawling up the other side, where security personnel blocked the door. "Hold on, Ezren."

Her arms tightened around him, and he swerved into traffic, weaving between the autocabs before erupting from the other side. The crowd scattered with a series of shrieks as he revved the engine and lurched up the long staircase to the mirrored wall of the shining building above them.

The security guards whipped toward them as their jetbike launched off the incline and through the floor-to-ceiling windows, glass exploding around them.

"Look out!" Ezren yelled just before they collided with the floor again, ambassadors and politicians dodging for cover.

Foster revved the engine once in warning before jolting forward toward the old-fashioned brown doors that two organizers were desperately trying to close.

But they banged past the antique wooden door as they drove over the threshold and onto the marble floor of the massive assembly hall. Grand stands of cushioned seats rose up in every direction, filled with representatives from Belethea, Obrone, Dreitis, and the twenty-four space stations.

Screams echoed through the impossibly high-ceilinged chamber as Foster turned the bike and drifted to a squealing stop on the smooth stone.

"What's happening?"

"Are we under attack?"

"That's Sterling/Hart!"

Ezren staggered from the bike, her breathing ragged, and blood seeping through the side of the nanite bandages drooping from the scraps of her torn topsuit. "We have an urgent message for the CIF concerning recent events on Otho."

Foster reached into his exosuit, passing her the cylinder and the data sphere just as security busted in the doors behind in full tactical gear. The black-suited soldiers swarmed them in a circle, their guns pointed straight at their heads. "Get on the ground!"

Foster was done with people shooting at them. Trying to kill them. He held up his hands, stepping away from the bike with a feral smile. "But we have an invitation." And they were fodding famous, after all.

"Where's Commander Liassidi?" Ezren curled her body around the cylinder, edging away from their pursuers. "Tell him Agent Shiro sent us."

"Don't listen to any of their lies!" Ambassador York strode through the door, his auburn hair askew, sweat dotting his flushed cheeks. "This is all just a publicity stunt by two criminal, cheating royalers who want to cling to the limelight." He gestured to his own security following him in blue tactical topsuits. "Remove these children at once."

A man lunged forward, reaching to steal the sphere from Ezren.

She turned to protect it with her body, and back-kicked him directly in the chest. Another tried to get her in a headlock, and she ducked him, dancing away while another grabbed for her arm. "They're trying to destroy the evidence!"

The soldier nearest Foster raised his rifle.

"Don't touch her." Foster surged between them, knocking the gun aside before kneeing the man in the diaphragm. He went down in a heap, but then two of the assembly guards seized his arms, dragging him backward. "We deserve a chance to speak!" He ground his teeth, the graze in his arm dripping blood onto the floor as they wrenched his hands behind him.

"Let them go," a cool, familiar voice boomed across the chamber, and the grip on his arms loosened. The assembly went quiet, and the soldiers froze in their pursuit.

Even Foster stopped struggling as all eyes turned to the doorway where he expected to see Shiro's commander.

But it was Calderon that looked back at him with an icy smile.

Mother suns. A chill ran down Foster's back, because at that moment, the truth sank in with sharp fangs.

Foster was on the same side as a murderer.

CHAPTER 34

8.18.43B: The Summit

EZREN COULD ONLY STARE at Calderon as he walked into the amphitheater, his silver hair perfectly coiffed and his brass goggs hanging around his neck. Four of his own security team flanked him in their three-piece suits, and a new chorus of hubbub raced through the gathered audience.

Ambassador York's face purpled, and he stabbed a finger in Calderon's direction. "This man was trying to hide a terranium operation on Otho and murder the witnesses from Baxter Research. Sterling/Hart are obviously working in concert with this corporate terrorist. It goes way beyond throwing the BRR. Don't let them—"

"*Sit* down." Another man strode into the room in a crisp black military uniform with four gold stars glittering on his shoulders. "All of you." Heavy, dark eyebrows underlined his wide forehead, and his brown dome gleamed under the bright lights. "Sterling/Hart are unarmed, and I've confirmed that they came directly from Otho's surface. Judging by their appearance"—his piercing stare scraped over their battered forms—"I'm extremely interested in what they have to say."

"But, Commander Liassidi, sir—" Ambassador York started.

"If you interrupt"—the Commander gestured with a hand,

and the soldiers released Foster and turned toward York, their weapons swiveling on a dime—"I will have you removed."

The room went silent around them, and Ezren exchanged a look with Foster. He gave her a nod, and she limped to the center of the floor, the lights bright in her eyes as her image projected from larger holos on the wall.

But this time, Ezren was no longer afraid. After all, this was where they were supposed to be. This was her job, and as she thought of her father fighting to give them a chance to get off Otho and expose the truth, a righteous fury burned within her. For the first time in a very long time, Ezren knew she was exactly where she was meant to be, doing exactly what she was supposed to do.

What she *could* do.

She tossed the data sphere to Foster. "Upload this to the holos so everyone can see."

Then she raised the dark cylinder and illuminated the interior black lights to show the luxies floating inside, pulsing red, orange, and purple. She said a silent prayer of thanks to the small creatures for holding on. Then, lifting her chin, she glared at the assembly with defiance. "Baxter Research has discovered complex alien life on Otho."

A gasp shot around the room followed by an immediate uproar.

"Not alien, manufactured!" Ambassador York screeched, lunging for the cylinder. "That's patented Baxter property."

Without thinking, Ezren shifted the cylinder under one arm and punched the man square in the jaw. Rage blotched his face, and he cocked an arm back to return the blow, but she was faster, grabbing him by the front of his one piece and slamming him to the floor.

"Enough!" the commander shouted.

Ezren stepped away from York with a grim satisfaction. It wasn't enough, but it would have to do for now.

"I *said* let her speak." The commander's intense gaze cut to York, but he was already scrambling to his feet.

"I'll not stand for this slander." York wiped a trickle of blood from his cut lip as he whirled for the door, his security gathered in a protective bubble around them. Stalking out of the chamber, he shot one last glare at Ezren and Foster, his voice a warning. "You'll hear from me again."

The clamor quieted, and with a nod from the commander, Ezren continued, "For years, Baxter has been holding scientists against their will to study and exploit these creatures." The data popped up onto the screens, showing holos of the missing scientists along with her father's familiar voice overlaying the scenes with their discoveries about the luxies. "The terranium and the accompanying syndicate rush were just part of Baxter's ploy to divert interplanetary attention. I know we're divided, but we have to come together on this." The luxies pulsed in her hand, and she let them plunge into darkness once more. "There's very little magic in this world to begin with, and we don't want to destroy the sparks we have."

"But what were you doing on Otho?" someone shouted.

"Yes, what does a royaler have anything to do with this?" another said.

From amidst the crowd, Ezren's gaze caught on Villegas's intense stare, her expression unreadable.

Ezren's hands balled into fists at her sides. "As many know, my father, Dr. Milo Hart, has been missing for the last four years." She glanced at Foster, and his jaw flexed. "When we learned that he was on Otho, we traveled there to find him."

"And ran straight into a fodding shaft storm," Foster ground out before raising his voice. "We barely survived Baxter's attempts to eradicate the witnesses—most didn't make it."

"Including over fifty Calderon Industries personnel," Calderon said, his voice carrying with an almost regal air.

Commander Liassidi gazed up at the holos, crossing his arms. "This is quite the sensationalist story. But I'm sure Baxter will have their side of it as well, especially considering the toxic and dangerous nature of Otho."

Ezren's shoulders fell, her eyes going wide. They needed *more* evidence? This felt like Calderon's trial all over again. What if Baxter went free? What if all of this had been for nothing?

"I'll back them up." Ezren and Foster turned to where Shiro limped through the door in his own battered topsuit. He stopped before the commander and snapped out a salute. "It's true, every word."

"And we have the holos to prove it," Grady said as he staggered in with Bex and Sylvia following behind. The holos around the room flashed with Grady's footage of their own plight on Otho, and he flashed his thousand-watt smile.

"We put together the highlights." Sylvia crossed her own arms to match the commander's posture, and Ezren was pretty sure she was the more intimidating of the two. Especially with Bex glaring over her shoulder. "But we've captured nearly the whole thing for further review."

For a moment, the assembled company watched the clipped montage in horror, and Ezren had to look away. Like the BRR footage, it was too raw. She wasn't sure if she'd ever be able to watch it. To relive it all.

Then she felt Foster's hands on her shoulders, his lips close to her ear. "Hang on, we're almost there," he whispered. "But there's one more thing from the data sphere."

She leaned into his chest, all the fight and energy beginning to fail her as the adrenaline seeped from her body. "I don't know if I can handle one more thing."

"They're messages from your dad. There's one for your mom, Sam, and... you." He slid his goggs from his dark brown waves and pressed them into her hand, the message tucked in the corner of the display. Ezren projected her father's words in front of her, unable to stop herself from poring over it right there.

Ezren,

I know I've asked a lot from you, and please know, that while there is a huge part of me that wishes I had stayed with you, Sam, and your mother. That I had never come here. That I could've abandoned this project and come straight home. There's a part of me that also feels like I was meant to be here. To protect these creatures and do what I can to fight the evil that threatens them. Not just them, but the values we hold as a human race—as a wanderer of galaxies. I know that may seem strange, but I feel called to this purpose.

I'm sorry for the sacrifices you made to be a part of this, but also know how proud I am of you. You've always been stronger and smarter and more capable than I could've ever dreamed, and it fills me with so much hope that I leave my life's work in your hands. Remember to believe in something bigger. Remember to hope, always. And please know that my love for you, Sam, and your mom has kept me going these years and it truly knows no bounds, in this world or the next. It puts my heart at rest to see you've found that love in your own life.

My heart forever lives in yours, and whenever you look up at the sky, know that I'm looking right back down at you.— Dad

P.S. Don't tell Foster I said that I like him. It might go to his head.

New tears pricked Ezren's eyes, and she squeezed Foster tighter. "Well, that rescue mission didn't exactly turn out like I thought."

"Yeah, I'm going to need some time to recover," Foster said

with his own dry rumble. Then he gently turned her shoulders and met her gaze while the system's most powerful people began to mutter around them. "But I'm glad we did it."

Ezren drew in a shaky breath. "You are?"

Foster nodded, tucking her hair behind an ear. "Yeah, I wanted it to be all about you and me, but I can no longer ignore that it's bigger than us."

"Our planet, our people, our system." Ezren's lips twisted to one side. "It's the right thing to do, but it still feels like so much."

Foster pressed his forehead to hers. "But we can do it, together."

"I guess if we can win the BRR and survive Otho, we might be able to pull this ambassador thing off." Ezren gave him a teary, rueful grin. "Maybe."

"Not maybe." He kissed her forehead. "Definitely."

The bang of the door echoed through the room, and Ezren flinched as Foster shielded her with his body.

"I was there too!" Gerard Y burst into the auditorium, and the audience erupted in a new wave of chatter. He jabbed a finger in the direction of the loose knot of security still standing around them. "Don't you lay a finger on my kids."

Bex raised an unamused white brow. "Kids?"

"Well yeah." Gerard slung an arm around Simon's shoulder with a smile that had to be worth a million creds. "Since you're obviously a package deal, I think I have to adopt all of you."

Simon's face lit up, and he turned to Bex with a triumphant smirk. "Best day ever."

Foster's shoulders relaxed with a tired grin. "You're a little late, Dad."

"Had to make an entrance." Gerard looked around at the gathering with an impressed whistle, propping his hands on his hips. "I mean how many times do you get to crash the Casolla ambassador summit?"

"I'll stand by them too," Villegas announced from the audience. They turned to see the austere ambassador in black ruffles standing from her seat, and Ezren thought she might die of shock right there. "We Beletheans may not have much, but we have grit and honor. I lay my own on theirs."

Ezren stared around at them then—Calderon, Villegas, Gerard—and thought she could almost feel the solid backing of Belethea herself. No matter what had happened in the past, or what would happen in the future, they would stand firm here.

"We'll be sure to take it all under consideration, Ambassador," Commander Liassidi said with barely concealed irritation. "But this is becoming a circus." He waved to one of his team. "Get these kids some medical attention. They're getting blood on my floor."

"And make sure they have a security detail," Sylvia added, putting a self-conscious hand to her wild curls. "I've lost count of how many people have tried to kill them."

Shiro edged closer to the commander's side. "I've got a full report ready for outbrief, but the Kalashnik's web is heavily involved."

The commander gave a sharp dip of his chin, and Ezren could see the gears spinning behind his dark lashes. "I suspected as much. They'll have our protection until we can figure out the full extent of the situation."

Ezren staggered toward Shiro, placing the cylinder of luxies in his hand. "Can I trust you with this?"

Shiro's face glowed as he pressed it to his chest, his hair a wild tangle and his expression earnest. "I'll make sure they're safe."

With a nod, Ezren turned toward the door, taking Foster's outstretched hand. Bex, Grady, and Gerard flanked them, along with a handful of guards. Sylvia moved to follow when Shiro caught her hand, and she let herself be pulled into one more kiss to Simon's low whistle.

Sylvia pulled away with a roll of her eyes. "Simon, don't make me come after you." She jogged to catch up with them at the door and feigned a swat at his shoulder. "Don't think I won't."

Simon held out a forearm. "I just want to give congratulations where it's due is all." She batted his arm away, and he offered his most innocent smile.

Their expressions fell as they passed Calderon though. The old man was standing placidly by, leaning on his cane as his lips curved on his sagging, wrinkled face. He nodded to them with a little bow. "My deepest appreciation for your assistance."

Foster waved the others on as Ezren stopped short. She felt his hand tightening in hers. *The enemy of my enemy is my friend.* No one said it, but the implication hung thick in the air between them. "This doesn't make us allies," she said, her jaw clenching.

"I never said it did." Calderon turned to Foster. "Have you given any more thought to my offer?"

Ezren locked eyes with Foster and gave him a nod as something else her father had told her echoed in her head. *Keep your enemies close.*

Foster issued a long sigh, but even as he did so, he seemed to stand taller. "It's not just me. Everything Ezren and I do, we do as a team."

Calderon's expression didn't so much as waver. "Naturally."

"And we're not doing the BRR. Ever again," Foster said.

"If you call the shots, you get to decide," Calderon replied.

Ezren glanced at Foster one more time. It was responsibility, but it was also control. And Foster was right, if they were together, they could handle it. Ezren lifted her chin. "Our legal team will be in touch."

With that, they walked out under the balmy, overcast Obronian sky, where Sylvia and the others awaited them. Emergency transport sirens trilled in the street and a crowd of cheering fans amassed on the stairway.

Something about the dappled sunlight and clean air nearly melted Ezren, and she stumbled on the step, the pent-up exhaustion and relief and emotion suddenly too much. She looked at Sylvia as Foster's arm curled around her, holding her up. "Please tell me we get a break after this."

"I'll do you one better." Sylvia's face creased in an empathetic smile. "How about indefinite rest and a cake?"

"You'll need to throw in coffee too," Bex said. "She looks like she's about to pass out."

"Don't forget a round of umbrella drinks on me," Grady said.

Gerard turned, walking backward down the steps. "First I need to call someone to pick up Davis from wherever he ended up, but I'll buy the second round."

"Coffee, drinks, sleep..." Foster pressed his lips to the crown of Ezren's head, his words soft in her ear. "Anything you want, as long as we're together."

"Always with you, Foster Sterling."

Only then, with five smiling faces staring back at her, did Ezren let the exhaustion take hold. As she crumpled to the ground, Foster caught her and cradled her to his chest, and she knew, at last, they were finally safe.

CHAPTER 35

09.03.43B Fifteen Days Later

FOSTER WALKED out onto Belethea's mauve surface toward the flat stretch of curling, experimental plants where Ezren perched on a belmoss-covered boulder. Her body seemed small atop her perch as she watched the navy clouds swirling across the sky, distant lightning forking between them. Though she wore a topsuit, her helmet sat beside her in the calm air. The memorial garden to Dr. Milo Hart stretched around her, overflowing with the violet and indigo blooms her mother's lab was planning to introduce to Belethea's hostile surface on a wider scale.

Foster paused, crouching at the commemorative stone that sat in the center. He ran his fingers over the words carved into its smooth polish.

Dr. Milo Hart
09.12.90B–8.18.43B
Discoverer and protector of the first complex alien life in the
Casolla system.
Beloved father, husband, and friend.
"Always remember to believe in something bigger."

. . .

Foster let out a slow breath and peered up at the sky where he could just barely pick out the pale orange circle of Otho orbiting Casolla's lava-scarred face. The fiery moon where, for the moment, the luxies lived unhindered by human presence. His gaze wandered to the bright points of the stations across the sky where the CIF were actively hunting down Ambassador York and his Kalashnik allies. It was still by no means a perfect situation—it would take time to normalize the black market and enforce the luxies' protections—but it was certainly the beginning Dr. Hart would've hoped for. Foster straightened and looked to where Ezren offered him a wistful smile.

"Is there room up there for one more?" he asked.

She patted the mossy rock. "Only for you."

He climbed up beside her, close enough to touch, but saying nothing. He took a deep, tangy lungful of air, letting the peace of home wash over them. With the intensity of the past weeks, this was badly needed. Breaking the news to her family had been tough on everyone, but the memorial ceremony had been a balm on a fresh wound. Thousands had shown up to pay their respects from across the system, including Foster's parents, and it seemed like after all the tension with the BRR, Casolla might finally be coming together once again. Though he knew it would still take the Harts time to recover from their loss.

"Sometimes I feel like nothing turns out like I expect it to," Ezren whispered.

"You didn't think Shiro and Sylvia would end up together?" Foster teased. "I think I could've seen it coming from the moment she first yelled at him for breaking into Carmella. Either that or kill—"

"You know that's not what I mean." Ezren nudged his

shoulder playfully. "Otho, Calderon, York. A year ago, I was a terraforming intern trying to make it through school. Then I was a royaler, and now we're Belethean ambassadors, and BRR *council members*." She wrinkled her nose, and Foster couldn't blame her. Though they'd refused to work for Calderon, even consenting to work beside him in an uneasy truce sent a chill down his spine. Ezren twirled a strand of her magenta-streaked hair between her fingers. "I mean, what's next?"

Foster took her hand in both of his and gave it a squeeze. "It is a lot."

"And my track record doesn't feel so great." She shook her head, entwining her fingers with his. "What if I chaff it up?"

"Well, we always chaff it up," Foster said, giving her a half grin.

"Foster," she groaned.

"Well, we do, but then we pull out the clutch save, and it all turns out right in the end." He pressed his lips to the back of her hand. "That's probably why the council approved us."

She let out a laugh that filled his chest with warmth. Real and full, like it used to be. The first real sign that they might one day get back to normal.

It had taken a few days, but Davis had made it back safely from Uvis Station in time for the memorial, which relieved Foster more than he would ever admit. Together with their Otho survival team, his dad had thrown them a celebratory survival dinner with a five-tiered coffee cake, and endless rounds of umbrella drinks. The day after, they'd parted ways, with Bex and Grady returning to Petraskis where he and Ezren would join them in time. For now though, he was ridiculously grateful that Sylvia had given him and Ezren space to breathe before they started in their new roles as full-time ambassadors. A mercy which Shiro claimed was his good influence, of course, though Foster secretly thought Turnip had that bizarre couple wrapped around her tails.

He didn't exactly know what came next, but one day soon, they'd have to announce that they were also the newest council members of the BRR, with voices that would decide its fate going forward.

But not today.

"I just..." Ezren's lips tightened, her gaze falling to the mauve spires in the distance as if looking for words. "I'm so used to finding ways to predict things."

"Like the weather?" Foster eyed a branch of lightning snaking through the jagged horizon.

"Exactly," Ezren said. "There's so much big stuff happening, but I don't have the slightest idea of how it's all going to turn out, and I'm kind of, well"—her gaze darted to him, her voice dropping to a whisper—"scared."

"Ah, so you're mortal after all."

She gave him a side-eye, a look he suspected she'd picked up from Sylvia. "I'm being serious, Foster."

"So am I," he replied, careful to keep his expression neutral.

She gave him a searching look with narrowed eyes before turning back to the sky with a quiet scoff. "You're not scared."

"I am," he said, sobering. "And when you'd left for Otho, I was chaffing terrified." He scraped a hand across his jaw, feeling her eyes on him. "But that's life, you know. Unknowns. Fear. And amidst all that, if we're lucky"—he met her gaze—"we get a few moments like this."

Putting a hand to her cheek, he leaned in and placed his mouth on hers. This time, it wasn't desperate or rushed. It was her lips and his fitting together like two puzzle pieces. His chest filled with the complete rightness of it—a snapshot of perfection amidst the chaos.

Reluctantly he pulled away, drinking her in as she looked up at him, her coffee-dark eyes warm and shining.

"Can we get more than a few?" she whispered.

"Oh yeah," he said. "We're *really* lucky." She let out another laugh that he'd never be able to get enough of.

"You're my everything, Ezren," he said. "You know that, right?"

She smiled up at him. "I don't know, maybe you should tell me again."

He leaned forward, gathering her to him, his lips in her ear. "Everything."

She nodded, her cheek brushing his. "I think you may be even more," she whispered.

And his mouth found hers again. Savoring the soft curve of her lips, the warmth of her skin, the sweetness of her taste. Even lost in the kiss, his head still whirled through all they'd been through. The race that had tried to kill them, the planet that had almost finished the job, and the temporary peace that would be their responsibility to maintain. Because they could.

Because they were bigger than just themselves.

They parted again, her gaze set on his like he was the only person in the 'verse. There was such love there, he felt it coursing around him, ensconcing them with warm, unbreakable arms. No matter what happened, they would always have this.

He squeezed her knee, and she jumped with a laugh that rang through the air, filling him like the very oxygen he breathed. Then together they turned to the teal sky, the curling towers of navy clouds scudding by, and the planets watching from above.

Gazing upward with Ezren, he felt simultaneously tiny and larger than life, and the truth of his own words sank into his bones. How so many people had conspired and sacrificed to make this moment possible. How infinitely lucky he was to be right here, right now—to have a lifetime of these moments stretching out before them.

In the breath of peace, they sat quiet together, soaking it in and watching the storms roll past.

ACKNOWLEDGMENTS

While I always knew Ezren and Foster's adventures didn't stop after the BRR, I never actually thought I'd get to write them. When Whimsical Publishing first released *Into the Churn*, this sequel was just a dream and a handful of notes in a file labeled "just in case." It was only thanks to Whimsical's amazing support, the incredible feedback from readers, and our wonderful street team spreading the word about these stories that we were able to make this book a reality. So I have a lot of people to thank!

First of all, I need to thank Micheline Ryckman for believing in this book. The passion and incredible work you put into Whimsical's stories never ceases to amaze me, and I'm so thankful we got to return to Belethea with these characters. I'm forever honored to be a part of the Whimsical family and can't wait to dive into our next adventure.

And of course, I have to thank my endlessly supportive family. To my parents, for always being in my corner, reading those extra rough first drafts, and letting me drink all your coffee. To my husband, for always making me laugh, keeping our house of chaos standing, and ever supporting this writing obsession of mine. And to my favorite wild boys, Decker and Dashiell, for keeping me on my toes, always being there with a sweet hug, and filling our lives with fun. I love you all to the ends of the 'verse!

To my beta readers—Mindy and Maddy—thank you for your sharp eyes in polishing this book from a dream to final draft in record time. I especially want to shout out my critique partners: Erin, for being right there with me on this writing journey, and Caleb, for going on four (how is that possible?!) years of weekly critique chats.

To my street team, for helping us spread the word about these characters, this world, and this story. With every share, review, and post, you all give this book wings. We would never have been able to do this without you, and your enthusiasm honestly makes me want to bawl happy tears. Your support is something I never could've dreamed of when I started writing, and in so many ways, I wrote this book for you. Special shout-out to Lee and her totally blime Ezren cosplay. My mind is forever blown.

And to everyone who has offered an encouraging word or recommended this book—in person, on social media, in your reviews—thank you so much for keeping me going on this writing journey. I so hope you enjoyed coming along to Belethea again with me, and I'm so grateful for each and every one of you.

ABOUT THE AUTHOR

Hayley Reese Chow is the award-winning author of Odriel's Heirs, Into the Churn, and other upcoming YA adventures. When not head over heels in a bookish world, she's also a full-time engineer, USAF reservist, avid traveler, and super nerd. Hayley currently dodges hurricanes in Florida with two small ninjas, her long-suffering husband, and her miniature ragehound. To see what she's working on next, check out hayleyreesechow.com or VSoc at @HayleyReeseChow.